WEAPON OF MERCY

WEAPON OF FLESH TRILOGY II
BOOK 3

BY
CHRIS A. JACKSON
AND
ANNE L. MCMILLEN-JACKSON

ILLUSTRATIONS BY
NOAH STACEY

This story is dedicated to our dearest friends, Joe and Kim, without whose love and support we never would have made it. We have shared so much and laughed so hard, and love both you dearly. You are, indeed, our safe harbor.

Thanks again to Noah, for the wonderful cover art, patience and inspiration. We owe you so much.

Weapon of Mercy

Weapon of Flesh Trilogy II
Book 3

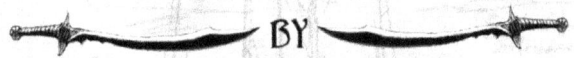

By

Chris A. Jackson
and
Anne L. McMillen-Jackson

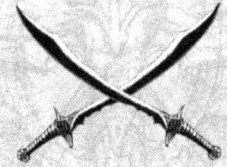

ISBN-13 978-1-939837-17-2

JAXBOOKS.COM

PRELUDE

What in the Nine Hells am I doin'?

Sergeant Benjamin peered around a corner, spied his quarry, and eased out onto the darkening street. He'd exchanged his constable's uniform and iron cap for a longshoreman's jacket and broad-brimmed hat. At a glance, he'd pass for just another laborer; the last thing he wanted was the man he was following to recognize him. *Especially since he's my boss!*

Chief Constable Dreyfus turned into *The Brass Hat*, a mid-scale pub popular with merchants and shopkeepers. Benj didn't frequent the place, preferring homey pubs where the ladies were friendly and the ale cheap. He licked his lips at the thought of a cool pint, but suppressed the craving.

He paused for a moment, wondering again if he was barking up the wrong tree. It might have been a coincidence that Miss Moirin went missing the day after Benj met with Dee, but Benj had been a cap too long to believe in coincidence. Something about Dreyfus' manner had rubbed him the wrong way, and there were too many rumors on the street of money being offered for information about Miss Moirin, and too many caps on the take. Someone must have followed Benj to the meeting with Dee, then followed Dee to Miss Moirin.

Problem is, only Dreyfus knew I was meetin' with Dee. He recalled that morning's conversation with the chief constable, trying to determine what had piqued his suspicion.

"Miss Moirin's been taken," Dreyfus had told Benj flatly. "Word came down from the palace that she fell for a trap."

1

"Taken?" The news had shaken Benj to the soles of his boots. The Hero of the Coronation, the woman who saved the emperor's life—saved Benj's life, in fact—taken? "I'll gather my people together and—"

"You'll do nothing, Sergeant." Dreyfus' rebuttal had taken Benj aback. "Our orders were to coordinate with her in our search for Baroness Monjhi's murderer, though she gave us nothing, and insisted we communicate through her *lackey*. We've *not* been ordered to try to find her. I'm telling you so you can redirect your efforts where we need you."

"But she *has* given us—"

"Drop it, Sergeant! We've more pressing issues. The emperor's appearing in public in a few days, and we've got security to deal with. Forget Miss Moirin and get on with your other duties!"

But Benj couldn't forget, and couldn't help but wonder why Dreyfus was so dead set against a few inquiries. What could he have against Miss Moirin? The chief might be a crotchety bastard, but he'd been upright and honest for all the years Benj had known him. He wouldn't...*couldn't* be on the take.

So what the hell am I doin'? Benj had no answer to that question other than his persistent gut feeling. *I should probably just go home and get details from Dee later.*

As was often his habit, Benj ignored what he should have done and strolled past the pub for a look inside. He glanced sidelong through the windows; lamplight gleamed on polished brass fixtures and glossy mirrors. The place was busy, folks tipping a glass before heading home for dinner, but the sergeant's professional eye spotted Dreyfus easily. He was talking to another man, accepting a glass from him. As they both settled into stools at the bar, the chief constable's companion turned, and Benj instantly recognized him.

"Otar?" Benj walked on past the window, stopped, waited a long moment, then walked back the other direction for another look. As sure as carts followed horses, the former captain of the Imperial Guard sat next to Dreyfus, a jovial grin stretching his face as he waved to the pretty bartender for a second round of drinks. "Why in the Nine Hells is Dreyfus talkin' to *him*?"

As far as Benj knew, Dreyfus and Otar had only consulted professionally. He'd never known them to be drinking buddies, and since Otar's public dismissal for refusing a direct order from the crown prince, he'd been shunned by anyone of consequence.

"But now he's chattin' with Chief Constable Dreyfus…" The sergeant's gut roiled again, and not just because it was dinnertime.

Benj took a position in a doorway half a block away and settled in to wait. If he'd learned anything in more than two decades as a constable, it was patience and to trust his gut. After an hour or so, Dreyfus emerged, smiling and well lubricated, if his gait and the flush of his face were any indications. Benj pulled his hat lower, turned as if to examine the nearby posterboard, and watched sidelong. The chief tottered off, and moments later Otar emerged and set off in the opposite direction, his gait somewhat steadier. Benj followed.

Halfway across Midtown, the former imperial guard captain entered *Lucky Gem's*, a gambling hall-tavern-brothel. Benj knew the place well. He didn't gamble, but enjoyed watching others lose their hard-earned money, and had once favored a lady who worked there.

Benj doffed his hat and longshoreman's jacket, tossed them into an alley, and walked in. He didn't know what might be going on here, but he sure as hell was going to find out.

CHAPTER I

Heat infused Lad's flesh as he confronted the three men in the common room of the *Tap and Kettle*. The magic of his runes primed him—*Move! Attack! Kill!*—exactly what he had been *made* to do.

The huge mastiff at Norwood's side growled deep in its chest, drawing the attention of the few guests still lingering over their ale. Dogs didn't like magic, and Lad undoubtedly reeked of it.

The dog first, then Sereth, then— No! Lad drew a deep, calming breath and let it out slowly, suppressing the violent urges. *That's not who I am anymore.* Besides, slaughtering three men and a dog in the common room with guests looking on wasn't likely to improve the inn's business.

But why would the captain of the Royal Guard, the guildmaster of Twailin's assassins, and Dee—who should be in Tsing with Mya—be here? Even be together? His mind leapt to the only likely conclusion.

"What kind of trouble is Mya in now?"

"Mya?" Norwood blinked and looked from Lad to Dee. "Who's Mya?"

"Moirin," Dee corrected, his voice tense. "Some of her friends call her Mya. Just a nickname." Then he turned to Lad. "How did you know she was in trouble?"

"It's the only thing that makes sense." *Because the Assassins Guild in league with the captain of the Royal Guard certainly doesn't.* He didn't know what they wanted of him, but he was pretty sure he wasn't going to like it. The magic tingled along his skin again, eliciting another low growl from the dog. He motioned them toward one of the private rooms in the back of the inn. "Gentlemen, if you'd follow me, we can relax in—"

"We aren't here to *socialize!*" Annoyance edged Dee's voice, uncharacteristic in Lad's experience. Fatigue and stress etched his face. "Miss Moirin's been—"

"Dee, calm *down.*" A hint of the harsh guildmaster he'd once been honed Lad's words. He cast a glance to the lingering guests, then fixed his eyes on his former assistant. "This isn't the place."

The muscles in Dee's neck bunched and twitched. The dog wasn't the only one wound as tight as a watch spring.

Finally, Dee nodded. "Fine."

Lad ushered them into the private room and closed the door. Norwood moved a chair into the far corner and sat with his cane across his lap and his massive dog at his side. Sereth leaned against the cold fireplace mantle and crossed his arms, his face unreadable. Dee stood with fists clenched.

"Now, what's this all about?"

"Miss Moirin's been kidnapped!" Dee eyes shone as hard as flint.

"Kidnapped?" Lad's brow furrowed. Mya's magical enhancements matched his own, exceeding them in some respects, and she was as paranoid as hell. Who could possibly have gotten past her guard?

"Yes, *kidnapped!* Abducted! Taken!" Dee glared at him. "What about that don't you understand?

"I understand kidnapped, Dee. Just relax and tell me how *anyone* managed to abduct Moirin, and why."

Dee ran a hand through his dark hair, took a deep breath, and nodded. "Miss Moirin was…recovering something for the emperor, something that was stolen by Hoseph."

"Hoseph?" Lad's gaze darted to Norwood. The captain was only alive because Lad had saved him from that murderous priest. *Is that why he's involved in this?*

"Yes. There are…*people* working with him. They set a trap for her. Maybe for me, too. We don't know."

"We? Who is 'we'?"

Dee spoke deliberately. "The people who work for Moirin. We don't know for sure why they took her instead of just killing her, but we think they might want to interrogate her about…her associates."

Captain Norwood cleared his throat and sat up straighter. "Gentlemen, please. It would save us all a lot of time if you'd stop beating around the *godsdamned* bush and speak plainly." He pointed to

5

Lad, but looked at Dee and Sereth. "I know what Loren is—or was—and by association, can guess what you two are as well. So, let's just get it out in the open: Assassins Guild."

Dee's eyes widened, and Sereth's fingers twitched to his sleeves.

Lad pictured Lissa asleep in her bed just down the hall and fought against the instinct to kill the three men. He stepped between the assassins and the captain, his eyes narrowed at Sereth. "You will do *no* violence in my home. I don't know why you're all here together, but you'll all have your say. Captain, please continue."

Norwood cleared his throat again. "Despite what I *know* about Loren, I *also* know that he's saved my life at least once, perhaps twice. What's more, I *suspect* that he's responsible for saving the empire itself. For those reasons, I'll never tell a soul what *else* I suspect he's done. Miss Moirin has saved the life of our new emperor. That she is somehow associated with you all only reaffirms my theory that there's a clandestine war going on, and you three are on the *right* side of it."

The captain shrugged his broad shoulders and sighed. "Let me assure you all that I'm *also* on that side. I've been commanded by my emperor to aid Master Dee in any way I can. That's my *only* concern here."

"You have a keen mind, Captain. Thank you for being frank." Lad cocked an eyebrow at Dee. "What I still don't know is what all this has to do with me?"

"What does it have to *do* with you?" Dee stared in disbelief, his face flushing. "You've got to help us get her back!"

Lad shook his head. "I can't help you. This isn't my war, Dee."

Dee's face flushed an even deeper crimson. "You *have* to help! You're the one who put her in this position in the first place!"

"I *know* that, Dee." Putting the Grandmaster's ring on Mya's finger had seemed the obvious choice to Lad. Not only would she make the perfect Grandmaster—an assassin with a good heart—but the position and ring would grant her the power and safety she'd sought her entire life. "How could they capture her while she wore the ring?"

"Hoseph burned the contracts."

Ahhh. Lad had never signed a contract, which was the only reason he'd been able to kill the previous Grandmaster.

"But why me? What about the Tsing guild? You implied that she controlled at least some of the factions. What about the Hunters?"

"They traced her to a dead end. They're good, but not like you. They don't have your skills. She saved your *life*." Dee's tone was beseeching now. "You told me that yourself."

"And I saved her life during five years as her bodyguard more times than I can count. I may have put the ring on her finger, but I didn't force her to take a job retrieving some stolen bauble for the emperor."

"It's not a bauble, it's a *boy*!"

"A boy?" That surprised Lad. Mya wasn't the sentimental type.

"Yes. Hoseph kidnapped three boys to use as leverage against their father. Does that sound familiar to you? Do you remember how it felt when that little girl of *yours* was held captive?"

Lad moved faster than Dee could blink. Face to face, he stared into Dee's eyes, holding the reflexive violence at bay, dashing the heat of the magic with cold will. "*Don't* bring my daughter into this," he growled between clenched teeth.

Dee looked him straight in the eye. "Do you remember that it was *Moirin* who helped you rescue her?"

Lad reined in his temper. The two most painful moments in his life were Lissa's abduction and Wiggen dying in his arms. He had lost his wife to guild business; he wasn't about to risk the rest of his family. Even for Mya.

"No, Dee, I can't help you. Lissa is *exactly* why I'm staying right here. I need to protect my family."

"Bullshit."

Lad's eyes snapped to Sereth. "What?"

The Twailin guildmaster still leaned against the mantle, his expression inscrutable. "Your reasoning is bullshit. I told Dee I wouldn't argue his case here, but I have my own case to make. You wanted out of the guild, so you're out. But do you really think that hiding out here makes your family safer?"

"I'm not *hiding* from anything! And I'm not going to Tsing. I'm staying here, Sereth." Lad's tone brooked no argument, but he got one.

"Oh, I don't doubt you'll do exactly what you want to do, Loren. None of us can force you to help. You know it, and we know it. But this goes way beyond Moirin. The entire Twailin guild is at risk, hundreds of people who are *my* responsibility." Sereth abandoned his relaxed stance, standing stiff in front of the fireplace, his hands deliberately open and away from his weapons. "Moirin has been taken and is likely being tortured for information. How long until she spills everything she knows about the guild here? Hoseph has already threatened to destroy us because we backed you. If he's interrogating Moirin, he'll get what he wants from her eventually. But consider what *else* she knows: You, the *Tap and Kettle*, your family…"

Lad's blood ran like ice water. "Think like an assassin" was Mya's axiom, and he'd been thinking with his heart, not his head. Mya knew Lad was alive, where he lived. Once Hoseph had pried that information out of her, the priest wouldn't stop hunting him until… *Forbish and Josie, Tika and Ponce, Lissa…*

No! Lad closed his eyes and willed his pounding heart to calm.

"We *need* you!" Dee pleaded. "You *know* what they'll do to her. You told me what they did to Kiesha."

"Kiesha?" Norwood's eyes snapped to Dee's, then to Lad's. "The woman in the emperor's dungeon…" He clenched his jaw and swallowed hard.

Lad's gut roiled as he recalled the mangled flesh that had been Kiesha. She had murdered Wiggen, but not even that justified what the emperor had done to her. Death had been a mercy. How long would Mya last before her immunity to pain failed and the screaming began?

"I have to protect my family," he said, but his vehemence had faded.

"But you can't be everywhere at once," Sereth said. "If we go to war with Hoseph and the Tsing guild, no place will be safe. The only thing that *will* protect the people you love is to prevent Hoseph from winning. That means saving Moirin. I owe you more than I can ever repay, Loren, and I give you my word that I'll protect your family while you're gone."

"I'll second that," Norwood affirmed. "If Master VonBruce is willing, the Royal Guard will work with his…private security people to cover all possible threats."

Sereth looked sidelong at the captain, then nodded. "Agreed."

"So you don't have to worry about your family," Dee insisted. "You *have* to help. Morin needs you. You can't just let her be tortured to death and still call yourself a human being."

"Maybe I'm not." Lad sighed. "I was wrought of flesh and magic into a *thing* made to kill for others. I swore I'd never go back to that. I'm not a killer."

"I'm not *asking* you to kill," Dee said, his tone calmer now. "Just help us save Miss Moirin."

Lad gave Dee a sour look. "And you think that's possible without killing, Dee? Really?"

"No, probably not."

"I'll tell you one thing, Loren," Norwood said. "If you chanced upon that motherless bastard Hoseph and happened to remove his head from his shoulders, I'd not call it murder. I'd call it a service to the empire."

"Moirin's already got a writ of immunity from the emperor in that regard," Dee said. "Hoseph is fair game."

"Imperial permission to kill..." Lad snorted a sardonic laugh. "How *convenient*."

Though none of the three men said another word, Lad bowed beneath the unrelenting weight of their silence and offered up one last weak argument. "We'll never get there in time. How do you know she's not already dead?"

"She was only taken night before last," Dee explained. "Duke Mir's wizard brought me here with magic. We'll return the same way in the morning."

Lad sighed in defeat. "I can't believe I'm even considering this."

"You'll help?" Dee's face flushed with relief.

Lad fixed him with a level stare and finally nodded. "I'll do my best." Lad forestalled Dee's outburst of gratitude with a raised hand and a glare. "Now get the *hell* out of my home so I can spend one last night with my family. Come back in the morning with your wizard, and I'll go with you."

"Yes." Dee nodded to the others. "Yes, of course. Thank you."

Norwood stood and stuck out a beefy hand. "Rest assured, Loren, I'll do everything I can to keep your family safe."

"I'll hold you to that, Captain." Lad shook his hand, then Sereth's. "And you, Sereth."

Sereth flashed him a rare smile. "You have my word."

Lad ushered them out and closed the door firmly. He dreaded breaking the news to Forbish, but the thought of saying goodbye to Lissa was worse. He'd sworn to never leave her again.

If I'm ever to keep her safe, I have to go. He knew it was the truth, but it didn't make it any easier.

Shink-Shink-Shink...

The quick, repetitive sound of metal on metal dragged her up from the depths of blessed unconsciousness. The stench of blood—*My blood...*—wrinkled Mya's nose, and dull pain sang like distant screams along her nerves.

Shink-Shink-Shink...

Cold stone beneath her back, hard restraints encircling her limbs, the bitter taste of opium on her tongue, blood, pain, and that incessant sound...

Where...what's happening?

Her mind drifted through a haze as thick and impenetrable as an early morning fog on the Twailin waterfront. Recognition came slowly, chilling—she was lying on the Grandfather's table, submitting to his knives as part of the trap to capture Lad.

I can't do that to Lad, she thought. *He's my...what? Friend? Lover? He kissed me, and put a ring on my finger.* She clenched her hand and felt a void where that finger had been. *Gone... Lad's gone...* When she tried to recall his face, she saw another's: dark hair, smooth skin, and gentle eyes. *Dee...*

Shink-Shink-Shink...

That sound...familiar and strangely nauseating. *Why...* She felt something tugging, like someone pulling at her clothes. The pain wasn't a dream. It should have been. *No pain...*

Mya heaved open her eyes and reality crashed in. Instead of the Grandfather standing over her, Kittal, Master Alchemist of the Tsing Assassins Guild, turned the crank on his vile machine, peeling away her skin, and with it, her magic. A low, inarticulate moan escaped her throat, a plea to sink back into the fog of oblivion.

Shink-Shink-Shink…

The incessant sound stopped. Without a word, an assistant proffered a fluid-filled jar; they had the routine down pat now. As Kittal lowered a bloody strip of wriggling flesh—*My flesh…*—into the liquid, the runes tattooed upon the skin flared as if lit by an internal flame.

My skin, my runes, my magic. How long until I have none left?

"Okay, that's enough. No more tonight." Metal clattered on metal and Kittal sighed. "What's her condition?"

"Alive and semi-conscious." Berta, one of Kittal's assisting Alchemists, put cool fingers to Mya's throat. "Her breathing and heartbeat are fast, but strong."

"Good. Clean her up and give her a restorative. We've harvested about all we can here. Tomorrow we'll start on her back. Tieg and Kelsey, turn her over in the morning. Do it early. I want everything ready by the time I arrive."

Turn her over… Mya fought to think though the drug-induced haze, to parse out what that meant. She was strapped down on her back, restrained by padded metal bands. To turn her, they'd have to remove those restraints. *They'll have to release me!*

Mya swallowed the restorative that Berta held to her lips, then gagged at the bitter taste of opium. Berta must have laced the elixir with the narcotic—*Kindness, mercy, or orders?*—but oblivion was the last thing Mya wanted right now. Immediately she felt just a little better, perhaps a little stronger, certainly much more relaxed as the pain ebbed. She longed to just close her eyes and drift away, let the drugs ease her into a painless sleep.

No! Mya struggled against the drug, as if swimming against a current that swept her out to sea. *Hate them! Focus! Stay awake…* She had a chance, if only she could stay awake, control her mind, and devise a plan. She had one slim hope. Three small words.

Turn her over…

CHAPTER II

Dee stifled a yawn as he stared dully out the carriage window. He'd stayed the night at Sereth's, but hadn't slept much. Instead, he'd spent half the night filling the guildmaster in on the events in Tsing, enemies and allies, plots and plans.

Sereth had given nothing back but a flat apology. "Sorry, Dee, but I can't tell you what kind of precautions I'm taking. If you were captured…"

Dee couldn't blame him. If he was taken, Master Inquisitor Lakshmi would extract from him any information she wanted. *Just like she's trying to do to Mya right now…* His morbid imagination had kept him awake for the rest of the night.

His thoughts turned to the present as the Royal Guard carriage rumbled into the courtyard of the *Tap and Kettle*. Two young men stood there, their faces falling into hostile frowns as the carriage jerked to a stop. They looked so alike that it gave Dee pause. *Twins…* He remembered reports from security details sent to watch the inn. *Tika and Ponce, Lad's nephews.*

Norwood opened the door and stepped down, his huge dog on his heels. Dee followed. Master Woefler came out last and slipped on a cobble.

A cringe wrinkled the wizard's youthful features as he scraped dog slobber from his shoe. "Dogs are such *revolting* creatures."

"Loren's inside," one of the young men said with a scowl.

Dee ignored their animosity and followed Norwood up the steps. *Let them be angry. Mya's more important than their feelings.*

Only one table in the common room was occupied this early, a pair of merchants eating a hasty breakfast. The serving woman glanced up from pouring blackbrew, her amiable countenance transforming into a glare.

From near the kitchen door, Forbish, the *Tap and Kettle*'s innkeeper and Lad's father-in-law, frowned, doubling his already numerous chins. "One moment, Captain Norwood." He turned and pushed open the door, leaned in, and said, "They're here."

A moment later, Lad emerged, a cherubic toddler perched on his hip.

Lissa. Dee had never seen the girl. Fine brown hair curled softly against a plump cheek, pink lips smiling up at her father. How ironic it seemed, such a picture of innocence in the arms of the most lethal assassin the world had ever known.

Dee felt a pang of guilt for asking Lad to leave her again. Not until now—with Mya gone—did he truly understand the depths to which one's soul sank when a loved one was in peril. But guilt wasn't about to make him change his mind about needing Lad's help.

Lad kissed his daughter and handed her over to Forbish. The baby immediately started to fuss, quieting only when Lad brushed her gossamer hair and whispered to her. Straightening abruptly, the muscles of his neck and jaw rigid, as if leaving her took every fiber of his strength, he whirled toward the back room and strode off without a word. Dee exchanged a worried glance with Norwood, and they followed. Only when the door to the private room closed behind them did Lad face them and speak.

"I'm ready."

Dee exhaled silently. He'd been afraid Lad would balk. "Master Woefler, if you please."

"Certainly, but might I suggest, Captain Norwood, that you take your drooling beast out of the room." Woefler's nose wrinkled. "I'm not sure how it might respond to my use of magic."

"I *am* sure, and I'd rather not clean up the mess." The guard captain held out a hand to Lad. "So long, Loren. Rest assured; I'll protect your family until you return."

Lad shook his hand. "Thank you, Captain."

Norwood left, his massive dog on his heels.

"I don't believe we've been formally introduced." Woefler smiled and nodded politely to Lad. "I'm Master Woefler, wizard to Duke Mir and your transportation to Tsing today."

Lad just stared at Woefler, his face blank.

Dee broke the tense silence. "Please, Master Woefler? Time is of the essence."

"Very well, then." Unperturbed by the affront, eyes twinkling with intrigue, Woefler pulled up his sleeves and worked his spell. The familiar oval of darkness appeared in the middle of the room. "All right, Master…Loren, is it? Please take hold of Master Dee's hand, and move only forward, not back. Bad things might happen if you try to back out of the portal once engaged."

"You didn't tell me that the *last* time we did this," Dee said, already nervous about repeating the magical journey through the ether.

"I didn't?" Woefler looked nonplused. "Well, it must have slipped my mind." He waved a hand dismissively. "No matter. Just take my hand, and Master Loren's, and we'll be off."

Dee grasped Woefler's hand and held his other out to Lad. He tried not flinch at the awkward feel of Lad's mutilated hand. Only the thumb and forefinger remained fully intact, but the grip was firm, and the injury didn't seem to bother Lad.

"Gentlemen, follow me." Woefler stepped into the darkness.

Dee followed, concentrating on moving only forward, closing his eyes in an attempt to avoid the disconcerting feeling of being in two places at once. The aromas of food and blackbrew told him they'd arrived, and he opened his eyes to the Blue Room of *The Hyacinth* café.

"Welcome back, Master Dee, Master Woefler." The emperor's archmage, Master Keyfur, stood from the table, his rainbow-hued robes swirling in a riot of color. Lifting a strip of crispy bacon, he waved it like a magic wand toward the food-laden table. "Breakfast is served!"

"I'm sorry, Master Keyfur, but we've already eaten." Dee released Lad's hand and tried to ignore the amazing spread of dishes. All he'd had this morning was dry toast, but his nervous stomach rebelled at the thought of food. "And we've got to hurry if we want any hope of recovering Miss Moirin alive." He started for the door. Thankfully, Lad followed without argument.

"Well, *I'm* not in a hurry, and I'm positively famished!" Woefler waved amiably. "Good luck to you both."

"I arranged a carriage for you. Call on me any time if you need magical assistance, Master Dee!" Keyfur called as the door closed between them.

Out on the street, Dee called up to the hackney driver, "The corner of Eastwatch and Holloway streets in the Dreggars Quarter."

"That's quite a drive, sir. It'll cost a bit."

Dee fished a gold crown from his pocket and held it up. "This is yours if you get us there quickly."

"Well, climb aboard and hang on to your seats!" The driver grinned and reached for his whip.

They boarded the carriage and it lurched into motion, clattering over the cobbles at a reckless pace. Dee tried not to fidget as he looked out the carriage window, watching the elegant facades of the Heights give way to the more functional buildings of Midtown. He felt Lad's gaze upon him—those mica-colored eyes gleamed faintly in the gloom—and shifted uncomfortably.

Finally, as they crossed one of the bridges that spanned the river, Lad broke the uneasy silence. "What's really going on here, Dee?"

"What?" The question took Dee off guard. "I told you what's going on. Hoseph and two factions of the Assassins Guild took Mya in a trap. We lost the trail, and you're going to help me find her."

"Not that." Lad's eyes bored into him. "There's more than you've told me. In all the years I've known you, you've rarely worn a weapon. Now you're carrying two hand crossbows and a dagger."

Dee's fingers twitched toward the compact crossbows tucked into special pockets in his coat, silently cursing Lad's uncanny knack for observation. "We're fighting for our *lives* here, Lad. You may not believe it, but I actually *am* an assassin. Mya wouldn't have chosen me to watch her back if I wasn't."

Lad smiled without humor. "You always were quick to take offence about that, though I meant none. But there's still more to this than you're telling me. Mya's been in trouble before, and you've never been so…wound up about it."

"I feel guilty about Mya. That's all." Dee looked back out the window. "She threw me to safety and sent me to find help. If I'd stayed with her, she might not have been captured. She saved my life at the risk of her own."

"It's more than guilt, Dee." Lad cocked his head. "Are you in love with her?"

Dee froze. *How...* Were his feelings writ so plainly on his face? He opened his mouth to deny it, but Lad would surely spot the lie. He closed his mouth and looked away.

"Don't tell me, then," Lad said into the silence. "I owe you for what you did for me when I was guildmaster, Dee, but if you took me away from my family just because you love Mya, I'll kill you."

The utter lack of emotion in Lad's voice sent a chill up Dee's spine. Any other might have used a threatening tone. Lad didn't need to threaten. He was just stating a fact. His only concern was for his family, and it transformed Dee's fear into anger.

"Your family isn't the *only* one that matters, you know." Dee matched gazes with Lad for a tense moment, biting down hard on his temper. "I wasn't *lying* to get you here. To me, it's about saving Mya's life, but that doesn't mean there's no risk to the Twailin guild and your family as well."

Lad held his gaze a moment longer, his pale, luminous eyes inscrutable, then shifted to look out the carriage window.

Dee released a breath he hadn't realized he'd been holding. *I just faced down Lad, and I'm still alive...* His concern for Mya had made him bold; he never would have spoken like that when he was Lad's assistant. *Careful, Dee. You may have survived this round, but he's still the most lethal killer you know.*

Mya stirred from a fitful sleep riddled with nightmares, unsure what had awoken her. The light sheet draped over her supplied little warmth, and a shiver wracked her body. A bone-deep ache had invaded her overnight from the enforced immobility and tight restraints.

Restraints... Turn her over... She fought through the residual lassitude of opium. *They'll turn me over, and to do that... Yes!* She remembered now her unexpected chance to escape. Desperation surged up, clearing the cobwebs from her mind.

Metal clicked on metal, and a hinge creaked. Light brightened behind her lids, but she kept her eyes closed and her breathing even. Her plan was simple, but required patience and observation. *Focus! How many?*

Boots scuffed along the floor, then the door closed, and keys rattled.

"Get a dose ready. I'll check her."

"Right."

Two men… Tieg and Kelsey. The names popped unbidden into Mya's head. *Kittal told them to come early.* Hopefully, it was early enough that everyone else was still abed.

She could hear their breathing, but faintly; before her mutilation, she could have heard their heartbeats. *Lost skin, lost runes, lost senses… What else have I lost? Strength, speed, agility?* Only days ago, killing two Alchemists would have been child's play. Now doubt clouded her confidence, blunted her concentration, dulled her edge.

Can I fight? Can I take them?

Her inner voice shrieked at her, igniting her nerves and honing her rage. *What alternative do you have? Kill them, or die screaming as they peel you like an orange. Hate them. Hatred will carry you through. Hatred is your only weapon.*

I can do this. Don't hold back. No pity. No mercy… Kill or die screaming. Mya focused all her senses, sought to feel the very air around her. *Just…don't…move.* She lay utterly still as one of the Alchemists pulled the sheet off and slapped her lightly.

"Huh. She didn't even twitch." Kelsey—Mya recalled his voice—pinched her shoulder hard. "Seems like she'd be awake by now. How much did Berta give her last night?"

"I don't know. You'll have to ask Berta."

"I'm not going to go wake her up and we can't wait until she gets here. Kittal won't be happy if we're not ready to go when he arrives."

"And if we kill his prize with an overdose, he'll use that skinning tool on *us.*" Tieg sounded tense. "You're senior. It's your call. Do I give her this or not?"

Kelsey sighed. "Wait a minute."

The wisp of steel on leather caught Mya's ear. Before she could brace herself, agony blossomed in her thigh as a blade pierced skin and flesh, pressing even into bone. Despite her stoicism, Mya jerked, her muscles straining against the bonds. An involuntary gasp parted her lips, but she managed to bite back the scream that longed to leap from her throat. *Limp! Go limp!* She forced her muscles to slacken, let the gasp escape her throat as a sigh.

"She's certainly still got *some* drug on board or she'd be screaming. You better halve the dose."

"Half it is." The blade slid from her flesh, and a needle pinched her shoulder. "There. Give that a minute and we'll flip her over."

The last thing Mya needed was more drugs, but half a dose was better than a full one. She fought against the rising fog, cursing silently all the curses she knew as the two Alchemists bustled about the room, preparing for the day's skinning. Sounds muddled, and the light behind her eyelids swirled in hypnotic patterns. She felt herself slipping into darkness, scrabbled to grab on to something—anything—to remain cognizant. *Focus! Don't let it take you! Hate! Hate them...*

"Check her again."

Pain lanced through her leg once more, this time dulled, but enough to bring her mind to scalding clarity. She didn't even twitch. Instead, she let the hatred take hold. Her back tingled as the magic rose in her remaining runes, her rage rising to fever pitch.

Wait for it, Mya...

"That's got her." The voice seemed distant. "Get the restraints."

Keys jingled like the chimes of freedom, and the restraints came off one by one: ankles, thighs, hips, arms, wrists, and finally her neck.

The Alchemists chatted as they worked. "Kind of a shame, really."

"What do you mean?"

"I mean, she's...well, she *was* quite lovely." Hard hands gripped her legs.

"Yeah, well, you've got to break some eggs to make an omelet, they say, and whatever Lakshmi wants, Kittal gives her." More hands gripped her under the arms. "Ready?"

"Ready."

Godsdamned right I'm ready, you torturing bastards. Mya stoked her hatred, willing it to burn away the opium fog. *Wait...*

"On three, then. One...two...three!"

As they lifted, Mya opened her eyes. A face hovered over hers, blurry, but clear enough. Kelsey's eyes widened, his mouth opening to shout. Only a strangled gasp escaped as she latched onto his throat with both hands.

At the same moment, Mya snatched one leg free of Tieg's grasp and lashed out blindly. Her foot connected with something solid. His grip vanished and glass and metal crashed to the floor over by the wall.

Mya embraced the rage, madness rising like a wellspring from her battered soul. Squeezing with every ounce of her strength, she dug her fingers deep until flesh split and fragile bones cracked. She tried to flip up and off the slab, but the drug made her clumsy. She fell with a bone-jarring thump to the stone floor, dragging Kelsey down with her, her blood-slicked hands still locked around his throat. Tighter and tighter she squeezed until a crimson stream spilled from his mouth, and his eyes rolled up.

Metal clashed behind her. Tieg struggled to rise amidst the shards of glass and metal implements, one hand clutching his shattered and bleeding jaw. She lurched up on wobbly legs, egged on by the mad voice in the back of her mind—*Kill! Murder the torturing bastards!*—and flung herself at the Alchemist. He cried out as she crashed into him, and they fell in a tangle, her fingers groping and grasping, her legs twisting and clamping around him. *Kill...murder... vengeance...*

Mya plunged her thumbs into his eyes, extinguishing Tieg's horrified gaze. The Alchemist bucked and fought, but she clung tight, squeezing her legs together. Deeper and deeper she pushed. *Hate him! Kill him!* Her world narrowed to just the two of them, locked in an embrace of life and death.

Pain lanced into her side, but it didn't matter. Nothing mattered but her rage.

Once...twice...thrice, she bashed the Alchemist's skull against the unyielding stone floor. Blood spread in a widening pool. Death spasms wracked his body, but she smashed his head down one more time for good measure before pulling her fingers from their bloody sheathes and releasing him.

Pain pulsed through the fog of opium, and Mya blinked down at the dagger protruding from her side. *A weapon... I should keep it...*

With a weapon she could fight or, if that failed, take her own life. Her unsteady fingers fumbled pulling it out, and she hissed between clenched teeth. Blood—too much—flowed from the wound. Would it heal? Could she stand, walk, escape?

Don't ask stupid questions, just do it!

Gripping the edge of a table, Mya pulled herself up. She shook her head to clear the drug-induced haze, and the room swam around her, then steadied, an abattoir, blood dripping from her fingers... *I did that... Oh gods...* She nearly toppled, her blood-slicked hands scrabbling for purchase on the stone slab.

No! Focus! Escape or you're dead!

Mya took a breath and tried to take stock. The two Alchemists were dead. She had a weapon. She was unfettered. *All good.* The chill air reminded her she was naked. She looked down, and a gasp caught in her throat. Waxy scars covered her chest, abdomen, and legs. Only where the restraints had held her immobile did narrow bands of her familiar runes dance and swirl. Bile burned Mya's throat, and she retched dryly.

How can I fight...live...survive without them? Despair threatened to overwhelm her.

Forget it! her inner voice chided. *Get out!*

Mya looked at the corpses, considered their clothing and boots.

No time! Get out!

She fumbled with the sheet they'd used to cover her, cutting a ragged hole in the middle and pulling it on like a poncho. Blood smeared the fabric—hers or theirs, she didn't know or care. Stumbling to the door, she pressed down on the handle and it opened. Peering out, worry niggled at her. *What am I forgetting?* She glanced back at the gore-spattered room and her bloody footprints. *Leaving a trail...* She wiped her feet as clean as she could. Still the worry niggled, but nothing came to mind beyond the imperative to escape.

A single oil lamp turned low lit the empty corridor. Straining to listen over her pounding heart, Mya picked out the distant clatter of metal, wood, and porcelain. The scent of food clenched her empty stomach. It was early; perhaps they were all eating breakfast.

Careful... Quiet... There'll be guards or servants...

Mya edged out into a hallway, closing the door quietly behind her. The floor seemed to tilt like a pitching rowboat, and she leaned against one wall for support. Cautiously, she staggered past four closed doors, two on each side. She ignored them; she needed to find a way out, not explore. If she opened a door into a barracks, her escape and her life would be over.

The hallway teed into another, and she peered around the corner to her left. The dining room must be through the open door at the end of the hall, though she couldn't see the source of the chatter and clatter. In the other direction, the hallway sported several closed doors before turning left. Stepping out into the open would risk being spotted from the dining room, but she had nowhere else to go.

Mya crept out with her back to the wall, both for balance and to keep a narrow profile. The dim lighting would help, but if someone happened to glance out from the dining room, a woman wearing a bloody sheet would raise an immediate alarm. A burst of laughter froze her in her tracks, her heart pounding in her chest, but when no one appeared, she moved on. She passed the closed doors, praying they wouldn't open and belch out an army of assassins, and finally reached the corner.

So far, so good.

She leaned out far enough to peer around with one eye and immediately jerked back. Two assassins with loaded crossbows guarded a rising stairway at the end of the corridor, dashing her hopes. She recalled how easily she had avoided the guards beneath the brick factory, sprinting up the wall and effortlessly evading their bolts. In her current condition, she'd be lucky to get three steps before they shot her down.

Shit! Nowhere to go… Mya glanced back at the dining room and the closed doors, and despair tried to claw its way into her heart.

Think, Mya! Maybe I can hide… When they found her missing, guards would begin searching. Perhaps she could use the distraction to strike and flee in the confusion. *But hide where?*

Mya checked the nearest door, but the latch didn't budge. *Keys!* Tieg and Kelsey had used keys to enter the lab and unlock her restraints. *That's what I forgot!* Cursing silently, she staggered to the next door. The latch yielded to her touch.

Thank you…

She opened the door and peered into the dark, sweltering room. It wasn't a barracks, so she slipped inside and closed the door behind her.

Acrid scents bit her nose even before she sorted out the room's vast, cluttered, and confusing contents. In the center, flame-fed cauldrons bubbled and hissed, throwing up pungent steam that rendered the air thick and hard to breathe. Wide tables lining two walls supported all manner of glass contrivances. Liquids bubbled above blue alcohol flames and flowed up spiral glass tubes in defiance of gravity.

Mya grimaced. Alchemy—half chemistry, half magic, and totally beyond her ken. It didn't matter. There was no place to hide in here. Turning back to the door, she stubbed her toe on a thick iron grating in the floor. *A drain?* Memories surfaced of wading through sewers with Dee. *Maybe...* It was barely as wide as her shoulders from corner to corner, but she might just fit through.

Kneeling, she tugged at the grating, but the wrought-iron bars were as thick as her thumb. There was no way she could break it. The mortared edge, however, was crumbling, probably due to long years of exposure to harsh chemicals. Her dagger fit easily into one of the cracks, and gentle pressure popped out a piece of mortar as long as her finger.

Yes!

Mya pried out piece after piece of the fragile mortar, dropping each through the grating. *If I hide my tracks, they might not figure out where I went.* She worked frantically, expecting the door to open any moment. When the last piece lifted free, she lay the dagger aside and gripped the thick iron with both hands.

Please... she prayed to any god willing to listen. Drawing a deep breath, she heaved, but the grating didn't budge.

"Come on, Mya..." Bracing her feet, she heaved again, straining until her head felt like it would explode. Gasping for breath, she gave up. *I need a crowbar, or...*

Mya snatched up the dagger and wedged the tip into the crack around the grating. Hammering the pommel with her palm, she levered it back and forth, repeating the process half a dozen times around the seam. Still the grating remained fixed in place. Her vision blurred with tears.

"Come on, come on, come on!" She wrenched at the blade...and it snapped off an inch above the floor.

"No, no, no!" Mya reversed her grip and smashed the pommel down on the broken tip of the blade as hard as she could, heedless of the noise, then again, and once more. "Please, please!" On the third impact, something cracked, and the grating shifted.

Mya sat back on her heels, her head spinning. Staring at the grating, she couldn't remember why she'd been trying so hard to break it loose. Over the reek of chemicals, a familiar scent wormed its way into her drug-addled mind. The stench of blood—her hands and the sheet she wore were red with it—reignited the memory of Kittal's vile machine slicing off her skin.

Escape!

Mya heaved on the grating. This time it came up, and she lay it down to one side. *Hurry!* She peered down into the darkness, but couldn't see the bottom, though she'd heard bits of mortar splash into water not far below. The sides of the drain were caked with filth.

Now's not the time to be squeamish.

Mya clenched the broken knife between her teeth and lowered herself down into the slimy orifice. When her eyes were level with the floor, she wedged one leg across the shaft and dragged the grating back into place. Maybe, if they were in a hurry, they wouldn't notice the missing mortar. Even if they did, few would be willing or able to follow. Most men wouldn't even fit down the drain.

Mya wormed her way down into the depths of Tsing's sewers, biting back her revulsion as tiny creatures skittered over her skin in the darkness. Her feet splashed into ankle-deep water. A pipe, barely larger than the shaft, stretched away in both directions. Contorting herself, she started scrabbling forward. *You're alive, Mya! Just keep crawling! Keep crawling or die. This has got to come out somewhere!*

Benj looked at his pocket watch, cursing the whole notion of mornings. He had just enough time for one more interview before heading down to headquarters. Yawning, his tucked the watch back into his pocket. "Too bad I ain't gettin' paid for all this extra work," he muttered.

Lucky Gem's was quiet this early, though there were a few diehards playing cards and chatting up the sleepy whores. Benj had been coming over in his off hours, checking up on Otar and questioning the employees. So far, his efforts hadn't yielded much; Otar drank and gambled almost every night, rarely raising his head until mid-morning. Benj preferred a similar schedule, but he was doing all the work himself on this case. He didn't dare tell anyone else about the suspicious association between Dreyfus and the former imperial guard captain; if word got back to the boss, he'd lose his stripes, at the very least.

But who else could he tell who could do anything to help? *Someone outside the chain of command, maybe.* The thought brought Miss Moirin to mind, but she'd gone missing, and Dee hadn't shown up for their scheduled meeting. He was undoubtedly busy trying to find her. *No help there...*

Benj accepted a refill on his cup of blackbrew from Gem and nodded his thanks, scanning the room with a judicious eye. His gaze fell on a curvy redhead and something Gem had told him clicked into place.

"That the one you said Otar likes?"

"Aye, that's Jacie." Gem and Benj went way back, and she knew better than to withhold information. She shook her head and sighed. "She's a good earner, but she drinks up her pay. Not long for this business, poor lass."

"Thanks." Benj took his cup and sauntered over to where Jacie sat eating her breakfast, a short, broad-shouldered man talking to her over a cup.

"You're Jacie, right?" Benj sat down at the table, ignoring the glare from her companion.

"I might be." Her eyes lingered on the stripes on his collar as she shoveled a spoonful of lumpy porridge into her mouth.

"The lady's havin' her breakfast, mate," the man grumbled.

"I see that. And I'm talkin' to her, and you're buggering off." Benj grinned at him. "Don't worry, friend. This won't take long. You can have a go at her when I'm through."

"Bloody cap." The man picked up his mug and left the table.

"That wasn't very nice, Sergeant," Jacie chided. "He was a payin' customer, you know."

"Oh, I think I was bein' *very* nice." Benj fished a silver crown from his pocket and flipped it across his knuckles. Experience had taught him that silver brought out the best in people. "You see, *I'm* payin' you, too, and all you got to use that mouth of yours for is talkin'."

Jacie smiled amiably and continued to eat, her eyes following the silver back and forth across his scarred knuckles. "All right, Sergeant. What's on your mind?"

"Gem tells me that old sot Otar favors you."

"True enough." She shrugged. "What of it?"

"What does he talk about?"

She laughed. "Not much other than what he wants me to do. Fella's got quite an imagination. Always somethin' new."

Benj sipped his blackbrew. "Not much. That's more than nothin'. He ever mention anyone by name? Why he got dismissed from the Imperial Guard? How he feels about the new emperor? His old aunt in Miravore? Anything at all?"

"Oh, he's got no love for the new emperor, that's clear enough. Calls him all kinda awful names, usually when he's got a head full of whiskey."

"What about friends? Does he play cards with anyone regular? Have any visitors?"

"Not so much." Another bite of porridge muffled her next words. "He *does* keep odd company sometimes, though."

"What kind of company?" Benj sat up straighter. This was the first he'd heard that Otar had company at all.

"Well, we was headin' up to his room a few nights ago and this fella was already in there. I thought at first Oatie wanted me to do 'em both, but he just shoved me out of there like a bag of dirty laundry and locked the door."

"What did this man look like?"

"Like a Downwind beggar." Jacie wrinkled her nose. "Skinny, hair and beard cropped short, gray robes. He'd a scary look to him. I'm glad Oatie didn't want a threesome. The freaky ones creep me out."

Otar consorting with beggars? It didn't seem likely, given the man's former position. Maybe he'd picked up a drug habit and this had been his supplier. "Did you hear a name?"

"Nah, but Oatie seemed surprised to see him there. I heard him say through the door he'd told the guy never to come in the evenings." Jacie stopped eating and pointed her spoon at Benj to emphasize her next point. "I wondered how he got into the room in the first place. Oatie keeps it locked, and Gem don't give her pass key out to anyone *ever*."

"Robes and short cropped hair, you say?" A niggling suspicion tickled the base of the sergeant's skull. Reaching into the inside pocket of his jacket, he retrieved a copy of the flier he'd been passing around. He unfolded it and showed it to her. "Is this him?"

"Hey! That *is* him! Well, I'll be buggered!"

A saucy quip died on the tip of Benj's tongue as the impact of what she'd said struck home. *Hoseph talking with the former captain of the Imperial Guard?* His hands shook as he folded the flier and tucked it away.

Standing, he dropped the silver crown on the table. "Thank you, Jacie."

"Any time, Sergeant." She snatched up the coin and grinned. "Easiest silver I made in a long time! Come see me if you want me to work for it next time."

"I just might." He gave her a tight smile. "No word to Otar about what we just spoke of, now. Or anyone else for that matter."

"Oh, I got a real short memory, Sergeant." She winked at him. "I hardly remember my own name some days."

Benj hurried out of *Lucky Gem's* and along the street toward the constabulary, his mind awhirl. Unconsciously, he touched the pocket holding the flier. Hoseph, the most wanted fugitive in Tsing, implicated in the attempt on the emperor's life, was meeting with Otar, and Otar was Chief Constable Dreyfus' new drinking buddy.

And Dreyfus is in charge of security for the emperor's big public announcement.

Cold dread roiled Benj's gut, his time-honored instinct kicking in. This was big, way bigger than a constable sergeant could deal with.

The question is, what in the Nine Hells can I do about it?

Chapter III

The heat and noise of the blacksmith's shop faded as Lad followed Dee down a steep flight of stairs. At the bottom, a long corridor ended at a door guarded by a man and woman, both armed to the teeth. From their calluses and scars, he judged them well versed in the use of their weaponry. The guards scrutinized Lad, but simply nodded to Dee, knocked on the door, and opened it.

Inside, several assassins crowded around a wide table strewn with maps, inkwells, and blackbrew mugs. A few others stood by attentively. Lad scanned all their faces. At Dee's glance, he shook his head. None of these were among those who had seen Lad when he and Mya ran into a patrol of Enforcers their first night in Tsing. Dee had agreed to keep Lad's identity a secret if possible. With any luck, he'd never encounter any of them, and his assumed identity would hold up.

"Dee! Good! You're back." A tall, raven-haired man with a warrior's build waved them over to the table.

Noncey, of course, Lad thought, noting the man's numerous weapons. He hardly needed Dee's introductions—his descriptions had been spot on—but nodded politely. Master Hunter Embree also fit the profile of his vocation, his analytical eye roving over Lad from head to toe, lingering on his old scars and his maimed left hand. The Master Enforcer, however, was not what he expected, lithe and beautiful, with faintly pointed ears peeking from beneath her shimmering blonde hair, rather than scarred and brutish as most Enforcers seemed to be.

"And you must be Bloodhound." Embree stepped around the table and held out a hand to Lad. "Funny that Mya never mentioned you."

"No, it's not." Lad shook the hand, matching the Hunter's attempt at a crushing grip exactly and interpreting the effrontery in Embree's eyes. The Master Hunter had failed to track down Mya and regarded his presence as an insult. Lad couldn't have cared less. "I'm not a member of your guild."

"Well, if you can find Mya, I don't care if you're a member of the *Prostitutes* Guild." Clemson shook his hand as well, her smile friendly.

"So, do we call you Bloodhound?" Noncey shook his hand and grinned. "You must be pretty good to have earned a nickname like that."

"Yes, and yes, I am." Lad was willing to be polite, but he wasn't about to offer explanations. The sooner he found Mya, the sooner he could go home.

"Fair enough." Clemson gestured to the map-strewn table. "Let us show you what we've got so far."

"Please." Lad shared a glance with Dee. "Time's not on our side *or* Mya's. I'd like to see the place where she was kidnapped before any potential clues degrade beyond use."

"We already searched the place thoroughly. The trail ends in a laundry, and there's no trace of where they went from there." Icy distain rimed Embree's words.

"With all due respect, Master Embree, *I* haven't searched it." Lad met the man's eyes without fear or rancor. "I don't have to prove myself to any of you. If you don't want my help, I'll leave."

Embree wrinkled his nose. "Well, if *balls* was all it took, you'd have found her already!"

"There's no harm in letting him try," Noncey said sharply.

"None at all." Clemson nodded curtly to Dee. "Use my carriage. Jolee, go with them."

"Yes, Master." A huge woman stepped forward with a covert wink and tusky smile at Dee.

"I'll go as well," Embree turned to another assassin. "Orvis, coordinate our search patterns with the Blades and Enforcers."

"I don't need any help." Lad glanced at the massive Jolee. "Or protection."

"You don't understand." Embree took a step forward, his posture stiff. "I'm Master Hunter here, and I say I'm going with you. I can save you time by showing you what we've already found."

"Can we just stop the pissing contest and get moving?" Dee snapped.

Lad looked at Dee in surprise. His time in Tsing had changed the meek assistant into someone willing to stand up to both Lad and a master, technically his superior. Lad nodded to Embree. "You're right, of course. Time is our first priority."

Embree flashed a tight smile. "Good. Let's go."

In moments, they were in a carriage headed back across the river into Midtown. Thankfully, Jolee perched on the vehicle's boot, since she wouldn't have easily fit inside. The three men rode in silence. Embree eyed him throughout the ride, but Lad ignored him. He wasn't here to make friends. He was here to find Mya and go home.

Down one of the more industrial streets of Midtown, they pulled up in front of a brick factory. The smoke belching from its stacks trailed the scent of brimstone and ash across the city on the sea breeze. In the courtyard, workers loaded huge wagons as teamsters struggled to keep their heavy draft horses in check. A burly man with a bushy red beard glared as they walked into the factory proper, but didn't stand in their way.

"Is this a guild-owned business?" asked Lad as they followed Embree through the sweltering factory.

The Master Hunter shook his head. "We found no connection. The foreman said some strangers came in offering a lot of money to rent some space. The owners apparently didn't even know about the old smuggler's hideout beneath the building. They were pissed off about the damage we did in our raid, but a few gold coins and a warning shut them up."

Finally, they came to a door guarded by a single man in a worker's apron. An assassin, no doubt; his hands sported the wrong calluses, and he looked far too clean to be a real laborer, not to mention the numerous small weapons that Lad spotted hidden about his person. Nodding to Embree, he opened the door and stepped aside. Through an office and a concealed door, then they descended a long stair, the air cooler with every step. At the bottom, the way teed into a dank passage.

Dee pointed to the left where the corridor led into darkness. "That's the way we came in, through a partially flooded sewer tunnel to the river."

Lad could smell sewage and mold. He nodded and turned to follow Embree the other way, where two more assassins guarded an opening.

Dee continued his account. "There were Alchemist guards at the door when we arrived, but Mya took them out."

Lad fingered the splintered wood of the door frame and inspected the door itself, leaning against the wall beside the opening. "She broke down the door?"

"Yes."

Lad stepped into the vaulted room and swept the chamber with his gaze. It had been beautifully appointed once, but now everything—the lush carpets, the furniture, the tapestries, and even the stone walls—were pocked and torn. The room stank of scorched vegetation, and bits of charred vines and burned leaves crunched under his feet.

Dee pointed to a tattered bed. "The boy was there. When I lifted him, overhead tapestries fell, releasing thousands of little black seeds. They sprouted everywhere, and vines grew *fast*." His voice quavered before he swallowed hard and continued. "Mya threw me and the boy clear, but she was entangled and couldn't rip free." He pointed to a spot on the carpet. "She was right there when last I saw her."

Lad knelt where Dee indicated. The leaves on the charred vine were burned beyond recognition, but he crumbled a piece and tasted it—bitter, ashy, with a hint of mustiness. A distant memory surfaced. "Dragons' bane vine. Not very common, but effective at restraining without killing. These here were sprayed with winter-cap mushroom tea, the only way to make it release its hold…barring fire, of course. That's how they got her out."

Embree cocked an eyebrow. "Well, you *do* know something…"

"It's also something an Alchemist would know." Lad brushed through litter on the floor: burned vines, tattered carpet, and bits of shredded cloth. A spot of color caught his eye, a thumbnail-sized swatch of dark silk. Holding it to his nose, he sniffed. It stank. He looked back down the long passage into the darkness. *They came in through the sewers.* "Do you remember what Mya was wearing?"

Dee's brow furrowed. "Of course. Black trousers, a maroon silk shirt—"

Lad held up the swatch. "This color?"

"Yes!" Dee snatched it, stared at it as if he might conjure Mya out of the tiny piece of cloth. "The vines were stuck to her clothes. She tried to tear them loose."

"How did you know?" Embree asked, his tone skeptical.

"It stinks of the sewer." Lad started a slow circuit of the room. A gaping hole on the back wall was hinged on one side with a stone slab of identical shape except where the edges were chipped and crushed. A dark tunnel extended beyond. "You think that's where they took her out?"

Embree pointed to a smudge on the wall near the door. "Yes. A blood trail led us to it."

"And Jolee broke it open," Dee added. The huge Enforcer cracked her knuckles. "We weren't far behind them, minutes at most."

Lad paused at the rust-colored smudge, sniffed it, scraped some off with his thumbnail, and let it melt on his tongue. "This isn't Mya's."

"Oh, come on! You expect me to believe that you can identify her blood by *taste?*" The derision in Embree's voice spoke volumes.

"I don't expect you to believe anything." Lad stepped into the tunnel, waving the others back. Sniffing the stale air, he detected the scents of numerous people—probably the Alchemists who took Mya and the Hunters who tracked them—as well as the one scent he sought. Dropping to his knees, he put his nose to the floor and breathed deep, shifting about until he located the source…a dried drop of sewer water. They'd carried Mya along here, and her dripping clothes had left a trail. "You were right. They took her this way." He stood and strode down the tunnel.

"Wait!" Embree trotted up alongside. Plucking a crystal from a pocket, he brought it to light with a word and held it up to illuminate the tunnel. "The last thing we need is for you to fall in the dark and break a leg."

Lad opened his mouth to protest—he could see better in the dark, and never tripped—but then reconsidered. The others had to see, and the fewer of his preternatural abilities the man knew about, the better. He couldn't risk any of them learning his identity.

"Keep the light behind me," he told Embree. "I don't want to be blinded and miss a step."

"Of course." The Master Hunter followed a step behind, light held high, while Dee and Jolee brought up the rear.

They walked quite a distance, Lad continually inspecting the floor, walls, and ceiling for more hidden passages, but to no avail. The faint scent of sewerage, however, persisted. Eventually they arrived at another stone door, this one sporting a locking mechanism. Embree threw the bolt and pulled it open.

"This is where we lost the trail. It's a laundry in the Wharf District."

Lad stepped through the door, and his heart lurched with recognition. The room reminded him of the abandoned laundry where he'd taken Wiggen after rescuing her from the Twailin Royal Guard prison. *Wiggen... That was the first time we...* Blinking hard to clear his eyes, he forced his attention back to his task.

Barrels, bins, and tools cluttered the periphery of the large, low room. In the center, three massive cauldrons bubbled atop coal-fueled furnaces, lye-scented steam wafting up into wide vents. A sweat broke out on his brow with the oppressive heat and humidity. Wiping it away, he surveyed the area, assessing the operation.

The dirty laundry came down through chutes into bins on wheels, which would be emptied into cauldrons and agitated by mechanical stirrers. Heavy mechanisms tipped the contents of the cauldrons into large strainers set over drains in the floor, and the strainers would be lifted by chains up through trapdoors in the ceiling, presumably so the clothes could be dried and folded above. Though coal dust and lint littered the corners, the center of the floor was relatively clear, scuffed clean by many feet.

Lad advanced slowly, trying to detect any hint that Mya had been here or where they might have taken her. The sewage smell was nearly overwhelmed by the lye odor, but suddenly he caught a stronger whiff of it. On hands and knees, he squinted at the floor. Leaning close, he inhaled, shifted a few inches, and inhaled once more. Again and again he repeated this, finally sitting back on his heels.

"They stripped her and dropped her clothes here." He traced the patch, perhaps two feet across, with his finger.

"Why would they strip her?" Dee's voice shook.

Embree snapped his fingers. "Because she stank like the sewers, just like you did, Dee. A smell like that would attract attention." He knelt, sniffed the area, nodded, and looked at Lad with surprised admiration. "Bloodhound indeed!"

"Stuff her in a laundry bag, carry her outside, and disappear. No one would think twice about someone carrying laundry out of a laundry!" Jolee's thick brow furrowed.

Embree nodded as he got to his feet. "That's the problem. No one *did* notice anything, and we've got no way to track her."

Lad stared at the floor, thinking. *They stripped her...* An incongruous memory surfaced of Mya disrobing in the dark room of an inn during their trip to Tsing. *Clothes...* The kernel of an idea formed. Sweeping his head from side to side, he sniffed and peered about. "There are other ways of tracking someone. If we could find her clothes..."

Embree scoffed. "Her clothing wouldn't do us any good. To track her with magic, we'd need something personal. Clothes don't work."

"That depends." Lad searched, peering under bins and rooting through the piles of bagged laundry. He wasn't sure how much Mya had confided to anyone in Tsing, and he didn't want to give away her secrets. "What I'm looking for isn't really *clothing*. It's a strip of black cloth, looks like plain linen, but—"

Dee's eyes snapped wide. "Her wrappings!"

Lad stared at Dee, wondering again about the relationship between Mya and her assistant. *If he knows about her wrappings...*

"Wrappings?" Embree looked from Dee to Lad and back. "What kind of wrappings?"

Dee glanced at Lad with a look somewhere between guilt and defiance and stammered, "Mya wore...enchanted wrappings under her street clothes to...um...keep her cool. She has for years. She only took them off...uh...rarely."

"Why didn't you tell me this when she first went missing?" Embree scowled. "If we can find them, we can use them to track her!"

"I...honestly didn't *think* of it." Dee's jaw clenched.

Embree cast about the room, his eyes drifting to the furnaces. "Mightn't they have burned them?"

"Why risk having the wet clothing douse the fire and draw someone down here? They don't look enchanted, they'd stink the same as her other clothes, and her kidnappers would have been in a hurry. And, like you, they wouldn't think they could be used to track her." Lad pointed to the cauldrons. "The easiest thing to do would have been to throw them in one of those."

"Which means..." Dee dashed for the stairs, Lad and Embree on his heels. "They may still be here!"

At the top, they hurried past a startled woman sitting at a table sorting papers, through another door, and into the laundry proper. Here, however, they stopped short. Dee groaned as he gazed out across the vast and crowded facility.

Dozens of workers rinsed, wrung, and hung laundry on hundreds of wheeled racks. Once a rack was full, another employee wheeled it away and hooked it onto a slowly moving chain overhead. The taut chain lifted the racks up and away through a gap in the ceiling. On the far side of the huge room, the racks descended back through another opening, and workers removed the now-dry laundry, folding it on rows of long tables.

"Mya was taken three nights ago, correct?" Lad asked. At Dee's nod, he approached a worker hanging laundry. "If something was washed three night ago, would it still be here?"

The woman laughed. "In *this* humidity? Course it's still here! We ain't got magic to dry things, just the sea air! Takes four days to run the process. Probably on a dryin' racks upstairs," she waved a hand vaguely overhead, "or bein' folded."

Lad flipped her a coin and returned to the others. "Embree and Jolee, check the folding tables. We're looking for a long strip of black linen about three inches wide. Dee and I will look upstairs."

"Right!" Thankfully, the Master Hunter didn't argue. As he and the Enforcer hurried off, Dee was already dashing up the stairs.

Lad followed, but Dee had stopped at the top of the stairs, staring up in shock.

"This is going to be like trying to find one particular leaf in a forest!"

Lad had to agree.

A lofty network of huge gears propelled the rack-laden chain on a serpentine track up through the rafters—fully three stories high—past rows of high, open windows. Thousands upon thousands of garments, sheets, and other washables flapped in the sea breeze, and water dripped like rain to be funneled away by floor drains.

"You go that way." Lad pointed to the series of stairs and catwalks that scaled the four walls. "I'll go this way."

Lad started searching, musing as he peered through the draped laundry. Had Dee learned about Mya's wrappings by accident, as Lad had, or was the situation more...intimate? Did he also know what her wrappings concealed? That was a secret Mya had previously killed to keep. If Dee did know, then perhaps she had finally learned to trust someone besides herself.

"There!" Dee's excited shout drew Lad's attention. "There it is!"

Lad looked where Dee was pointing and spotted a long black streamer fluttering among the other garments. It was near the top of the run, well away from the walls and several turns from its eventual descent to the lower floor.

"Good eye, Dee!"

"But how do we get it?" Dee craned his neck. "There's no way up there, and it won't be lowered to the folding room for hours!"

"I'll get it." Lad examined the three-dimensional maze of chain, gears, and racks. "Just keep everyone out of here. I don't want Embree or Jolee to see me do this."

"Yes...yes, I will." Dee hurried down to stand guard at the stairs to the lower level.

Dashing to one of the great gears, Lad shimmied up the slowly revolving vertical shaft to the next level, flipped up over the slowly rotating gear, then climbed two more above that, carefully avoiding where the chain meshed with the massive teeth. If he got a hand or foot caught between a cog and the chain, he'd be maimed once again, and he was already short three fingers.

The chain clanked slowly past. Two hooks suspended each rack, one after another in an endless procession, preventing Lad from swinging hand over hand along the chain.

Well, if not underneath, then on top of it.

Lad leaned far out, grasped the chain between two racks, and let go of the gear shaft. Though the chain was under tremendous tension, it swayed as it carried him along. Flipping and twisting, Lad swung himself atop the chain, balancing on the rough iron links like a performer on a tightrope. He was on the right level, but the wrappings hung five rows over.

The chain ran immediately below the ceiling joists here, so instead of leaping between the rows, Lad hopped up onto the nearest of the heavy wooden frames, then down onto the next pass of chain. Four more like that and he was on the right one. Stretching out his left leg as a counterbalance, he leaned out, caught sight of the wrappings only half a dozen racks ahead. Running lightly down the chain to the requisite rack, he sat sideways on the chain, flipped backward to dangle by his knees, and snatched up the length of dark cloth, rolling it into a tight ball.

One step closer to Mya...and home.

Hanging there like a bat in a belfry, Lad tucked the cloth firmly into his belt. Watching carefully, he waited for a break between the racks on the lower levels of chains, then straightened his legs and plummeted headfirst toward the floor, flipping in midair to land on his feet.

Dee stared at him wide-eyed, mouth agape, and Lad realized that, despite their lengthy association, Dee had never seen him use his magically enhanced talents. Well, if they were going to work together to rescue Mya from assassins, he was going to have to get used to it.

"It's not like I *flew* or anything!" He strode past Dee without pause. "Stop staring and come on."

On the main floor, Embree tore through the stacks of neatly folded clothing, while Jolee kept the irate workers at bay by merely standing there with her tree-trunk arms crossed, a scowl on her brutish face. Dee whistled and waved, pointing toward the exit.

"Sorry for the disruption." Embree tossed a few coins at the enraged foreman as they exited the building. "Did you get it?"

"Yes." Lad looked up and down the bustling street. "Now we need a—"

"HACKNEY!" Jolee's bellow rattled windows. Stepping in front of a carriage, she snatched the traces and planted her heels. The matched pair of horses snorted and tried to rear, but she held them firm.

"Hey!" The driver nearly pitched forward out of his seat. "You can't just—"

"Shut up!" Jolee snarled. "We're hiring you."

"I already got a fare! Just you let loose of my team!"

"Dire business, I'm afraid. My apologies." Embree motioned the others forward as he fished in his belt pouch. Gold glinted toward the driver, and the man snatched the coin from the air like a bat plucking a moth from the sky. The two passengers, a man and woman wearing merchants' garb, squawked in protest until more gold passed hands. The assassins boarded, Jolee mounted the running board, and Embree ordered, "Corner of Eastwatch and Holloway in the—"

"Wait!" Dee interrupted. "We need to go to the *palace*. The emperor's archmage will help us."

The Master Hunter frowned. "You want to get the godsdamned *emperor* involved? We can *hire* a mage for this, someone we've used before who'll keep their mouth shut."

"You think a hired wizard is better than the emperor's archmage?" Dee argued. "Besides, if you've hired this wizard before, how you know that Lakshmi and Kittal haven't gotten to him first?"

"*Her*, actually, and I don't," Embree conceded, his face flushing scarlet. "But—"

"The emperor *offered* to help! He ordered his entire staff to spare no effort."

The Master Hunter glared and lowered his voice. "You're exposing the *guild* to imperial scrutiny, Dee."

"Make up yer mind, gov! Ain't got all day!" the driver bawled.

"No more than it already is!" Dee hissed back through clenched teeth. "We can't take half measures in rescuing Mya. If we've got access to the best wizard in Tsing, someone we *know* won't betray us to the other factions, we should use him!"

Lad had to concede that Dee made a good point, but this wasn't his argument. Dee was facing down a guild superior once again...for Mya.

Embree's eyes hardened. "I know the Grandmaster trusts you, Dee, but make sure you're thinking with your head not your dick." He rapped on the door, and Jolee stepped off the running board. Embree stepped out and ordered the driver, "Take them to the Imperial Palace," then lowered his voice again to speak to Dee. "If Mya doesn't make it, you'd best remember not to flout a master's wishes so casually. I'll let Clemson and Noncey know where you've gone. Send word. We expect to be kept *informed*. This *isn't* just about you, Dee."

"No, sir, it's *not* about me." Dee stared him straight in the eye. "It's about our *Grandmaster*." He banged the roof and shouted, "Drive on!"

They rumbled away, leaving the Master Hunter red-faced, and Jolee hiding a smile behind one massive hand.

Dee caught Lad's eye. "What are *you* staring at?"

"You." Lad frowned, his suspicions confirmed. When it came to Mya, Dee was over the top. He held out the rolled wrappings. "Just remember what I told you about putting me in danger unnecessarily, Dee. If you *really* want to get Mya back, you've got to start thinking with a level head."

"I *am* thinking with a level head." Dee snatched up the ball of cloth, clutching it in a white-knuckled fist, his eyes hard as he banged again on the roof of the carriage. "Faster, driver! Another gold in your hand if you don't spare the whip!"

"She *what?*" His mind still ringing with the chime that had summoned him, Hoseph couldn't believe his ears. "I *told* you to kill her!"

"Yes, you did. Now calm down!" Lakshmi stood firm in the face of his tirade, her wizened brow knitted and her rouged lips set in a disapproving frown.

"Calm *down?* You let the most dangerous creature in Tsing escape from your grasp, and you want me to calm down? I've had *enough* of your incompetence!" Hoseph stalked forward, the pearly light of Demia's magic flaring from his palm. *I'll send her soul to the afterworld for this!*

Lakshmi's hand shot out and latched onto his forearm, her bony fingers digging into his flesh. Hoseph tried to wrench free, but she held firm, her grip like iron. His rage wavered, clouded with uncertainty. *How...* He tugged again, but couldn't break the old woman's grasp. *How can she be so fast, so strong?*

"You will drop that invocation and back away from her this instant, Hoseph, or I will *end* you."

Kittal's hissed threat drew the priest's glare. Greenish liquid swirled in a tiny glass vial in the Master Alchemist's hand. One flick of his wrist would send it jetting at Hoseph, undoubtedly with lethal results.

"Blessed shadow of death..." Hoseph growled the mantra like a curse. Faced with Lakshmi's startling speed and strength, and Kittal's deadly alchemical threat, he could do nothing but capitulate. He banished the invocation, the glow fading from his palm. Lakshmi's grip slackened, and he wrenched his arm free, stepping back.

"Now, if you wish to be part of our effort to recapture Mya, we could use your help." Lakshmi examined one glossy nail as if afraid that she'd broken it on Hoseph's arm. "If you would rather throw another *tantrum*, please do so elsewhere. You *can* track her, can you not?"

"No, I cannot," Hoseph scoffed.

Kittal eyes widened. "But you did before! You found her in that orphanage she was staying in."

The priest shook his head. "I can recognize the unique pattern of her soul, even when she's in disguise, but she's got to be in sight. I can't simply conjure up her trail from thin air. *You're* the assassins. Can't *you* track her?"

"That's the job of Hunters," Lakshmi reminded him. "No matter. I'm acquainted with a tracker who knows the sewers. He hunts gullywhumps for the constabulary when they become problematic."

"The sewers?" The thought of delving sewers infested with packs of feral humanoids was bad enough. Pursuing Mya in that dark, dank environment was suicidal. "You intend to hunt through the sewers for a woman who can best any assassin in the guild? Are you insane?"

Kittal waved aside his concerns. "She's drugged and weak. She was dosed just this morning. She must have escaped before the drug took full effect. Also, much of the magic that makes her so formidable has also been removed."

That took Hoseph aback. "What do you mean, removed?"

"I mean removed, excised, stripped from her. As you surmised, Mya gained her abilities through rune magic, tattoos inscribed on her skin. I've removed about a third of them."

Hoseph's nose wrinkled. "Why?"

"For *me*, Hoseph." Lakshmi smiled, a crimson gash of triumph. "The experiment I told you about worked. Kittal grafted Mya's tattoos onto me. Her magic is now mine!"

Hoseph didn't know whether to be intrigued or appalled. He rubbed the bruised flesh of his arm, confirmation that Lakshmi now possessed at least some of Mya's strength and speed. "If she was drugged, weak, and secure as you said, how did she get free? Are you sure she wasn't rescued by the other masters?"

"The evidence suggests that she escaped on her own," Kittal said. "It looks like her restraints were released before she had fully succumbed to the drug, allowing her to murder two of my assistants when they were repositioning her. She crawled through a drain in one of the labs that empties into the sewers. She's probably lying unconscious somewhere nearby. The sooner we can find her, the less dangerous she'll be. The three of us are a formidable force. Once we have her, you can transport us all back here."

"The *three* of us? Why don't you already have your assassins scouring the sewers?"

A pained look stiffened Lakshmi's features. "We've had some morale problems, and haven't told everyone that Mya has escaped. The last thing we need is a mass exodus."

"To the Nine Hells with your morale problem!" Hoseph had had enough of their folly and shortsightedness. "As *formidable* as we may be, and as weak as *she* may be, we're talking about *Mya* here. I'll accompany you, but you'll bring along a team of your best Alchemists, Kittal, fully armed. I don't care what you have to tell them."

Lakshmi and Kittal shared a look, then the Alchemist nodded. "Very well."

Thoroughly disgusted, Hoseph resolved that, regardless what Lakshmi and Kittal wanted, Mya wouldn't leave the sewers alive.

CHAPTER IV

Y ou've found her already?" Master Keyfur swung wide the door to his chambers, his face alight with elation.

"No, Master Keyfur, but we have a chance. And a favor to ask." *Please let him be able to do this!* Dee wasn't concerned about losing face with the guild masters, he just wanted to put all the power he could into finding Mya.

"Of course, I'll do whatever I can. You'd best come in." With a dismissive wave to their imperial guard escort, the archmage ushered Dee and Lad into his chambers. Stretching out a hand to Lad, he said, "I'm sorry we didn't have time for introductions this morning. I'm the emperor's archmage, Master Keyfur."

"Dee's told me of you." Lad shook the wizard's hand. "I'm called Bloodhound."

"Please," Dee interrupted, not about to let pleasantries take up their invaluable time. "Can you locate someone magically?"

Keyfur nodded. "Yes, but I would need something of Miss Moirin's, something highly personal to focus the magic."

Dee held out Mya's wrappings, reluctant to let them go. How many times had he unwound them—like unwrapping a gift—to reveal her beautiful tattoos. *Stop it! Focus!* "Here. She wore these beneath her clothing for years."

Keyfur's countenance brightened. "I recognize them from the coronation! Not the usual lady's undergarments, but under the circumstances..." He took the wrappings from Dee and stroked the soft fabric. His eyes widened. "They're enchanted, you know."

"Yes. Is that a problem?" If the magic of the wrappings interfered with the location spell, they were sunk.

"Oh, I should think not." Keyfur shuffled over to a tower of shelves crowded with books, knickknacks, and magical paraphernalia. "Now, where did I put that lodesphere?"

Dee shifted impatiently.

"We'll find her, Dee." Lad was staring at him again. He'd been doing that a lot, and it unnerved Dee to an uncommon degree.

"I can't stop thinking of what they might be doing to her."

"You're not doing her any good working yourself into a panic. Relax."

Dee gritted his teeth. "Could you relax when Lissa was taken?"

A muscle twitched in Lad's neck. "No, but I *did* manage to think straight, which is how we got her back."

Dee nodded. Lad was right. He took a deep breath and exhaled slowly, trying to calm his nerves.

Still Lad stared. "It's good that you two found each other. Mya needed someone."

"I know she needed someone." Dee flicked a cold look at Lad, but bit his lip. *Because she loved you and you left her alone in Tsing!* He couldn't, however, maintain his anger. Lad was the only reason they had any hope of finding Mya at all.

"Here!" Keyfur hustled over to a low table and motioned them closer.

Dee walked cautiously, eyes straight ahead. The last time he was here, the otherworldliness of the wizard's quarters had driven him to distraction. Lad seemed unconcerned by the shifting artwork, the mutable furniture, the nauseating writhing of the carpet underfoot. *Not surprising, I guess, since he's half magic himself.*

Keyfur piled Mya's wrappings in the center of the table and nestled a glass sphere within the folds. Inside the sphere hovered a human finger, as plump and pink as if it was still living. The proximal end, however, had been cleanly severed, rings of skin and muscle distinct around white bone. Dee's stomach churned, and he concentrated on the wizard.

Keyfur dropped a tome onto the table and flipped through the pages. "I don't perform this spell often, and I want to ensure I get it right. Ah, here we go!" Muttering an incomprehensible phrase, he plucked the colorful feather from behind his ear and waved it over the glass sphere. The finger within twitched, then swiveled and pointed a new direction, quivering at a downward angle. "There! It should be pointing at her now."

"Do you have a map?" asked Dee.

"Indeed I do!" Keyfur scooped up the cloth-nested sphere and strode to a wide table littered with glassware, books, trinkets, and crockery. He pushed hard on one edge, and the entire tabletop flipped.

Dee braced himself for the crash as everything atop it fell to the floor, but...nothing did. Leaning down, he peered beneath and found everything stuck in place, even the liquids in the glassware. *Okay, magic can be handy,* he conceded.

"So, we're here, of course." The table's new top displayed an amazingly detailed, three-dimensional map of Tsing. Keyfur rested the bundle of wrappings and the sphere atop the palace. "The map is accurately oriented, so we can get the general direction to Miss Moirin."

Lad sighted a line from the end of the pointing finger down across the city: The Heights, Midtown, over the river to the Dreggars Quarter. "She could be anywhere on that line?"

"That's a big area." Dee tried to keep his voice from quaking.

"Don't despair, Master Dee. The precision increases as you get nearer to the target," Keyfur explained. "The angle between two blocks from this distance is tiny, but from only a hundred yards away, it's huge."

"All right." Dee pointed to the glass sphere. "Can we take this? Will it work for us?"

"Um...no. I have to maintain the magical energy." The wizard barked a sudden laugh and grinned. "I guess I'm going with you! I owe Miss Moirin my life, and I'll not let a bunch of fiends harm her."

"This is apt to be dangerous," Lad warned.

Keyfur considered him with a jaded eye. "So am I, Master Bloodhound. Magic can be both a formidable weapon and a potent defense."

Dee felt a sudden flush of confidence, but also a twinge of concern. Keyfur might be good to have along, but they could hardly enlist the help of the Assassins Guild also. *No choice...we can't waste time.*

"We need to go immediately. Can you come with us?"

"Give me two shakes to gather some things and I'm with you!" Keyfur grinned and started rummaging through his shelves, tucking this and that into his robes.

Dee exchanged a glance with Lad, who only shrugged and said, "Never hurts to have a wizard on your side, I suppose."

Dee could only pray that he was right.

Keep crawling... Keep moving...or die. Scrabbling through the muck, Mya's hand came down on something soft and yielding. Before she could snatch her hand away, pain lanced through it.

"Shit!"

Her curse echoed through the tunnel, involuntary and loud. She snatched her hand back and peered fearfully around, to no avail. The darkness was too complete; she may as well have been blind. Recollections of the torture surfaced unbidden, and with them, a gut-wrenching dread.

Did they take my eyes? Hesitantly, she reached up to her face and found the orbs intact. *No,* she remembered, *they took my skin...my runes.* That was why she could no longer see in the dark, could feel the pain of the bite.

Mya sucked at the wound, tasted the metallic tang of blood. *Hungry...* She blinked in the darkness, her thoughts skipping through memories, dreads, nightmares without rhyme or reason. The only constant was the need to keep moving.

Yes... Keep moving. Find a way out...or die.

Unfortunately, the way out continued to elude her. Disoriented beyond reckoning, she had no idea how long she'd been crawling through the stinking tunnels, how many insect and rat bites she'd endured, how many times she'd risked a mouthful of the fetid water to quench her thirst, only to retch it back up. Had she escaped hours ago...or days ago?

Keep moving...or die.

Mya scrambled on.

She didn't notice the darkness gradually give way to gloom, and the gloom to shadows. Only when a sliver of diffuse sunlight stabbed down ahead did she realize that the tunnel opened up. She froze for a moment, trying to think what the light could mean. Was it good or bad? Crawling forward through the mire, she squinted into the light, felt a faint waft of air upon her cheek. Light and air seemed foreign concepts to her drug-addled mind until it finally hit her.

Light…air…a way out!

Scrabbling out of the small tunnel into a vaulted chamber where several large pipes came together, she reached up toward the light. It seemed miles away, far out of reach. She could make out the bars of a storm drain, hear street sounds. Her hand strayed into the radiance, and she stared at it in shock. It looked like the claw of some subterranean creature, blackened with filth and blood. Mya looked down; the rest of her wasn't any better. The sheet was torn and no longer white, and foul muck smeared her legs and feet. She gave up reaching for the light. It wouldn't come down to her, and she had to keep moving.

Suddenly she felt exposed. Why in the Nine Hells was she standing in the light? *Someone could see me!* Darkness meant safety; the Assassins Guild had taught her that.

Keep moving…

Mya plunged back into darkness, walking now, feeling her way along the curved wall of a larger tunnel. She could move faster on her feet than she could crawling, though the footing was treacherous. She didn't know where she was going, or even what she was fleeing. All she knew was that if she stopped, she would die screaming.

Farther on—minutes at least, hours maybe—the sound of splashing stopped her. Another rat? *No*, she decided. *Too big. But what else could be down here?*

"This way!"

The distant voice echoed off the tunnel walls, igniting Mya's frazzled nerves. Her breath caught in her throat and her heart raced. Voices meant people, and people brought pain and shearing blades that parted skin from flesh. Snapping her head right and left, she tried to determine where it had come from.

Ahead? Behind? Panic raced through Mya's bleary thoughts. *It doesn't matter. Move, Mya! Move or die…* Lurching into motion too fast, her head spun. She stumbled to her knees with a loud splash.

"What was that?"

No, no, no!

More voices, but Mya couldn't hear their words over the pounding in her ears. Ahead, a pearly white light glimmered on the slimy wall of the tunnel.

Move…run…get away!

Mya scrabbled to her feet and staggered back the way she had come as the sounds of pursuit closed in.

"Drat! It's doing it again!" Keyfur splashed to a stop at the branching tunnel, glaring down at the disembodied finger in the glass sphere under the light of Dee's glow crystal. The wizard frowned and swung this way and that.

Lad bit back a terse comment. He was fast losing faith in Dee's wizard and his grotesque device. First it had directed them *beneath* the streets of Tsing—no real surprise, since the other masters had subterranean strongholds as well—but then the signal had started shifting, both further down and laterally. Suppositions abounded: Were Mya's captors moving her? Had she escaped? Had they killed her and thrown the body into the sewer?

Dee had vehemently rejected that last suggestion and urged them on. But the movement of the target wasn't the biggest problem.

"Double drat!" Keyfur shook the glass sphere. The finger wavered, pointing first one direction, then another. This vacillation had occurred intermittently both above and below ground. One signal was clearly stronger, held position longer, but even so, the wavering didn't inspire confidence.

Lad would have preferred working alone, but he couldn't follow a trail until they picked up evidence of someone's passage. And the environment—dripping water, tremors from the streets above, the scratching of vermin, and the noxious reek—all interfered with his senses. *Like garrote weather*, he thought, remembering the tumultuous downpours of Twailin.

Keyfur swung the glass sphere and pointed down the right-hand tunnel. "This way!"

A distant splash froze Lad in his tracks. He grasped his companions, pulling them up short. "What was that?"

"I didn't hear anything," Dee said impatiently.

"More of those vile creatures, you think?" Keyfur whispered.

"Can you run them off with that light spell, like you did before?" Dee fingered his weapons.

"Shhh." Lad cocked his head to listen. No, this wasn't the rhythmic, flat-footed *Splat! Splat!* of the gullywhumps they had previously encountered. It was unsteady, erratic, scrabbling, and moving away fast. Lad glanced at the guiding finger pointed rock steady in the direction of the receding noise. "Come on!"

Lad hurried down the tunnel, the splash of his companions loud behind him. In his own flickering shadow, he almost missed the disturbance on a slime-covered stone. He stopped and squatted to look closely, and knew. "It's her."

Dee dropped to his knees beside Lad. "How do you know?"

"Shine your light here." Lad pointed to the impression in the muck, a clear handprint. "Small fingers, the right size, and look." He traced the outline. "It's missing a finger on the left hand."

Dee caught his breath. "Why would they—"

"To take the ring." Putting the ring on Mya's finger hadn't protected her as he'd hoped, but only made her a target. *Just like Wiggen...*

"Why would they..." Keyfur snapped his fingers. "If that's true, it might explain the interference in my spell! It points to the finger left behind and Miss Moirin as she moves on."

Dee splashed to his feet. "We have to—"

"Shhh!" Distant splashes echoed through the tunnels at the edge of Lad's hearing, many of them, and they were coming closer. "Someone or some*thing* else is down here."

"We've got to *hurry*, then!" Desperation edged Dee's voice, but his free hand plunged beneath his coat and came out holding a small crossbow. He clicked it open, loaded and ready.

Lad nodded his approval. At least Dee was thinking clearly. "Yes. Be ready. Follow me as quietly as you can, and try to keep up."

He started out, concentrating on the sound of bare feet sloshing through the mire. He didn't dare call out Mya's name for fear of alerting the unknown others, still distant but closing. Then he realized that he didn't need to shout. *Mya can hear a pin drop from a hundred paces.*

Lad cupped his hands and whispered "Mya! Stop! It's Lad and Dee!" Listening, he detected no slowing of her pace, not even a hesitation. Still, he knew it was her.

He came to a branch in the passage. Here, the two sources of sound diverged, Mya had gone left, and the other still distant source was to his right. *She must have heard them.* Lad barely hesitated, continuing after her at his best speed. *She knows she's being hunted and doesn't know friend from foe.* Suddenly, her splashing footsteps changed to a scrabbling crawl. *If she wiggles into a space too small for us to follow, we'll lose her!*

Lad dismissed stealth and caution, dashing forward at full speed, his senses and reflexes slamming on full. Tiny creatures skittered and scuttled from his path, their pinprick eyes staring at him. Dying wavelets in the mucky water verified Mya's recent passage; he was close now. Around a series of twisting turns, a smaller drain pipe yawned halfway up the wall to the left, a clear scuff mark on the rim. Lad gauged the diameter on the run, judged it to be large enough, and barely slowed as he dove in. The pipe was too small for a crouching run, so he scrabbled along on fingers and toes. The echoes of Mya's flight sharpened in the confined space.

"Mya! Stop! It's Lad!" he hissed in a stage whisper. The tunnel curved, then straightened, and he spotted her, scrambling away from him on all fours. Filthy and bare footed, she looked to be wearing nothing but a torn sheet. "Mya! It's Lad!"

She stopped and turned, eyes wide, pupils huge, but there was no recognition in her gaze. In fact, her eyes weren't even tracking him. She didn't seem to see him at all.

What's wrong with her? he wondered, for he knew her senses were as sharp as his.

"Mya! It's me, Lad!" He slowed, approaching cautiously, eying the broken-tipped dagger she clutched in one grimy hand. "Don't—"

The dagger slashed at his face.

Lad caught Mya's wrist, but she launched herself at him in the confined space, punching, clawing, and kicking with feral ferocity. He'd sparred with her many times, even fought her in earnest once, and knew instantly that something was very wrong. Her blows, though faster and stronger than those of an unenhanced human, were sluggish and weak by Mya's standards. He blocked and countered her frantic attacks easily, wondering if she'd gone utterly mad. Then he caught the scent of opium on her breath and sweat. *She's drugged! That explains it.*

Lad twisted the dagger from her grasp and clamped his arms around her, pinning hers to her sides. "Mya! Stop! It's me! You're safe!"

"Nooooo!" A piteous wail tore from her throat, the cry of a wolf with its paw caught in a trap.

"Mya, it's Lad!" He crushed her to him, his mouth close to her ear as she thrashed. He spoke in the low, gentle tone he used when Lissa cried and called for her mother who would never again come home. "Come on, stop fighting me. Dee's here. We'll get you out."

She stopped struggling, but still quivered like a leaf in a hurricane. "D...Dee? Who..."

"It's *Lad*, Mya. We're here to get you out. You're safe now."

"Lad?" Dee's voice echoed up the pipe, the light of his glow crystal reflecting off the pipe's walls. "Are you in there?"

Lad ground his teeth. "Yes!" he called back, wishing Dee hadn't used his real name in front of Keyfur. "I've got her! We're coming out." Slowly, he eased his arms from around Mya, but kept hold of one hand. Thankfully, she didn't try to kill him or flee again. "Come on, Mya. Come with me. We're getting out."

"Out..." She blinked, clearly dazed and confused. "Yes...out."

Together, they crawled toward the light.

Chapter V

"Get that light out of my eyes!" growled Lad as he crawled toward the end of the drain pipe.

Dee ignored the command, thrusting the glow crystal forward to see the figure crawling behind Lad. "Mya?" His gut twisted at the sight of her, mucked and bedraggled, peering fearfully at him, pupils wide despite the direct light. She tugged reluctantly at Lad's hand, her mouth set in a rictus of panic.

"Dee, lower the light and step back!" Lad held up a hand to fend of the glare. "I need you to help her out. She's been drugged. Move slowly, don't frighten her."

Dee handed the glow crystal to Keyfur and dropped his crossbow, trying to move with slow deliberation as he held out a hand. "Here, Mya. It's Dee. Take my hand."

"D...Dee?" She blinked at him and put a trembling hand in his.

"Come on. We're getting you out of here." Gently he pulled her toward him, cringing as she came fully into the light.

Her skin and the sheet she wore were filthy, spotted with muck and rusty stains. *Blood? Hers?* He lifted her gingerly out of the pipe and stood her up in the larger tunnel. She stumbled, and he caught her, inadvertently pulling aside the sheet. He caught his breath at the pale, waxy scars covering her legs and abdomen. *Scars?* That didn't make sense; Mya healed instantly. Through the filth, he could see only a few of her beautiful tattoos, writhing like trapped serpents upon the scant unscarred flesh. His jaw clenched, and his composure crumbled.

"Oh, gods, Mya!" He clutched her close, ignoring the reek of sewage and blood. The vacant terror in her eyes and uncontrollable trembling cut him to the core. Rage boiled through his veins. *They skinned her…stripped away her magic! I'll fucking kill them all for this!*

"Dee." Lad gripped his shoulder and nodded down the corridor. "Not now. We've got to go. There's someone coming."

"Lakshmi! Kittall!" A moan of panic escaped Mya's throat, and she strained against Dee's embrace. "They're coming for *me*!"

"It's okay, Mya." Dee assured her. "We've got you. You're safe."

Lad stooped and grabbed Dee's dropped crossbow, shook the water from the mechanism, and waved them forward. "We've got to get back to the branching passages before they do, or we'll be cut off."

"Why can't we go that way?" asked Keyfur, pointing further down the tunnel.

"It's a dead end." Lad breathed in the fetid air deeply and shook his head. "No fresh air flow. It either dips below the water level or peters out into small passages."

Keyfur gaped at Lad as they hurried forward. "Bloodhound indeed! You're more than you appear to be, sir."

Lad stopped and held out his arms to bring them to a splashing halt. "Let's hope *you're* more than you appear to be, Master Keyfur, because it's too late." Lad nodded into the darkness down the tunnel. "We're cut off. They're coming."

Dee's heart pounded in fear and rage. He'd just gotten Mya back, and the torturing animals who had taken her, who had *broken* her, were coming to take her again. He'd be damned to all Nine Hells before he let that happen. He pushed Mya behind him, but kept hold of one hand, loathe to let her go.

Lad held up the crossbow. "I'll keep this one, if you don't mind. I know you have another."

"Sure! Careful, the bolts are—"

"Poisoned. I know." He turned to Keyfur. "Put away the light; it only gives away our position and makes you a target. Dee, stay back and protect Mya."

The wizard fished a peacock feather from his cloak and waved it, fading completely from view and plunging them into darkness. "There'll be light aplenty the moment I have a target. I suggest you shield your eyes."

"Dee..." Mya staggered against him. "They...drugged me. I can't...fight."

"I've got you, Mya." Dee wrapped an arm around her trembling shoulders and pressed them back up against the slimy tunnel wall. How ironic it seemed to be protecting Mya when she had shielded him from harm so many times.

Mya moaned deep in her chest. "We need to *run*, Dee. Can't let them take me..."

"Shhh, we *can't* run," he whispered. The approaching splashes were audible now, and a diffuse glow grew from around the nearest corner. Dee drew his second crossbow and pulled the trigger that cocked the weapon. "You're safe. We won't let them take you."

A hissing whisper rose above the splashing footsteps. "More than just her now. Someone's picked up her trail."

Dee's grip on his crossbow slickened with sweat. *Torturing filth... They did this to her—took her skin, her beautiful runes. I'll kill them for it. Just give me one clear shot.*

The glow from around the corner brightened, diffusing the shadows farther down the tunnel.

"No, no, no..." Mya whispered, tugging at Dee's hand. "Got to move...run or die!"

"Did you hear something?" a woman's voice asked above the splashing.

"No, I—"

"Careful now! These prints are fresh. Someone's—"

A piercing light swept into the tunnel, a glow crystal held aloft by a man in a slouch hat and leathers. He rounded the corner, eyes on the floor. Several more figures followed, crossbows and blow guns at the ready.

Dee picked out Lad from the shadows, lying at the curved juncture of wall and floor, looking like a heap of refuse. Keyfur, of course, was nowhere to be seen. Dee hunkered back against the wall, pulling Mya close, thankful for his choice of dark clothes and the filth that blackened her sheet.

The approaching group's attention seemed to be on their guide, and the light he held shone in their faces, blinding them to anything in shadow. Dee squinted beyond the light and spotted an elderly woman in their midst. *Lakshmi!* Torture was an Inquisitor's specialty.

No doubt she had been Mya's tormenter. Dee raised his crossbow, took aim, and slowly began to squeeze the trigger.

Another man rounded the corner into the light, and Dee caught his breath.

Hoseph!

Dee shifted his aim to this new, more urgent target. *I've shot you twice, and you lived, you bastard, but not this time.* Again he applied pressure to the trigger.

Crack!

Dee flinched, thinking at first that he'd misfired, but it hadn't been his crossbow. *Lad!*

Down the tunnel, the man in the fore gasped and fell, dropping his glow crystal into the soupy water. The light dimmed, wavering across the damp walls and the startled faces of the assassins. They froze in their tracks, eyes searching the darkness, their fingers twitching on triggers.

Distracted from his own shot, Dee struggled to pick Hoseph out from the milling figures in the gloom. *There!* He raised his weapon…

Multi-hued light erupted from nowhere as Keyfur materialized in the center of the tunnel. Lashing his peacock feather like a whip, he sent a rainbow of light sweeping across the faces of the two crossbowmen in the fore. Their eyes exploded from their sockets. Screaming, they fell, but not before one of them got off a shot. The bolt's tip gleamed red as it sped down the tunnel.

In a blur of motion and a spray of fetid water, Lad leapt up and slapped the bolt off its trajectory. Spinning through the air past Keyfur, Dee, and Mya, the bolt struck the slimy floor beyond them and erupted in flames.

Shit! Dee and his companions were now backlit by the blaze. Taking aim at Hoseph, he squeezed the trigger. The envenomed bolt flew true, but Lakshmi spun and shoved Hoseph aside. The bolt struck another assassin in the throat, and he went down.

Shit! Shit! Shit! Dee released his grasp on Mya and drew a new bolt.

"Protect Mya!" Lad called out, racing toward their foes.

A scintillating translucent wall of colored light shimmered across the tunnel in front of Keyfur just as three more crossbowmen fired. One bolt disintegrated against the magical barrier. Lad deflected the second, which hit the tunnel wall in a hissing spray of acid. The third, he caught and sent streaking back at them.

Miraculously, Lakshmi plucked the returning bolt from the air. She stared at it for an instant, as if surprised to find it in her grasp, then threw it back. Her aim wasn't as good as Lad's, however, and it shattered against the mucky wall of the tunnel in a shower of sticky strands that sizzled and popped.

Then Lad was among the assassins, hands and feet deadly blurs. Two Alchemists went down before the others could even react. A third died as she tried to shoot him at close range with a blow gun, her own weapon shoved through her mouth and out the back of her spine.

Dee cocked his crossbow, slapped the bolt in place, and took aim, but Lad was a blur in his line of fire, so he didn't dare a shot at Hoseph or Lakshmi. Hells, he didn't even know if his shot would penetrate Keyfur's rainbow barrier. A curse died on his lips as glass shattered and a swarm of tentacles erupted from the floor of the tunnel around Lad.

Godsdamned Alchemists! But Dee couldn't let himself be distracted. Lad could hold his own. His finger twitching on the crossbow trigger, he scanned for the one figure he sought. *There you are!*

Hoseph hung back against the wall away from the others, his attention focused beyond the maelstrom of Lad fighting the writhing tentacles. A shiver ran up Dee's spine as the priest's gaze passed over him, and he clutched the little crossbow with both hands. He could *not* miss this time.

"I've got you now, Hoseph," he murmured, his finger tightening on the trigger.

"Hoseph?" Mya's horrified whisper was followed by frantic splashing.

Mya! He whirled to see her stumbling back, eyes wide, her face twisted in fear. Spinning awkwardly, she staggered down the tunnel.

"Mya! No! Stay here!" Dee took a step toward her, then realized she couldn't go far. The tunnel was a dead end.

Firming his resolve, Dee turned back to the fight, squinting through the rainbow barrier as he raised his weapon and steadied his aim. Where Hoseph had stood, however, there was now only a swirl of black mist that dissipated even as Dee watched. Dread gripped his gut. He'd seen that trick before.

He'll pop back in behind me! Slamming his back against the slimy wall, Dee scanned the flickering darkness. Mya staggered past the dying fire of the incendiary crossbow bolt, but he couldn't see any sign of Hoseph. *How in the Nine Hells can I spot black mists in a dark tunnel?*

Without warning, a pulse of energy slammed through Dee, despair darker than the blackest night gripping his soul. Every horrible moment of his life played out in his mind, drowning him in sorrow, guilt, and regret. He fired blindly into the darkness beyond Mya, then fell to his knees. His crossbow splashed into the fetid mire.

He's here! Dee recognized Hoseph's spell, but was powerless to combat its debilitating effect. Slumping forward, he clenched his fists to his bowed head and prayed for a quick death, anything to stop this misery.

Mya's scream cut into the fog of his despair like a slap in the face. Forcing open his eyes, Dee espied her lying in a heap just beyond the flickering flames, curled in a fetal position, her shoulders quaking.

Mya... Got to get to her...before... Dee struggled to rise from the muck, but his body refused to answer. He crawled forward, but the morass of guilt, shame, and self-loathing weighed him down like a leaden net. *It's not real! It's just a trick! It can't hurt me!* What *would* hurt him—would tear his heart asunder—was if Hoseph murdered Mya.

Then the shadows beyond Mya moved, and a pearly light blossomed in the darkness. Hoseph slogged forward through the water, death glowing in his hand. In the dying light of the withering alchemical blaze, he reached down for Mya.

"No!" Dee heaved up and launched himself at the priest, grabbing Hoseph's forearm as he bowled into him.

The two men sprawled in the muck. Hoseph's glowing hand twisted and groped at Dee, coming within a fingerbreadth of his face, but Dee refused to let go. Hoseph's free hand slammed into the side of Dee's head, and still he clung, fighting through the gut-wrenching despair. If he let go, he and Mya would both die.

them in the Sphere of Shadow and be done with their incompetence! But without Lakshmi and Kittal, he had little hope of ever attaining his previous position as the emperor's spiritual advisor and the right hand of the Grandmaster of the Assassins Guild. He would be forced to flee, find refuge in some distant temple of Demia and live out the rest of his days as a mere priest. *No, that will never do.*

"If we're not in imminent danger, then we can proceed afoot. Demia's gifts are not to be squandered."

"Fine." Lakshmi hurried on, all but carrying the injured assassin, her stride smooth and sure.

They didn't speak again or slow down until they reached Kittal's headquarters. After washing the muck from their boots, the Master Alchemist ushered Lakshmi and Hoseph into his living quarters, a suite of sparsely furnished rooms.

"Six of my best Alchemists dead." Kittal strode across the room to a sideboard. "Who the hell was that…man who attacked us?" He poured liquid from a decanter into two tiny glasses, handed one to Lakshmi and downed the other.

Hoseph dismissed the slight; he didn't take alcohol anyway. "The man, if he *is* a man at all, was Lad. And it's worse than you know. If Master Keyfur was there—"

"Wait!" Kittal's hand shook as he refilled his glass. "That was no lad, it was a full-grown man, and he fought like—"

"Not *a* lad, *the* Lad!" Hoseph cut in. "Saliez's living weapon. The Tsing Guildmaster who, with Mya, slaughtered *five* imperial blademasters and murdered our Grandmaster."

"Lady T told us he was dead." Kittal downed his dram of liqueur and reached for the decanter again.

"Obviously a lie that Mya fed her." Hoseph sighed and began to pace, too overwrought to sit down. "I believed it myself. It seemed plausible. After all, the man was rather dim-witted and dangerous in the extreme; not the safest combination. Mya must have sequestered him somewhere, a card to be played only in dire need."

"Well, she played him, and he waded through my people like a scythe through wheat!"

"The *truly* dire news is the involvement of Master Keyfur." The wrinkles in Lakshmi's forehead deepened. "Mya is clearly working closely with the emperor. How much has she told him of the guild?"

"After the coronation, she could tell him any lie she wanted!" Kittal downed his third dram of liqueur. "Maybe *she's* his spiritual advisor now."

"Kittal, stop drinking. You're losing perspective." Lakshmi scowled disapprovingly, and Kittal put his glass aside without argument.

Hoseph sighed in frustration. "The *point* is, if Lad and the emperor are both helping Mya, she'll be nigh unstoppable."

"I must agree. We'll never get near her again." Lakshmi trailed a finger around the rim of her glass, then looked to Kittal. "Do you intend to relocate this operation now that Mya's free?"

The Alchemist shook his head. "I don't think that's necessary. Mya was unconscious when she was brought here and drugged when she escaped. The sewers are a labyrinth, and the drain she used has already been sealed with solid rock. Besides, I'm running short of places to retreat to, and moving all the labs would be a monumental task."

"How could they have tracked Mya down so quickly?" Hoseph asked.

Kittal shrugged. "Magic, I suppose, considering the emperor's archmage was with them."

"It doesn't matter." Lakshmi waved a hand dismissively. "You can bet your last penny that she's in the palace by now, utterly out of our reach."

"It wouldn't matter if she was staying in the swankiest inn in Tsing under her own name! Mya's got *Lad* protecting her now." Hoseph cleared his throat to cover the quiver of fear in his voice, recalling all too vividly the bloodbath in the palace dungeons. "We've got to focus on the heart of our plan: getting rid of Arbuckle. If we can do that, all Mya's plotting falls apart."

"We know he'll be in public for the announcement of his New Accords, and, thanks to the information provided by you," Lakshmi inclined her head toward Hoseph, "we know what security measures will be in place. We've devised a plan—"

"Which *now* will no longer work." Hoseph scowled, counting off their failures on his fingers. "Mya's alive and free. Lad's guarding her. And the emperor and Mya are in cahoots, so both Lad *and* Mya, as well as Master Keyfur and five hundred imperial guards, will be in the Imperial Plaza to protect him."

"So I've had my people working day and night making explosives, potions, and poisons for nothing?" Kittal's face flushed. "The emperor will be protected from the instant he steps out of his carriage to the moment he returns to it. Nothing will pierce that cordon short of—"

"Kittal!" The epiphany struck Hoseph like one of the Alchemist's explosions. "That's *it*!"

The Master Alchemist couldn't have looked more startled if Hoseph had kissed him. "What's it?"

"The *carriage!*" Hoseph ignored the masters' baffled looks as he formulated a plan in his mind. "This just might work!"

"Gods of Light, the *stink*!" The imperial guard officer reeled back from the carriage as Keyfur stepped out.

"Thank you for your assessment, Lieutenant, but when one delves the sewers, one often comes out smelling like them!" Keyfur glared at the woman and gestured toward Lad, who was maneuvering a senseless Mya out of the carriage while trying to keep her filthy sheet in place. Thankfully, she'd fallen into a fitful sleep. "Now, might I suggest you assign an escort for us *before* Miss Moirin expires? And, send for Master Corvecosi. She's been drugged and is in a bad way."

Lad admired the wizard's spunk, and had grown to respect the man. His magic had certainly proven effective. When they made their way back to the surface, Keyfur had insisted they bring Mya directly to the palace.

"It'll be utterly safe, and the emperor's healer will provide the best of care."

Lad hadn't argued. He didn't know what kind of care the guild might be able to provide, but he doubted it could best that of the imperial healer.

"Of course, Master Keyfur." With a nervous glance at Lad and Mya, the lieutenant snapped her fingers twice, and a corporal and four guards formed up. "I'll inform Captain Ithross immediately! The emperor will want to know she's safe."

"And send a runner to the palace chamberlain. We'll need a hot bath for her." Keyfur's order received an enthusiastic nod from the lieutenant, who sent a guard dashing off.

Lad smoothed the sheet in place to cover her as much as possible and followed the escort to the postern door. Keeping Mya's secret wasn't high on Lad's priority list, but he'd do his best. The muck covered her arms and legs, hiding her runes, but he'd glimpsed her scars beneath the sheet. Scars meant that whatever torture they'd inflicted had destroyed enough of her runes to impede her healing magic at least partially. He didn't know how much magic she'd lost, but if all the blood staining the sheet was hers, she was lucky she was alive.

"Need us to carry her, sir?" the corporal asked, though the guards seemed reticent to come close.

"No. I've got her." He carried her easily. "She's drugged and disoriented. Waking up in the arms of a stranger might set her off." Twice during the carriage ride, she'd snapped awake and lashed out reflexively. The last thing they needed was a dead guard on their hands.

"This way, then."

Flanked by the guards, they followed the corporal through corridors and up two flights of stairs. They walked at a steady but staid pace, and the guards began to glance at Lad nervously. Realizing why, he started feigning fatigue on the second stair.

"Not far now, sir," the corporal assured him as they continued down another hall, finally stopping at a door.

They were ushered into an opulent room furnished with plushly cushioned chairs, a breakfast table, and a huge bed. Already, a large copper tub had been set in front of the floor-to-ceiling window, and servants poured in bucket after bucket of steaming water.

Loathe to foul the pristine white coverlet on the bed, Lad ignored the nervous stares from the servants and propped Mya up in one of the chairs adjacent to the tub. She stirred and mumbled incoherently, her eyes fluttering open for a moment before sagging shut again.

"Shhh," he whispered to her while the servants finished. When the tub was full, and they started arraying soaps and towels, he said, "We need some privacy for the lady, please. Master Keyfur, if you'd stay..." The wizard had already glimpsed Mya's runes, and Lad thought he could be trusted with the truth.

"Of course." Keyfur ordered the guards and servants out, and returned to Mya's side.

"We should clean her first, I suppose." Lad started to lift the disgusting sheet, but stopped as Keyfur raised a forestalling hand.

"We should wait for the emperor's healer, Master Corvecosi. He'll want to assess her condition, and he'll not appreciate us usurping his duties."

"I guess there's no rush." Torn between the desire to help Mya and the need to keep her and his own secrets, Lad vacillated between helplessness and unease. He was no healer, and the imperial guards stationed outside the door set his nerves on edge.

"May I ask," Keyfur looked curiously at Lad, "why you and Master Dee call Miss Moirin 'Mya?'"

"Just an old nickname," Lad said casually, adopting the excuse Dee had used with Norwood. "We've known her for a long time."

The wizard seemed to accept this, and started to say something more, but a quiet commotion outside interrupted by a light rap on the door, Keyfur opened it to usher in a dusky-skinned man with a round, friendly face. He carried a voluminous black satchel in one hand.

"Ah, yes, I see that my services are most certainly required here." He bustled over, nodding politely to Lad. "I'm Master Corvecosi, the emperor's healer. You must be Miss Moirin's associate, Master Dee. I'm honored to meet you." He held out a hand.

"I'm not, actually. I'm another of her associates." Lad shook the man's hand, oddly soothed by his friendly manner and melodic accent. "I was brought in to help find her. They call me Bloodhound. Dee, I'm afraid, was...taken during her rescue."

"Oh. I'm so very sorry to hear that. Master Dee performed valiantly in the service of both Miss Moirin and the emperor." The healer's eyes shifted to Mya. "But we must see to the living, yes?"

"Please." Lad motioned him over. "She's been injured and drugged, and is confused when she wakes. Her wounds seem to be healed, but Master Keyfur said we should wait for you before cleaning her up."

"And quite right he is." He touched her wrist, then lifted one eyelid.

Mya moaned and started to lash out, but Lad caught her wrist, whispering softly, "Shhh. You're safe. I'm here."

"Do you know what drugs she's been given?" asked Corvecosi.

"I smelled opium and something else, I think," Lad offered.

"Indeed." The man sighed. "Well, I dare not give her anything, not knowing what might be running through her veins. She doesn't appear to be bleeding or in pain, but I need to see the extent of her injuries. Help me remove this…garment."

Lad held Mya upright while Corvecosi gently lifted the foul sheet over her head. He tensed at sight of the long rows of waxy scars, much worse than he'd imagined. *Oh, Mya…*

Keyfur caught his breath. "Gods and devils, what did they *do* to her?"

"Torture…" Visions of Keisha flayed in the former emperor's torture chamber rose unbidden.

"More than torture, I believe." Corvecosi traced a professional finger down the precise parallel lanes of scar tissue. "She looks to have been carefully and professionally *skinned*, and then healed." The scant few runes remaining on the bits of unscarred skin writhed like trapped serpents. "But these markings…" He looked to Keyfur. "These are *magic*."

"Indeed they are. Perhaps some kind of curse or—"

"Runes." Lad judged it time to nip any erroneous assumptions in the bud. These two would learn the truth soon enough anyway. "You both know of Miss Moirin's…capabilities. She's had these tattoos for years, magical enhancements that imbue her with special abilities; strength, speed, and healing, among others. That's one reason she wears those enchanted wrappings, to keep them hidden." He fixed first Keyfur, then Corvecosi with pointed stares. "*Please* don't tell anyone she has them."

"Her secret's safe with me." Keyfur shrugged. "It certainly explains a lot."

"My only concern is her *health*, Master Bloodhound. My patients' secrets remain their own." The healer's eyes returned to Mya. "She has scars from stab wounds as well, in her leg and her side here. The…skinning seems to only have been done on her front side. I see no bleeding or suppuration despite the fetid conditions you found her in." He nodded to Lad. "Help me get her in the tub."

"Let me do it, please. She knows me."

"Oh, by all means." Corvecosi took a cautious step back.

Lad lifted her, whispering again as she stirred in his arms, "It's all right. I'm here. You're safe."

"Dee…" The murmur was faint and forlorn.

Mya gasped and opened her eyes as Lad lowered her into the warm water, but there was more surprise than distress in them, and she didn't strike out.

"It's just a bath. You're fine. Just relax. We have to clean you up." She calmed at Lad's gentle words, sighing as the warmth enveloped her. "There. See? It feels good, doesn't it?"

"Good…" Mya seemed to melt into the water, her eyes drifting closed. "Warm…"

Lad cradled her head so she wouldn't slip beneath the surface and nodded to Corvecosi. "Go ahead."

While the healer carefully and thoroughly bathed Mya's body, Lad laved water over her hair, rinsing away the caked filth. Keyfur found a bottle of fragrant soap, and applied some. Lad worked it into a lather, then rinsed it clean. Mya moaned, but didn't fight him. He washed her face with a damp towel as gently as he would his daughter's, while Corvecosi finished up with her fingernails and toenails, scouring away the last of the dirt.

"There." Corvecosi stood and lifted a thick towel from the rack beside the tub. "Lift her, and I'll dry. We don't want her catching a chill."

Lad complied, and as the now gray water ran away, they beheld the full extent of her scars.

"Gods of Light…" The calm professionalism on Corvecosi's face darkened to anger. "It's amazing that she's alive." He dried her carefully, then gestured to the bed. "Now, let me see how she fares."

Lad placed her on the bed, and Corvecosi examined her carefully, checking her pulse, pinching her skin here and there, listening to her heart and breathing with a curious trumpet-shaped device. Lad was relieved to see that Mya's back was unblemished by scars, her runes intact. He estimated that about a third of her skin had been removed, and wondered why they'd done it so meticulously. Only one reason came to mind: *Remove her magic so she can feel pain, then torture her for information...*

Corvecosi straightened and sighed. "She's remarkably well, considering her trauma. She's dehydrated and needs rest and food. As far as her scars go, I can't—"

"Well, I can do something about *that*, at least." Keyfur fished a small black marble from a pocket and held it up for the healer's inspection. "With your permission, of course."

Corvecosi frowned. "She's been through a lot, Master Keyfur. Taxing her with your magical trinket might be dangerous."

"What is that?" Lad asked.

"It's called a fleshforge. It heals virtually any wound, as long as it's recent, and will even regenerate missing tissue. Miss Moirin recovered it from my predecessor during the coronation, and saved my life with it." He looked to Corvecosi. "It will heal her scars, and maybe even her missing finger. I don't think it will tax her strength."

The healer nodded, but his frown remained intact. "Very well."

"Thank you." The wizard poured a glass of water from the pitcher beside the bed and nodded to Lad. "Sit her up, please."

Lad did so, and watched as Keyfur roused Mya, slipped the sphere into her mouth, and held the glass to her lips. She swallowed the water greedily, her throat pulsing as she drank it down. Finally, with a sigh, she relaxed.

Immediately, Mya's flesh ran like melting wax, the thick scars smoothing into tiny patches of healthy pink skin that expanded and spread like wildfire. Slowly, her runes shifted their positions onto the new skin as if renewing their symmetry. From the void between two of her fingers sprouted a pink nub that lengthened into a perfect new digit, even sporting a smooth nail.

When the healing was complete, Lad started to lay her back onto the bed.

Keyfur touched his arm. "Not yet. Wait a moment."

Mya's eyes fluttered open and she suddenly looked stricken, her mouth gaping as she retched. Keyfur caught the tiny black sphere as she hacked it up, wiped it clean, and tucked it into his pocket.

"Disgusting, I know, but it's effective."

"Nothing short of miraculous," Corvecosi agreed, checking Mya's breathing and pulse again as Lad lay her back.

When the healer was finished, Lad tucked the crisp sheets around Mya and drew up the coverlet. She seemed to be resting more peacefully now, her damp hair tousled atop the down pillow, her face relaxed in deep sleep.

"Just remember, healing is one thing, trauma is another." Corvecosi gathered up his bag. "I'll send someone should stay with her. She'll probably sleep through the night, but she should drink and eat as soon as she's able."

"I'll stay with her." Lad pointed to the divan. "I can sleep there."

Keyfur smiled and bowed. "I'll retire to my chambers for a bath, then. Don't hesitate to call on me if you need any assistance whatsoever."

"Thank you for everything, Master Keyfur." Lad shook the wizard's hand again. "When Miss Moirin's better, I'll contact you about getting back to Twailin."

"Please do." As the wizard reached for the door, however, a commotion arose outside.

Without a knock, the door flew open and a squad of imperial guards entered, nearly bowling the wizard over. Lad tensed, his senses flaring as a wave of heat washed through him. Had he been betrayed? Had the emperor somehow identified Lad as his father's murderer? The guards scanned the entire room, scrutinizing Lad professionally, but without any overt hints of aggression.

Not an attack. Threat assessment, Lad realized when a middle-aged man wearing a slim gold circlet on his brow stepped into the doorway.

Corvecosi and Keyfur both bowed low, murmuring, "Your Majesty."

Lad followed suit, stifling his uneasiness with the glowering guards. This wasn't about him, it was about Mya.

The emperor strode toward the bed, ignoring everyone else in the room. His face lined with concern, he reached one hand out toward the peacefully sleeping Mya.

Lad moved to intervene before the sovereign's fingers brushed the coverlet. "Majesty, I don't—"

An imperial guard officer lunged between them, pulling a dagger from his belt in the restricted space. "Back, you—"

As the tip of the dagger clear the sheath, a hundred alternatives blazed through Lad's mind. Most ended with everyone in the room save him and Mya dead. *No! No killing!* Once it started, it would never stop. He'd never get home, never see Lissa again. But he'd be damned to all Nine Hells if he'd let the man stab him.

Lad clapped both hands onto the flat of the blade, immobilizing the weapon.

Before the officer could even show his surprise, the emperor's icy command stopped the impending violence. "Captain! Stand down! There is no threat to Us here!"

"Majesty, I—"

"*Please*, Majesty, I beg to differ." Lad released the captain's blade, but didn't back away. "I intervened because Miss Moirin is not herself. She's been drugged and is disoriented. She's lashed out violently when touched." He met the captain's glare with a solemn look. "I didn't want her to harm you inadvertently."

The emperor stepped back and looked at him. "We thank you, Master…"

"I'm called Bloodhound, Majesty." Lad bowed. "I'm an old friend of Miss Moirin's. I was brought here to help find her."

"And did so, We see. You have Our thanks again." The emperor edged closer to the bed, gazing down at Mya. "How is she, Master Corvecosi?"

"Dehydrated and under the influence of an unknown mixture of drugs, Majesty, but alive and otherwise healthy." The healer bowed politely. "She needs rest."

The emperor's shoulders dropped as his tension eased, "Thank the Gods of Light." Emotion ran deep in the sovereign's voice, profound relief, regret, perhaps more. After a moment's contemplative silence, he stirred and looked around the room as if seeing everyone for the first time. "And where is Master Dee? We'd like to commend him on his loyalty to his mistress."

"Dee was lost during the rescue, Majesty. He was…taken by Hoseph"

"Hoseph?" The muscles at the emperor's jaw twitched beneath his beard as he gazed down at Mya. "One more atrocity heaped upon that man's soul…"

Everyone stood in silence for a moment, no one daring to move or speak while the emperor gazed upon Mya. Whatever thoughts ran through the man's mind, Lad couldn't tell, but one thing was clear, he cared for Mya more than a ruler for a mere servant. Finally, the sovereign shook himself as if stirring from deep thought.

"Do all you can for her, Master Corvecosi. And you, sir," the emperor turned to Lad, "are welcome to stay in the palace. We'll order a room prepared for you."

"I'll stay with Miss Moirin, if it's all the same to you, Majesty." Lad nodded to Mya. "It would be best if she woke to a familiar face."

Several unreadable emotions flickered across the emperor's face, then he nodded in acquiescence. "Very well. Master Corvecosi, We would speak with Miss Moirin when she's cognizant."

"Of course, Majesty." The healer bowed.

After one more lingering look at Mya, the emperor departed with his entourage of guards, healer, and archmage in his wake. When the door closed, Lad was finally alone with Mya.

So that was Tynean Tsing III. Aside from some physical similarities with his father, there was little other resemblance. *And he obviously cares for Mya.* Lad stood by the bed, considering her. Mya always had a plan, always watched out for herself. He smoothed the hair off her forehead, wondering if her plans included a close relationship with the emperor.

Mya gasped at his touch, and her eyes fluttered open. "Dee?"

"Shhh," Lad whispered. "It's me, Lad. You're safe. Just relax."

Mya blinked at him, her confusion clearing a bit, only to cloud over as she frowned. "Lad? I remember…Dee…and Hoseph."

"Yes. Just relax now. Sleep. You're safe. We'll talk later."

"Safe?" Her brow furrowed, but she nodded and closed her eyes, slipping back to sleep.

For her sake, Lad hoped she didn't dream.

Dee drifted in a sea of sensory deprivation, long past fear. He couldn't tell how long it had been since Hoseph had abandoned him; time meant nothing without a point of reference. Only one fact seemed certain.

I'm alone.

He'd been alone much of his life, so that was really nothing new. Even when making love to Mya, he'd been alone, for she hadn't loved him back. Even so, he'd do anything to see her again, hear her say his name, feel her touch.

Stop it, Dee, or you'll drive yourself mad! Mya's alive! He had to believe she was alive. *Lad will get her out of the sewers and restore her to her rightful place as Grandmaster. Maybe…she'll come for me.*

And so, Dee drifted…and thought…and remained alone.

Or not…

At first, he thought his mind was playing tricks on him, making him imagine…not voices, but rather something like echoes of voices in his mind. They were distant and faint at first, but approached like the whisper of a growing breeze through the leaves. Hope and fear alike rippled through him. If Hoseph had marooned him here—wherever *here* was—might he have done so to others, too?

Whispers in a hundred languages grew louder, nearer, looming like a nebulous shadow over his mind. Emotions—rage, anguish, fear, love—threatened to sweep him into a wild maelstrom.

Then one clear, deafening message resounded. **Join us…**

It wasn't an offer or a plea. It was a command.

Panic threatened, but Dee's curiosity and a longing for anything but an eternity of solitude won out. *Where am I?*

Here, with us…everyone…

Who are you?

We are everyone… We are one…

Unable to refuse or resist, Dee joined with them, became them, and they him.

In a rush of a thousand minds, he understood…everything.

And he felt strangely welcomed.

Dee was no longer alone.

CHAPTER VII

*B*lock, step, turn, strike...

The imperial bedroom, once he'd moved some furniture back to the walls, was more than large enough to accommodate Lad's morning exercises. He went through the routine in utter silence to keep from waking Mya.

Lunge, step, kick, spin...

Exquisitely aware of his body, he flowed through his ritualistic dance of death—martial exercises learned in his youth, perfected over a lifetime of training, and recently modified to accommodate his maimed hand. Between the exertions of their foray into the sewers and an uncomfortable night sleeping on the divan, he needed to loosen his muscles, relax his mind.

Kick, strike, block, sweep...

A rustle of sheets snapped his attention to the bed. Mya had tossed and turned all night, mumbling curses and intelligible words— Lad didn't want to think about what she dreamt—but this was different. She was waking.

Mya moved under the blankets, stretching and tossing her disheveled mop of hair. Her brow furrowed, she rubbed her eyes, then opened them. Her startled gaze flicked around the room. "Where..."

"The palace."

She lurched up onto her elbows, blinking away sleep. "Lad? What the..."

"You're safe, Mya." Lad strode to the bedside and poured her a glass of water. "How do you feel?"

She watched him as if she didn't believe he was real. "Confused, and...thirsty!" She took the glass in a shaking hand and gulped it down, coughing and clearing her throat as he took it back. "Tell me what the hell happened! I was...hurt, and escaped, but..."

"Just take it easy, Mya. I'll answer as many of your questions as I can. You've been through a lot."

"But...Lad...what the hell are you *doing* here? I thought I'd *dreamed* you. I..."

"I came to help find you." A smile quirked his lips. "Let me send for breakfast, and I'll explain."

Lad went to the door and popped his head out, startling one of the guards stationed there. "Miss Moirin is awake. Have breakfast for two sent up, please."

When he turned back, Mya sat propped against the ornate headboard with the blankets pulled up to her chin, her forehead scrunched in thought. "How *did* you find me? I remember...escaping, and dark tunnels...rats...the sewers! How did you track me down in that labyrinth?"

Lad fished her wrappings from his pocket and held them out. "You broke one of your own cardinal rules, Mya; never possess anything that can be used for magical tracking. Luckily, when they captured you, you reeked of sewage. They dumped all your clothes, and your wrappings with them. Keyfur used them to track you down."

She reached out and took the wrappings. Her eyes went wide at the sight of her unscarred arm, and she glanced beneath the covers. "Wha— What happened to..." She closed her eyes tightly and clutched the wrappings in a white-knuckled fist. "They...bound me and...cut me..."

"And you *escaped*, Mya!" Lad said, driving home the point. "You're safe now. You can thank Master Keyfur and his fleshforge for healing your scars and regrowing your finger."

Cautiously, Mya peered again at her arm, flexed her renewed finger. "But not my runes."

"No, not your runes."

Mya considered her pale flesh, the widely scattered runes, then looked at him again. "Wait a minute! How'd you here so quickly? It's weeks to Twailin, and I wasn't crawling around in the sewers *that* long!"

"Force of will," Lad told her. "*Dee's* will. He convinced the emperor to help find you. Keyfur and Duke Mir's wizard, Woefler, transported him to Twailin, then he badgered me into coming back to Tsing to help." He paused, then added, "He loved you very much, you know."

Mya's face reddened. "He told you that?"

"He didn't have to."

Mya sniffed and looked away. "I *told* him not to, and he fell in love with me anyway. I should have sent him away, but…"

"But you needed him."

She nodded. "I needed him, but I didn't love him."

"We can't control how other people feel about us, Mya."

Her eyes snapped to his, sharp and lucid. "I know that!"

Lad nodded. "Is it because of the emperor?"

Mya looked confused. "Is *what* because of the emperor?"

"Is the reason you didn't love Dee because you have feelings for the emperor? The emperor certainly has feelings for you."

Mya snorted in derision. "What could have *possibly* put *that* thought into your head?"

Lad shrugged. "The way he rushed to see you when we brought you in. The way he looked at you. The tone of his voice when he spoke of you. The fact that he ordered Corvecosi to do whatever it takes to make you well again."

"I saved his life and rescued two heirs to the throne. He considers me to be a loyal servant to the empire, that's all." Mya's jaw muscles clenched, and she pointed to the robe draped over a nearby chair. "Hand me that robe."

"Of course." Lad handed over the silk garment and turned his back. Maybe she really didn't know how the emperor felt about her. It wasn't his business. "If you want to put on your wrappings, I can—"

"Not now."

He listened to her scramble from the bed and struggle with the robe. A sharp breath and a stumble brought him around in time to steady her. "Take it easy. Master Corvecosi said that you need rest and food. You may even still have some drugs in your system."

"I'm fine!" Mya cinched the robe tight and jerked her arm from his grasp. She leaned back against the bed, her arms folded, her eyes avoiding his, her breathing labored.

They were both rescued from the uncomfortable silence by a knock at the door.

"Breakfast," Lad said, and another thought struck him. He leaned close and spoke low. "Before they come in, the story is that I'm an old associate of yours from Twailin, called Bloodhound."

"All right." She pulled the robe tight to cover the few scant runes revealed at her neck.

Lad admitted two servants bearing heavy trays. They set the table with quiet efficiency, uncovering a mouthwatering assortment of dishes: eggs, toast, ham, pastries, blackbrew and tea, fresh juice, and pots of honey and jam.

"Blackbrew or tea?" one asked.

"Blackbrew," Lad said, and Mya also nodded.

Fragrant steam curled up in wisps as the man filled their cups. When the silver utensils were perfectly arranged and linen napkins placed with a flourish, the servants withdrew.

Lad steadied Mya as she walked to the table, and they sat. "Quite a spread. I hope you're hungry."

"I could eat a mule without taking off its tack and harness." Mya sipped blackbrew, the cup trembling in her hand, and started eating, slowly at first, then with more relish.

Lad sipped blackbrew; it was good, but not as good as Forbish's. The rest of the food was excellent, far richer fare than he was used to.

They ate in silence for a while, and Lad gauged her covertly. Her hands steadied, and the tension in her shoulders finally eased. Pouring her a second cup of blackbrew, he finally asked the question he desperately needed answered.

"I don't want to upset you, Mya, but did they destroy your runes so they could torture you for information? Did you tell them anything about the guild or Twailin?" *Or me?*

Mya's fork clattered to her plate and she clenched a fist before her mouth. Her voice came out quiet and chill with terror. "They…didn't want information."

"What then?"

"They wanted my magic. Lakshmi wanted my runes for herself." She lifted her cup and her hand shook once again. "Kittal skinned me and grafted them onto her."

"*What?*" Lad rocked back in his seat, revolted and disbelieving. "Why?"

"Because Lakshmi's *old*, Lad; far older than she looks. She thought my runes might keep her alive when all of Kittal's potions were failing."

The fight in the sewer replayed in Lad's mind, the old woman amidst the assassins catching the crossbow bolt he threw, moving with strength and speed inhuman. *Mya's runes.* It explained her abilities, but... "Do you think that would work? Your runes might heal her of injuries and ills, but would they prolong her life?"

Mya looked up at him then, her eyes gleaming with sheer malevolence. "They might, until I get my hands on her. Then I'll see how *she* likes being strapped to a table and skinned when I take my runes back!"

Lad reeled back in shock at her bloodlust, but Mya had been through a lot. *She needs time...* Then another thought occurred to him. *Take her runes back... Lakshmi's wearing her skin!* "That explains the problem with Keyfur's tracking device. It was homing in on two targets."

Mya looked at him sharply. "What?"

"It kept pointing us in two different directions when we were in the sewers." He sat up straight. "It pointed first one direction, toward you, then another direction. We thought the weaker signal might be your finger that they cut off, but—"

"My skin! Lakshmi's wearing my skin!" Mya lurched up from the table on shaking legs. "We can track her!"

"Calm down." Lad rose and reached out to steady her.

"Don't touch me!" Eyes wide, she jerked away and nearly fell.

Lad stepped back and held his hands up, trying to look unthreatening. "It's all right, Mya. I'm not going to hurt you." He gestured to her chair. "Sit down and eat. You need food and rest. We can send a message to Master Keyfur, but you're not leaving this room."

"You..." She glared at him, but sat back down.

"Now eat!" Lad pointed at her plate.

Mya ate silently for a moment, avoiding his gaze. Abruptly, she dropped her fork. "I thank you for finding me, Lad, but don't think for a minute that you can dictate to me."

"I'm not dictating to you. I'm following Master Corvecosi's orders. Once you're stronger, you can do whatever you want."

"Don't try to talk me out of this!" Mya spoke through clenched teeth. "I'm going to kill them, *all* of them!"

"I'm not trying to talk you out of anything, Mya." Lad recognized her smoldering rage. He'd seen it in himself not so long ago. He'd been so filled with anger and hate after Wiggen's death, so intent on avenging her murder, that he'd hardly recognized himself. He'd killed without provocation, bent others to his will with no regard for anything but vengeance. He knew he couldn't dissuade Mya, and didn't know if he should even try. He could, however, give her one piece of advice. "Just think this through before you act, please."

"Think it *through?*" She stood slowly, steady this time. "I did my thinking strapped to a stone slab while they stripped my skin from my flesh, Lad. I'm going to kill them for what they did to me, and you are not going to stand in my way."

"No, I'm not." He cocked his head and studied her. Mya lashing out was nothing new, but her continued vehemence disturbed him. The glint in her eye seemed not so much fervor as madness. "A man I respect recently told me that there are things in this world that *need* killing. I agree. Just don't let your quest for vengeance turn you into something you don't want to be."

"All I want to *be* is Grandmaster of my guild! I can't be that with traitors opposing me at every turn! The equation isn't difficult. Either they die or I die, and I do *not* intend to die."

"Then don't, but consider the Grandfather and the previous Grandmaster. Would you make yourself into something like that just for revenge?"

Mya's face darkened, but she didn't answer.

Lad stood slowly. "I put the Grandmaster's ring on your finger because I thought you'd be the perfect leader for the guild, an assassin with a good heart. If you let this change you...*poison* your heart, what kind of Grandmaster will you be?"

"How can you think for an *instant* that this *couldn't* change me?" Mya's eyes sought to pierce his with their intensity, her lip quivering with barely suppressed emotions.

Fear, rage, vengeance... Maybe something else, I can't tell. Mya wasn't acting like herself, she wasn't showing any of the tells he knew so well. Lad endured her glare, gauging her fragile frame of mind. This ordeal certainly had changed her. He hoped it hadn't made her something that he would one day be forced to kill.

"What's this about, Sergeant?" Captain Ithross burst into the small waiting room by the palace postern door. "Do you have a message from Chief Constable Dreyfus?"

How in the Nine Hells does he always manage to look so...shiny? Benj had put on his best uniform and even shaved to come to the palace, but his best didn't hold a candle to the captain's. The creases in the man's pants looked sharp enough to slice open a finger, and his breastplate positively gleamed.

"No, Captain. I've come of my own accord."

The captain's eyebrows rose. "You've bypassed the constabulary's chain of command?"

"Yes, I did." Benj glanced at the two guards stationed by the door, certain that they would never consider going over their captain's head. *But who else might they be reporting to?* Long years of watching fellow constables take bribes and kickbacks had honed his paranoia to an edge as keen as the captain's pressed trousers. "And what I've got to tell you is highly...uh...confidential, so..."

Ithross frowned, but waved his guards out. After the door shut behind them, he turned on Benj with a stony mien. "Now, what is so *confidential* that you couldn't send it through proper channels or say it in front of my guards?"

"I couldn't go *through* Dreyfus because it's *about* Dreyfus, and a possible conspiracy to murder your boss."

"*What?*" The captain's eyes narrowed. "Accusing Chief Constable Dreyfus of treason and conspiracy to commit regicide is a serious charge, Sergeant. I hope you have evidence to back it up."

"I'm not accusing anyone, Captain." Benj bit off a sharper retort, knowing belligerence wouldn't get him anywhere. He hadn't wanted to come here, but Dee hadn't shown up for their scheduled meeting, undoubtedly busy searching for his missing mistress, and Benj had nowhere else to go. "If you'll *listen* instead of jumping to conclusions, I'll tell you what I've discovered."

Ithross clenched his jaw, but then nodded. "Very well, Sergeant. Let's hear it."

Benj first told him what he'd learned from Jacie. At the mention of Hoseph, the captain's face paled, but to his credit, he kept his mouth shut until Benj finished with the connection between Otar and Dreyfus.

"This does *not* bode well." Fingers flexing around his sword hilt, Ithross looked as if he wanted to hack something to death. "The emperor's public appearance is tomorrow. It can't be rescheduled. The easiest solution would simply be to arrest them both, I suppose."

"With all due respect, Captain, that's just cutting off your nose to spite your face!" These imperial types were always so eager for action without investigating facts or considering consequences. "Arresting Otar would just tip off Hoseph, and accusing Chief Dreyfus without evidence would be *worse*. He *could* be just a dupe."

"I suppose…" Captain Ithross didn't looked convinced.

"Look, my job is to investigate, so let me do the investigatin'. Your job is to protect the emperor, which is why I'm here. You keep on protectin' him. Maybe you can—I don't know—change things and not tell Dreyfus."

"And with all due *respect*, Sergeant, I'll do as I see fit with respect to the emperor's safety, and I won't be consulting you!" His face hardened again. "For all I know, you're feeding me lies to implicate your boss to usurp his position!"

"Right you are," Benj said with an approving nod. "Paranoia's a healthy thing in our business, Captain. I trust you because you're pretty much above suspicion, but you've got no reason to trust me. Other than my thirty years as a cap in this city…" He grinned without humor.

"Yes, well, thank you for bringing me this information, Sergeant. I'll take the appropriate steps."

"Good." Benj started for the door. "I'll be back to my job, then. If you want to get in touch, send a message to the *Copper Pot Pub*. My flat's upstairs."

"I will, Sergeant…"

"Benjamin."

Ithross' brow furrowed. "Sergeant Benjamin…the constabulary liaison to Miss Morin?"

Benj stopped short. "Aye, that's me. Unfortunately, her people have been scarce lately. Busy lookin' for her, I guess."

"You've not heard…" Ithross grinned, his shift in expression changing his entire demeanor. "Miss Moirin's been recovered. She's here in the palace."

"What?" Benj snapped. "When? Does Dreyfus know?"

"Just yesterday, and nobody's been told." He nodded as understanding dawned. "We'd best keep that to ourselves for now. If Dreyfus is compromised… Anyway, she's recovering from her ordeal here. She was in a bad way when they found her."

"Well—" Benj bit back a delighted expletive. *No wonder Dee didn't show up last night. He's celebratin'.* "That's somethin'! Mind if I speak with her?"

"I don't see why not. I'm told she's up and about this morning." Ithross opened the door and ushered him out. "Leave your weapons with the guards here, and someone will escort you to her chambers." With that, Ithross strode off down the hall.

"Weapons, huh?" Benj sighed and started the laborious process of disarming himself. When his sword, four daggers, sap, pair of brass knuckles, and belt-buckle knife lay on the table, Benj gave his pockets a pat, and nodded to the gaping guards. "Well, I think that's it. Let's go then. I gotta get to work today."

Mya flung the parchment down onto the window-side table in frustration, and clutched the window frame as her head spun.

"*Damn* it!" She gritted her teeth until the room stabilized. Corvecosi had told her that she wasn't yet well; one night's sleep and one good meal wouldn't expunge the trauma, fatigue, malnourishment, and the slurry of drugs still working their way out of her system. But that wasn't her only frustration. She glared daggers at the note she'd just received from Master Keyfur.

Miss Moirin,

I regret that I am unable to meet with you today due to my current heavy schedule of duties. I would, however, be delighted to entertain you in my quarters tomorrow afternoon. An escort will bring you here at three o'clock, if that is satisfactory.

Sincerely,
Archmage Keyfur

Encouraged by the prospect of tracking Lakshmi, she'd sent the request for a meeting to Master Keyfur right after breakfast. His reply was more than disappointing.

"Patience! Relax! Rest! Wait!" she muttered, clenching her fists. How could she relax knowing she had the means to find the Master Inquisitor and couldn't do it? *Lakshmi could realize the same thing any minute and take steps to block the location spell!*

Sitting here alone was driving her mad. She'd sent Lad off to inform the masters of her survival and Dee's loss, sick of his staring at her and coddling her. *Rest...relax...calm down...you're safe. Bullshit!*

Mya glowered out at the palace gardens. She'd appreciated their beauty during the post-coronation party, dancing with nobility among the flowers, basking in the emperor's praise. Now the scarlet bougainvillea and crimson hibiscus seemed to her like splashes of blood, the floral scents devolved into the alchemical reek of her torture chamber, and the twitter of birds mimicked the squeaking of Kittal's skinning machine.

With no one to talk to and nothing to do, her thoughts spiraled down dark paths of vengeance and murder. *I'll kill them all for this... I'll skin Lakshmi and get my runes back!*

A knock at the door tore her away from imagined screams and blood and the tug of Kittal's machine, strips of flesh writhing in jars, her runes alight...

She whirled to the welcome interruption. "Yes?"

The door opened, and a man in full armor filled the aperture, the elaborate crest emblazoned on his breastplate proclaiming him to be a knight. His short beard was flecked with gray, and his scarred hand rested on the hilt of a well-used sword. He didn't look threatening, but didn't seem very amiable either, His flinty eyes scanned the room before centering on her.

"Sorry to disturb you, Miss." He bowed shortly. "His Majesty Tynean Tsing III will see you if you're well enough."

Lad's comment about the emperor flashed through Mya's mind. Heat flushed to her cheeks, more from annoyance than anything else.

"Of course, but I'll need clothes." Her wrappings were once again snugged around her body under the silk robe, but it wasn't fit for an appointment with the emperor. "I'm not dressed appropriately for a stroll through the palace."

"You misunderstand, Miss Moirin. His Majesty is *here*." He nodded to the hallway behind him. "Now."

"Oh, I…" Mya tightened sash of the robe and tugged the sleeves to cover the edges of the wrappings. She couldn't refuse the emperor, of course, but the assumption that he could just barge in anytime set her teeth on edge. She bit back her sharp response. "Of course."

The knight strode in, and two more warriors followed, a burly man and a flaxen-haired woman, both as fully armed and armored, wearing the same livery as the knight, though significantly younger. They spread out, eyes sharp, hands on weapons. Either this was some kind of military action, or she'd done something while drugged that warranted additional security. She vaguely recalled lashing out— at hallucinations or real people, she wasn't sure—and tucked her hands firmly by her sides; it wouldn't do to have escaped the assassins only to be killed by imperial knights.

The emperor entered, flanked by four imperial guards, and Mya curtsied low. "Your Majesty."

"Please rise, Miss Moirin." The sovereign strode to the center of the room, his stone-faced guards close by. "It does Our heart good to see you up and looking well."

"Thanks to Your Majesty." Mya tried to smile, but her mouth wouldn't cooperate. "Without Master Keyfur's assistance, I would never have been found."

"After your service to the empire, it was the least We could do." His smile came easier than hers, but when he stepped closer and his guards shuffled along as if joined at the hip, his smile faltered. The emperor stopped and said, "Guards, stay where you are. Miss Moirin is quite lucid and no danger to Us."

No danger... Mya appreciated the sentiment, but her mood only plunged deeper. In her current condition, she'd hardly be a threat to a chambermaid, let alone a man protected by imperial guards and knights.

"Please forgive my escort. Captain Ithross insists that Sir Fornish and his squires attend Us in addition to my usual guards. It's hard to fault someone who's only trying to keep one alive." The emperor extended a hand toward the window. "Please."

"Of course, Majesty." Mya joined him there, the stares of the anxious guards pricking her back. More discomforting was the notion that Tynean Tsing felt something for her. It was foolish of Lad to think so, but how often had she relied upon Lad's skill at reading people? He wasn't often mistaken.

The emperor smiled amiably and asked, "How are you feeling?"

The question grated like a rasp on raw flesh. Everyone wanted to know how she felt, from the guards to Corvecosi, to Lad, and now the emperor. She wanted to scream out the truth, that she felt helpless and weak, that she felt like running away, finding a dark corner and curling up in a ball to hide, but that would only earn her ridicule.

"Well enough, all things considered, Majesty." The lie came easy. "Eager to be back at work."

The emperor chuckled. "We thought you'd say that. Your dedication is to be commended, but Master Corvecosi said you're not fully recovered yet."

"I'm just a little tired," she countered, fighting to keep her voice calm.

"Understandable. And We feel somewhat responsible for your plight." His amiable countenance darkened. "You suffered this...misfortune as a result of the mission you undertook for Us.

It's only right that We aid your recovery. You must stay as long as you wish, Miss Moirin, as Our guest."

"I..." Mya swallowed hard. Luxurious though it might be, the guards stationed outside her door made her feel like a prisoner. Of course, she couldn't say that. But she was tired and weak, and the palace was safe. She couldn't speak to Keyfur until tomorrow anyway. "I'd be grateful for another day's rest, Majesty. Thank you."

"You're more than welcome. We only want to see you well again." Abruptly, his broad smile fell. "And please accept Our sincere condolences for the loss of your assistant. Master Dee was tireless and quite vehement in his pursuit of your rescue."

"He..." Mya stifled her reflexive response. Her smothering guilt over Dee's loss was too painful and too fresh. Talking about it with Lad was one thing—he understood loss—but divulging such personal and agonizing details to a roomful of strangers was unthinkable. "He'd been with me a long time, Majesty."

The emperor sighed. "Yes, well, we survivors must forge on, mustn't we?"

"Yes, Majesty." Mya watched Tynean Tsing carefully. She wasn't as astute as Lad in discerning motives, but she'd spent a lifetime bluffing and talking her way in and out of situations. The emperor's thought had seemed unfinished, and now he looked out the window, seemingly serene except for his fingers twitching within the full sleeves of his elegant tunic. *What does he want from me?*

Turning a blazing smile on her, the emperor said, "And if you're feeling well enough, as a show of Our gratitude, We would like the honor of your company at dinner this evening."

Mya gaped at him. The last thing she wanted was an evening of fawning nobles and courtiers. And frankly, in her current mood, she'd likely spend the entire time struggling to keep her mouth from getting her into trouble. *But how can I beg off?* If she claimed illness, he'd insist she stay in the palace even longer.

"I appreciate the invitation, Majesty, but I'm afraid I have nothing to wear." Mya plucked at the sleeve of her robe.

"Oh, *that's* no problem." He waved a hand dismissively. "The Imperial Tailor is already working on a gown for you. More than one, in fact. Your efforts in Our service seems quite detrimental to your wardrobe."

Shit! She had no other way to refuse, and dare not insult him. *Better just get it over with.* "Then it would be my pleasure, Majesty. Thank you."

"Excellent. We will see you this evening, then." He held out a hand.

Mya took it, curtsying properly, then blanched when he bent to kiss her knuckles. *Gods, was Lad right?* She knew little of court manners, but the gesture seemed overly familiar.

With a smile, Tynean Tsing strode from the room, followed by the guards, Sir Fornish, and the squires. The door closed, and she was once again alone.

Mya stared at the sky beyond the window and balled her fists. *I'm no less a prisoner here than I was in Kittal's torture chamber.* Pressing a hand against the glass, she fought the urge to smash it, leap down to the gardens below, climb up over the wall, and run, just run and never look back. *Run or die…*

Another knock at the door rescued her from the maelstrom of anxiety. Perhaps the emperor had reconsidered his ill-conceived invitation. "Yes!"

The door opened and a guard peered in. "Miss Moirin, there's a constable here to see you. A Sergeant Benjamin."

"Sergeant Benjamin?" *What the hell's he doing here?* Her pulse quickened as she considered the possibilities. *Hoseph? Dee? Lad?* "Send him in!"

The guard nodded and admitted the sergeant.

"Miss Moirin!" Benj stepped into the room looking cleaner and more professional than she'd ever seen him. His tobacco-stained smile was broad as he strode over and stuck out a beefy hand. "Damn, it's good to see you breathin'!"

"Thank you, Sergeant." His honest regard lightened her heart. She matched his grip easily, though a few days ago she'd have had to hold back to keep from breaking bones. "I intend to keep breathing for some time yet. How did you know I was here?"

"Old Ithross told me you was back. Is Dee here, too? He missed our last two meetings without even a note."

The shroud of guilt threatened to suffocate her again, but she pushed it aside. "Dee…is gone. Hoseph took him during my rescue. I don't know if he's dead or being held captive somewhere."

"Damn it to all Nine Hells! I'm sorry." Benj's face reddened, his eyes narrowing. "Hoseph can...*take* people?"

Mya swallowed hard. "Yes. I saw them both just...puff into mist."

"That man needs a short talk with the emperor's new neck chopper, he does!" Benj made a face and sighed. "Well, that makes what I've got to tell you even more important!"

Mya stiffened and stared into his earnest face. "What?"

The sergeant's frown turned into a predatory grin. He looked over his shoulder at the door and lowered his voice. "I got a line on Hoseph."

The news struck her like a bolt of lightning. "*Where!*"

"A gambling house I know, *Lucky Gem's*, down in Midtown. They rent rooms. One of the ladies spotted him in the company of the former captain of the Imperial Guard, no less."

"The former captain..." Mya's mind snapped to the implications like the crack of a whip. "He's working him for information about the emperor's security."

"That's not all," Benj continued. "Former Captain Otar's been hoistin' a few drinks with Chief Constable Dreyfus lately. That's why I come here, to tell Captain Ithross. I was gonna get word to Dee, but..."

"Tell me where this place is."

"Corner of Red Leaf and Wattle. He's got a room on the second floor corner. Jacie's the young lady who spotted Hoseph in Otar's room, identified him from that sketch you gave me. I'd assign someone to watch Otar, but I can't spare anyone. Hoseph could pop in and out without us ever knowin' anyway. I think he's gonna try for the emperor tomorrow."

"Tomorrow?" Mya's thoughts stumbled. "What's tomorrow?"

"His Majesty's gonna announce his New Accords in the Imperial Plaza at midday." Benj snorted a laugh. "Like he didn't learn a thing the last time they tried to kill him there."

No wonder Keyfur is busy. Mya bit her lip and considered the plaza. The rebel assassins had tried for the emperor there before and failed. Lakshmi and Kittal wouldn't repeat that fiasco. *But they might try something different.* "Don't ask me for my sources, but you should check for hidden explosives in the area. Alchemical ones, like they used on us at the orphanage."

The sergeant's eyebrows shot up, but he just nodded sagely and didn't press her.

"Security *should* be impossible to breech, if Ithross learned anything from the last time, but if Hoseph knows what measures are being taken…"

"Damn straight. The assassins didn't have information from Otar and Dreyfus last time," Benj agreed. "Ithross said he'd take precautions, but I was hopin' you could…um…maybe make an appearance. With you there, Hoseph would never have a chance of getting close to the emperor."

Mya stiffened and clenched her fists, felt the weakness in her grip. *No danger to anyone… Weak and slow…* "I'm not in the emperor-saving business, Sergeant. I just happened to be in the right place at the right time at the coronation." At his crestfallen look, she explained. "That's the job of the Imperial Guard and soldiers. I'd just be in their way. Hoseph has never participated in these assassination attempts. He'll sit someplace safe and send someone else out to take the risks. Hell, he only murdered Lady T once she was alone in the carriage, then he disappeared. Besides, if I attend this event and I'm recognized, Hoseph and his accomplices will know I'm back in the game. To have any chance of killing that bastard, I'll have to surprise him."

"How?" Benj looked dubious. "Hard to surprise someone who can come and go like a fart on the breeze."

"I know, but I also know someone who can catch a fart on the breeze, tie it in a knot, and paint it blue." Mya grinned at Benj, though there was more malice than mirth in it. "And he hates Hoseph just as much as we do."

Chapter VIII

Lad followed his imperial escort down the corridor to Mya's room, struggling to keep his eagerness in check. *Home...Lissa...and away from assassins, emperors, and guards. A quick goodbye and I'm on my way home.*

At Mya's door, he smiled amiably at her guards. "I'd like to see Miss Moirin."

"Let me ask if she's up for guests." One of the guards knocked.

"Yes?" She was awake, at least.

The guard opened the door. "Your associate's here to see you, Miss Moirin."

Mya looked up from the small bag she was packing. "Yes, I need to see him."

The guard ushered Lad in and shut the door, but before he could even say good morning, Mya snapped, "Where have you been?"

"Lots of places. When I came back last night, you were out, so I went to bed. They had a room set up for me, though it was too soft and I could do without the guards." Was Mya irritated with him? Perhaps she still didn't feel well. Lad assessed her carefully; she certainly looked better, her hands were steady, her color good. Indeed, she looked like she'd just stepped out of a salon: nails burnished, skin rosy, brows perfectly shaped. Her hair had been returned to its natural deep red and neatly trimmed. The cobalt-hued gown she wore fit perfectly, and even more clothes lay on the bed ready to be packed. "Gifts from the emperor?"

Her eyes narrowed dangerously. "Yes. Don't change the subject. Tell me where you were all day yesterday."

91

"I visited the masters, just like you asked me to. They were worried about you, but I told them you were alive and safe."

"How much did you tell them about what happened to me?"

"Only that they tortured you, and that you were recovering. And I told them about Dee. That hit pretty hard, especially Jolee."

"Yes." Mya's face flushed and she looked away. "Dee was well liked." She rolled up a nightgown and stuffed it in the bag. "And after that?"

"I walked around the city. It's changed, or the people have. The mood's different, hopeful."

"That's the new emperor's doing. So, why didn't you come back here?" Still, she seemed upset.

"Because you needed rest, and my being here wasn't going to help that." Lad shrugged. "I came back in the evening, then, since you were busy, I figured I'd speak to you this morning."

"Well, at least you're back now. We've got a lot to do."

Lad didn't like the sound of that. "*You've* got a lot to do, Mya. I came to say goodbye."

"*Goodbye?*" Mya dropped the silk robe she was folding and stared at him. "What do you mean?"

What did she think he meant? "I'm going back to Twailin."

"No!" She clenched her jaw. "You *can't* leave yet."

"I *can*, Mya." He cocked his head, hoping he'd misunderstood her commanding tone. "I'm not in the guild anymore. I don't answer to you."

"That's not what I mean!" She rounded the bed, glowering at him. "The job's not *done* yet!"

"Mine is. I promised Dee I'd find you, and I did." He pointed to the dress she wore. "If you're well enough to get dressed up and dine with the emperor, you're well enough to be Grandmaster. You don't need my help, Mya."

"I *do* need your help! I'm not..." Mya's face flushed a deeper crimson, and her hands balled into fists at her sides. Her voice fell to a hoarse whisper. "I'm not what I *was*, Lad. I can't do this alone."

"You're not alone. You've got three factions of the guild on your side. You can—"

"That's not the *same!*" she argued. "None of them can do what you do. *I* can't do what you do, not after Kittal stripped away half of my runes!" Her voice shook with emotion.

"You don't know that."

"I *do* know it," she countered. "I'm slow and weak, I feel pain, and the healing magic… You saw my scars!"

"I feel pain, and have no healing runes left at all. Besides, you have no idea how fast or strong you are, unless you've been sparring with your guards since yesterday."

She glared at him, but anger was better than fear and self-doubt.

"No? All right, let's see how slow and weak you really are." He nodded to her gown. "But you should take that off. I'd hate to damage the emperor's gift."

"Here?" Her ire shifted to shock and suspicion. "Now?"

"Why not?" Lad pushed the divan up against the wall. "You've got your wrappings on, and there's enough room for some light sparring if we're careful."

"But…" Doubt clouded her eyes again.

"You *have* to know your capabilities, Mya." He frowned and shrugged. "Or would you rather test them when Hoseph pops in behind you?"

Mya's hands flexed and fidgeted, her nails clicking, one of her tells. *She's nervous.*

"Fine." She glared at him while she reached behind and loosened the gown's stays, then turned away, struggling for a moment with the long sleeves before stripping the garment off and tossing it on the bed. The black linen wrappings hugged her like a glove.

Lad kicked off his shoes. He'd already exercised this morning, so his muscles were loose. "Do you need to warm up?"

"No. Let's just get this over with."

"Okay." Lad squared off with Mya in the center of the open space and assumed the first pose of his long-practiced routine. "Begin whenever you're ready."

Mya mirrored his stance, took a deep breath, and began the sparring cadence slowly, methodically, almost tentatively. He blocked her strikes and kicks without thought, and countered barely faster than her pace. She blocked, wincing as his foot hit her forearm.

"You'll have to get used to feeling pain again." Lad blocked two more strikes and flicked out a foot to rap her lightly on the ribs.

Mya stepped back, one hand lowering to touch where his kick had tapped her.

Lad paused. "Come *on*, Mya. You were faster than this when you attacked me in the sewers."

Her lips thinned into a hard line, and she resumed, diverging from the standard cadence in a flurry of ineffective strikes and kicks. Spinning with the impact of Lad's counterstrike, she lashed out with a backhand.

Lad leaned back and watched her knuckles pass a finger width from his nose, felt the breeze of the strike. He caught the next one and smiled at her. "Better."

Mya broke his hold and snapped a kick at his chin. Lad whirled away and let loose a roundhouse kick, but she ducked and spun low, pushing off the floor with her palms and scissoring her legs across his planted foot.

Oh, very good! She wasn't quite as fast as before, but her innovations were as sharp as ever. *Let's see how good...*

Lad sprang off the floor in a flip, his foot evading her trap. As with any fully evasive maneuver, however, once he was committed, his trajectory was predictable, his landing point fixed. If he'd truly wished to escape, he'd have bounded backward out of her reach, but this wasn't an evasion, it was a test. He suspected Mya's problem was a lack of confidence, not ability, so he'd left an opening for her. If she could exploit it, maybe she could show herself what she was capable of.

She whirled as he flipped, building momentum for the kick he'd hoped for. It was well timed and powerful...but predictable. As Lad flung out his hands to intercept her foot, however, Mya twisted and lashed her other foot right at his head.

Lad jerked back barely in time, the edge of her foot grazing his cheek, genuinely surprised—and pleased—by her counterstrike. Overbalanced, he tucked and rolled to his feet, grinning and holding out his hands for her to stop.

"There. Now you know."

Mya stood poised, blinking as if surprised at her own performance. She looked down at her hands, breathing hard, and nodded. "Yes, I... Thank you."

"You're welcome." Lad slipped into his shoes. "And goodbye. I'm off to see Keyfur about getting home."

"You can't." Mya snatched up her dress, talking as she flipped it over her head and wriggled into it. "Keyfur's busy until this afternoon."

Lad frowned. *She'll say anything to make me stay.*

She waved at a letter on the small table. "If you don't believe me, read that. I wanted to talk to him about tracking Lakshmi. But there's something else you need to consider before you run off to Twailin."

Lad eyed her suspiciously. "What's that?"

"Hoseph undoubtedly recognized you in the sewers. He knows you're not dead." Mya worked her shoulders to settle the dress into place and began tightening the stays. "And he may have taken Dee for questioning. He could know where you live, about your family, your daughter, everything."

Lad clenched his hands so hard his knuckles cracked. She was right, but he couldn't let her manipulate him. "All the more reason I need to be with them. You've got more than half the Tsing guild on your side, and much more experience running them than I do. You also strategize better than I do. You don't *need* me here."

"Yes, Lad, I *could* do this without your help, but I can do it better and faster *with* your help." She cinched the last stay and regarded him with knitted brows. "The sooner I win, the sooner your family's safe. Help me neutralize the threat, both to me *and* your family, before it manifests."

"Neutralize the threat?" Lad wrinkled his nose. "Don't mince words, Mya. You want me to help you kill Hoseph."

"That's *exactly* what I want." She slipped her feet into her dainty shoes and faced him with her hands on her hips. "This is kill or die, Lad. We kill Hoseph, or your family is at risk. Help me kill him and win this war. Only *then* will Forbish and Lissa and your nephews be safe. Once that's done, you can go home and be an innkeeper, and I'll never bother you again."

Lad couldn't argue with her logic, but he didn't trust her. Mya always thought ahead, always had ulterior motives, always looked out for herself. And she wasn't just out to win the guild war, she was out for vengeance. She wanted his help and would do anything to get it. Had her warning about his family's safety actually been a subtle threat? If he left her to face this alone, would her quest for vengeance extend to more than Lakshmi and Kittal? Perhaps not, but he couldn't risk being wrong.

"Very well, Mya, I'll stay and help you."

"Thank you." She finished packing the small bag, hefted it, and headed for the door. "I received some information that might help us track down Hoseph, and I've got a task in mind for you. I'll fill you in on our way out."

"One thing's for damn sure," Benj said to Jorren as they strode the perimeter of the Imperial Plaza, "security's tighter than a banker's purse strings."

"In a brute force sort of way, I suppose." Jorren eyed the phalanx of armored cavalry lining the streets to the east and west of the square, and the gleaming ranks of imperial guards surrounding the platform from which the emperor spoke. "At least they're not all facing the same *direction* this time."

Benj stifled a grin at Jorren's derision. Despite outperforming all other candidates when competing for a squireship, he'd been passed over in favor of a noble's son. He'd borne a heavy chip on his shoulder ever since. Benj was secretly glad things had turned out the way they had; Jorren made a far better constable than a knight. He was smart, observant, and reliable, one of the few caps Benj trusted completely.

"True," he agreed as he gazed around, assessing the upgraded security measures. The stage itself was shielded from view behind, above, and to both sides by blue canvas. In addition to imperial guards and knights, regular army soldiers were stationed at every window of every building, and archers manned the rooftops. While these troops watched for threats to the emperor, the constabulary had been tasked with keeping an eye on the teeming crowd. The division of labor made sense. "At least Ithross is smart enough to admit that his guards don't know the city or the people."

"I guess you can't blame him for that. He's probably only out of the palace once a month or so." Jorren paused to peer down a sewer drain before moving on.

"True enough…the poor sod." Benj raised his voice as the crowd erupted in more cheers, responding to some point the emperor had just made. He wasn't listening to the speech, which had just begun and was to continue for at least an hour. "Dressed up in finery and standin' in one spot day after day ain't no way for a fightin' man to make a livin'." Benj spat a stream of tobacco juice into the gutter.

"I'll bet he saves a bundle on shoe leather." Jorren chuckled. "And they *do* make an impressively shiny wall. Not much is going to get past half a thousand imperial troops."

Hoseph can. Benj wished again that Miss Moirin was here. Though she'd doubted that the priest would show up, his gut told him otherwise. He wouldn't breathe easy until the emperor was safely back in the palace.

The crowd thinned as he and Jorren approached the northeast corner of the plaza. Beyond the cordon of imperial guards, three identical imperial carriages sat in a row along the street behind the stage.

"Why three carriages, I wonder?" asked Jorren.

"Probably a shell game. If someone targets a carriage, there's only a one in three chance they'll pick the one with the emperor aboard."

Jorren nodded. "Of course."

Benj wondered if Ithross had devised this new precaution because of the sergeant's warning. He approved of the tactic, but something about the carriages nagged at him. Jorren had already spun on his heel and started back along their route, but Benj waved him on. "Cover our section for me. I want to look at somethin'."

The corporal cocked an eyebrow, then nodded. "Sure, Sergeant." Benj was breaking protocol by leaving his patrol area, but Jorren knew better than to ask questions. He turned and started back south, his stride slow and deliberate, his eyes watchful.

Benj approached the nearest imperial guard officer. "Sergeant Benjamin, Tsing Constabulary. Mind if I have a stroll along the back of the stage?"

The man checked a list and squinted at Benj. "*You're* Dreyfus' first sergeant?"

Just doin' his job, he reminded himself, biting back a sarcastic retort. "I am."

"Put your hand on this." The officer rolled up the scroll and held it out. "We're checking everyone. Archmage Keyfur's orders."

Benj gritted his teeth and put his hand on the parchment. Nothing happened. He didn't want to know what would have happened if he wasn't who he'd said he was.

"All right, Sergeant, you can pass through." The officer stepped aside.

Benj grunted his thanks and passed through the cordon. The area behind the stage was clear save for the carriages, and the windows of the surrounding buildings were shuttered. Archers were silhouetted atop the roof, crossbows at the ready. Benj didn't see how any attack could come from that quarter.

Abreast of the three carriages, he leaned down to peer under the back of the stage, the only side that wasn't draped with a canvas skirt. It had undoubtedly been checked already, and nobody hid under there. Benj turned to the carriages, identical right down to the teams of white horses and the banners that fluttered from the corner posts. Dark curtains on the carriage windows would hide the occupants. Liveried drivers sat in their seats looking bored. They ignored Benj as he strolled by. Try as he might, Benj couldn't find a single thing amiss.

You're barkin' up the wrong tree, Benjamin...

Another roar of applause drew his attention to the rear curtain of the stage. A fold in the curtain indicated the only entrance or exit to the stage. Onstage the emperor was at risk. Once back here again, he'd be safely out of sight and out of reach.

Safe... Benj looked along the path the emperor would take: through the curtain, down the stairs, and then to one of the carriages, surrounded by his guards the whole way.

Safe... So what the hell's bothering me about... He turned and squinted, his teeth grinding.

The carriages... Benj examined the carriages again. What was it about them that roiled his gut? *Something...a conversation with someone...but who?* Someone had died in a carriage. He caught his breath. *Baroness Monjhi!* Miss Morin had told him that Hoseph materialized *inside* the baroness' carriage to murder her.

That's it! The emperor was always surrounded by guards and knights, even in the carriage, so Hoseph couldn't pop in while the carriage was in transit. *But who boards the carriage first?* If Hoseph was waiting inside when the emperor stepped aboard, he could kill him and disappear before the guards realized what was happening.

But Ithross surely knew about Hoseph's disappearing act. Benj's report of how Baroness Monjhi died had been sent to the palace. *But did they read it?* he wondered. *Do they know?*

Well, there was an easy way to counter the threat: Put a guard in each carriage. *And maybe we snag Hoseph at the same time!*

Benj started toward an imperial guard lieutenant, then stopped and looked back at the three carriages. *How can he know which one?* Hoseph might have inside information, maybe even someone inside the Imperial Guard, but rumor was that all palace staff were under extra scrutiny since these assassinations attempts started, so it was unlikely. So, he would have to be watching from somewhere when the emperor left the stage.

And if he is watchin, and I create a big hubbub by tellin' the guard, he'll be scared off.

The Imperial Guard wouldn't be subtle if there was a potential threat to the emperor. They'd call in a phalanx of knights and put them in and around all three carriages. The emperor would be safe, of course, but the chance to bag Hoseph would vanish. And unfortunately, Benj couldn't call in his own people without alerting the Imperial Guard.

Which means it's up to me...

All he needed was a moment. If he could surprise the priest when he popped in, one quick dagger thrust would end this. He had no illusions about attempting to apprehend someone who could kill you with a touch.

Benj knew his plan was way out of line, but then, he'd never been one for rules. Usually that meant drinking on duty and roughing up ner-do-wells for information, not endangering the emperor's life to nab a killer. *In for a penny, in for a crown, Benjamin.*

He strolled back to the carriages and realized he had a problem in common with Hoseph. "Which carriage?"

Stopping at the first, he opened the door and peered inside. Nothing. At the second, he found a small box of pens and inkwells lying on one of the cushioned seats. If Ithross was smart, he might place decoys board each carriage to throw off any observers. *Maybe he's not so dumb after all.* At the third carriage, however, Benj spotted the one thing that gave it all away; tucked in the corner of one seat lay a thin circlet of gold.

Benj grinned. *Heavy things, crowns. He probably can't wait to take the thing off and put on the simple circlet.* Benj closed the door and strolled away. Now all he had to do was get inside that carriage without drawing attention.

"Are you sure this is where you want to be, miss?" The imperial coachman wrinkled his nose at the little bakery on the Midtown corner. "I can bring you to your home, or wait…"

"This is fine. We're just going to get a bite to eat." Mya gestured Lad toward the bakery. "No slight to his majesty's chief, but I'm *dying* for a proper pastry. No need for you to wait. We'll hire a hackney."

"As you wish, miss." The driver looked dubious, but lashed his reins, and the carriage rumbled off.

Mya watched until the coach rounded the corner. Lad flagged down a hackney and stood by the open door, so she tossed in her bag and stepped aboard. The door shut behind her before she'd even sat down, and Lad called out an address to the driver from outside.

"Wait! What are you doing?" Mya hissed, leaning out the window. "Get in here!"

Lad shook his head. "You've told me everything I need to know. I'm going to work, and it's in the opposite direction from where you're going."

"But I thought you would—"

"You'll be fine, Mya. I know you don't like carriages any more than I do, but you're safe. Nobody knows you've left the palace. I'll see you later." With that, Lad turned and strode off down the street.

Mya gritted her teeth as the carriage jerked into motion. *Deathtraps!* But she could hardly walk to Embree's headquarters, especially in these toe-pinching shoes. *And I don't even have a weapon!* She yanked the curtains shut and wedged herself into a corner, one hand on the door latch. *Damn him! He could have stayed with me until I was safe!*

By the time the carriage pulled to a halt in front of the *Black Goose Inn* in the Dreggars Quarter, Mya's nerves were as tight as over-wound watch springs. She stepped out of the carriage and paid the driver, dragging in a deep breath to ease the tension and slow her pounding heart. *Don't show weakness, Mya. You're Grandmaster! In control! In charge!*

Head high, she entered the inn.

"Well, *hello*, ma'am. We've been expecting you." The innkeeper smiled and beckoned to her. "We've got the private room you requested all ready, right this way."

Of course they were expecting her. Mya nodded and followed, inspecting the place with feigned nonchalance. An old woman sweeping the floor caught her eye and winked, and a few other faces looked familiar. *Safe…I'm safe.* The inn wasn't unlike her old home, the *Golden Cockerel*, in Twailin. There, of course, Paxal had always been behind the bar, tossing her a smile and anticipating her every need. Here she was surrounded by strangers, but still she found the environment vaguely comforting. The innkeeper—either an assassin or, like Paxal, deep in the guild's confidence—ushered her down a hall to a door, knocked, and opened it.

The three masters looked up from a broad table, then stood as Mya entered the office.

Thanking the innkeeper, Mya closed the door and strode forward. *Confidence. Strength. You're Grandmaster!* She held up a hand to forestall their questions. "I'm fine. We've got a lot to do, but first," she held out a hand to Noncey, "give me a dagger."

Noncey swallowed, but complied without pause, removing a dagger and sheath from his belt and handing it over hilt first.

Mya took the weapon, unsheathed it, and felt instantly better. "Thank you." She admired the blade for a moment, beautiful layered steel and razor sharp. "I'm afraid I lost the ones you gave me before, Noncey."

"No matter, Grandmaster." His lips quirked into a weak smile. "I've others."

Mya sheathed the dagger and steadied herself with another deep breath.

"Good to have you back, Grandmaster." Clemson gestured to an empty chair.

"It's good to *be* back." *And to be alive...* She sat down, clutching the dagger under the table. *Safe! I'm fine!* "Let's not waste any time. I assume you got my message yesterday. Tell me what's been done."

Mya listened patiently as the masters explained the deployment of their forces. They knew their jobs and performed them well. Embree had sent several people to watch *Lucky Gem's*, as she had ordered. "Excellent! Now, what about the guild wizard I asked you to bring in?"

"Unfortunately, the wizard we usually contract with isn't available." The Master Hunter looked apologetic, but Mya wasn't interested in apologies.

"What do you mean, isn't available?" She gritted her teeth to keep her emotions in check. "Why not?"

"We can't find her. She wasn't at her home or shop. Maybe she's away, or maybe Lakshmi and Kittal got to her before we did. I don't know."

"Damn!" Mya clenched her hands on the dagger, fighting to rein in her temper. *Another godsdamned delay!* She'd hoped to start tracking Lakshmi immediately, but it looked as if she'd just have to wait for Keyfur. "Well, I guess I'm going back to the palace this afternoon."

"We're better off with the archmage, anyway. At least we know *he's* not in league with Lakshmi and Kittal, and he can do the job." Embree looked thoughtful for a moment, then asked, "If you don't mind my asking, Grandmaster, who did you want to find?"

"Lakshmi."

Embree looked even more confused. "But what do you have of Lakshmi's that would allow us to track her with magic?"

Mya had wracked her brain for some way to explain this without revealing her secret, but saw no way to avoid telling her masters the truth. They already knew she was magically enhanced, but to reveal her runes... She'd killed to keep that secret safe.

You have to trust somebody, Mya...

"It's not what I have of hers, but what *she* has that was mine." All three of them looked perplexed, but Mya soldiered on. "What I'm going to tell you, I've kept secret for years...but it's time I take you into my confidence."

The three masters stiffened like bird dogs on the hunt, but uttered not a word.

"You've all seen me do things that...normal people can't do. These...abilities are imbued through rune magic in the form of tattoos." Mya unbuttoned a sleeve and rolled it up above her elbow, then pulled her wrappings up far enough to show them the writhing black runes on her skin. "Lakshmi discovered this and decided that she wanted them for herself."

"She...*what?*" Clemson's eyes widened.

"Kittal...surgically removed about a third of my runes and grafted them onto Lakshmi. She's now..." Mya swallowed the bile that threatened to surge up her throat, "...wearing quite a lot of my skin."

Noncey blanched. "That's *disgusting!*"

"So now you'll understand my next order, and let me make this *perfectly* clear: Lakshmi and Kittal are under a death sentence. There will be *no* forgiveness, *no* amnesty, *no* deals, and *no* compromises. I want the two of them, *and* Hoseph, dead!"

"Understood," Clemson said, and the other two nodded.

Embree leaned back in his chair, fascination and revulsion vying for dominance on his face. "But why would Lakshmi want your magic? She's no fighter."

"To keep her alive. She's evidently very old, and Kittal's potions apparently aren't doing enough anymore." Mya flexed her hands on the dagger beneath the table, envisioned using it to reclaim her skin from Lakshmi. She shook off the image and forced herself to calm down. "The only fortunate consequence of what Lakshmi did was that we can now track her the same way Dee and Master Keyfur found me." She fingered the dark wrappings at her wrist. "Using these."

"But, Grandmaster, if Lakshmi is wearing some of your skin…" Embree faltered, cleared his throat, and continued, "couldn't they use that to track *you*, just as you intend to track her?"

Mya's heart skipped a beat, and the room swam around her for a moment. *Run! Run or die!*

"Grandmaster? Are you all right?"

"All right?" Mya swallowed her terror and fought down the urge to leap up and flee. "Not really, but I will be. I hadn't considered that, Embree, so thank you for thinking of it. We should…take precautions."

Embree nodded. "I'll set up a cordon for two blocks around the inn to watch for anyone suspicious, Grandmaster."

"And I'll have Blades guarding you round the clock," Embree added.

Lad! I need Lad! But Lad had a job to do, and being her bodyguard, though comforting, wasn't a good use of his skills. *But if not Lad, then who…* She looked at Clemson, and the obvious answer popped into her mind.

"Jolee." The huge Enforcer could take more sheer punishment than anyone else in the guild. "If you assign Jolee as my bodyguard, I won't need to draw on any other resources, and I *know* I can trust her. Besides, she has just as big an axe to grind against Hoseph and the others as I do."

"She's yours, Grandmaster, and you're right." Clemson pursed her lips. "Do you think that Dee *is* still alive?"

Mya rubbed her eyes. She'd been avoiding this topic, but it had to be addressed. "I don't know if he's dead or alive. All I know is Hoseph took him. We've got to assume that they have Dee and are…extracting information from him." The remembered sound of Kittal's skinning machine buzzed along her nerves.

Noncey nodded. "That's what Bloodhound said, and why we moved headquarters."

"Where *is* Bloodhound?" Embree asked. "He's damn good at his job! Maybe he can help us track down Dee."

"He's the best," Mya agreed. "That's why I've assigned him to watch Otar. He's familiar with Hoseph, has dealt with him before. If *anyone* can catch that..." She fought again for control.

"But I've already stationed my people—"

Mya held up a hand. "No insult to your Hunters, Embree. Bloodhound won't interfere with your people, and they probably won't even know he's there."

"As you wish, Grandmaster."

"I've got one more thing I want you all to look into." Mya gripped the dagger's hilt so hard her knuckles popped. "In my...time with Lakshmi and Kittal, I noticed that they have a certain...rapport. Kittal has devoted untold resources and effort to keep Lakshmi alive. I want to know why. Does he owe her for something? Does she pay him for his efforts with information? Or maybe she holds something over his head?"

The three masters exchanged blank looks and shrugs.

"Well, look into it. Ask your older members what they know about the two. Beating them means knowing them, and I don't like mysteries. If we find them, we find the last Tessifus boy, and their entire plan for reinstalling an Imperial Grandmaster falls apart. And maybe we find Dee alive as well." She stood, and they followed suit. "Now I'm going to change into something that doesn't have a godsdamned corset."

Hunkered in a dark corner of the emperor's carriage, Benj couldn't decide whether to hope that his supposition was correct or a colossal blunder. If he was right, and Hoseph popped into the carriage, Benj would have to kill him without hesitation, which almost felt like murder. *And if I'm wrong, I've got to explain to the emperor why I'm hiding in his carriage.* Being mistaken, if he was lucky, would only cost him his career. If he wasn't so lucky, he'd end up in the palace dungeons, or get a sword in the chest from an over-zealous guard.

Another prolonged roar of cheers and applause shook the carriage. The emperor's speech should be coming to a close soon.

Waiting for the murderous priest to appear felt like waiting for the hangman's noose to tighten around his throat. Benj fingered the dagger at his belt, fighting to stay attentive. A nip from his hip flask would have steadied his nerves, but he dared not. Explaining himself would be hard enough without whiskey on his breath.

Another resounding cheer, even louder and longer than the previous, echoed around the plaza. *The bloody speech has got to be over.* The emperor would be descending the steps behind the stage in moments, turning toward the carriage, striding across the short distance surrounded by his guards, and...

A breeze wafted through the carriage, but it billowed the curtains outward, not in. The shadows deepened, tendrils of ebony mist swirling out of nowhere, forming into the vague shape of a man. Benj gritted his teeth and drew his dagger. He was no stranger to the simple magic of light stones and message crystals, but this—flesh forming from mist, killing with a touch—scared the shit out of him.

Even wizards bleed, Benj reminded himself as Hoseph solidified into flesh and blood before him. *At least he's facing the door...*

Even as the last of the mists faded, the priest plucked a small vial from the belt of his robe and raised it to his lips. Benj didn't know what was in that vial—*magic, no doubt*—but he had no intention of letting Hoseph drink it. Lunging from the shadowed corner, the constable grabbed the priest's wrist, thrusting his dagger into the man's back.

A guttural cry rang in the confined space—from his own throat or Hoseph's, he couldn't tell. They slammed into the carriage door, and the latch splintered. Daylight blinded him for a moment as they tumbled out. Benj hit the cobblestones hard, taking the impact on his shoulder, his iron cap cracking against the stone, but he had been in more street fights than most soldiers had seen battles. He jerked the knife out of Hoseph's back and thrust again, feeling the blade bite deep. Shouts rang out: his own, the guards', Hoseph's. Once again Benj pulled his bloody dagger free, warm blood slickening his grip, but as he thrust a third time, a pulse of darkness swept over him, dredging up horrors from every corner of his soul.

Deaths, murders, beatings, interrogations—all in the name of the empire—blood on his hands, too much blood, the smell of it, the *taste* in his mouth. His grip on the priest turned to water, his dagger clattering to the cobbles. An unrepentant howl of anguish tore from his throat. Benj rolled, thrashing to flee the monster within him, the brute, the thug, the murderer.

No…not real! Magic! Benj wrenched his eyes open. *Kill him! Kill the bastard!*

Hoseph lay on the cobbles only an arm-span away, bleeding and gasping. Suddenly, he began to dissolve into black mist.

No! Reactions honed by a lifetime on the street kicked through the agonizing fog clouding Benj's mind. Pulling another dagger, its hilt solid and real in his grasp, Benj rolled into the swirling mists and thrust down as hard as he could. A jolt numbed his arm as the blade cracked against the cobbles. Hoseph was gone.

Gods damn it! Benj dragged a breath into his ravaged throat. Shouts and threats, cries and warnings, rang out around him. He tried to get up, but something hard hit him between the shoulder blades, pinning him down.

"Don't fucking *move*!" an imperial guard bellowed, the tip of her sword pricking the back of Benj's neck.

"Not movin!" He dropped his dagger. "I'm a constable, for the gods' sake!"

"I don't give a damn *what* you are! You move, and I'll put this blade through your neck!"

"Fine!" Benj could see nothing with his face pressed to the ground, but the cacophony of shouted orders, stamping feet, and clanking armor sounded like all Nine Hells had broken loose. Nearby, a door slammed shut, a whip cracked, and iron-shod hooves and wheels trembled the cobbles under his cheek. When the clatter of carriages had faded, the pressure of the blade on his neck eased a trifle.

"Get him up!" ordered the officer who had pinned him. "Disarm him."

"I'm Sergeant Benjamin of the constabulary! Call your captain over. Ithross knows me!" Benj didn't protest as they hauled him to his feet and took his weapons. Ringed by naked blades, fighting them would have been suicide.

"Make a lane! Make way for the captain!"

The crowd of grim imperial guards parted. Captain Ithross shouldered his way through, his eyes wide and his knuckles white on the hilt of his sword. "Sergeant *Benjamin?* What in the Nine Unholy Hells is going on?"

"Captain! It was Hoseph! He appeared in the emperor's carriage." Benj pointed to the bloody dagger lying on the street. "I put a blade in him, but he faded away to mist before I could finish the job." He didn't bother adding that he'd been hiding in the carriage.

The captain's eyes narrowed, flicking from the broken door of the carriage to the bloody dagger lying on the cobbles. "Did anyone see this?"

"I saw...something, sir!" A guard saluted and stepped forward. "I heard a commotion and saw him," he stabbed a finger at Benj, "tumbling out of that carriage with some fellow in brown robes. I started to shout, but then...some kind of magic hit me. Felt like it turned me inside out, it did. When I looked up again, the robed fellow was gone."

"Well!" Ithross looked at Benj. "Release him, Lieutenant. We'll be taking you to the palace to discuss this, Sergeant."

"*Thank* you, Captain." Benj straightened his tunic and caught sight of Jorren at the edge of the crowd of imperial guards, looking worried. "I'll need to leave word for Chief Dreyfus. Don't want him to think I've just skipped town."

"Very well."

Benj waved Jorren over and explained what happened. "Give Dreyfus the news, Corporal. Cover my watch."

"Sure, Sergeant." Jorren nodded knowingly; he'd only tell Dreyfus what was necessary.

"Captain." Benj grinned at Ithross and held up his bloody hands. "I'm all yours."

Chapter IX

Hoseph materialized on the floor of Kittal's office, curled into a fetal ball of bloody robes and agony. *Demia, end the pain!* Gasping for breath, he coughed up blood and groaned. His head felt like it would explode, and his back blazed with pain from the stab wounds.

"Hoseph! What *happened* to you!" Lakshmi and Kittal rushed over and knelt beside him.

"Someone…" Hoseph coughed more blood, fighting to stay conscious. "Someone was waiting…in the carriage."

Fumbling with the vial still clutched in his hand, he twisted the cap free and dashed the elixir onto his tongue. The pain and nausea eased in a heady wash of mint. The stab wounds pinched closed, the flesh knitting together with a tingle. He could suddenly breathe again, and strength returned to his limbs. Hoseph heaved a sigh of relief. *Not yet into your embrace, sweet Demia…* He recapped the vial and started to tuck it away.

"What's *that?*" Kittal grabbed his wrist before he could hide the potion. "That's one of *mine*! How did you… Who gave this to you?!"

"No one *gave* it to me!" Hoseph jerked his wrist free and struggled to his feet, still dreadfully weak, his robes matted with blood. The potion had saved his life, and he wasn't about to give it up. "I needed it, so I took it!"

"You *thief!*" Kittal flushed with rage.

"You weren't about to give it to me, and without it, my efforts to bring our plans to fruition would be impaired." Hoseph stepped back from the irate Alchemist.

"Don't you try to talk your way out of this! You *stole* that!" Kittal held out a shaking hand. "Give it to me this instant!"

"No." Hoseph tucked the bottle away. "I need it."

"Oh, no doubt you do! It's highly addictive! How much have you been taking?"

"Enough. Now, can we *please* focus on something important! The emperor's still alive. Someone was hiding in the carriage."

"This *is* important!" Kittal folded his arms in defiance. "You have no idea what that elixir will do to you if you use too much. When it runs out, you'll wish you'd never been born!"

"Then you'll have to give me more."

"I will *not!*"

"Kittal, please!" Lakshmi stepped between them, resting one wrinkled hand on the Master Alchemist's arm. "We can deal with Hoseph's thievery later. We have more important things to attend to now. We need to know what happened."

"How can we trust the word of a *thief?*" Kittal's his face twisted into a mocking sneer.

"Kittal!" Lakshmi flashed him a warning glare.

"Oh, fine!" The Master Alchemist whirled away with a dismissive flick of one hand. "Regale us with your *failure*, Hoseph. You were stabbed? How could *that* have happened?"

"As I *said*." Hoseph checked his temper. "Someone must have suspected what I planned to do. Duke Tessifus might have told them that I materialized inside his carriage, or we may have a leak through one of your people."

"Typical! Blame us! Maybe your own informant betrayed you!" Kittal snorted in disgust.

"Taking the Tessifus boys was not *my* idea!" Hoseph countered.

"Would you both calm down and swallow your pride for a moment!" Lakshmi glared at them. "We'll get nowhere if we fight. We must work *together*."

"You don't understand! They *saw* me! Before this I was wanted for *suspicion* of being involved in plotting regicide. Now they have incontrovertible evidence."

"And now getting to Arbuckle will be virtually impossible, thanks to *your* failure!" Kittal glared at Hoseph.

"Kittal!" Lakshmi stabbed a finger at the Master Alchemist. "Stop it! None of us are blameless here. We agreed on this plan, and we *all* failed to see the damning flaw. If we want *any* hope of putting the guild back on track, we need to *cooperate*. We need to be *honest* with each other."

"And not steal from each other," Kittal muttered with a dark look at the priest.

Hoseph rounded on the two masters, his temperance at an end. "If you want my cooperation, you need to stop treating me like an outsider. I may not have signed a blood contract, but I'm as much a part of this guild as *either* of you. More so, in fact! You never even *met* your own Grandmaster, didn't even know who he was! I had his utmost confidence and advised him constantly! I know every guildmaster in every city throughout the empire. I was privy to every plot and plan he devised. So if you intend to bring the guild back to its former glory, you *need* me. You need to recognize me as integral to the guild, not just some underling at your beck and call!"

Hoseph caught his breath—*Sweet shadow of death, soothe me*—and fought for calm. This had been building for a long time. He'd been the right hand of the Grandmaster, his sole liaison to the rest of the guild, and he would be again.

To Hoseph's surprise, neither of the masters spoke for several breaths. He braced for another argument, but then Lakshmi inclined her head in a solemn nod.

"You're quite right, Hoseph. The blood contracts are gone anyway, and you *have* been an integral part of this guild. I...*we*," she said with a significant look at Kittal, "will henceforth recognize you as a full-fledged guild member, not in the chain of command, of course, but with an equal say in all our endeavors."

Hoseph hesitated. The concession surprised him. *But can I believe them?* Lakshmi was a Master Inquisitor, skilled at weaving lies. *I have no choice. They are my only means of attaining my former position.*

He returned her nod. "In the interest of trust, I'll tell you why I need this." He plucked the vial of elixir from his sash. "My frequent forays through the Sphere of Shadow have...worn on me. I suffer severe headaches and nausea each time I travel. The elixir cures them."

"No." Kittal shook his head. "It *does* mend flesh to a certain degree, but it doesn't *cure* the underlying malady. It merely treats symptoms, drawing on your body's reserves to do so. Over time—"

"Over time, I'll need more." Hoseph shook the bottle, already less than half full. He hadn't realized he was getting so low. "You say it's addictive, so be it. My instantaneous travel is *essential* to the successful operation of this guild."

Kittal opened his mouth to speak, but Lakshmi raised a hand. "He's right, Kittal, and though he stole it, his reasons were not selfish. Hoseph employs his divine gifts for the good of the guild. Enough elixir to serve *our* needs is a reasonable request."

"I'll not be held responsible for what it does to you in the end, Hoseph," the Master Alchemist warned.

"I'm not asking you to take responsibility." If it meant getting more elixir, Hoseph would agree to any plot they cooked up.

"Fine, I'll assign someone to start preparing more, but use it sparingly. The formulation takes time."

"I only use it when necessary," Hoseph assured him.

"All well and good, but this doesn't get us any closer to our goal." Kittal looked frustrated. "We *must* eliminate Arbuckle, but we can't bypass the palace's defenses, and after today's…incident, they'll increase his security even more."

"We've tried and failed four times now, thwarted each time by security measures we didn't know existed," Lakshmi agreed.

"Two of those instances involved Mya," Hoseph reminded them.

"You're lucky *she* wasn't waiting in that carriage for you," Kittal pointed out. "Or that…living weapon creature."

Hoseph hadn't thought of that. "They may have been in the other two carriages for all we know, but yes, it *was* lucky."

"So, we agree that the emperor's defenses are virtually impenetrable." Lakshmi tapped a lacquered nail to her wizened lips. "Perhaps we've been going about this the wrong way. We've been trying to get *through* the emperor's security. It's like trying to bash down an iron door—impossible! But perhaps there's a way to *weaken* the door."

"How do we do that?" Kittal asked.

"We've already removed his blademasters…" Hoseph snapped his fingers. "We need to draw off Arbuckle's remaining defenses."

"Again, how?"

"The emperor's security is three fold," Hoseph explained. "The army, which includes his knighthood, the Imperial Guard, and his single remaining mage, Master Keyfur. If we stir up enough trouble, we may be able to draw one or more of them away."

Kittal looked thoughtful. "Perhaps, but we have to consider the reason for our previous failures. Either someone somehow figured out our strategy, or we have a leak. If it's a leak, I doubt it came from within the guild, but we can look into that. Your informant, however..."

"Will you tell us who it is?" Lakshmi asked.

Hoseph saw no reason not to at this point. "Former Captain Otar of the Imperial Guard."

Lakshmi arched a pencil-thin eyebrow. "I'm impressed."

"It wasn't difficult to gain his cooperation. He has no love for the emperor. I've had him pumping Chief Constable Dreyfus for information, but..." Hoseph considered for a moment. "He has no loyalty to me other than the gold I pay him. More than anything, he wants his old position back. He may have betrayed me to get back into the emperor's good graces."

Lakshmi pursed her lips. "That *is* possible."

"If you can't trust him, maybe it's time to clean up that loose end," Kittal suggested.

"I agree." Hoseph thought some more. "Perhaps we can make this play into our new strategy, cause some disruption. Perhaps even enough to draw the Imperial Guard out of the palace."

"Riots, violence, something like the Night of Flames?" Kittal seemed eager now. "My Alchemists can help with that."

Hoseph smiled, a conversation of long ago coming to mind. "That will certainly help, yes, but there's also the army to consider. If *they're* in the city, no amount of rioting will draw out the Imperial Guard."

"How do you plan to get rid of the army?" asked Lakshmi.

"Simple." Hoseph smiled. "War."

Benj sat still and tried not to fidget, worried that the ornate little chair they'd put him in might collapse at any moment. The two imperial guards stationed at the door—one the officer who'd nearly put a sword through his neck—glowered at him. *They can't still think I tried to kill their boss.*

His throat was sore from giving an account of his actions in the plaza three times now: first to Ithross, then again to some court fop in rainbow-hued robes who constantly waved a feather around, and lastly to a portly little scribe with a pen that skittered along the pages of his ledger as fast as Benj spoke. The sergeant didn't like the idea of his words being written down. Once something was written in a book, it could come back years later to bite you on the ass.

Shifting in a futile attempt to get comfortable, he sighed when the guards' hands twitched toward their swords. "Oh, just calm down. Bloody chair's about as comfortable as an iron maiden."

"We can arrange one if you'd prefer," the officer said flatly. "Just sit still and shut up."

He met her scowl with a sardonic grin and folded his arms. "Maybe you'd *prefer* I let someone murder the emperor on *your* watch next time?"

"I said *shut up!*" Tendons flexed in her neck.

So that's it. They're sore because I upstaged them. Benj rolled his eyes and looked away, but the gaudy paintings, frilly curtains, and wallpaper the color of a trollop's silk stockings unsettled his stomach. Closing his eyes, he replayed the tussle in the carriage. Two inches up and left, and his dagger would have pierced Hoseph's heart. *Two inches, Benj. You must be losin' your edge.*

The door opened, and Captain Ithross entered in the company of several more guards. Behind them, Emperor Tynean Tsing III himself strode into the room. Benj lurched to his feet, caught flat footed by the sudden and unannounced appearance of the emperor. He tried to bow, but his ass had gone numb and he almost pitched over. Cursing under his breath and feeling like a new recruit, he steadied his legs and tried again.

"You may rise, Sergeant Benjamin." The emperor's voice sounded different in person than when he spoke in public, calmer and more melodic, almost friendly.

"Thank you, Majesty." Benj snapped to attention and fixed his gaze over the sovereign's shoulder; he knew better than to be lulled into complacency by a kind voice.

"It is We who should be thanking *you*, Sergeant." The emperor took four long strides forward and stuck out a bejeweled hand. "Thank you for Our life."

Benj stared at the hand, utterly flummoxed. With no clue about palace etiquette, he didn't know if he should shake it, kneel and kiss the imperial seal, or just bow. He settled for the first and third options together. "Just doin' my job, Your Majesty."

"We thank you nonetheless." The emperor released his hand and took a step back. "We've heard your testimony and that of the witnesses as to what happened, as well as Captain Ithross' account of your conversation yesterday. We appreciate your quick thinking and decisive action, but We wonder..." His eyes shifted to his captain, then back to Benj "...why you didn't simply inform Our guards of your suspicions?"

"And create a big hubbub?" Benj frowned and shook his head. "That'd of tipped Hoseph off sure as...well, sure enough."

The emperor's brows arched. "You put more value on apprehending a criminal than on the life of your sovereign?"

"No, Majesty, not *more*." Benj had prepared for this question, at least. "But, with all due respect to Your Majesty, it wasn't my job to protect your life. Our orders were only to watch for trouble, and Hoseph is nothin' *but* trouble. He's is our most wanted criminal right now. I couldn't pass up a chance to get him."

"But if your surmise had been *wrong*..."

"I'd probably be in your dungeon or skewered by one of your fine guards." Benj nodded toward the young woman who had nearly put a sword through his neck. "But right or wrong, I didn't put your life in any *more* danger, Majesty."

The emperor frowned. "Only your own."

"That *is* part of my job, Majesty."

"We see." The emperor looked to Ithross again, then back to Benj. "You have a keen mind and courage, Sergeant. How would you like to become a member of Our Imperial Guard?"

"I...uh..." Benj would sooner spend a month in the palace dungeon than get stuck in one of those tight-laced uniforms standing a post staring at bilious wallpaper all day, but he dare not insult the emperor. "With respect to the Imperial Guard, I don't think that'd be a proper fit. I'm a street cap. I'd be a fish out of water here."

"Yes, well…" The emperor smiled and glanced at Ithross, whose mouth twitched at one corner. "Our Captain said about the same, but We wanted to make the offer. We shall think of some way to properly reward you." His face sobered. "But there is also Chief Constable Dreyfus to consider."

"Consider, Majesty?" Benj blinked in surprise.

"Yes. There is now evidence, though circumstantial, that Chief Dreyfus knowingly or unknowingly leaked information to Our enemies. At the very least, he must be brought in for questioning."

And if he's not a snitch, I get raked over the coals for goin' over his head to the emperor. "With Your Majesty's permission, I'd ask to speak freely on that subject please."

"By all means, Sergeant."

"I suggest we wait and watch Dreyfus and Otar like we don't know a thing. If we do anythin' to either of them now, the jig is up. We lose the advantage." His eyes flicked to Ithross, saw the affront there, then settled his gaze back on the emperor. "Let me set some trusted people to watchin' them both, see if I can piece together enough evidence to either make a real case or exonerate my chief. Might even get another shot at Hoseph if we play our cards right."

The emperor pursed his lips and turned to Ithross. "Captain, your thoughts?"

"He's got a good point, Majesty." Ithross sounded like a schoolboy giving a speech, wooden and emotionless.

"Then We'll proceed as you propose, Sergeant Benjamin. Arrange communications with Captain Ithross. We would like to be kept informed."

"Of course, Majesty." Benj bowed.

"Thank you once more for saving Our life, Sergeant. You have Our gratitude."

Benj grinned and touched the rim of his iron cap in salute. "All part of wearin' the uniform, Your Majesty."

Mya paced the palace waiting chamber, her footsteps silenced by the plush carpet while her inner voice screamed in frustration. *Two godsdamned hours stuffed in a godsdamned carriage because the entire city's celebrating the godsdamned emperor's godsdamned speech, and now another godsdamned hour waiting on that godsdamned wizard!*

Exactly how long she'd been waiting, she didn't know, for there was no clock in the room. It didn't help that her feet were still cramped into dress shoes and her waist throttled by a corset. Her runes no longer blocked pain, and though her blisters would heal slowly, she longed for the comfortable leathers Clemson had procured for her. Unfortunately, a visit to the palace called for formal attire.

How do nobles dress like this every damn day?

The dress she wore was the same one the emperor gave her for their dinner. Hadn't that been an unpleasant surprise. She'd expected his dinner party to be crowded with preening nobles, but had been escorted into an intimate dining room with a table set for two. With only two footmen serving them and the guards banished to the hallway outside, she'd recalled what Lad had said—*The emperor certainly has feelings for you*—and immediately felt uncomfortable. She'd spent the entire dinner scrutinizing the emperor's every word, expression, and movement. He was an attentive host, gracious and concerned for her, but thankfully he hadn't revealed any personal feelings. He'd only prattled on about these New Accords he was going to announce today.

Mya sighed and tried not to fidget. The real problem with waiting was that it gave her too much time to think, time for her anxiety to dredge up memories: the smell of blood, the press of restraints, the delirium of drugs, the squeak of Kittal's skinning machine, the look of panic on Dee's face as he faded into mist…

Run…run or die…

Mya bit back the nagging voice, refusing to be dragged down into that pit of guilt, paranoia, and despair. She needed to stay focused, stay busy, be Grandmaster. Instead, she was stuck here waiting…waiting…waiting…

Footsteps in the hall outside stopped Mya's pacing.

The door latch clicked, and one of the guards leaned in. "Master Keyfur's here, Miss Moirin."

About godsdamned time! With a sigh of relief, Mya girded her hopes. "Please, show him in."

Keyfur swept in with his usual flashing grin. "Miss Moirin!" He swept his rainbow robes in a fluid bow. "It's delightful to see you so radiant. I'm sorry to keep you waiting, but we've had *quite* an eventful day!"

"Yes, I know." She bit back her impatience. "The emperor's announcement's thrown the whole city into chaos. But I've come about something—"

"Oh, more than just the announcement!" The archmage took a deep breath and let it out slowly, as if trying to decide how much to say. "It's not common knowledge among the populace, and the emperor wishes to keep it so, but there was another attempt on his life at the Imperial Plaza. High Priest Hoseph appeared in the emperor's carriage."

"Hoseph!" *The horror on Dee's face as black mists devoured him.* Mya shook off the vision. "Sergeant Benjamin was right!"

"Indeed he was! And he intervened in the nick of time!"

A flare of hope dispelled the dark hatred that filled her. "Did he manage to *kill* the bastard?"

"Alas, no, but he marked him well with a dagger." Keyfur flicked a hand. "Hoseph dissipated into vapor before the sergeant could finish the job."

"Damn!" Mya flexed her hands as if she could strangle Hoseph from afar. "That priest has more lives than a cat!"

"Indeed, but you didn't come here to discuss the emperor's close call with mortality." The wizard cocked his head inquisitively. "You have an air of urgency about you. What can I do for you?"

"I need you to find someone for me, the same way you found me."

"Ah, my prowess with divination has become legend, I see!" He chuckled and shrugged. "Honestly, one of my predecessor's trinkets does most of the work. Who do you wish to find, if I might ask? Master Dee, I hope?"

Mya grimaced. "No, I have nothing to trace Dee with. I'm looking for the woman who tortured me."

Keyfur's face fell from hope to concern, and he started to say something.

Mya didn't want to hear it. "Before you think this is simple vengeance, this woman also holds the last Tessifus boy, and *maybe* Dee."

"Well, well!" His face transformed again, eager and intrigued. "Yes, of course I'll help. We need a focus. What do you have that was hers?"

"Nothing, but she has something that was mine."

"Um...I don't think that will work. It must be—"

"Let me explain, Master Keyfur." Mya took a deep breath. "You saw me...my condition when you found me. My scars... In fact, I owe you a great deal for using your fleshforge to heal them."

"It was the *least* I could do."

"Well..." Mya gritted her teeth, the memory of Kittal's skinning machine singing along her nerves. "The *point* is, those scars were inflicted to harvest my runic tattoos. This woman I seek took them for herself. She's wearing my skin."

Keyfur looked slightly ill. "That's...morbidly fascinating, and also explains the difficulty we had in locating you."

"Bloodhound told me about that. It's what gave me the idea to use the same magic to find her."

Keyfur's dark brow furrowed in consternation. "Yes, well, that poses a problem."

"What problem?"

"The signal of the location spell will be confounded by your presence. Considering that you possess more of your flesh than...this woman does, the interference will be overpowering, especially if you're near when I'm searching."

"Oh, I'll *be* there, all right." *I have to be there.* Mya quelled the vision of removing her runes from Lakshmi's wizened body.

"I'll need your wrappings and some time to discern some way to cancel out your signal."

"Of course." Mya started loosening the stays of her gown.

"Then I...uh..." Keyfur stared at her as she unlaced her dress. "Um...what are you doing?"

"Giving you my wrappings. I need to find this woman as quickly as possible!"

119

"Uh, well, I...shouldn't I call a maid to...help you..." He fluttered a hand at her dress as she shrugged out of the cumbersome sleeves.

"I'm not so frail that I need a *maid's* help to undress."

"But...um..."

Mya snorted in derision and wiggled the gown over her hips, then started unwrapping the dark linen from her wrist. "You've seen my runes."

"It's not your *runes* I shouldn't be looking upon, Miss Moirin!" The wizard gaped as she uncovered one arm and started on her upper torso.

"I don't have time to waste." She freed her other arm and paused. "You *could* turn your back..."

"Oh, of course!" He whirled so fast that his feather fell from behind his ear.

"So, how long will your experiments take?" Mya finished uncovering her torso and started on her legs.

"I...don't know. I'll have to do some tests. It would be easier if you were far away, but I daresay that'll be impossible."

"Yes, it will be." She finished with the wrappings and flung them over his shoulder.

Keyfur gasped as if he'd been knifed, then laughed nervously. "My apologies, Miss Moirin. I'm...not used to women who...well...have so little regard for modesty."

"I don't have time for frivolous notions, Master Wizard." Mya wriggled into her dress. It would be a drafty ride back to Embree's headquarters without scanties, but she could manage. "And I'm afraid *modesty* is one of them."

CHAPTER X

Otar's final breath escaped in a sigh as his soul fled like a dove on the wing. Hoseph drew back his hand, the light of Demia's grace fading from his palm. Where the Keeper of the Slain would send the former captain's soul wasn't his concern; whichever god—if any—the man worshiped would give him his due reward or penance. This quiet, painless death was the priest's final gift, due payment, and all anyone could hope for in the end.

Hoseph looked around the squalid little room, wrinkling his nose at the noisome odors of alcohol and lust. *At least I won't have to come here anymore.* But he had tasks to accomplish before he could leave.

A careful search revealed nothing that would incriminate him. Eager to finish, he fished a pouch from his robe and tucked it carelessly under the lumpy mattress. Satisfied, he flipped Demia's talisman into his hand, whispered the invocation, and faded into mist.

He paused in the Sphere of Shadow, wondering what had become of those he left here. Unlike the souls he sent to Demia—like Otar just now—those he stranded here never passed on to their final judgement. Legends told of a demon or godling banished to this place eons ago, stranded here to roam the shadows alone as punishment for some dreadful deed. Hoseph had felt its powerful presence on occasion, but Demia's talisman kept him safe. Not so for the souls he abandoned here; they were consumed.

He wondered briefly what oblivion would be like, the cessation of existence, body *and* soul, with no hope of a spiritual afterlife. Unnerved by the concept, Hoseph hastily concentrated on his next destination, mentally invoked the talisman, and materialized in Chief

Magistrate Graving's study. The room was empty at this early hour, as he'd intended. No one saw him stagger with the blinding pain, nausea, and weakness of the transition. A dab of Kittal's elixir erased his discomfort.

Settling into a dark leather chair with a view of the door, he waited, listening to the faint clatter and thump of the waking household. As the rising sun lightened the room's lofty curtains, the chief magistrate burst into the room like a bull into a cow byre, snorting and scowling. He slammed the door and was halfway to his desk before he spotted Hoseph, and his expression shifted from determination to distress in a flash.

"By the Nine Hells, what are *you* doing here?" Graving hustled back to lock his study door.

"I came to solicit your aid, Chief Magistrate." Hoseph smiled. "Due to Arbuckle's persistent efforts to keep breathing, our tactics must evolve."

"*Our* tactics?" Graving bustled to his desk. "You mean *your* tactics, don't you? Your *failed* tactics!"

Hoseph cocked an eyebrow. Graving was rarely so openly confrontational. "If you find our previous tactics ineffective, you should have no objection to aiding our new efforts."

"Well, *something* has to be done!" Graving's chair creaked alarmingly as he sat. "Have you read that maniac's New Accords? He's curtailed the authority of the judiciary drastically, relegating us to little more than *tax* collectors!"

"*What?*" Hoseph had not read Arbuckle's new laws in detail, but if what Graving said was true, this was a complete restructuring of the judicial system. Tynean Tsing II had relied heavily on his magistrates, demanding that punishment for even the tiniest infraction be swift and ruthless. "Who will adjudicate offenses? Who will enforce the law?"

"The *law?* Fah!" Graving's face curdled. "What little of it remains will be enforced by the constabulary and, when necessary, the military. As for adjudication, Arbuckle has pulled a number of knights and paladins out of retirement to serve as *judges*! He's out of control!"

Good, Hoseph thought. The more upset Graving was, the more helpful he'd be, and his help was crucial. "Then you have a vested interest in helping us remove him from the throne."

"Not *another* assassination attempt!"

"Not right away. My colleagues and I have realized our mistake. Despite the removal of his blademasters of Koss, Arbuckle's security is still too formidable to penetrate."

Graving frowned, but his eyebrows arched in curiosity. "How do you propose to circumvent it?"

"We don't. We've devised is a plan to *weaken* his security before our next attempt."

Graving's brows rose further. "How? The Imperial Guard is dedicated solely to his protection, and with half the knighthood in residence, that protection is doubled. And if you want to talk sheer numbers, the First Army barracks right here in the city, and the Second Army is only two days away in Miravore."

"You needn't know all the details," Hoseph said. "Ignorance of our entire plan will protect both you and us if the emperor suspects something and questions you under magical compulsion. We only need your aid in removing the army and Arbuckle's knighthood from the equation."

"Remove the..." The magistrate's brow furrowed. "How?"

"What else are armies for?" Hoseph smiled and spread his hands. "War."

"*War?* With whom?" Graving snorted in disgust. "No kingdom would be foolish enough to attack Tsing!"

"No?" One thing Hoseph had learned in his tenure as the Right Hand of Death was that fools were never in short supply. "You said once before that our southern border is far from stable, that Morrgrey would take advantage of any lapse in our defenses."

Graving's eyes narrowed at having his own words thrown back at him. "Yes, I did. Morrgrey has long coveted the highland province of Twailin."

"Precisely. And you, Chief Magistrate, are going to help me convince the sultan to take it."

"You can't be serious!"

"I'm completely serious! The emperor would have to order the armies to march, and the majority of his knighthood with them, leaving only the constabulary and the Imperial Guard to keep order and protect him."

Graving paled. "But…the army will take *weeks* to arrive! Twailin might fall!"

Hoseph flicked a dismissive hand. "Duke Mir is an ardent supporter of Arbuckle. We'd be better off without him."

"But what of the populace?" Graving's chins quivered as he spoke. "You're willing to destroy the empire for this plot of yours?"

"I'm willing to do what I have to do to restore Tsing to its former glory!" Hoseph reined in his temper. "If the Morrgrey do take Twailin, they won't slaughter the populace. They're not savages. Once Tessifus is on the throne, the Tsing army will beat the Morrgrey back. The empire will remain intact, and Tessifus can claim victory. Commoners and nobles alike will sing his praises."

"And the New Accords?" Graving looked skeptical. "As soon as Tessifus repeals them, the commoners will revolt."

Hoseph shook his head. "All in good time, Chief Magistrate. We will let the New Accords stand for a while, then start phasing them out gradually. The commoners will be the proverbial frog in the pot of water, slowly heating until it boils. Before they know what's happening, they'll be cooked."

"But I'm not an ambassador. And how can I convince the Sultan of Morrgrey to do anything from *here*?"

"I only need you to convince the Morrgrey ambassador to present us to the sultan. I'll do the convincing."

"Present *us*?" Graving's eyes nearly popped out of his bulbous head.

"Yes, *us*! Though wrongfully accused, I *am* a wanted man. The ambassador would never agree to meet with me, much less present me to the sultan. *You*, however, are the Chief Magistrate of Tsing, a man of great respect."

"But I don't have time to travel to…" The magistrate's objection trailed off as Hoseph dangled his talisman between them.

"We'll be there and back in no time."

Graving stared at him for a long moment as if considering an outright refusal, then pulled paper and pen from a drawer of his desk and began scratching a note. "Very well. I'll send a missive to the ambassador and ask for an immediate audience. Come back in, say, an hour."

"Oh, that's all right." Hoseph settled back in his chair and stretched out his legs. He had no intention of allowing the chief magistrate to run off or double-cross him. "I'll wait right here."

Lad lay stretched out atop the roof of *Lucky Gem's*, the morning sun hot on his back, his ear pressed to the warm slate shingles above Otar's room. He ignored the thousands of sounds of the busy, vital city, focusing fully on the room below, listening for anything out of place. Aside from the sounds Otar entertaining a young lady the previous night, he'd heard nothing but the occasional snore or rustle of sheets. An ordinary person's attention might have drifted with boredom, but Lad was anything but ordinary. He also had a lifetime of training in the art of patience.

Right on time, three sharp raps on Otar's door announced the maid's arrival. Lad had come to appreciate her punctuality over the last couple of nights. After her midmorning wake-up visit, Otar would drink the cup of blackbrew she brought, then go downstairs to eat, drink, and gamble. The Hunters stationed in the gambling hall would take up the daytime surveillance, freeing Lad to report back to Mya.

Otar didn't respond to the knock. *Must still be drunk,* Lad thought as the maid pounded harder and called out. He smiled at her muttered curses as her key clattered in the lock.

The door creaked open. "It's mornin', Master Otar."

Otar was usually snorting and groaning at this point, but the room below remained silent save for the maid clomping across the floor. The hairs on the back of Lad's neck rose.

"Master Otar?" Sheets rustled, and the maid drew a sharp breath. "Lords and heavens preserve me!"

Her exclamation tensed Lad's every nerve. He strained to listen, but above her hard breathing, hurried steps, and the click of the door latch, he heard only a single heartbeat...the maid's.

"Damn!" Lad inched to the edge of the roof and peered over, but Otar's window drape was closed, as always, which was why he was listening here instead of watching from across the street. He'd heard nothing untoward during the night, but then, he hadn't been paying such close attention that the cessation of the man's heartbeat had caught his ear. "Mya's going to have a fit."

Feet rumbled up the stairs—*Three people, two women and one man*—and hurried down the hall. The door creaked open, and they entered the room.

"Don't touch anything," a man said.

"This is my place! I'll touch what I want!" That was Gem, the owner. Lad recognized her voice from his brief visit to the gambling house the first day he'd come here.

"No, you *won't*, Gem! Now let me...." Footsteps crossed the room. "Shit!" The man's voice was low and harsh. More footsteps, back toward the door. "Gem, lock this room and don't let anyone in. I'll be right back."

"I don't want no corpse in my place! I don't care if you—"

"If anyone touches that body, I'll have your whole staff in the lockup! Now do as I say!"

Lockup? He'd thought the man might be one of Embree's Hunters, but the Assassins Guild didn't have a lockup.

When the door's lock clicked home, Lad edged over to the south side of the roof and peered down to the front door. A tall man hurried out and down the street. Lad considered breaking in through the window to have a look for himself, but in broad daylight, he'd risk being spotted.

Best wait. Only minutes passed before the tall man returned in the company of two constables, and Lad realized his mistake. *Of course they had someone here!* Mya had learned about Otar meeting Hoseph from a constable. Lad skittered back to his position over Otar's room as their heavy boots ascended the stairs and thudded down the hall. The door didn't open.

"Stand watch here. *No one* goes in there, you understand?" It was the tall man again.

"Aye, Corporal. Nobody goes in."

"Good. I'll be back with the sergeant as quick as I can."

Lad pressed his ear to the roof. Two hearts beat strongly as the constables muttered back and forth. Lad considered whether he should go tell Mya that he'd failed, or wait to see who else showed up. *Damn it!* Lad had no doubt that the Hunters posted in the gambling hall had already figured out that something was wrong. Mya would know soon enough.

Wait...wait and learn. He'd already lost their only connection to Hoseph. He had nothing better to do.

"Another one, Chief!" A breathless constable burst into the constabulary headquarters, his soot-streaked face worried. "Yonsen's Brewery on the corner of Grayson and Filcher just went up in flames!"

"What?"

Benj cringed at the chief's tone and stood from his desk.

"That's three fires in three days!" Dreyfus stalked out of his office and glared at the huge map of Tsing tacked onto the wall behind Benj's desk. "Two might be a coincidence, but three? Damned rabble! As if they didn't do enough damage during the Night of Flames!"

Benj thrust a pin into the map at the site of the fire and stepped back. The first two had been a clothier in the Heights and a warehouse in Midtown. *This ain't like before.* "Yonsen's don't fit that pattern, sir. It's *south* of the river. It's a family business. Nobody had an axe to grind with them, least of all the common folk."

"Hoodlums are burning *my* city, Sergeant! I don't care *who* they are! I want the culprits found and strung up by their balls!" Dreyfus glared around the room as if his own people were to blame. "Put every cap on the street. Canvass those neighborhoods and beat the godsdamned truth out of someone! I want descriptions of these arsonists! They're probably wandering the city now, looking for a new target!" The chief whirled and stalked back into his office, slamming the door hard enough to rattle picture frames.

Benj beckoned to one of his men. "Corporal Tobin, take a squad to the brewery and start askin' questions, but mind your manners.

We break these New Accords His Majesty's so proud of, there'll be hell to pay."

"Aye, Sergeant!"

As the corporal hustled his squad out, Benj stared at the map. *Why the sudden upsurge of arson?* There had been no rioting reported, no throngs of vengeful thugs or revelers, and almost no violence following the emperor's announcement of his New Accords. In fact, the city seemed happier than ever. No, this was no Night of Flames. This was different.

"Penkin, send someone to the archivist's office and get everythin' you can on these three businesses."

"Thinkin' we got a bit of targeted mayhem, Sarge?" The corporal jotted down a note and handed it off to a bright-eyed private who dashed out the door.

"Maybe, maybe not. Hard to find a pattern with only three points. One thing for sure, it weren't a dreggar."

"How do you figure, Sarge?" Penkin asked.

"Burn a brewery in their own neighborhood?" Benj snorted. "They'd sooner chop up their own kids and bake 'em into pies!"

"Didn't some old codger do just that a few years back?" Penkin's dusky face pinched in a look of disgust. "Sold the pies to some high-class eatery in the Heights?"

"Yeah, but it weren't kids, remember?" Benj still had nightmares about the horrors they'd found in that man's cellar. "The trollop population took half a year to recover."

"That's right." Penkin winced. "They never did find all those pies, did they?"

"Nope, and nobody was gonna tell all those fancy folks who ate 'em neither."

Penkin turned back to his desk, and Benj continued to stare at the map. A clothier, a warehouse, and a brewery... The door flying open again broke his concentration. *Not another one.* But Jorren Arryx stood in the doorway, and Benj's stomach lurched. *Uh-oh.*

He'd assigned the corporal to watch Otar at *Lucky Gem's* in his off hours, low key and in plain clothes. But here he was, not only in uniform, but with his shirt misbuttoned. Jorren had changed in a hurry.

"I…need to talk with you, Sarge." Jorren spoke low and glanced around, then noticed the new red pin in the map. "Another one?"

"Yep. Just this morning. Yonsen's Brewery south of the river." Benj gritted his teeth and shifted focus. "What's up? Wait. Let's go for a walk. Damn desk makes my arse hurt."

"Sure, Sarge." Jorren followed him out. They walked a half block along the busy street before Jorren said, "Otar's dead."

Benj stopped cold. "What? How?"

"I don't know yet. One of the inn's maids found him in his bed about half an hour ago, stone dead, and no sign of violence."

"Drank himself to death, maybe?"

Jorren shrugged. "He looked healthy enough last night. Tipsy, but healthy. He took Jacie upstairs just before midnight, and she came down later with no fuss." They resumed walking. "I called in two caps I trust and stationed them at his door, then came here. Gem's upset and wants his body out of there, but I told her to bide until we could have a look."

"Good work." Benj was already considering the repercussions. He'd been the one who suggested they watch Otar instead of bringing him in for questioning. *Ithross'll have my head!* "I've got to tell Captain Ithross. He'll want to see the scene, I'll wager."

"Do you want me to hold off the investigation until you bring him?"

"Yeah. Tell Gem I'll pay for her trouble, but don't let anyone touch that room. I'll be there as soon as I can."

"Sure, Sergeant." Jorren touched the rim of his iron cap and started to turn away, but Benj grabbed his arm.

"Keep this *quiet*, Jorren, and your eyes open! I don't want Dreyfus to find out, and I don't believe for a second that Otar died of natural causes."

"I'm on it, Sarge!" Jorren hurried off, his long-limbed stride taking him around a corner in moments.

Benj swore under his breath and started back to headquarters. He'd have to make up some tale to cover his absence for the rest of the day, but with fires flaring up all around the city, that wouldn't be hard. Just when everything was starting to look brighter, all hell was breaking loose.

A drop of sweat fell onto the map covering Noncey's desk, darkening a building on Esson Street in Midtown.

"Sorry." Mya wiped her face. Without her wrappings, the oppressive heat was sapping her strength and making her clothes feel sticky, but right now, comfort was low on her list of priorities.

"No problem." Noncey drew a kerchief from his sleeve and dabbed up the moisture, then handed it to Mya.

"Thanks." She mopped her brow and tapped her fingertip at three dispersed locations on the map. "Midtown, the Heights, and the Dreggars Quarter. Why are you so interested in these three? Tsing must have fires every day."

Clemson said, "Because they were obvious cases of arson and have 'Alchemist' written all over them. No apparent cause, and the entire structure in flames in a matter of minutes."

Noncey squinted at the map, incredibly detailed, right down to street names. Most of the buildings were numbered—guild designations—and the Master Blade flipped through the pages of a thick ledger, running his finger down a list. "This last one was Yonsen's Brewery."

Clemson crossed her arms and frowned. "That brewery was old when I was just an apprentice; I collected some of my first protection fees from Martin Yonsen. Young Harry runs the place now. He always pays on time, and he's not in debt to anyone. It was a family business for six generations."

"And will be sorely missed," Embree added. "They made a damn fine bitter."

"So, what do a high-class clothier, a grain warehouse, and a brewery have in common?" Mya asked.

"Nothing that we know of, Grandmaster." Noncey fingered the ornate buckle of his belt. "None are guild businesses, so *we're* not being targeted. Maybe some grudge. It might not even be Kittal's people at work here. There *are* other alchemists in the city."

"Anyone hurt or killed?"

"Yes." Embree tapped the map at the Heights. "Two tailors at the clothier were badly burned. We're trying to get their accounts of what happened, but there are still caps all over the place. Nobody was hurt at the warehouse, but it was full of sugar and cornmeal—all destroyed. One woman we spoke with said it was more an explosion than just a fire. Blew out windows."

"And the brewery?"

"Yonsen and his people are okay except for a few burns. They tried to put the fire out, but it's a total loss." Noncey rubbed his eyes. They'd all been working long hours.

And now this... Mya massaged her aching temples and mopped her forehead with the kerchief. The inn that was Embree's headquarters was comfortable enough, but her sleep the past few nights hadn't been restful. She was anxious to track down Lakshmi and Kittal and conclude this business, but she hadn't heard a peep from Keyfur yet.

"We'll get more from Yonsen once the caps leave off," Embree assured her.

"Offer to help them rebuild," Mya said. "Loan them what they need with no interest."

Clemson's eyebrows arched. "Why?"

"Because our reputation could use some bolstering, and a brewery, as mundane as that sounds, is important to the Dreggars Quarter. If word gets around that we helped Yonsen, we'll earn a good name among the locals."

"The guild never worried about our reputation with commoners before," Clemson said.

"I know, but we're not the same guild we were before. Trust me on this. We changed how things worked in Twailin, and it paid off tenfold." Mya wiped the sweat from her brow again. "Besides, if they were paying us protection, we should be protecting them. Now, what are the chances this *is* Kittal's handiwork?"

"The method fits, but what motive he could have to burn three unrelated businesses is beyond me," Embree said.

"Terror," Clemson said firmly. "Terror, fear, and intimidation are my business, though Enforcers usually accomplish it more subtlety than burning a building down. I'd say Lakshmi and Kittal are trying to make it look like the emperor's New Accords caused this."

Mya wrinkled her brow. "The nobility lashing out against the Accords? Kind of the opposite of the commoners' attacks during the Night of Flames?"

Noncey shrugged. "Yonsen's got no ties to politics or the nobility, but if the other business owners were supporters of the emperor…maybe."

"The brewery *could* be a diversion," Embree mused.

"Maybe. Take a closer look into the other two businesses for some kind of connection." Staring at the map, Mya sighed, willing some pattern or understanding to well up from the chaos, but her mind seemed a muddle. "I need some air and something to eat."

Shoving away from the desk, she crooked a finger at Jolee—her new constant companion—and headed toward the door. "Blackbrew and a pastry, Jolee. I'm buying."

Chapter XI

Ah, you're back.

Lad peered over the roof edge to get a better look as the tall man returned, this time dressed in a constable's uniform, the insignia of a corporal on his shoulder. He put his ear back to the roof and listened, but nobody climbed the stairs to Otar's room, so he settled down to wait yet again.

It was nearly midday when a carriage stopped at the front of the establishment. This wasn't usual; most of *Lucky Gem's* clients arrived on foot. Lad scooched over and peered down as a constable sergeant in a stained tunic stepped out and ushered another man dressed in plain but finely tailored clothes toward the door. *Sergeant Benjamin, Mya's contact,* he concluded, recalling her description. The man in civilian clothes carried himself like a soldier. Even at this bad angle, Lad finally recognized him.

"Captain Ithross? What are *you* doing here?" Obviously, Benjamin had also told Ithross that Otar had met with Hoseph. That the captain was here in street clothes might mean he didn't want to be recognized. Regardless, it gave Lad an opportunity to get into that room.

He was down to the street in a flash, and around the corner to the front. His eyes adjusted to the dim lighting inside *Lucky Gem's* with one blink. He drew little attention other than a glance from the bouncer and a lascivious head-to-toe inspection from a woman leaning over a gaming table. There were no constables in sight, and no Captain Ithross. Lad crossed to the stairs, and the sounds of cards, dice, laughter, and conversation faded as he ascended.

The two constables posted outside Otar's room watched him approach, hands on their swords. Lad stopped in front of them. "I need to speak with Captain Ithross."

The guards looked at one another, their startled glances confirming Lad's guess; Ithross wanted to remain incognito.

"Don't know any Captain Ithross. Now you best—"

Lad raised a forestalling hand. "The captain knows me. I'm Miss Moirin's associate. He'll recognize me."

The constables still looked skeptical. "Your name?"

"I'm called Bloodhound."

The constables smirked, but Lad didn't respond. "Stand right there," one ordered before cracking open the door and leaning in to say, "Some dreggar says he needs to speak with you, Captain. Says his name's...Bloodhound?"

"*What?* Show him in."

"Yes, sir." The constable gave Lad a curious look and opened the door wide. "In you go."

Lad stepped into the room and breathed in the sickly sweet stench of death that hung in the hot, still air. The captain, Sergeant Benjamin, and the tall corporal all stared at him. He nodded respectfully to Ithross, "Captain," then turned to the sergeant. "You must be Sergeant Benjamin."

"Who's this?" The sergeant eyed Lad critically.

"Master...uh...Bloodhound." Ithross seemed perturbed with the pseudonym. "The man who found Miss Moirin."

"Oh! Well!" Sergeant Benjamin grinned with tobacco-stained teeth. "Any friend of Miss Moirin's is a friend of mine!" He stuck out a scarred and calloused hand. "Call me Benj."

"Pleased to meet you." Lad matched the pressure of the man's grip carefully.

"Bloodhound, eh? You must be the one she said could catch a fart on the breeze!"

The two constables in the hallway sniggered before the sergeant closed the door on them.

"I...have certain talents," Lad admitted.

Ithross narrowed his eyes. "But what are you doing here?"

"I'm afraid that's probably my doin', Captain." Benj nodded to Lad. "I told Miss Moirin about Otar meetin' Hoseph here."

"Yes, and she assigned me to watch Captain Otar in hopes that I might spot Hoseph." He looked over at Otar's pallid face. "It seems I failed."

"It seems we *all* failed here." Ithross flicked a sharp look to Benj, and the sergeant flushed.

"Aye, we did, but now we got a puzzle to put together, so—"

"Would you mind if I have a look at the body?" Lad broke in, eager to find out as much as he could before they spoiled the evidence. "Miss Moirin wasn't exaggerating. I *do* have certain skills."

Ithross frowned anew. "I don't know if—"

"What's the harm, Captain?" Benj interjected. "We're all in this together, right? We all want the same answers. It's not like he could *kill* the man, after all."

"He wouldn't be *dead*," Ithross said coldly, "if we'd followed my recommendation."

Sergeant Benjamin flushed scarlet. "You're right, I screwed up. I'll formally apologize and genuflect to His Majesty later, but what's done is done. We need to know how this man died, and this fella *might* be able to help us. We'll be right here to watch him."

"Oh, very well! Take a look, Bloodhound." Ithross waved a hand at the bed.

"Thank you." Lad knew almost as much about death as he did about killing. He went to the bedside and examined the body without touching it, but found no obvious signs of struggle or contortion. The man looked peacefully asleep. Lad pinched the skin on the corpse's forearm and watched it retract slowly, then peered into the milky eyes. Lastly, he opened the mouth and sniffed. Stepping back, he said, "There's no sign of struggle, injury, or trauma, and there's no smell of poison. Alcohol, yes, but not strong enough to have killed him. He died in the early hours of the morning. I'm guessing it was Hoseph. I've seen him try to kill using his magic and, though I've never seen the result, I've been told it looks like a natural death."

"It does," the sergeant said with a scowl. "Lady Monjhi didn't have a mark on her." He jerked his head at the tall corporal. "Jorren, let's have a look around."

"Yes, sir."

Lad stood by and watched as the two constables conducted a meticulous search. He had to admit, they knew their business.

Rummaging through the dresser, the corporal pulled out a leather pouch and said, "Sergeant."

Benj took the hefty purse and bounced it in his palm, jingling the coins inside.

Lad recalled from his youth a pouch that jingled like coins but yielded a deadly surprise when it was opened. "Careful, Sergeant. We're dealing with people well-acquainted with both poison *and* magic."

"Good point." Benj opened the drapes and window, then held the pouch outside to pull the strings. Nothing happened. Pulling back into the room and peering into the pouch, he let out a low whistle. "I guess they pay imperial guards a lot more than constables."

"Otar was receiving a pension from the crown," Ithross said. "Not a fortune, but it would keep a man comfortable."

"I imagine Hoseph was payin' him, too." Benj handed the purse back. "Corporal, count it and log it as evidence."

The search continued until the sergeant shoved a hand between the mattress and the frame. "Oh ho, what's this?" Out came another pouch. This one clinked of coins as well, but also crackled like parchment. Benj took the same precaution as before, with no surprises. "More gold and a note." He retrieved the note from the pouch, unfolded it, read it, and wrinkled his nose in disgust.

"What?" Ithross snatched the note out of the sergeant's hand. A grim smile spread across his face as he read it aloud. "'Despite the failure of our attempt, the information provided by our friend in the constabulary was accurate and his fee well-earned. Please forward this to him with our compliments and our hopes to work with him again.' Well, Sergeant, this confirms it. Your commander was being paid to—"

"It doesn't *confirm* anything, Captain." Sergeant Benjamin snatched the note back and jingled the pouch of coins to the captain. "It takes more than a little gold to turn a man like Dreyfus. I know him. This stinks like a set up!"

"We'll let the emperor decide that." Captain Ithross pointed to the body on the bed. "We'll also have Master Keyfur examine the body to see if he can pick up anything not detectable by cursory inspection or"—he glanced at Lad—"*smell.*"

"Captain, you can't seriously think that Dreyfus would—"

Ithross cut short Benj's protest. "Sergeant, you'll accompany me to the palace. Tell your constables to keep this *quiet*. Master Bloodhound, you may go, but you'll keep these findings to yourself and your mistress only. Is that understood?"

"Perfectly, Captain." Lad didn't bother telling the captain that he didn't take orders from *anyone*. Instead, he nodded politely and headed for the door. He had all the information currently available, and Mya would want to know without delay.

Hoseph plucked at his sweat-dampened robes. Tsing was hot enough in summer; the jungle kingdom of Morrgrey was far worse. He and Graving labored up the steps of the royal palace behind the Morrgrey ambassador, who seemed to revel in the torrid climate.

The palace gleamed in the light of the high windows. From the brightly painted tiles underfoot to the gold and mother of pearl scrollwork that adorned the walls, the edifice was designed to impress visitors with the kingdom's wealth. Hoseph knew better. The capital city of Tolnyek was dying, a pit of squalor rife with disease and famine, testimony to Morrgrey's decades of ill luck.

So much the better, Hoseph thought. What he had to offer was exactly what the kingdom most needed to survive.

Ambassador Kovak didn't share the priest's confidence. His hands twitched nervously at his sides as they neared the gilded doors to the audience chamber. "The sultan does *not* like surprise visits. I risk much by bringing you here without due protocol."

"And you've been well compensated for your service, Ambassador." Graving smoothed the wrinkles from his jacket. "Besides, when your sultan hears our proposal, you'll probably receive a title for your efforts."

The great doors opened, and they strode down the length of the vast pillared chamber between rows of palace guards. Hoseph admired their golden breastplates, helms, and scale-mail kilts, scimitars glittering at their waists, spears at the ready. They looked every bit the proud and strong people the Morrgrey used to be, a blatant contradiction to their waning power.

Atop a broad dais at the end of the chamber, the sultan lounged on a low divan. He wouldn't have fit on a throne.

When he inherited the kingdom three decades ago, the sovereign had been the epitome of Morrgrey strength: tall, handsome, and broad shouldered, with olive skin and a luxuriant mane of ebony hair, commander of the Morrgrey navy, and a renowned sailor. Now impossibly corpulent, his skin sallow, his bald pate sheened with sweat despite the efforts of the fan-wielding slaves, the sultan labored with the exertion of merely breathing.

The only person I've ever seen who makes Graving seem slim by comparison, thought Hoseph as they neared.

Two younger men flanked the sultan, his sons and senior viziers. One wore the kilt and weapons of a warrior, the other the robes and accoutrements of a mage. Other viziers stood on the lower step, and scantily clad servants hovered silently by, trays of drinks and sweetmeats at the ready.

Stopping before the dais, the two visitors from Tsing bowed respectfully, while Ambassador Kovak fairly prostrated himself before his lord.

"Oh, Great Sultan, Scourge of the Southern Ocean, Wielder of the might of Morrgrey…"

Hoseph ignored Kovak's sycophantic blather, pandering to the delusional conceit of a ruler who refused to acknowledge that Morrgrey's day had come and gone. The kingdom's downfall began centuries ago, when the gold from her mines dwindled. Then, as if the gods weren't satisfied with one torment, a quirk of nature shifted the rains to the north, reducing her verdant rainforests to savanna and withering jungle. The rivers that supplied Tolnyek dwindled, and the great river delta silted in, stranding the king's ships and strangling trade. The life-giving rains now fell onto the highlands to the north, making Twailin the breadbasket of the Tsing Empire. The desperate plight of the forsaken kingdom was exactly what Hoseph intended to take advantage of.

Kovak rose finally from his obeisance and swept an arm toward the guests from Tsing. "Your Highness, I bring emissaries from

Tsing with a proposal of great interest. May I present Chief Magistrate Graving of the Imperial Judiciary of Tsing—"

"Your Highness!" Graving stepped forward, interrupting the ambassador. "Thank you for consenting to see us on such short notice. I promise you won't be disappointed with our proposal."

"Yes, yes." The sultan waved a pudgy hand. "And who is your companion? His dress is that of a priest."

Hoseph had exchanged his unkempt disguise for the crimson robes of a high priest of Demia for the occasion. Although it pleased him to be recognized for what he was, they had intended to delay his introduction until the proposal had been made. News of the events in Tsing had undoubtedly traveled this far by now, and wanted men were not generally welcome at court.

"My apologies, Your Highness," Graving demurred. "May I introduce High Priest Hoseph of the Temple of Demia."

"Highness!" The sultan's war-garbed vizier stepped forward, drawing his wickedly curved scimitar and signaling the royal guard with a flick of his fingers. "This man is wanted by the Emperor of Tsing on charges of attempted regicide!"

The sultan's eyes widened. "You *dare* to bring a traitor and would-be assassin to my court?"

The royal guards stiffened and stepped forward, their hands tightening on sword hilts and spear shafts. The sultan's other son drew something from the sleeve of his robe, and roiling flames blossomed in his palm.

"Uh…uh…well…" A fat drop of sweat rolled down Graving's cheek. For once, the pompous magistrate was speechless.

Sweet shadow of death… Inconspicuously clutching his talisman, Hoseph stepped forward and bowed low. "Your Highness, I am no traitor. I was at the emperor's side when assassins struck him down, assassins sent by an unworthy son who coveted his father's throne! I was a convenient scapegoat, nothing more. The nobles and judiciary of the empire have seen through this treachery and recruited me as advisor to their most-just cause."

"What is this cause?" boomed the sultan. "And what does it have to do with Morrgrey?"

"To unseat the usurper."

The sultan's eyes narrowed, and his two viziers exchanged a wide-eyed glance.

"We seek assistance from you in our quest for justice, and are willing to compensate you handsomely for your support."

The sultan pursed his lips and flicked a hand. His guards stepped back, and the two viziers resumed their positions, sword sheathed and flame extinguished. Hoseph breathed easier.

"What would this *support* entail, and what compensation do you offer?"

"Your objective and reward are one and the same, Mighty Sultan: the province of Twailin."

The sultan snorted in derision. "Do not jest with me!"

"It's no jest, Highness," assured Hoseph. "To remove the usurper from the throne, we must weaken his defenses. Your role in this would be to draw off the Tsing armies by attacking Twailin. The incursion must begin immediately."

The renowned Morrgrey temper flashed in the sultan's eyes. "I am *not* a fool! My forces cannot stand against Tsing's armies. We would be slaughtered!"

Hoseph smiled. "Your forces will never clash with Tsing's armies, Your Highness. Once the imperial forces are drawn away from the city, we will make our move. Duke Tessifus, the rightful heir to the throne, will immediately be crowned emperor, and will order the army back before they arrive at the city of Twailin. You'll only have to deal with Duke Mir's forces, which number no more than a thousand, along with a few constables and royal guards."

The sultan pursed his lips. "And what assurance do I have that we get to *keep* the lands we take? You could betray us after we aid you."

No fool indeed, Hoseph thought, for that was exactly his plan. But he was also no fool, and had prepared a rebuttal. "Tsing cannot *afford* a war, Your Highness. Truth be told, the capital is plunging toward anarchy! The weakling usurper has enacted decrees that empower the very rabble in the streets with the same rights as the highest noble."

"Preposterous!" The sultan looked duly shocked. "Ambassador Kovak, is what he says true?"

Kovak bowed low. "It is, Your Majesty. The commoners feel free to riot and burn, while the nobility see their power wane day by day. The situation is untenable, and whispers of an uprising are heard even in social gatherings."

"So you see," Hoseph said smoothly, "when the usurper is eliminated, Tsing will be hard-pressed to suppress open rebellion, and will require all our armies at home. As for compensation, the province of Twailin is rich in farms and fields. Once it's yours, her fruits will flow downriver to Southaven and thence to far ports to the south. Unlike your mines, these resources are renewable and without limit. Food will flow into your people's larders, and gold will flow into your coffers."

"Perhaps," the sultan countered, "but to take Twailin, we would have to take control of the mountain passes. Tsing has a treaty with the ogre tribes there, while we do not. Forging one would be costly. Your offer may be generous, but not generous enough."

Just like all greedy men; offer them silver, and they want gold. But Hoseph had anticipated this as well. Every man has his price, and it was common knowledge that the sultan craved more than gold and lands. "We *do* have something more to offer that Your Highness might find of interest…"

Graving looked at him askance, eyebrows arched skeptically. He had no idea where Hoseph was going here. That was no surprise, since Hoseph hadn't told him.

"Your fascination with the arcane is widely known, and you've succeeded at empowering your bloodline with magical talent." He gestured to the robe-clad vizier.

The sultan snorted, but looked smug at the compliment. "A man's progeny are his greatest achievement! Many of my wives possess the gift, and many of my children have inherited their talents to one degree or another."

"And I'm sure that their skills are of tremendous use." Hoseph bowed graciously. "I offer you even *more*. Magic to imbue a city's walls to repel any assault, to fortify an army with preternatural strength and speed. Indeed, the means to instill magic into *your* very being: strength, vitality, even immortality."

"Impossible!" The sultan looked to his son, who just shrugged.

"No, Mighty Sultan, it is not. I'm sure your esteemed vizier has heard of the legendary runemage, Corillian." Hoseph turned to the sultan's robed son expectantly.

141

"I have." The man said, his eyes alight with interest. "He vanished decades ago."

"True. He vanished into Krakengul Keep, where he perfected the art of rune magic. Corillian is now dead—killed in an unforeseeable tragedy—but the keep survives in a remote region of Twailin province. As part of your compensation, I'll show you where it is. Take Twailin, and the keep's secrets will be yours."

"A foolish promise." The sultan waved a pudgy hand dismissively. "If we take Twailin, we'll seek it out on our own."

Hoseph smiled and shook his head. "You would never find it. All roads and paths to the keep are obscured by Corillian's magic. I alone can take you there."

The sultan and his robed son exchanged intrigued, but skeptical, glances.

Come on... Hoseph had thought the sultan would jump at the opportunity, but he obviously needed more convincing. "I can show you the keep, transport you there by the grace of Demia, to prove my claim."

"I think not!" the sultan protested, but his son leaned over and whispered into his father's ear. One of the sovereign's brows arched, and then he nodded. "My son, Junan, will accompany you."

"That will be fine." Hoseph beckoned the mage closer. "Please rest your hand on my shoulder." Cupping the elixir vial in one hand and the talisman in the other, Hoseph waited until Junan was in place, then invoked Demia's grace.

Slashing rain soaked his robes, and a keening wind buffeted his unsteady legs. Hoseph covertly sipped the elixir, but he needn't have worried about being noticed.

Junan stared up at the massive keep in rapt fascination. Veils of rain limited their sight, parting only to tease with glimpses of the vast structure looming over them like a cliff. Stepping closer to the bleached bones of the incautious or unlucky who had ventured too near, Junan raised his arms, murmuring arcane words that were whisked away on the wind. A warm yellow glow bathed the wizard's hands, and the very walls of the keep responded, a golden tracery of runes appearing on the stone. After some time, Junan extinguished the magical light and returned to Hoseph.

"It is as you say. The very stones are enchanted."

"All the secrets of Corillian can be yours." Hoseph smiled and nodded respectfully. "For the good of Morrgrey, of course."

The vizier's eyes narrowed. Though his face remained stoic, the corners of his mouth twitched. "Let us return."

"Of course." Hoseph invoked Demia's talisman again, and a moment later they stood dripping on the floor of the audience chamber. Hoseph staggered, but a sip of elixir steadied his stance and banished the headache and nausea. When his vision cleared, Junan was already whispering in the sultan's ear.

After an extended quiet conversation, the sultan nodded, and the vizier resumed his position at his father's side.

"My son tells me that the keep is protected by magic." The sovereign frowned. "That is a problem. It could take years, perhaps a *lifetime*, to breech the wards."

"Or it could take a week," Hoseph countered with a shrug.

"Possibly." The sultan pursed his lips. "I must consult with all my viziers this evening. I'll give you my answer in the morning."

And that answer will be yes! Hoseph resolved. He would not leave the outcome to fate and the whims of the sultan's sycophants. *Tonight, Mighty Sultan, I'll see you again...in your dreams.*

Mya doffed her hat and wiped the sweat from her brow as she entered the *Itty Bitty Bakeshop*. *Gods, I miss my wrappings!* If Keyfur didn't finish with them soon, she'd have to look into having another set made. Truthfully, she didn't know which bothered her more: the heat or the feeling of having a target painted on her back. Jolee's massive presence helped with the latter, though she couldn't watch over her day and night.

"Afternoon, ladies." The young woman behind the counter grinned and dusted her hands. "Be with you in two shakes."

"We're in no rush." Mya strode to the rear corner booth, thankful that the shop wasn't busy at this hour. She sat with her back to the wall, while Jolee wedged her bulk sideways into the opposite bench seat so she could keep an eye on both Mya and the door.

The smiling young woman arrived a moment later. "What can I get for you?"

Though Mya had been using the bakery as a message drop for weeks, the woman always managed to look as if she'd never laid eyes on her. Of course, she was paid well for her discretion, and knew who she was dealing with.

"A Morrgrey doublebrew and the biggest cinnamon apple pastry you've got."

"Doublebrew," Jolee grunted, her eyes never leaving the door. "Sweet, with milk."

"Right away." The woman bustled off.

Silence hung heavily between Mya and Jolee. This was the first time they'd been really alone together since Jolee had become her bodyguard. Mya studied the hulking Enforcer's silhouette, somehow different now, grimmer, even more menacing. *She doesn't smile anymore.* Not many assassins did—the war was taking its toll—but previously, Jolee had always sported a genuine if somewhat hideous grin and a bawdy joke. *What's changed her?* Mya wondered, then realized that she already knew.

"I'm…sorry about Dee, Jolee. I didn't want him to get hurt."

Jolee's eyes snapped to hers for a moment, then away. "Dee did what he had to do, Mistress. It wasn't your fault."

"Of course it was. He was taken trying to rescue me."

Jolee frowned, her tusks grinding. "It's war, Mistress. People die."

"He might not be dead, you know."

"Might be better if he was, if Lakshmi's got him."

"I know."

Jolee looked to her again. "Aye, I imagine you do."

Another silence, but this one more companionable. The waitress delivered their blackbrew and a pastry big enough for three hungry laborers. Mya pinched off a bite and pushed the plate to the center of the table.

"I miss him," Mya confessed. It felt strange to say the words. She'd been so caught up in maintaining her composure in front of the masters, trying to convince them that she was still their confident and competent Grandmaster, that she hadn't allowed herself to feel.

"Me, too." Muscles bunched at Jolee's massive jaw. "We were lucky to have him for a friend."

"Yes, we were," Mya whispered.

The jingle of the bell as the door opened snapped them both from their reverie. Mya tensed, clutching the hilt of a dagger under the table and suppressing the urge to leap up.

Jolee shot a look at the door, then sighed. "Just a beggar kid."

Mya caught a glimpse of a ragged mop of hair, a filthy shift, and a twisted leg, and was out of her seat before she even realized she was moving. "Gimp!" She knelt and gripped the girl's shoulders. "Gods, it's good to see you!" Truth be told, she'd not thought of her urchins or Paxal at all since her ordeal, she'd been so busy.

Gimp grinned. "We been lookin' *everywhere* fer you!"

Laughter bubbled up from Mya's throat unbidden at the girl's scolding tone. "Where's Pax? Is everyone okay?"

"We're all fine, Miss." The girl proffered a wrinkled and folded piece of paper. "We got a new place with the money Dee gave. I come to leave a note like he said to, but—" She looked past Mya at the towering Jolee. "Where is he?"

The knife of guilt twisted in Mya's gut, and she saw Gimp's startled reaction to her anguished expression. She knew what she had to do, but telling her urchins that Dee was gone loomed up before her like an unassailable fortress. *Face it, Mya,* her damning inner voice insisted. *Dee would want his friends to know what happened.*

She stood and took the girl's hand. "Take me to Paxal, Gimp. Jolee, pay the reckoning and come along."

The emperor frowned as he looked at the note they had found in Otar's room. "Well, this is certainly damning, Captain."

Ithross bowed shortly. "Exactly my thought, Majesty."

Don't say it, Benj pleaded inwardly. *Don't...please...*

"It seems We have no recourse but to arrest Chief Constable Dreyfus on charges of conspiracy to commit regicide."

Benj's stomach flipped. He'd held his tongue so far for fear of getting tossed into the dungeon for insubordination, but now he had no choice. He couldn't let them arrest Dreyfus on such flimsy evidence. "Um…Your Majesty…can I put in a word or three here?"

"Of course, Sergeant. You were the one to bring this situation to Our attention in the first place, but you must admit," he waved the letter, "this doesn't look good."

"Thank you, Majesty." Benj cleared his throat. "With all due respect to Your Majesty and Captain Ithross, this so-called *evidence* is just too easy for me to buy on credit."

"Too *easy*?" Ithross looked stunned. "There was nothing easy—"

"Please, Captain, We would hear what Sergeant Benjamin has to say. He is, after all, a career investigator. Sergeant, what do your instincts tell you?"

In for a penny, in for a crown! His favorite mantra seemed particularly apropos, considering who he was talking to. "Well, first, Majesty, that little pouch of gold ain't enough to buy Chief Dreyfus."

"It might not have been the first," Ithross argued.

"I don't care if it was ten times that much. It ain't enough to risk facin' the gallows…or that head-loppin' contraption that Your Majesty prefers."

"It's called a guillotine, Sergeant, and your point is well made, but the note clearly states that the gold was payment for information."

"But to who?" the sergeant protested. "The chief wasn't named, and their 'friend in the constabulary' could mean anyone."

"Majesty please! Sergeant Benjamin suggested restraint before, and look where it got us!" Ithross glared openly at Benj. "This all fits! Dreyfus gives information to Otar, who passes it on to Hoseph, who uses it to attempt to kill Your Majesty. Then Otar dies of drink before he can get the final payment to Dreyfus."

"Exactly! Too godsdamned *easy*! Majesty, please listen." Benj was warming to the subject now, his suspicious instincts kicking in. "I'd bet a year's pay that your archmage don't find enough alcohol in Otar to kill him. And if he doesn't, then *Hoseph* killed him. And if *that's* the case, this so-called evidence is a frame job! Why else would anyone leave a note? Why not just tell Otar to thank Dreyfus when he handed over the gold? No, he left that pouch under Otar's mattress for us to *find*, I'd wager. If Dreyfus was on their payroll, and Hoseph wanted to keep him as an informant, but get rid of Otar, he'd scoop up anything that could implicate the chief and leave Otar's corpse to tell no tales. This whole thing stinks like my granny's shit bucket!"

The emperor blinked and leaned back on his throne. Ithross' mouth dropped open, and he glared daggers at two guards trying unsuccessfully to stifle smirks.

"Pardon the language, Majesty, but *think* on it!" Benj knew he was right; he could feel it. Dreyfus was a dupe in this. "Otar was bein' paid by Hoseph for information. That I get. He was madder than a wet tomcat at bein' dismissed, and was out for revenge. Not to mention that the gold helped him pay for his booze and trollops. But *Dreyfus*..." Benj shook his head. "He's got no axe to grind, nothing to gain but a bit of gold, and *everything* to lose, including his *life*. He may not like these New Accords of yours, but he's no rebel, and he's no traitor! Otar may have been milkin' him like a dun cow, but *conspiracy*? I don't buy it for a second."

Silence fell on the audience chamber.

"You suggest this is an attempt to implicate Dreyfus?"

"I do, Your Majesty."

"Why would they want that?"

"No bloody idea, Majesty. I can see *how* they did it, but not *why*. Unless..." Benj scratched his head and considered the last few days. "Unless they're just out to make general trouble. We got new cases of arson sproutin' up like daisies on a dung heap since you announced your Accords. The constabulary's spread thin checkin' them out and tryin' to prevent new ones. If you arrest the Chief Constable now...well, what kind of message does that send to the common folk?"

"Message?" Tynean Tsing said, his brows arching.

"They'll think they can't trust the constabulary, that we're for *sale*, traitors. Think that'll help in keepin' the city quiet? You arrest him, and you'll kill morale in the constabulary, cause chaos in the ranks, and sow distrust on the streets. Not a good thing when we got trouble flarin' up."

The emperor tugged his beard, and Ithross looked taken aback. Finally, the emperor spoke. "Your assessment of this, Captain Ithross?"

"It...*could* make sense if Hoseph and his...associates are trying to foster general unrest, Majesty."

Tynean Tsing nodded. "Agreed. And if they're successful, We'll have nobles and commoners alike beating down Our doors demanding action. We *need* the constabulary to show the people that we're *all* on the same side." The emperor looked to Benj again. "Any suggestions, Sergeant?"

"Bolster the constabulary with soldiers, Majesty. The more boots on the ground, the better. It might not stop more violence, but it'll show people you're tryin'."

"And what about Dreyfus?" Ithross asked accusatively.

What about *Dreyfus?* Benj was putting his head on the block here. He'd already screwed up once. If Dreyfus did turn up guilty, Ithross would come down on Benj so hard he'd never get up again. "Let me put a tail on him."

"Won't he recognize his own constables?" the emperor asked.

Benj grinned. "Not the ones *I'm* thinkin' of, Majesty. They could follow a tomcat through a henhouse without 'em knowin'."

"Very well, Sergeant. Keep Captain Ithross up to date on developments. Captain, send word to Commander Dask of the First Army to assign a company of infantry and a phalanx of cavalry to Chief Constable Dreyfus for additional patrols." The emperor's brow furrowed, his eyes stern. "And *both* of you; any information on the identities of these the arsonists or anyone associated with Hoseph is to be brought to Our attention immediately, day or night. Is that understood?"

"Yes, Your Majesty," chimed both men.

Benj looked at Ithross, and the two shared a nod of understanding. He thought the captain too tight-laced for his own or anyone else's good, and Ithross undoubtedly considered Benj an undisciplined lout. *Fair enough.* They were both on the same side, even if they didn't agree on tactics.

Chapter XII

Shadow coalesced into flesh in the darkest corner of the sultan's audience chamber. Staggered by pain, Hoseph leaned against the wall and dabbed his diminishing vial of elixir onto his tongue. The agony behind his eyes eased…but didn't quite vanish. He took a couple more drops. So much travel through the Sphere of Shadow in one day while transporting others was taking its toll, but there was yet work to be done.

The audience chamber was blissfully empty at this late hour; the palace slept, save for a few guards standing their posts or patrolling the hallways. Hoseph crept past the dais onto the wide balcony and peered over the balustrade.

The sleeping city of Tolnyek spread out below him, fetid and reeking in its decay. Beyond loomed the black mass of jungle, a ceaseless, verdant predator fighting to claim the city. Just as ceaselessly, the Morrgrey people fought back, a testament to their strength and stubbornness. It was a fight they would eventually lose. However, like a great wounded beast, the kingdom was yet dangerous, and Hoseph needed it to fight one last battle before it died.

The priest leaned back on the balustrade and looked up at the massive tiered pyramid of the palace. A gilded crest gleamed in the moonlight, four colorful spires at the cardinal points thrusting like lances toward the heavens. Somewhere in this vast structure slept the sultan. Unfortunately, all Hoseph had been able to tease out of the ambassador was that the royal family occupied an entire upper floor. Of course, that family included the sultan's ten wives and a multitude of children.

Like looking for a needle in a haystack...blindfolded. But where to start looking?

Hoseph climbed up onto the balustrade, clinging to the awning's corner post, and leaned out for a better view. The sultan's personal bedchamber would undoubtedly sport a balcony, and would command a view. *Start from the top...* Picking the highest balcony he could clearly see, he invoked his talisman and slipped through the Sphere of Shadow. Blinding pain assaulted his skull and he staggered against the balustrade. A quick dose of elixir quelled the distress, but warmth tickled his upper lip, and his hand came away bloody.

Blast! Pressing a kerchief to his nose, he considered another dose of elixir, but when he held the vial up to the moonlight, it shone only a quarter full. *Best ration it.* Hoseph tucked the vial away and crept forward. Beyond the fluttering drapes were only the low divans, chairs, and tables of a sitting room, none sufficient to accommodate the sultan's bulk. There was nothing to do but keep searching.

Six balconies and six transitions through the Sphere of Shadow later, Hoseph collapsed to hands and knees, pressing his forehead against the cool stone while blood trickled from his nose. He had once cut a crossbow bolt from his hipbone, but never had he experienced agony like this. *Sweet Keeper of the Slain!* With trembling hands, he dabbed the elixir on his tongue, fighting the urge to upend the vial over his mouth and quaff the whole thing. Pain, nausea, and weakness ebbed slowly, and he sat back on his heels, wiping up the puddle of blood and tears from the stone before him.

I can't do this much more... Demia, sustain me. Give me strength. Aid your humble servant's quest.

As if in answer to his prayer, a guttural snort sounded from beyond the gossamer drapes. Hoseph stood and edged toward the opening, peering cautiously into the chamber. A lazy breeze billowed the gauzy drapes, bringing the scent of sweet incense and a sound like a creaky bellows. The sultan lay atop a massive bed beneath a canopy of fine mosquito netting. The bed could have accommodated six —and probably had, given the tales of the sovereign's unbridled youth. Despite being propped up on a mound of pillows, the sovereign's breath came in labored gasps.

If he lay flat, he'd probably choke to death on his own fat.

Thankfully, there were no guards present, though they were undoubtedly posted outside the door. Hoseph trod quietly toward the bed and gently parted the mosquito netting. The sultan lay in the exact center of the expansive bed, well out of reach. Unfortunately, to delve the man's dreams, Hoseph had to look directly into his sleeping face.

Demia, please let him be a heavy sleeper.

With his talisman in one hand, Hoseph knelt gingerly on the bed and inched forward. The sultan snorted and grunted in his sleep. The priest froze, poised to flee into the Sphere of Shadow, but the sovereign didn't wake.

Closer…closer…closer he crept until, finally, he peered down into the face of the sultan. Sweat sheened the ruler's thick jowls, its acrid scent overpowering the sweet incense.

Hoseph closed his eyes and reached out with that secret sense bestowed upon Demia's favored, the gift of delving dreams. *Dream… Dream, and show me your soul…*

Hoseph saw visions of youth, the sea, women, and power, the sultan's deepest longings. Into these dreams Hoseph delicately wove images of his own: Krakengul Keep glowing with magical runes, arcane wonders, riches beyond compare, exotic women. He constructed a picture of the sultan in his youth, standing on the prow of a huge Morrgrey war galley gleaming with the runes he'd seen on Corillian's keep, an emperor warrior, long ebony hair streaming in the sea breeze.

Dream of power…dream of vitality, prowess, immortality…

Finally, he added an image of the sultan riding at the van of his army, the walls of Twailin falling to Morrgrey forces, the duke's palace opening to its new master, and Mir's head on a pike.

Take it…take what is rightfully yours…take Twailin…

Lad crouched on a rooftop, drinking in the essence of Tsing.

Look, listen, breathe in the night, feel it in your veins… Remember!

The warm breeze bore a million scents, the sultry air a thousand sounds, the very tiles beneath his feet trembled with the heartbeat of the city. Countless lights shone in the night, each as sharp in his sight as a sliver of glass. He knew he was being seduced, but couldn't resist the temptation. He loved his family, cherished his daughter, but this… This was what he was *made* to do.

Rising, he dashed silently across the roof and leapt, sailing over the quiet street below like a feather in the wind to land on the next building. After a brief pause to listen, he scampered across the tiles. Crouching again, he crept to the edge and peered over to spot his quarry.

Chief Constable Dreyfus strode down the street with a slight wobble in his gait from the drink he'd taken with his supper, but steady and aware enough to greet a passing squad of constables and soldiers. They outnumbered the civilians at this time of night. The soldiers were new, and although Mya wasn't sure why the emperor had ordered them to bolster the constabulary, her spies had told her that they were asking a lot of questions about the recent fires.

Mya had accepted the news of Otar's death with anger and frustration, but no blame. She assigned Lad to watch over the chief constable, reasoning that if Hoseph killed Otar to cut out the middle man, he might intend to work directly with Dreyfus from now on.

The chief constable rounded another corner, and Lad raced across the block of buildings to a new vantage. Dreyfus crossed the street, walked halfway down the block, mounted the steps to his townhouse, and worked the key in the latch.

The guild had a startlingly complete file on the man, a career constable with a reputation as a harsh disciplinarian and a bad man to cross. He'd lived alone for the last several years, since his wife and children left him, employing only a single manservant. He ate his breakfasts in, his dinners out, and slept on the second floor in a room with one window facing the street. He enjoyed alcohol, but rarely to excess and never while working. Perhaps most telling, the guild had failed to bribe or coerce him despite numerous attempts. In Lad's mind, that made the note they'd found under Otar's mattress even less likely to be genuine.

Little of this mattered to Lad. His job wasn't to judge the man, but to watch and hopefully discover what link, if any, there might be between Dreyfus and Hoseph. Having failed to even detect Hoseph's deadly visit to Otar, much less intervene, he'd resolved to keep a closer watch on the chief constable. That, however, wouldn't be easy.

Situated in the center of the block, the townhouse shared walls with two adjoining neighbors. The front of the home was well lit by street lamps and in direct view of passersby. That made getting in through the door or any of the three windows difficult and dangerous. Also, the roof wasn't gabled, so it sported no handy attic vents that might provide access.

The back, then.

Working his way to the corner of the block where the streetlights were dimmer, Lad paused to gauge the distance, then backed up and took a running leap. The roofs of the townhouses were shallow-pitched, slate-shingled, and coated with slimy black mold, but Lad landed like a spider on a pane of glass. After pausing again to listen, he crabbed along the slick surface to the chief constable's roof and pressed his ear to the slate. Beyond the scrabbling of a few mice in the attic, he picked out a couple of voices far below, barely audible.

"…tonight, Vetri. I'll just…with some tea and a book."

"Very good…kettle on and…for the night."

The faint tremors of footfalls traversed to the back of the house, and Lad followed. He would wait until the servant left, then slip in. A pump squeaked and something clanked. Lad leaned over the eaves just far enough to view the back door. The latch clicked, and the door opened, spilling light into the dim alley.

"Good night, sir," the servant said. "Sleep well."

"Goodnight, Vetri," Dreyfus replied, his voice faint from the front of the house.

Lad watched Vetri step out of the back door. The servant snugged a cap on his head, locked the door, pocketed the key, and strode up the alley.

Now for a closer look. Lad lined himself up with a small second-story window, gripped the moldy slate eaves, and flipped over the edge. He swung once, twisted and let go. One foot landed on the narrow lower windowsill, and he grasped the upper with his fingertips. Crouching there, his body splayed to keep his center of weight close to the wall, he checked the window. It was secured with a simple turn latch. He'd have to break or remove a pane to get in this way, leaving a trace he couldn't hide. That wouldn't do. Leaning out, Lad spied a window opening into the ground-floor kitchen, but it, too, was secured with a latch.

The back door then, he decided, but just before he released his grip, the sharp rap of brass on brass announced someone at the front door.

A caller at this hour? Mya hadn't mentioned that Dreyfus had any nocturnal visitors, but she had told him Dee's supposition that Hoseph needed to see a location before he could magically transport himself there. If this was the priest's first visit to Dreyfus, perhaps Lad would get the opportunity he'd been waiting for. *There are things in this world that need killing.*

Lad sprang up to grip the eaves, flipped over, and scrambled back across the roof to the street side. Creeping to the edge, he peered over and frowned in disappointment.

A woman stood on the landing. She wore a hat, so Lad couldn't see her face, but he scrutinized the rest of her. Her clothes were high quality, simple and elegant, her shoulders perfectly square, and her back straight. Her hands were those of a woman of middle years, well-groomed and clean with gleaming lacquered nails and two gold rings.

The door opened and the chief constable's voice, weary but curious, asked, "Can I help you, madam?"

"No, Chief Constable, you cannot, but *I* can help *you*." The woman's speech was cultured and articulate, with the barest hint of a quaver. She was nervous or afraid and trying not to show it. "We have a mutual acquaintance who recently met with a…mishap."

"Who are you and what are you talking about? Nobody I know has—"

"Please, Chief Dreyfus!" She looked up and down the street, her head jerking birdlike. "What I have to say is not something to be discussed on your stoop."

"I'm not about to let a stranger into my home!" Dreyfus sounded annoyed now. "It's late, and—"

"Please! This can't wait! If they find me here…" Her voice now shook noticeably. "My name is Rose. The acquaintance I speak of was formerly the captain of the Imperial Guard. He's been murdered!"

"What?" Dreyfus sounded genuinely shocked. "I don't know what you're talking about, but... Come in."

The woman stepped inside, and the door closed.

She's talking about Otar. Lad had to hear this conversation, but their voices were low and indistinct. Scrambling back across the roof, he glanced to make sure the alley was empty, then leapt. Rebounding off a windowsill across the alley, he landed by the chief constable's back door with two slim lockpicks already in hand. He worked his picks in the lock, felt the tumblers, and applied just the right amount of twist to elicit a soft telltale click. Gently pressing the latch, he slipped inside and silently closed the door behind him. He crouched in a hallway that stretched from the back of the townhouse to the front, the woman's voice now clear from the sitting room.

"...can't tell you my sources, Chief Constable."

"You'll forgive my skepticism, Miss Rose, but I think if Captain Otar was murdered, I would have heard of it. He *was* formerly head of the Imperial Guard."

"And yet, murdered he was, I assure you." Her hard shoes clacked on the floor, and Lad slipped into the entry to the kitchen in case she stepped into the hall. "Perhaps you weren't told because of your association with the man."

"Otar and I were only acquaintances."

"You should be aware, Chief Constable, that others are convinced you had a more, shall we say, *profitable* relationship with the late captain."

"*Excuse* me?" Dreyfus sounded irritated again. "What's that supposed to mean?"

The woman's voice had shed its fearful timbre and taken on a confidential tone. "Evidence was found in Captain Otar's room that implicates you in a treasonous conspiracy against the crown!"

How does she know about that? Lad wondered. Ithross said he'd take the evidence to the emperor, but Lad couldn't imagine a leak from there. Would Sergeant Benj warn his boss? Unlikely, since that would put him in trouble with the palace. Corporal Arryx seemed too straitlaced to disobey orders. *Who is she?*

"*Treason?* Does someone accuse me of participating in the assassination attempt on—"

"Shhh! Don't say any more names! There's magic afoot that keys upon a spoken name, and we're dealing with those who employ the best wizards in the empire. We don't want your enemies to know that you've been warned."

"Enemies? But...but I've done nothing *wrong*!" A heavier tread clomped across the floor; Dreyfus had begun pacing. "What's this so-called evidence?"

"Gold and an incriminating note that implied you were being paid for information."

"This is ridiculous! I only ever had a few *drinks* with Otar! This is completely fabricated!"

"Exactly! Which is why my patron insisted that you be warned. If you don't take care, you'll end up in the palace dungeons or share poor Captain Otar's fate."

Patron? Lad furrowed his brow. Was there a third party involved in this? Then it struck him; there *was* one other who would know of the evidence—the person who planted it. *It's got to be Hoseph!* The prostitute had also been in Otar's room that night, but to Lad's thinking, it was more likely that Hoseph had popped in, killed Otar, and planted the evidence.

"Who do you work for?" Dreyfus demanded.

"It's too dangerous to give you a name!" Miss Rose sounded panicked again. "Suffice it to say that I work for people who want to keep you alive and doing your job." Her hard shoed clacked across the floor again. "Forgive me my impropriety, Chief Constable, but my nerves are an absolute wreck. Might I trouble you for a spot of sherry?"

"*Your* nerves?" The chief constable stopped pacing and glass clinked. "I could use a dram myself. Gods, I never thought..."

"None of us do until our necks rest upon the emperor's guillotine."

Glass clinked again. "Who *are* these enemies you speak of?"

"Look to the palace," she whispered. "Who benefitted most by Otar's dismissal? Who might want him dead for fear of his reinstatement? Who has failed utterly to find those who threaten the life of our sovereign and would want a scapegoat?"

"Ith—" Dreyfus checked himself.

Ithross? Lad smiled, finally understanding. *She's lying to him.*

"This is monstrous! I'll go to the crown with this! I'll have him—"

"Chief Constable, *think* please. Will the crown accept your word over the captain of the Imperial Guard?"

Dreyfus merely grunted.

Lad had dealt with enough Inquisitors to recognize their subtle techniques and manipulations. The fabricated evidence hadn't gotten the chief constable arrested, so Lakshmi sent this woman to plant doubt and distrust between Dreyfus and Ithross. *But why? What benefit would they reap from a fight between the constabulary and the Imperial Guard?*

The click-pop of the kettle heating on the stove caught Lad's ear. It would soon boil and whistle. *Time to leave.* He crept to the back door and was about to slip out when the woman's voice brought him up short.

"Heed my warning, Chief Constable." Skirts rustled and her hard shoes clicked on the wooden floor. "Thank you for the sherry. I'll be in touch."

"Thank you for the warning, Miss Rose. You've given me much to consider."

Lad slipped through the door and relocked it. He'd intended to spend the night hidden in the house in case Hoseph showed up, but this visitor warranted a change of plan. If she was an Inquisitor, she might lead him right to Lakshmi. He swarmed up the back wall of the townhouse, from window frame to window frame, then leapt to the eaves and flipped up to the roof again. Dashing to the front, he looked down to the street. Dreyfus' visitor was already half a block east, walking briskly. Lad started to follow, but froze as movement in the shadows across the street caught his eye.

A tall man in a longshoreman's jacket and hat stepped out from the cover of an alley and started after the woman. He moved quickly and with reasonable stealth, keeping well back. The hat hid his face, but Lad caught his reflection in a shop window as he passed near a lamppost.

Corporal Arryx. He wondered how long the constable had been watching Dreyfus, chagrinned that he hadn't noticed him earlier. The corporal couldn't have overheard the conversation inside, but he, too, had obviously decided that this late-night visitor was worth following.

Lad stalked them both, leaping from rooftop to rooftop, a ghost in the night. A few blocks away from the chief constable's house, the woman waved down a solitary passing hackney. She boarded, the driver applied the whip, and the coach clattered off toward the Heights District.

"Damn it!" Corporal Arryx cursed, looking helplessly after the carriage.

Lad leapt overhead in high-speed pursuit, leaving his fellow stalker far behind. Corporal Arryx was good, but he wasn't *made* for this.

CHAPTER XIII

Despite the misgivings of some of my viziers," the sultan of Morrgrey scowled at his two eldest sons, "I've decided to accept your proposal. My armies will march on the morrow. We will be in Twailin province in days and spearhead for the city."

Hoseph smiled and bowed low. "Thank you, Your Majesty!" *And thank you, blessed Demia.* Though the night's exertions had left him utterly spent, the exertion and pain had been worth it. He had his war.

"However..." the sultan held up a hand, "the success of this operation will depend on information—Twailin's fortifications and preparedness, the deployment of imperial troops from Tsing, their marching order and estimated time of arrival. My son Galak will lead my army in the field, and has drawn up a list of what is needed and a schedule for when the information must be provided. If you *don't* provide it, I will order my armies to withdraw, and personally beg the emperor's forgiveness, naming you *both* as seditionists."

Galak, with a grim mien and one hand gripping his jeweled scimitar, stepped down from the dais and proffered a scroll.

Hoseph glanced at the list and grimaced. *Sweet Shadow of Death, does he want me to hold his hand during the attack?* The information on Twailin would have been simple to obtain if he'd had the cooperation of the guild there, but the cowards had gone into hiding. *Which means I'll have to do it myself.* This was turning into more time and effort than he'd planned on, but there was no recourse. They couldn't proceed without Morrgrey's help.

"I'll deliver the information on schedule, Your Highness." He bowed stiffly.

Graving shot Hoseph a nervous glance, then bowed also. "We will of course provide everything you require, Mighty Sultan. The Empire of Tsing is in your debt. We *won't* forget our greatest ally."

"Then our business is concluded." The sultan waved a hand in dismissal.

They backed out of the royal presence.

Ambassador Kovak paced anxiously in the entry hall. "Well?"

"Everything is proceeding perfectly, Ambassador," Graving said with a satisfied smile.

Hoseph flicked the skull talisman into one hand and held out the other. "Shall we return to Tsing now?"

"Yes, at once." Graving took his hand and gripped Kovak's with his other.

Even as the mists consumed them, Hoseph cringed inwardly in anticipation of the pain that awaited him on the other side of the Sphere of Shadow. Briefly, he considered stranding his companions in here to ease his agony, but decided against it. He still needed Graving, and the sudden disappearance of the ambassador on the eve of a Morrgrey invasion would cause an investigation.

As the blissfully benign Sphere of Shadow solidified into the chief magistrate's study, pain and nausea drove Hoseph to his knees. He gagged, retched, then emptied his stomach onto Graving's luxurious rug. His ears rang as if demons howled inside his head, and his head felt like they were clawing to get out. Someone gripped his shoulder, and Graving and the ambassador expressed their distress and concern in muted voices that seemed to come from afar.

Hoseph ignored them, fumbling for the vial of elixir at his belt. He pulled it free and popped the tiny stopper. One drop and the pain and illness would vanish. With a trembling hand, he raised the vial and tilted it into his mouth. Nothing. Hoseph shook the vial, pleading silently for the sweet relief, the minty wash of respite, but still felt nothing. Blinking away tears, he stared at the vial.

The elixir was gone.

Tap, tap, tap.

Sounds in the darkness... Wet tunnels... Crawling... Things biting in the dark... The stink of blood... Squeaking rats, or was that Kittal's skinning machine... Glowing runes and writhing strips of flesh...

My flesh...

Tap, tap, tap. "Mya?"

Mya tried to move, but something—sticky, clammy—bound her arms and legs. Panting, her heart racing, she fought to free herself. Eyes flying open, she looked wildly around. Not bound, but tangled in a sweat-dampened nightgown. Not in the dungeon, but in a room in Embree's headquarters. The air bore a scent of the river, not the sewers. With an exasperated sigh, she sat up and flung off the clammy sheet.

"You okay, Miss Mya?"

"Wha—" Her eyes snapped to the two diminutive shapes hunkered under her window. Nestor and Knock met her shocked gaze with wide, concerned eyes. Mya had forgotten that she'd recruited her urchins to watch over her again. Jolee had to sleep sometime, and Mya didn't yet completely trust any of her other assassins. "Yes, I'm fine."

Someone tapped on the door. "Mya, are you awake?"

"Lad?" She banished her nightmares and climbed out of bed. It must have been the tapping at the door that invaded her dreams.

Nestor trained his crossbow on the door, and Knock smacked her axe handle into her palm, baring her short tusk.

"It's okay." She gestured for the urchins to lower their weapons, then said loudly, "Come in."

The door opened, and Lad entered. Enticing aromas wafted from the pot and covered dish on the tray he bore. "Blackbrew and breakfast?"

"Gods, yes." She turned and pointed to the tiny table near the window. "Delivering breakfast? I guess you really *are* an innkeeper now." When Lad didn't reply, she turned back to find him staring at the urchins.

"You're recruiting *children*, Mya?" Tendons bunched at Lad's neck.

"This is Nestor and Knock. They're...friends of mine."

"They're armed bodyguards." Lad strode to the table and put the tray down heavily, rattling the dishes, his eyes never leaving the urchins.

"Who's he?" Nestor still held his crossbow, but it was pointed at the floor.

"Knock!"

"A *friend*." Mya gestured to the door. "You two head home. Tell Pax to send Gimp and Sticks tonight."

"Yes, Miss Mya." Nestor unloaded the crossbow and propped it against the wall, then followed Knock out.

Mya shut the door and turned back toward the table, trying to avoid Lad's mica-hued eyes, blazing with anger and pinning her like a bug under a cup.

"*Children*, Mya? You're using *children* for guild work?"

"Yes, I am!" she snapped back, her temper piqued. "After you left me here *alone*, I needed help, and used whatever resources I could find."

"But you're putting children in *danger!*"

Guilt tightened her gut. *He's right,* whispered the voice in the back of her mind, but she thrust it aside.

"You have no idea what you're talking about." Mya stomped to the table and tried to pour a cup of blackbrew, but her hands were shaking so badly she spilled it. Putting the cup down, she rounded on Lad. "They were starving in the street when I found them. I gave them food, clothes, a roof over their heads! They lived in danger every day before they met me. Yes, protecting me is dangerous. Hoseph *murdered* one of them trying to get to me, and I have to live with that, but there's no telling *how* many would have died on the street if I hadn't taken them in."

Lad took a breath, seeming to force calm. "But you don't need them anymore. You have assassins at your command now. Let them go."

Mya barked a laugh. "Let them go *where?* Back to starving to death on the street, stealing and mugging people for money?" She clenched her fists on her hips and stared him down.

Lad didn't say a word, but his jaw muscles clenched and unclenched rhythmically.

"They don't *want* to go back to what they were. With me, they have a purpose. Did you see that girl, Knock? She saved the *emperor's* life, though nobody will ever know it! What kind of life do you think she had on the streets? Yet when she met Jolee yesterday, her eyes lit up as bright as the sun. She saw that someone like her could *be* someone, have decent clothes and a life worth living. She'd never have found that on the street. They wouldn't leave if I *told* them to. Ask Paxal if you don't believe me."

Lad's eyes flicked up and down as if assessing her. "I believe you, Mya, but I don't like it. It's dangerous."

"You don't *have* to like it. It's *my* call. You're not in the guild anymore, remember?"

"Neither are those children."

She gave him a cold smile. "They're tougher than you think, and street smart in ways that even Embree's Hunters can't match."

You're pushing away one of the only friends you have, her conscience nagged.

Mya swallowed her anger. She didn't want to fight with Lad. He was a father who had lived through his own child in danger. His concern was understandable. "Besides, I only use them as spies, mostly, watching and reporting what they see. They don't work with anyone but me, and they don't know enough about guild business to be in any danger that way. They don't even know this is guild headquarters. When they're older, I'll let them choose for themselves the life they want. But for now, just leave it be."

Lad stared at her for a moment longer, then nodded. "Fine."

Mya dropped into a chair beside the table, poured cream in her blackbrew, and downed a gulp. The steaming brew burnt her tongue, but helped to clear her fatigue. "How did your night go?"

"Better than yours, I think." Lad sat down and poured himself a cup of blackbrew. "I see you're still not sleeping well."

Mya squinted at him. "How the hell do you know that?"

"Your hair's all over the place, you've got dark circles under your eyes, and your face is pale and puffy." He cocked his head at her glare. "You asked. Don't kill the messenger. I'm on your side, remember? And I brought you blackbrew."

Mya finger-combed her hair and sighed. "You're right. I'm a mess. I think not having my wrappings is part of it; I'm not used to the heat. And when I *do* get to sleep, I have nightmares."

Lad shrugged. "Well, *I* can't help you sleep soundly."

Dee used to do that... Mya studied Lad's face, but it was completely devoid of guile. *Why does it always seem like there's both too much and not enough between us?* "Forget it. I'll be fine. I just need some time." She finished her cup of blackbrew and reached for the covered dish. "Tell me about your night. If you really want to cheer me up, tell me you killed Hoseph."

"Sorry, no Hoseph. However, Dreyfus *did* have a visitor."

Mya ate sweet porridge and drank another cup of blackbrew while Lad gave his report. At the mention of Miss Rose, she dropped her spoon. "You think she's an Inquisitor? Tell me you followed her!"

"Yes, and I wasn't the only one. That constable corporal, Jorren Arryx, was watching from outside."

"That doesn't surprise me. Sergeant Benjamin's sharper than he looks. Do you think Arryx saw you?"

"I don't think so," Lad said with an uncharacteristically sheepish expression. "He's good, though. I don't think the woman spotted him either, but he was left behind when she caught a hackney. I followed her to a big place in the Heights—three floors and half a city block. It looked like an inn, but there was no signboard identifying it as a business. A lot of well-dressed people came and went, and there was music inside. No doorman on the stoop, but one just inside the door; I saw him when Miss Rose went in. I watched all night, but she never came out again."

"Excellent! I'll have Embree find out what it is." Exhilaration, better than a whole pot of blackbrew, surged through her. "I think you're right. She *must* be one of Lakshmi's people! I don't know why they'd want to frame Dreyfus or start a fight between him and Ithross, and I really don't care. If we can track this woman to Lakshmi and Kittal..." Mya sat back in her chair, visions of vengeance playing through her mind. *I'll kill you myself...*

"Mya?" Lad's tone was strange, his eyes narrowed and his brow knitted.

"Sorry. I got lost there for a minute." She got up and went to the vanity, poured water into the basin, and dampened a cloth to scrub her face. "I'll assign people to watch that house today while you rest, but I want you to go back tonight to have a look inside."

"I'll go if you back me up. The place could be full of assassins, after all."

"What?" Mya stopped scrubbing and met his eyes in the mirror. "You work best alone. You always said that."

Lad shrugged. "It's a big place. I could use an extra set of eyes, but I can't risk your assassins seeing what I can do, so it has to be you. Besides, we reconnoitered together when we first came to Tsing. We made a good team."

Mya turned around to face him. Unconsciously, she rubbed her arm, as if she could feel the thin tracery of runes beneath her sleeve. "But...I'm not what I used to be."

"No, you are what you are. That's more than most, less than a very few, and all you have to work with."

"How philosophical!"

"I just need you to watch from the street. Are you saying that you can't do a job you'd assign *children* to do?"

"I wouldn't send a *child* out to watch your back!"

"No?" He shrugged. "Maybe you need to take a lesson from them. You're tougher than you think, Mya. And stop clicking your nails together; you don't want to show people you're nervous."

Her temper flared. He'd often warned her that her unconscious tells gave away her feelings, but right now it just made her mad. "You have no *idea* how tough I am, Lad."

"No, I don't, and you need to learn it for yourself."

"Look, I appreciate you coming here to help me, but that doesn't give you the right to judge my methods or think for one *second* that you know me better than I know myself."

Lad cocked his head. "I don't claim to know you better than you know yourself, Mya. I'm just giving advice. Just like *you* gave *me* advice—*good* advice—when I was drowning in guilt over Wiggen's death. You told me what I needed to hear, and I'm telling you what *you* need to hear."

"What if I don't *want* to hear it?" Mya knew she was being petulant and argumentative, but she couldn't help it. She was as mad at herself as she was at him, probably because he was right and she just didn't want to face it. Despite their disputes, she'd missed Lad. It felt good to have someone she could speak with honestly.

"That's why *I'm* the one telling you." He flashed her a smile. "I'm not in the guild, remember? And you can't kick my ass."

"I can't kick your ass?" She arched an eyebrow. "Care to test that theory in the sparring room?"

Lad grinned and waved toward the door. "I thought you'd never ask."

"What the hell now?" Sergeant Keesen muttered to Benj as the line of caps filed toward Dreyfus' office.

"Damned if I know," Benj admitted. The chief had called in all his senior sergeants for this meeting, but hadn't said what it was about. "Maybe the emperor's come up with some *new* New Accords."

"Would that mean the New Accords are now the Old Accords, or would that be the Old New Accords?" Sergeant Tobas grinned. "Gonna be hard to keep all these accords straight."

Benj and the others chuckled ruefully. Adhering to the new rules of conduct wasn't easy. Asking commoners politely for information came hard to street caps used to demanding, threatening, and even knocking a few heads when necessary. Two caps had already lost stripes for reverting to old habits.

"Shut up and settle down!" Dreyfus barked as they filed in. "And close the door."

The sergeants fell silent and shuffled into positions where they could all see their commander. Dreyfus didn't look happy and, unless Benj missed his guess, had spent a sleepless night. Dark circles puffed beneath his eyes, and stiff, gray hairs that had eluded the razor sprouted from his cheeks. Of course, Benj hadn't shaved at all this morning, but the chief was usually all prim and proper when he came through the door.

"We had *three* more fires last night: an inn on the riverfront in the Wharf District, a cobbler's in Midtown, and a chandlery in the

Dreggars Quarter. The only two districts that haven't been hit are the Temple and Downwinds."

"Does that make priests and beggars our prime suspects, Chief?"

Dreyfus surged to his feet, his scarred hands pressed atop the cluttered desk and his face flushed. "One more wisecrack, Tobas, and I'll have you walking a beat in the Downwinds with only one stripe on your collar. I didn't call you in for jokes! I called you in to tell you we're putting all our efforts, and I mean *all*, into finding these arsonists. All other investigations are hereby put on the backburner."

Where did this come from? Benj raised his hand. "But Chief, I'm workin' on the Hoseph—"

"Are you *deaf*, Benjamin? I said *all* other investigations are put aside. You all listen close! No more running off to do the imperial guard's job for them. If they can't keep the emperor locked up safe behind palace walls, that's *their* problem! We've got buildings going up in flames and people being burnt to death. We've got a company of soldiers to help us now, so let's put them to work. I want answers, and I want them yesterday! Do you lot get me, or do I need a dozen new sergeants?"

"Yes, sir!" they all said. Clearly, the chief was in a mood, and heads would roll for anyone who didn't toe the line.

"Then get out of my office and do your godsdamned jobs!"

The sergeants filed out. Only when the door closed did the grumbling begin. There were dozens of ongoing investigations, and sergeants took it hard to see their work thrown out like the contents of a chamber pot.

Benj stared at the chief's door, wondering about the man inside. A chill ran up his spine. *Could I have been wrong? Could he really be part of some conspiracy?* He knew he could lose his job over it, but he had no intention of throwing away *all* of his investigations.

"What was that all about, Sarge?" Jorren stood with the blackbrew pot in one hand and a cup in the other, looking at the parade of disgruntled sergeants. "Someone cut pensions?"

"Nothin' so catastrophic as that, but somethin's got his goat. The chief's putting a hold on all investigations until we can cap a lid on these arsons." Benj studied the corporal, who looked impossibly bright and spry considering the late night he must have had. "Didn't expect to see you so early. Any news?"

"Some." Jorren sipped his blackbrew and nodded to the door. "Want to stretch your legs?"

"Sure." Benj waited while Jorren downed his blackbrew, then followed him out. They walked in silence for a short distance before Jorren spoke.

"Dreyfus had a visitor last night right after he got home. A well-dressed lady."

"A high-priced trollop?" Benj hadn't ever heard that Dreyfus had any lady friends, but men had needs, and there was no shortage of women, or men for that matter, to fulfill those needs for a few silver crowns.

"I don't think so. She didn't look the type, even for a Heights courtesan, and if she was, it was the shortest dalliance in human history. The curtain wasn't completely closed, so I could see them talking in his sitting room, but I couldn't hear. She was only there a few minutes."

"Get a look at her?"

The corporal shook his head ruefully. "Other than a finely dressed, middle-aged woman, I can't say much. It was dark, and I didn't want to get too close. I tried to follow her, but she hopped a hackney, one of Chocky's. I've got a cap trying to find the driver."

"Good. Find out where she went and maybe we'll find out who she is." Benj looked over his shoulder in the direction of the constabulary headquarters. "Dreyfus was in a real mood this morning and looked like he hadn't slept. Maybe she gave him bad news."

"About his friend Otar maybe?" Jorren frowned. "You think we've got a leak among our circle of friends?"

"That would be bad." Benj thought about the caps who knew about Otar's death and shook his head. "Not on our end. Gem'll keep her people quiet, and I don't think Miss Moirin's man would leak it."

Jorren raised his eyebrows. "Ithross?"

"Ha!" Benj shook his head and spat into the gutter. "Not a chance. The timing stinks like a leak, though, don't it?" He ticked off on his fingers. "We find Otar dead and a note implicating Dreyfus.

Then a woman visits him late at night, and the very next day the chief cancels all investigations except for the arsons. Blackmail, maybe?"

"Maybe there's an investigation someone wants stopped. Stopping just one would look suspicious, but stopping all of them might look like he's concentrating his forces on the arson investigation."

All the maybes bobbed in Benj's mind like apples in a barrel. "Hells, *maybe* this mystery woman has nothing to do with anything. Could've just been bad news. You know, *coincidence*."

They stopped and looked at one another, then shared a scoffing smile. "Nah."

"We should keep right on investigating, I think." Benj said.

Jorren grinned at him. "Seems reasonable."

"Go ahead then, but keep it off the record and quiet."

Jorren's smile faded. "I may need some money to get the hackney driver to talk, and I don't think Dreyfus will appreciate me drawing from the constabulary's kitty."

"Here." Benj pulled out his belt pouch and handed it over. "I'm likely as not to just spend it on wine, women, and song anyway."

"I didn't know you were a music lover," Jorren said, trying to keep his face straight.

"Depends who's singin'," Benj replied with a wink. "See you later, then."

"Later, Sarge." Jorren touched the rim of his iron cap and strode off.

Benj watched him go, then turned the corner to work his way around the block back to headquarters. Jorren was as sharp a cap as he'd ever known. He hated risking getting him into trouble for breaking orders, but he wasn't ready to give up on this investigation. His gut told him that there was some thread connecting his boss' strange behavior to Hoseph. Benj intended to find that thread, pull it, and see what unraveled.

Hoseph stumbled from the carriage, clutching the door to keep his knees from folding. The jolting ride had made his head pound in time to his racing heartbeat and threatened to empty his stomach again. Gritting his teeth against the disgraceful weakness, he closed the carriage door and shuffled out of the road.

The social club that disguised Kittal's headquarters stood across the street. The age-old, members-only establishment catered exclusively to the gentry. Consequently, Hoseph couldn't just walk in. Instead, he headed toward the gleaming row of shops that lined the other side of the street, girding his fading endurance.

Just a bit farther…a few steps.

His hand trembled as he clutched the latch of *The Spice of Life* and pulled open the door. An aromatic mélange of a hundred spices assaulted him as he stepped inside, roiling his already fragile stomach. The shop hid one of the four alternative entrances to Kittal's headquarters.

"Can I help you, Brother?" asked the wizened shopkeeper.

"I was told you have a selection of rare incense in your cellar."

The old man didn't even bat an eye, but toddled over to a door and opened it. "Through here and down the stairs, sir. Someone will see to you."

Hoseph passed through the door and stared dubiously down the staircase. After collapsing in Graving's den, he had feared that another transit through the Sphere of Shadow without the elixir might kill him. Now, faced with trembling legs and a long stair, he wondered if he should have risked using the talisman.

Sweet shadow of death, give me strength. Leaning heavily on the rail, he descended step by shaky step. At the bottom stood two surly-looking assassins, arms crossed, eyes narrowed.

Hoseph drew back the hood of his robe. "I need to see Master Kittal at once."

"High Priest *Hoseph*?" The assassins exchanged a surprised look, and the woman who had spoken stepped aside while her companion opened the door. "Pardon us! We didn't recognize you."

He wasn't surprised considering his recent change in guise, and dismissed the apology with a grunt. He shuffled through the door and stopped. The room was crammed with iron-strapped chests, piles of leather bags, and rows of jars atop walls of shelving, all redolent of spices from around the world. There was no door.

"Which way?"

"Just through here." The woman stepped around a stack of chests to the back wall, moved a shelf that appeared to be on hidden wheels, and gestured to the dark space within. "Do you need a torch? The way's dark."

"No." Hoseph called the pearly glow of death to his hand and stepped past the assassin.

The way was indeed dark, but the floor was well trodden. The walls gleamed with moisture. When he reached out to steady himself, his hand came away coated with filth, but Hoseph could not have cared less. He'd never felt such fatigue, such weakness. Collapsing in Graving's den, vomiting and bleeding from his nose, had shaken his confidence, and even his faith. *Demia, I can't continue like this...*

There was, both figuratively and literally, a light at the end of the tunnel, however. Two Alchemists guarded the door at the other end, crossbows loaded with Kittal's alchemical bolts pointed at Hoseph's chest. Beyond that door, the Master Alchemist would give him more elixir.

The assassins recognized him and lowered their weapons. One turned and knocked a staccato beat on the iron-bound door behind them, announcing, "The priest's here."

The door opened to reveal two more assassins. They ushered him through and shut the door behind him. From here, Hoseph knew the floor plan well enough to find Kittal's office. Two additional guards met him at that door.

"Is Kittal in?" Hoseph muttered.

"Yes. Both masters are here." The guard knocked and opened the door.

Kittal and Lakshmi sat at a large desk perusing a map of the city. They looked up as he entered, and their eyes widened.

Hoseph waited until the door closed. "Kittal, I need more of your elixir immediately."

"*More?*" The Alchemist stood, looking shocked. "You *can't* have used up that entire vial yet!"

"Obviously I have or I wouldn't need more." He leaned back against the door, concentrating on staying upright. "My mission to Morrgrey was more…strenuous than I planned."

"You *really* shouldn't be taking so much." Kittal pulled out a chair. "I *told* you it was dangerous. Sit before you fall down."

Lakshmi peered at him. "You do look dreadful, Hoseph. Perhaps Kittal's right and you need to forgo the elixir."

"It's not the damned *elixir* that's killing me!" Hoseph bit back his anger and shuffled across the rug to the chair. He collapsed into it, pressing his palms to his pounding temples. "My transitions through the Sphere of Shadow have taxed me to the point of collapse, and I'm not finished. If I can't use my talisman, our entire plan fails!"

"I'll get you something." Kittal left the room, returning moments later with a vial in hand. "This is a different formulation, but should help. It'll also stave off your withdrawals. Take only one drop."

Hoseph clutched the vial in a quivering hand and dosed himself. His nausea vanished, his strength waxing as the pain waned. A dull ache lingered, like the memory of a bad dream, but it was nothing compared with the previous anguish. His hand still quivered as he tucked the vial in his pocket.

The Master Alchemist peered at Hoseph as if the priest were an intriguing specimen. "This debilitation is a magical side effect of the Sphere of Shadow?"

"Or the magic that takes me through it and protects me," Hoseph already regretted revealing his secret.

"What are your symptoms?"

"What does it matter? The elixir you gave me cures them. I just need—"

Kittal interrupted him. "You need to answer my question. The elixir only relieves the symptoms and heals the damage. With more information, I might be able to prevent the effect entirely."

Hoseph needed only a moment to consider the implications. *If Kittal can prevent the pain…* "Headaches, nausea, weakness, and occasionally nosebleeds."

"When did this start?"

"Sometime after the assassination of the emperor. It began slowly, so I can't pinpoint it more exactly. The frequency and severity of the symptoms have increased over time and are especially severe with many sequential transitions or when I transition with others. I've been using my talisman far more often than I used to."

"The transitions are accomplished with that skull talisman?" Kittal held out a hand. "Let me see it."

"No." Hoseph instinctively flipped the skull into his hand and clenched his fist around it. "It's a divine relic given to *me* by Demia, not just a magical trinket. None other may touch it."

Kittal shrugged and sat back down. "Have it your way, but don't take more of that elixir when you wake in the middle of the night with chills and sweats. It won't help."

"Then give me something that *will* help!"

The Alchemist glared and opened his mouth, but Lakshmi intervened. "Please, Kittal. Hoseph's skills are vital to our efforts."

Kittal frowned and nodded. "I'll see what I can do, but I'm warning you, Hoseph. There'll be a price to pay in the end."

"None too costly to achieve our goals."

Lakshmi cast a cautioning glance at her fellow master, then turned to Hoseph. "Was your mission to Morrgrey was a success?"

"Yes, but it's going to require more work than we thought, more travel." Hoseph patted the pocket with the vial of elixir. "The sultan insisted upon information about Twailin's defenses, Mir's troops, their state of readiness, and the deployment of Tsing's armies. Anything you can dig up without my help will ease my burden. At least we're one step further in our efforts to get Arbuckle off the throne."

Lakshmi shifted in her seat and studied her nails. "Yes, well, as to that, we've had a minor shift of plans."

"What's that?" Hoseph knew well enough now when she was hiding yet another failure.

"We hoped the note left in Otar's room would result in Chief Constable Dreyfus' arrest, but that didn't happen. Alternatively, we're trying to erode his allegiance."

Hoseph snorted in derision. "You've already tried and failed to recruit him. What makes you think he'll flip now?"

"We're not *trying* to recruit him. We merely need to nudge him in the right direction." She smiled sweetly. "We're pitting the constabulary against the Imperial Guard."

Hoseph leaned back in his chair. "And that's working?"

The Master Inquisitor smiled in satisfaction. "It'll take time, but with Kittal's help, we'll have the Chief Constable jumping at every shadow."

"Will it be enough to strip away Arbuckle's security?"

"Once the army is out of Tsing, I believe so, yes."

Hoseph allowed himself a rare smile. There was still work to do, but their plans were finally on the way to fruition.

CHAPTER XIV

Crouching in the dark, Mya fought to control her warring emotions.

What's wrong with me? She'd always loved the hunt—slinking through the streets, senses heightened, moving like a shadow within shadows—especially with Lad. She'd felt some of that old exhilaration during their stealthy dash across the city, matching his pace, shadowing his every step close enough to catch his scent on the sultry air.

It's nothing but a lie.

Lad had gone easy on her, slowed down so she could keep up, taken easy paths. The routes they had traveled when they first arrived in Tsing, she could never have managed now. She felt clumsy and slow, and even though her bruises from their morning sparring session were only a memory, his brutally honest assessment of her performance still stung.

"You've gotten used to not having to worry about getting hurt. Now you realize you can be, and you're overcompensating. Accept it, *plan* for it, but don't hold back. That will only get you killed." He'd held up his maimed left hand. "Sometimes you *have* to get hurt to survive."

She knew he spoke from experience. Lad had been immune to pain, injury, and even emotion, until he'd broken the magic that made him a slave. And yet, she'd seen him fight unflinching through injuries that would have staggered a seasoned warrior.

How does he deal with it? she wondered, but only for a moment. *Wiggen.*

That was how they differed. Lad had gained something when he lost his runes. Love had allowed him to embrace his loss.

I only lost... My runes, my confidence, Dee...

"What's wrong?" Lad's eyes were intent upon her instead of their surroundings.

"Nothing." The lie came automatically. "Why?"

"Your breathing changed and your skin flushed. I thought you might have spotted something."

"No, nothing. Just learning to deal with getting winded so easily."

He looked at her blankly for a moment, then shrugged. "Don't tell me if you don't want to, but pay attention. We're here." He pointed across a wide avenue.

Mya eyed the building across the street, a private, high-class social club, according to Embree. Digger's description had been more colorful: "Some kinda rich folks' play house, we figure. They go in, stay a couple hours, then come out with smiles on their faces." It sounded like the kind of place Lakshmi would use to glean rumors from society's upper crust.

Both Hunters and urchins had watched the place during the day, but Mya had pulled them back for tonight, not wanting to risk anyone seeing her and Lad.

"Once around," Lad whispered, creeping forth like a ghost.

Mya and Lad started working their way around the club, skirting the adjacent blocks in a wide cloverleaf pattern to inspect the place without exposing themselves to direct view. It was a potential assassins' hideout, after all. The stealthy reconnaissance came as natural as breathing, and Mya settled into the familiar comforting pattern; her physical skills might be diminished, but her Hunter's instincts were working fine.

The building occupied half of an entire block, bordered on three sides by cobbled streets and a narrow alley on the fourth. The street-side façades sported numerous large windows, the lower ones shuttered for privacy and the upper shrouded by curtains, some dark, some backlit. Laughter and music echoed within. The alley side had only a few small, dark windows and a servant's entrance.

Mya started into the alley, but Lad gripped her shoulder.

"Too dangerous. If someone comes out that door while we're in there, there's no place to hide."

You mean there's no place for me *to hide*, Mya thought despondently. Lad could have swarmed up one of the sheer walls like a spider. She bit back her sharp response and followed him on.

Finally, they arrived back where they had started. Other than a passing patrol of constables and a few vagrants sleeping in shadowed doorways, they'd spotted nothing worthy of notice.

"Where do you want me?" Mya asked.

Lad shot her an inscrutable look, then pointed to a two-story building diagonally across one intersection. "There. From the corner roof you can see two of the four sides and the main entrance. That's the best we can do with just two of us. I'll go in on the third-floor, second window from the corner. It's ajar and fairly dark inside."

"Okay." Mya had noticed several open windows, but had no idea why he'd chosen that one. *You* should *know!* She'd planned hundreds of incursions like this one; spotting the best point of entry was her business. *You're a Hunter, Mya, start acting like one.* "Give me ten minutes to get into position. If I spot anything before you go in, I'll whistle."

"Good. Keep an ear cocked once I'm in. If I need you, I'll try to make enough noise for you to hear."

"Okay." She turned to go, doubting very much if Lad would ever need her to come to his rescue.

"And Mya…"

She looked back at him.

"Don't kill anyone if you don't have to."

Such a Lad thing to say… "I won't, if you promise that you *will* kill if you have to. We're dealing with the people who strapped me down to a table and skinned me alive."

"I know."

"They'll do the same to you if they get the chance."

"I'll remember that."

"Good."

Mya worked her way around the block to the back of the building she would watch from, found a stout drain pipe, and started climbing. The rough iron brackets and weathered mortar bit into her fingertips. *It's just pain, Mya. Get used to it.* Near the top, a clatter caught her ear and she froze. A block away, a troop of constables and soldiers rounded a corner. Fortunately, they were watching the streets and alleys, not overhead. She hunkered in the shadow of the eaves until they passed, then clambered up and over the edge.

Distributing her weight evenly on the rain-slicked tiles and muttering a prayer that the earlier thunderstorm had truly passed, she gained the crest of the roof and edged forward. She was now in full view of the club's upper windows, but anyone looking out would be hard-pressed to see a darkly clad shape atop the dark roof on a moonless night. At the edge, she peered down and spotted Lad's faintly luminous eyes in the shadows. She gave him the all-clear signal, quite sure he could see her despite the darkness.

Then he moved.

Mya caught her breath as he dashed across the open street, a brief blur in the lamplight. He hunkered in the gloom under a window for a heartbeat, then skittered up the side of the building. She would have sworn he barely touched a single windowsill. What had taken her ten minutes, took him five seconds. He paused for a moment at the open window, then pulled himself up by one hand, eased the gap wider with the other, and slipped through.

Suppressing a pang of jealousy, Mya settled back to wait and watch, rhythmically shifting her attention in a long-practiced pattern of vigilance—left street, right street, windows, rooftops, alleys—all the while listening for any hint of trouble. A foursome left the social club, laughing and smiling, their steps unsteady from drink or some other intoxicant. They started up the hill, talking about their good luck at cards and poor prospects of finding a hackney at this late hour. As they passed the narrow alley behind the social club, the darkness in the adjacent shop doorway shifted. Squinting, Mya watched as the vagrant that she and Lad had previously spotted sleeping in the doorway lifted his head and scratched something in a small notebook.

Someone else was watching the club.

Had one of Embree's Hunters disobeyed her order to stay away? *Whoever it is certainly knows what he's doing.* She doubted he was one of hers, and fortunately he was on the wrong side of the building to have witnessed Lad's climb, but she needed to find out who this was.

She inspected the club again. Most of the higher windows were dark and quiet, the sounds of merriment from below undiminished. No sign that might suggest Lad needed help. She had told him she'd watch, but he could handle himself, and this bore investigation.

Time to hunt...

Keeping one ear cocked for any sign of trouble inside the social club, Mya edged to the blind side of her building and descended the drain pipe to the street. Rounding two blocks at a silent trot, she slipped into the far end of the alley behind the club, pressing against the rough brick wall to lessen her profile. As before, the alley presented a problem. Narrow and relatively clean, there was no place to hide if someone exited the back door of the club or came in from the other direction. It was also the only way she could get close to the watcher without him spotting her. There were only two ways to do it.

High or low?

The walls weren't close enough for her to reach both at the same time, and the few small windows were too widely spaced for her to climb from one to another. Lad could have bounded from one to the next like a cricket, but...

Maybe... Lad was right; she hadn't tested her capabilities. She picked out a path up the side of the wall, eyed it critically, and decided that this wasn't the time or place for such a test.

Well, if not up, then down. Mya dropped to the cobbles and crept forward on fingertips and toes, her ears perked for any sign of trouble.

The Heights District might be renowned for its magnificent mansions, high-class shops, and exorbitantly priced restaurants, but that reputation evidently didn't extend to their alleys. Though relatively clear of refuse and filth, the cobbles were far from clean and reeked of urine and worse. She tried to avoid the muck edging the passage and ignore the skittering insects. Her wrists and shoulders ached with the strain, and the gritty cobbles scored her fingers.

Dark...wet...pain...skittering...biting...keep crawling...crawl or die...

No! Mya shook off the flashback, blinking away tears. *You're an assassin! You can do this!*

Gritting her teeth, she continued on past the doorway, all the way to the wedge of shadow at the other end of the alley. When a gale of laughter echoed in from the street, she froze, eyes down, to wait until they passed. Two women, from their voices, and they would pass both her and the watcher.

He'll watch them. Now's my chance. The moment the women passed the alley, Mya stood up against the wall again and slipped a small mirror from a pocket. Edging it out around the corner, she caught a glimpse of the watcher's face in profile as he leaned out of the shadowed doorway.

Corporal Arryx? It seemed the constable had tracked Miss Rose here after all. *Well, damn!*

Killing him was out of the question, and not just because Lad didn't want her to. Bodies were difficult to dispose of, and killing a constable would cause problems. Still, she could tolerate no interference here. If one of Lakshmi or Kittall's assassins spotted Arryx, her only chance of tracking down their headquarters would vanish. She'd have to warn him off, but how could she get him off the street without drawing attention?

His pencil scratched like an insect skittering across stone. He was taking notes on the people who came and went from the club. That meant his attention would be on his work, at least for a moment, after each visitor passed.

More voices from the street, a muffled goodnight from within, and the front door to the club thumped closed. A threesome this time, two men and a woman, started up the street. Mya tensed, motionless in the dark. When they had passed the alley, she edged her mirror out again. *Timing... Don't kill him...unless he does something stupid.* She doubted he would—the corporal had been cool under fire when the orphanage was attacked—but there was always a chance.

After the threesome passed the shadowed doorway, Arryx leaned out to watch them, notebook in hand.

Mya moved.

Up and around the corner, she slipped into the dark alcove and dropped on him, one hand clamped on his mouth, the other pressing a dagger to his throat.

"Good evening, Corporal," Mya whispered in his ear.

Arryx dropped his notebook and reached for her wrist, every muscle in his body instantly tense.

"Shhh!" Mya held the flat of the blade against his neck. "It's Miss Moirin! If I wanted you dead, you would be, so just calm down."

He froze, and she removed the dagger from his throat.

"Now, when they round the corner, we're going to get up and step quietly into the alley for a chat. No noise and no questions. Nod if you understand."

His head bobbed once.

"Good." Mya waited until the trio was gone, removed her hand from his mouth, and tugged at his collar. "Up."

The constable complied, recovering his notebook as he stood, and she pulled him into the alley. There, she backed him into the wedge of shadow, still gripping his tunic and the dagger. He probably doubled her in weight, but he didn't struggle.

"How did you find this place?"

"A woman visited Dreyfus," he whispered. "We tracked her here. How did *you* find it?"

"I had someone watching Dreyfus, too. They followed her here. I've got someone inside now checking it out, and I can't have you lurking about. If someone spots you, it'll ruin everything."

"No one will spot me. I know what I'm doing."

"I spotted you, didn't I?" His face hardened, and she realized she'd said the wrong thing. "Look, you're good, but these people are better. If I spotted you, they can. And if they do, you'll die, and they'll know the constabulary's onto them."

"I was ordered to watch this place."

"So was I, and I think the *emperor's* orders supersede Sergeant Benjamin's." Not exactly true—she wasn't here at the emperor's specific command—but close enough. "Please, Corporal, let me do what I'm best at."

His eyes narrowed. "I will…if you tell me what you know about the woman who visited Chief Dreyfus."

"Not here." Mya flattened herself against the wall as another peal of laughter erupted from the street. When it faded she whispered, "I'll meet with Sergeant Benjamin and tell him everything we know. Okay?"

The muscles of his jaw worked as if he was chewing on her offer like a piece of tough meat. "Fine. *Marley's Pub*, eight o'clock tomorrow night."

"I'll be there."

"And you'll tell him everything you know?"

"Of course." She grinned. "Thank you, Corporal. Now, please make yourself scarce."

"Fine." He hurried off down the alley, his footfalls remarkably quiet for a constable.

Mya waited until he was out of sight, then made her way back to her post, a thin smile of satisfaction spreading across her lips.

And I didn't even kill him, she thought as she settled back onto the roof. *Won't Lad be proud...*

Lad peered through window into the dark room, inhaling the aromas of cologne, spices, and scented oil. A woman lay face down on the bed, motionless, nude save for a sheet draped across her hips, skin gleaming in the light of a single candle. Her breathing told him she was asleep, so Lad slipped through the window.

The woman's flesh glistened with sweet-smelling oil, the curve of her backside barely concealed beneath the sheet, her legs long and bare. Beneath the spicy redolence hung a subtle, musky, and eminently familiar scent.

Sex.

So the club provides carnal services. Lad filed the fact away and started for the door, but the musky scent and the sultry curves of glistening flesh ignited his memories. *Wiggen...*

Wiggen lying in the lamplight next to him, a sheen of sweat on her skin, breathing deeply, sated, smiling, happy, her fingers trailing lightly upon his chest. Not a night went by that he didn't miss her touch.

Lad tore his gaze away. *Focus. Extraneous thoughts during a mission are as deadly as a blade through the heart. Remember!*

Whether a client or an employee of the club, the woman hadn't slathered her own back with oil, so her masseuse would probably return shortly.

Lad reached for the door latch, but froze. Lost in his memories, he hadn't caught the quiet footsteps coming down the hall. He tensed as they approached. *One person, bare feet, carpeted floor, nobody else in the hallway...* The soft tread stopped outside the door, and the latch clicked.

Lad's eyes swept the room, but found few options. He could go back out the window and try to find another entrance, but he had no time to make sure there were no passersby. Waiting under a bed while they continued their dalliance above him was out of the question, and hiding behind the door would only work until it was closed. He looked up at the room's lofty ceilings, and another option popped into his mind.

The latch turned, and the door opened. As lamplight from the hall scythed through the room, Lad moved to the blind side of the door. A silver tray balanced in a man's hand came through first, the scent of opium wafting from the small water pipe atop the platter.

Lad tensed as the man stepped into the room, gauged the moment, and leapt straight up, arching his body over the door. Grasping the upper molding, he swung into the hallway, landed without a sound, and stepped aside, pressing his back against the wall.

The servitor quietly closed the door, completely unaware of Lad's acrobatic evasion. "Baroness, I brought you a present."

They cater to nobility.

Another fact filed away, Lad closed his eyes and took a moment to really listen. A threesome made love in the next room over, while across and down the hall a man laughed and a woman giggled girlishly. Snores, clinking glass, and heavy breathing from a few more rooms, but nobody else walked about on this floor.

Lad slipped down the hall, senses heightened to a fever pitch. Doors lined both sides of the hall, and he caught a few snippets of hushed conversations, but nothing suspicious. Left at the end, a stair, and another hall, also with doors on both sides, and another left turn. A glance around that corner revealed another less ornate stairway, and the layout clicked into his head: The rooms on one side of the hallway overlooked the streets, while those on the other side probably viewed a small inner courtyard. The carpeted stair with ornate bannister, obviously for patrons, descended on the south side, while the one to the north, narrow and unadorned, was for servants.

He descended the north stair, gauging each step for squeaks before applying his full weight. If this place was indeed a front for Lakshmi's Inquisitors, he'd most likely find evidence in the areas where clients didn't go. At the second floor landing he paused to listen, but it sounded much the same as above.

The sounds from below were distinctly different. Glass clinked, dice rolled, cards ripped in a shuffle, and some kind of bone or metal tiles clacked together. People laughed; had good-natured arguments about games, rumors, politics, and religion; and whispered about who was having illicit relationships with whom. There was no clanking of pots and pans or other kitchen noises, suggesting the cooks and scullery staff had been sent home for the night.

At the ground floor, the stair emptied into a short hallway, the air muddied with the scents of chocolate, vanilla, cinnamon, and baked goods, as well as rum, whiskey, wine, tobacco, and opium. One end of the hall ended in a bolted door that opened into the alley, with openings to the left and right. The other end sported a swinging door that, from the sounds, opened into the common room. *Well...can't go that way.*

The openings near the back door led into the kitchen and scullery. No one currently labored there, though five silver trays artfully arranged with delicate tidbits crowded one kitchen counter. Lad snatched a small tart from one of the trays and ate it, nudging the others to fill the gap. It was tasty, but he preferred Josie's almond cookies.

Finding nothing of real interest, he tried the scullery. To the left, a banister girded a steep, stone stair that descended to a wooden door.

Suddenly, the door at the bottom of the stair opened. Lad peered over the banister as a woman emerged bearing four bottles in her arms. Kicking the door closed behind her, she started up the stairs.

Lad pressed himself against the wall, waited until she neared the top of the stairs, then hopped over the banister and landed silently behind her. Backing into the shadows by the door, he held still until she topped the steps and left the scullery.

He listened at the wooden door, but heard no one beyond. An earthy scent lingered in the air. Carefully easing open the latch, he peered inside. A wine cellar, no surprise, lit by several oil lamps turned low, the rows of bottles and casks clean, dusted, and orderly. Someone was proud of their collection.

Lad stepped inside and closed the door behind him, muffling the sounds of the upper floor. Curiously, he could still hear the faint clatter of glass and metal, and voices, not from above, but nearby. He turned his head slowly, homing in on the new noises, and wove his way through the racks to the back of the room. The rear wall of the cellar was one long unbroken rack of bottles, but Lad wasn't fooled for a moment. The sounds were coming from behind the second rack from the left. Peering closely, he discerned faint wear marks on the stone floor; the rack swung outward. Reaching carefully between the bottles, he felt around until he found a slim seam in the stone, and smiled. A door.

He listened closely: two heartbeats just beyond the door, but no sound of shifting or movement; muffled voices farther away, the sharp clink of glass on glass, the thicker clink of pottery, the slow grating of a mortar and pestle, and the whisk of metal on stone as someone honed a blade.

Lad frowned. This sounded like an alchemy lab, but he would have sworn the woman he followed here was an Inquisitor. *Which means Lakshmi and Kittal are consolidating forces or at least sharing this hideout.* That was unusual, but not unheard of during war.

Lad ran his fingers lightly over the wine bottles and rack until he discovered the mechanism that opened the door. *Second row from the top, third bottle from the right.* If it also triggered an alarm or trap, he had no way of knowing, and even if it didn't, he'd have to kill the two guards on the other side if he opened it, which meant discovery.

Just bring the information back to Mya, he resolved. He was glad she wasn't with him. She'd done well enough sparring and during their stealthy excursion across the city, but he didn't know how she would react faced with a real threat. Her shaky self-confidence, lapses in attention, and thirst for revenge made her unpredictable. Only one thing was certain: Mya wouldn't stop until she either won this war or died.

And if she decides to mount an assault and kill everyone inside…

Would he help? Would he kill for her?

She killed for me…

In the palace dungeons, Mya could have given Lad up to the Grandmaster and become the Twailin guildmaster. Instead, she'd risked her life, fought with him, killed for him.

Because she loved me…

A thump from somewhere above snapped Lad out of his musing.

Talk about Mya's inattention… Spinning on his heel, he slipped out of the wine cellar and up the stairs. The back door, however, presented a problem. Locked and bolted from the inside, he couldn't use it without leaving it unbolted. He'd have to go back upstairs and find an unoccupied room, which was risky, or find a way out down here. Padding back to the kitchen, he examined the two high windows meant for venting heat. Though narrow, they were wide enough for him to slip through. They were also locked, but an unsecured window was less damning than an unbolted door.

The latch opened with only a faint click, but the crank that opened the window squeaked. A drop of oil from a bottle beside the stove silenced it and made the gears rotate easier. Lad cranked the window open, then climbed up onto the iron sink, chinned himself on the windowsill, and pulled down on the window. The mechanism ran backward. *Good!* He'd be able to close the window behind him. There were no sounds from the alley, so he wriggled out, pushed the window closed, and dropped to the cobbles. Hastening to the end of the alley, he flicked a quick signal to Mya, and met her at the downspout she'd used to gain the roof.

"Well?"

"It's a social club above ground. They cater to nobility and provide all manner of entertainment. There's also a concealed door in the wine cellar with guards on the other side. I heard the sounds of an alchemy lab beyond, but I couldn't make out anything in detail, and I couldn't open the door without giving myself away."

"An alchemy lab?" Mya's brow furrowed. "A social club seems more like a cover for an Inquisitor."

"And the woman I followed here was certainly an Inquisitor. Your enemies must be sharing resources. Interesting that they're working in the middle of the night."

"Busy making potions and explosives, I suppose." Mya bit her lip as she thought it over.

"What are you going to do?"

"Keep watching. See if my Hunters can recognize any of Lakshmi or Kittal's people coming or going, and track them to other hideouts. Until Keyfur refines his spell to locate Lakshmi, we can't be sure she's here. This is the only lead we've got."

Mya's forbearance surprised Lad. "You don't want to capture one of their people and interrogate them?"

Mya shook her head. "The last time I did that, I walked into a trap. If we can identify their hideouts, we can hit them all at once, leave them no place to run to. I've got to be sure of a win this time, or I lose everything."

Which means even more killing... But Lad couldn't judge Mya's methods. A decisive end to the conflict might actually save lives in the long run. "I'll watch the rest of the night."

"All right. I'll see you in the morning." Mya hesitated, as if she wanted to say something more, then bit her lip and hurried off down the alley.

Lad watched her go, considering her unmistakable tell. *She's holding back, but what?* Not too long ago he might have been able to guess, but he had no idea what might be going on in this new Mya's head.

Chapter XV

"*Marley's Pub?*" Embree wrinkled his nose. "It's a shithole on the edge of the Downwinds District, not fit for a dog. Why?"

Mya tapped the map on his desk. "Because I need directions. I'm meeting Sergeant Benjamin there tonight."

The Master Hunter looked at her as if she'd asked for his liver. "After dark? You're asking to get your throat cut."

"Rough place?"

"Rough *neighborhood*." He traced a finger along the line that separated the two southern districts. "The edge of the Dreggars Quarter is where Downwinders hunt. They'll cut you open for the stones in your kidneys. You go there, you better be ready for a fight."

Mya didn't want a fight at all. She couldn't take Lad with her; he was watching the social club. Jolee would certainly dissuade any ne'er-do-wells, but she was awfully conspicuous, and Mya didn't want to draw attention either. The only other way to avoid a fight was to look like she had nothing worth stealing. By evening, she had her disguise as good as she could manage, and collected her escort.

"How do I look?" she asked Jolee, fingering the neck of the raggedy canvas jacket. It covered her tattoos and concealed her sex—a precaution against anyone who might think they could take the one thing even penniless women had—and she'd taken special care in applying a thick layer of dirt, both to the clothes and herself.

Jolee wrinkled her prodigious nose. "You look bad and smell *worse*, Grandmaster. Bad enough for *that* neighborhood even."

"Not too much?" She looked down at her grimy bare feet. "I'm worried they won't let me in like this."

"At *Marley's*?" Jolee snorted a laugh. "Show 'em a silver half-crown, and they'd let you in if you'd been dipped in dung."

"Good, then." She led the way out the back of Embree's inn, checking the street before venturing forth. "Follow about half a block behind me, and keep out of trouble while I'm inside."

Jolee fingered her tree-sized cudgel. "I won't start anything, but if trouble comes to me, no promises."

"Fair enough." Mya started off to the south, one hand on the rusty kitchen knife thrust through her rag belt, her bare feet patting the slimy cobbles.

Mya had never been this close to the Downwind Quarter, and saw now that Embree hadn't exaggerated. Hungry eyes watched her, gauging her, assessing the value of what little she had and how much it would cost to take it. These people weren't just poor, they were starving, feral, and desperate. She could see why neither the guild nor the constabulary bothered with the Downwinds; there was nothing here but suffering. She'd asked her urchins about the area, and they'd all just shaken their heads.

"Once you get out, you never go back," Digger had said. "We was livin' high on the hog in the streets compared to them poor buggers."

Mya slunk past hovels, ramshackle tenements, shacks, and even lean-tos, some backed by a tottering edifice of great granite blocks and crumbling mortar. Two centuries ago, the old wall had been city's southernmost border. When Tsing expanded, building a new wall even farther south, the old one was torn down by the denizens for building materials. Some portions of it yet stood, serving as a wall for the sturdier buildings. *Marley's* was one of these.

The pub *did* have four walls and a roof, Mya conceded, though three of the walls were patched together from scrap lumber and the roof was a mishmash of broken tiles, slate, and moldy boards. The front sported no door, just a hanging leather flap. Two wiry fellows with cudgels and sharp eyes flanked the portal. They watched Mya as she approached, eying her slouched, uneven gait.

One of them flicked a hand in a shooing motion. "Off with you, Downwinder. You need money to come in here. No beggars."

"Not a beggar," she said, pitching her voice low. "Got money to spend." She showed them a silver half-crown coin in a grimy palm.

The two exchanged a glance and a shrug. "We catch you begging, you'll leave the worse for it."

"Won't beg." She nodded jerkily, and they let her pass.

The inside wasn't as bad as she'd feared. Granted, the floor was cobbles with filth filling the cracks, but the tops of the stones were swept. A salvaged ship's railing had been fitted with a wide plank to serve as a bar, and the tables were built of old timber or coarse stone. The bartender challenged Jolee for size and intimidation, with intriguing scar patterns etched into skin the hue of midnight, and long braids down his back. A single barmaid wove among the battered tables, serving customers who hunkered over their tankards. A few glanced at Mya and looked away without interest.

Apparently, she fit right in.

Sergeant Benjamin sat in the far corner, his chair leaned back against the wall, his boots on the table, and a tankard propped on his knee. To Mya's surprise, he still wore his constable's uniform, though his iron cap hung from his sword's hilt. She would have thought this neighborhood would chew up constables and spit them out.

As she worked her way toward him, his eyes passed over her without pause, then returned when she stopped right in front of his table. "Good evening, Sergeant." She grinned and leaned closer, lowering her voice. "Nice place you've found here."

"Who the—" His eyes widened and his boots scraped the edge of the table as he dropped his chair. "Criminy! Miss *Moirin*? You look like…uh…" He pushed out a chair with his foot. "Sorry, but I didn't recognize you."

"Kind of the point." She sat down. "You don't want to be seen with me any more than I want to be seen with you."

"Yeah, I get that." He downed his tankard and waved to the server for two more. "Speakin' of not bein' seen, you scared my corporal half into his grave last night, you know."

"It'll teach him to keep a sharper eye out."

"Jorren *is* sharp, but I doubt he would have spotted *you* even if he knew you was there." Benj paused as the server put two tankards on the table. The rough-looking woman palmed the four pennies he proffered and stomped away. Benj pushed one tankard across the table's scarred top and took up his own. "If you want to look like a Downwinder, you better drink up."

Mya sipped the tar-like liquid and stifled a cough. The ale, if that's what it was, tasted like scorched codfish oil and burned her throat.

Benj smiled. "Takes some gettin' used to, but it'll grow hair on your...uh...well..." He covered his gaffe with a pull from his tankard. "Sorry. Forgot who I was talkin' to, proper lady and all."

"Don't worry, Sergeant. I'm not half the lady I pretend to be." She grinned and took another careful sip. It tasted a bit better this time, and the burn settled into an intense warmth in her belly.

"So, tell me what you found out about this woman we're both tracking," Benj said, getting down to business. "Do you know why she visited Dreyfus?"

Mya told him word for word what Lad had overheard.

The sergeant looked dumbfounded. "How the hells did you get all that?"

"I can't reveal my methods, Sergeant." Mya smiled thinly. "What do *you* think about what she told him?"

His thick brow furrowed. "I think it's complete bullshit, and so do you! It also confirms that I was right about that phony *evidence* we found in Otar's room."

Mya nodded. "Bloodhound thought it was suspicious, too. He told me you took it to the palace. What did the emperor say?"

"Took some arguin', but he agreed not to arrest Dreyfus. We're just watchin' him for now. But that bit about Ithross..." Benj shook his head and drank more ale. "No *way* did he kill Otar."

Mya nodded. "True. Hoseph was the only one who could have done it. Otar was alive when his lady friend left, and nobody went into the room after that."

"How do you know—" Sergeant Benjamin held up a hand when Mya opened her mouth to interject. "Oh, never mind. Anyway, if this woman's tryin' to drive a wedge between the palace and the constabulary, it's workin'. Dreyfus must have swallowed her story hook, line, and sinker. He's madder than a wet hen. Yesterday he put a stop to all investigations except for these arsons. Now it makes sense; he's tryin' to get back at Ithross."

Mya blinked in surprise. "Why cancel *all* investigations?"

"Because if he cancelled only the investigations we're cooperatin' with the Imperial Guard on, someone'd sniff it out."

"Makes sense." Mya sipped her ale. "I've given you all I have, Sergeant. Now it's your turn."

"What do you need to know?"

"I don't know much about this social club, and I can't ask too many questions without arousing suspicion." She raised her eyebrows hopefully.

"I'm already lookin' into it, but I'm short-handed. It'll take some time."

"Be careful," Mya warned. "This club's somehow linked to Hoseph and his associates. If they get wind of someone asking questions, they'll bolt."

Benj nodded. "What else?"

"Keep your people away from the club. Follow Dreyfus. Leave Hoseph to me. That way we won't get in each other's way."

The sergeant looked as if he might argue, then tipped his tankard and finished his ale. "Fair enough. If Dreyfus has any more visitors, we'll track 'em down and give you the addresses. If you find out any more about this Miss Rose, you let me know." He looked at Mya's nearly full tankard. "You're not thirsty?"

"It's a bit thick for my taste." She switched tankards with him and smiled. The division of labor would work. "I appreciate the help, Sergeant, but tell your constables this: The people who are working with Hoseph are the same ones who took me. If they catch one of your constables, they'll find out everything they know, then deliver the body to you in fruit jars."

"Understood."

"Good." She started to get up, then hesitated, looking around the pub. "One more question: Why meet here, Sergeant?"

Benj grinned. "Jorren knew I'd be here tonight. I was born in the Dreggars Quarter, so they know me here. I show up to remind 'em that caps aren't all tight arses. Besides, that lad in the corner there can sing like a songbird. Stick around, if you'd like."

Mya turned to see a young man sitting on the back of a chair in the corner, an old lute in his lap, plucking out a tune and humming. People were shifting their seats to watch.

"Maybe once this is all over. Pick a place for our next meeting, one that doesn't require me to dress like a vagrant to get through the door."

"See, I *knew* you was a proper lady." He grinned at her and raised his tankard. "Let's make it *Blue Blake's* in the Wharf District, two days from now."

Mya hid her smile, nodded, and made her way out of *Marley's*. As she pushed aside the leather flap, the minstrel lad struck a pure chord on his lute and began singing with a voice that would bring tears to a critic's eyes. She shook her head in wonder. How strange it was to find pearls of such value in such a vile pub: a minstrel of marked skill, and a constable she felt she could honestly trust. It was too bad the ale tasted like scorched codfish oil.

Spin, kick, lunge, thrust...

Lad whirled low, one leg outstretched. Planting his right palm, he pivoted, tucked, and rolled. In the original sequence, he would have pivoted on his left hand, but his missing fingers affected the balance of that move, so he'd changed it.

Improvisation is the key in the perfection of a fighting style. Remember!

He'd been exercising for a quarter hour, so a light sheen of sweat dampened his skin, and his muscles were loose and limber. It felt good after a frustrating night lying still atop a roof, watching the social club for a woman who never appeared.

The Hunters posted around the club had been busier. When one slipped off to follow someone, another would quickly replace them, undetected by anyone but Lad, or maybe one of Mya's kids. He doubted if the assassins had spotted the urchins, however. They were more impressive than he'd expected. He never would have realized that the waifs panhandling or presumably sleeping in dark doorways were anything but street urchins. Though he still didn't like the thought of using children, he was forced to acknowledge their value. What surprised him most, however, was their devotion to Mya, and hers to them.

A key clicked in the door, but he ignored it. He'd identified Mya's footsteps descending the stairs to the sparring room.

"You didn't wake me." She sounded sullen, but Mya had never been a morning person.

"I didn't have any reason to." He continued his routine, noting the dark circles etched beneath her eyes, her disheveled hair, and puffy face. "I learned nothing new, so I let you sleep."

Mya closed and locked the door, then kicked off her shoes and joined him. It took her a moment to warm up and pick up the cadence, but eventually they moved along in perfect synchrony. Lad didn't slow his pace for her as he had before, and in minutes she was breathing hard, but she kept up.

Lad fell back into the intimately familiar rhythm of the dance. The world around him faded away, all his cares, frustrations, even the stone walls of the sparring room. All that remained were the smooth glide of muscles, the air whispering over his skin, the slap of bare foot or hand against the wooden floor, the beat of his own heart.

And Mya's.

Lad generally exercised alone, preferred it that way. Training his nephews, Tika and Ponce, required an abbreviated version of his Dance of Death, slower and without the acrobatic moves impossible for them. It pleased him to pass on his skills, but those repetitions didn't provide the mental and physical release of the full routine. With Mya, it was different. She didn't need him to hold back or check his movements. She even picked up his modifications; if she missed a move during a first round, she had it down pat during the second. Their seamless synchrony dredged up memories of their journey from Twailin to Tsing, how she'd coaxed him into resuming his exercises when he'd abandoned them in his grief over Wiggens' death.

She saved my life...

With a final whirl and stomp, the sequence ended. Lad was sweating and breathing hard, more from exhilaration than exhaustion.

Mya leaned over, hands on her knees, breathing deep, sweat streaming down her face and soaking her clothes.

Lad eyed her critically. "You're out of shape. You should do this before you go to bed as well. It'll help you sleep."

"Maybe." Her voice was husky from the exertion. "I always seem…to be busy…in the evenings, and when I came back last night…you were still out."

Lad huffed in exasperation. "You don't need me to exercise, Mya. You've always pushed yourself harder than anyone else. Why not now? What's changed? You're not injured. Your body can take it. You *need* it, now more than ever."

Mya jerked up, droplets of sweat flying from her short hair, a shower of tiny diamonds in the lamplight. She glared and opened her mouth as if to rebuke him, then clamped it shut. Closing her eyes, she breathed deep, then nodded and looked at him again. "Thank you. You're the only one who tells me the truth."

"Because you can't kick my ass."

Lad relished her snort of laughter and regarded her for a moment, looking for the caustic sarcasm she so often wore like armor. There was none. He'd take her at her word, then, and give her what she needed. Assuming the first position of the routine, he crooked a finger at her. "Again. I'll slow it down this time."

"No." Mya assumed the stance, her eyes straight ahead, expression determined. "Don't slow the pace. I need you to push me."

They moved as one into the routine, every twist, every turn, every strike, flowing with a synchronicity that made Lad's blood race. *Synergy… Rhythm… Two as one…* Whirling, he suddenly improvised, reaching out to grasp Mya's hand. As if she'd read his mind, Mya leapt, kicking out in a blinding scissor kick as he spun her around. If they'd been encircled by enemies, she'd have cut them down like a scythe. Their grips loosed at the same instant and Mya flew from him, tumbling and kicking off the wall, flipping over his head to land behind him. Back to back now, they resumed the sequence as mirror images, then side by side, then face to face. Again and again, one improvisation after another, following one another perfectly, until the climactic final kick and stomp and—

They stood like statues, inches apart, breathing heavy. Mya looked worn, but her eyes were bright, sharp, intense.

She stepped back with a smile, leaning over again to catch her breath. "That was…amazing."

"Yes." The damp fabric of her shirt clung to her, heaving as she panted, and Lad found his eyes drawn to the strong pulse at her neck, the diamonds of sweat beading there. Watching too long…

Mya stood, caught his gaze, and blinked at him. "What?"

"Nothing." Lad spun on his heel and snatched up a towel to wipe his face. It had been a long time since he'd felt such a sweet, satisfying exhaustion. *Not since Wiggen…*

Shaking his head, he dismissed the thought. *Training with Mya is* not *the same as making love to my wife.*

Still, Lad couldn't shake the feeling. He wasn't a fool; he knew what was happening. He was lonely for companionship, and Mya was, in some way, providing it.

Mya dried vigorously with a towel, her hair spiked like red flames. "Well, I'm ready for a bath. Come to my room for breakfast and I'll tell you what Sergeant Benjamin had to say." With a farewell flip of the hand, she strode out.

Lad watched the closed door, listened to her tread up the stairs, his mind oddly calm.

No, Mya wasn't Wiggen. Nobody ever would be. But…maybe…

Chapter XVI

Hoseph emerged from the Sphere of Shadow to behold the sweaty, flushed features of Chief Magistrate Graving. *As if the transition wasn't nauseating enough...* He dosed himself with elixir to quash the sickness and pain, not bothering to hide the action. The magistrate already knew that using the talisman taxed him.

"What took you so long? I sent a messenger *hours* ago!" Graving's chins quivered as he spoke, a sure sign that he was upset.

"Pay for a better messenger." Hoseph wondered if the man had been drinking. "I'm *not* at your beck and call. Now, what news?"

"It's begun," Graving said. "The emperor informed the senior nobles, his resident knights, military commanders, Chief Constable Dreyfus, and myself this morning that Morrgrey forces have taken several farms and villages in south Twailin province."

"Finally!" It had only been a few days since their visit to Morrgrey, but Hoseph had been champing at the bit for the news to hit Tsing.

"Seems odd to me, though," Graving said. "I have no idea how Arbuckle learned of the incursion so quickly."

Hoseph knew perfectly well how Arbuckle had gotten the news, having been the previous emperor's close confidant. He had counted on it, in fact. "What was his response?"

"He's mobilizing the First and Second Armies. They'll march as soon as preparations are complete. A public announcement will be made tomorrow morning, and the First Army should be on the way around midday. The Second will leave from Miravore as soon as may be. They'll be under the command of Lord ker Mishkall and Sir Fornish."

"So, they should arrive in Twailin in three weeks."

"About that. They're to march with all haste. If they encounter no trouble in the mountains, they'll reach the city in ten or twelve days, at most."

"And their orders once they arrive?"

"What do you *think* their orders are?" Graving sputtered. "If Twailin's walls have been breached, they're to retake the city. If not, they're to break the siege and destroy the sultan's forces. If the Morrgrey retreat, ker Mishkall is to fortify the city while Fornish pursues. Once Twailin is safe, both armies are to advance into Morrgrey and take Tolnyek."

Hoseph's eyebrows shot up. "Take Tolnyek? I didn't expect Arbuckle to have the nerve."

"He recited some godsdamned *history* lesson to us, citing the prevalence of invasions during the first few months of a new reign." The chief magistrate rolled his eyes. "Arbuckle intends to make an example of Morrgrey to discourage others from following suit."

Hoseph pondered the news and nodded. "This will work out well. If the troops are already prepared to continue on to Tolnyek, Tessifus can't be accused of war mongering, but can take the credit for defeating the enemy and ending the war. What about the Third Army?"

"He intends to keep them in the north." Graving's chins doubled in number as he frowned. "The city will be stripped of any fighting forces other than the Imperial Guard, the constabulary, the crews of a few naval vessels, and a few knights and squires."

"And Archmage Keyfur," Hoseph added. He'd never taken particular notice of Keyfur when the mage was merely another member of the Imperial Retinue, but the wizard's defense of Arbuckle during the coronation and his clever spells in the sewers gave Hoseph pause. *He could be trouble.*

"So, what's the plan from here?" asked Graving.

Hoseph smiled coldly. "Leave those details to me, good magistrate. What you don't know, you can't be compelled to reveal. Your task will be to rally the ranking nobles in support of Duke Tessifus once Arbuckle is…deposed."

The chief magistrate didn't look happy, but grunted in acknowledgement.

Without another word, Hoseph flicked the silver skull into his palm and faded into mist, eager to tell Lakshmi and Kittal the good news.

The Empire of Tsing was at war.

As Tsing woke to another sultry summer morning, Lad took a circuitous route home, taking his time, noting each street name and applying it to his mental map of the city. *An assassin can never have too much information about his environment. Remember!* He would never be able to assimilate all of Tsing during his time here, but he filed away streets, buildings, and even people as a matter of course. He had plenty of time to explore this morning. He was in no hurry to report the night's observations to Mya because he had nothing to report. Miss Rose had made no appearance at the social club or its environs...again. Despite his innate patience, he was getting tired of watching night after night for a target that never appeared.

A luscious scent and an empty stomach drew Lad to a street vendor. He waited in the quick-moving line, listening to the banter, watching the vendor slap sausages, fried onions and peppers, and a spicy sauce onto steaming flatbread with practiced movements.

"You, lad?" the olive-skinned man reached for a flatbread, his eyes flicking up expectantly.

Lad suppressed a smile at a distant memory, his first attempt at simple commerce and the misunderstanding that had given him a name. "One. The works. Medium pepper." *So easy...simple...obvious.* His smile faded as he recalled how that first encounter had ended. *Violence...it follows me like a hound.*

The man's hands went through the motions, and Lad handed over three pennies. He continued his route, enjoying the spicy meal and pondering the situation. He'd provided a detailed description of Miss Rose for Embree's Hunters, but none had reported her leaving the social club during the daylight hours either.

So, she's either still holed up inside, has already left wearing a damned good disguise, or there's another way into that room behind the wine rack.

Lad understood Mya's strategy, but the delay galled him. Embree's Hunters had watched for days, tracking innumerable people to other potential hideouts, and still she wanted more information. Without a decisive action soon, this cat-and-mouse game could continue indefinitely.

Which only prolongs my stay in Tsing.

Lad briefly wondered if Mya was stalling just to keep him here, but dismissed the notion. She was a far better tactician than he, and the other masters concurred with her strategy. He would do as he'd promised and help her rid the guild of Lakshmi, Kittal, and Hoseph. He agreed with her there—it was to his benefit as much as hers.

As Lad strode through a broad square, popping the last spicy bite into his mouth and licking the grease from his fingers, a commotion caught his attention. A crowd bustled around one of the many posterboards. Their raised voices, curses, gasps of surprise, and oaths pricked his senses like nettles. He walked over, listening and watching.

"War? Can't be serious!"

"The bastards!"

"Wouldn't trust no Morrgrey as far as I could toss one!"

Lad worked his way to the fore, the hairs rising on the nape of his neck. The poster bore the imperial seal—an official announcement—and the words printed there ignited his every nerve.

Twailin...

Ignoring the protests, he snatched the sheet from the board, slipped through the crowd, and dashed out of the square. Cries of anger and astonishment rang out behind him, and Lad realized he had just made a spectacle of himself. He slowed down, cursing his lapse of caution, and jogged down the hill toward the river at a human pace. Across the Dunmire Bridge and through the bustling streets of the Dreggars Quarter, he arrived at Embree's headquarters sweaty and breathless, not from the run, but from the news he clutched in his hand.

Lad burst into the common room, ignoring the hands that twitched toward weapons. The Hunters knew him now, though they didn't care for this upstart from Twailin.

He stepped up to one Hunter he recognized. "Where is she?"

The woman frowned at him. "Office, but I wouldn't—"

Lad didn't care what she wouldn't do, dashing to Embree's door and thrusting it open without knocking. Before he'd taken two steps into the room, a huge hand clapped onto his shoulder, stopping him cold. *Jolee.* A dozen ways to break her hold and render her unconscious or dead flashed through his mind, but he quelled his reaction. *She's only doing her job.*

"Let him go, Jolee." Mya stood behind the desk with a dagger in her hand. She flashed an irritated look at Lad and slammed the blade back into its sheath. "You should knock."

"Yes, you *really* should!" Noncey tucked a throwing star back into his sleeve. "I could have killed you by accident."

Lad bit back the impulse to tell the Master Blade that he couldn't have killed him on purpose, much less by accident. None of that mattered. Jolee released him and he strode forward, thrusting the flier toward Mya.

"Morrgrey's army has crossed the southern border of Twailin province and is headed toward the city. Tsing is at war! I've got to go back right *now.*"

Mya took the flier, and her eyes flicked back and forth across the page. The masters watched her without a word, strangely calm with the news.

Clemson shook her head and broke the silence. "Morrgrey doesn't have half the military strength of Tsing. What are they thinking?"

"They're not stupid, but it's a stupid move," Noncey argued. "The question is *why?*"

Embree straightened and stretched. "At least our courier got out before the army. Guildmaster Sereth will have some advanced warning of the army's arrival. It's going to put a damper on profits for a while."

"Courier?" Lad blinked in surprise.

Mya remained silent, her gaze still on the bulletin, but she wasn't reading; her eyes weren't moving. Then she brushed an errant strand of hair behind her ear.

Lad recognized the gesture and stiffened. "You already *knew* about this!"

Mya's eyes flicked up, the muscles of her jaw bunching and relaxing rhythmically, her lips slightly pursed. She was angry, but he didn't care.

"You *knew*, and you kept it from me?" Heat flushed his skin, but he clenched his fists against the rising magic. "Mya, this isn't *my* godsdamned war! I've got to *go*! You can't keep me here!"

"I don't care who the hell you are," Embree snapped. "In *my* headquarters, you speak to the Grandmaster with respect, or I'll—"

"Calm *down*, everyone!" Mya barked, her eyes hard. "I need to speak to Bloodhound alone, so if the rest of you would excuse us…"

The three masters stood, their faces set in stone, and silently filed out.

"You, too, Jolee," Mya ordered, waiting until the door closed before rounding on Lad. "Don't *ever* barge in here and question me in front of my people!" Her voice was low but shook with anger. "My hold on the guild is *tenuous*! The last thing I need is you undermining my authority."

Classic Mya, lashing out, shifting blame to anyone but herself. But he wasn't going to play her game. He leaned on the desk and stared her straight in the eye. "You can't keep me here."

"I'm not *keeping* you here. I'm working out the details." She spat out the words like venom. "I only learned about this last night, and if you haven't noticed, I've been *busy*." She waved to the map pinned on the wall, festooned with notes and markings.

Lad wasn't about to let her change the subject. "I need you to contact Keyfur to arrange transportation. I can't stroll into the palace myself and ask for the archmage."

"All right! I'll send a message, but don't get your hopes up." She took a breath, controlling her anger. "With a war brewing, Keyfur's probably busy, and I imagine Duke Mir's wizard is up to his eyeballs. I can't *command* them to take you home."

As Mya shuffled through the papers on the desk, found a blank piece of parchment, and penned a note, Lad considered his options. She was right, war would preclude his needs. He could grab a horse and leave, but even riding day and night it would take at least a week to reach Twailin, and he'd have to change horses, avoid trouble and the Tsing army, and traverse the mountains. Too much could go wrong. He'd wait for Keyfur's answer, then decide.

Mya folded the note, scrawled something on the outside, and sealed it with wax, then went to the door, opened it, and gave it to Jolee. "Have a messenger deliver this immediately." She whirled and strode past him, still obviously upset, but no longer livid.

Lad took a deep, calming breath. *Patience.* "Thank you."

"You're welcome. Now go away." Mya took up a stiff stance behind the desk, her back to him, her eyes fixed on the map of Tsing. "I'm busy with guild business, and you're not guild."

Thank the gods for that. Lad went to the door, but stopped with his hand on the latch. "By the way, there was still no sign of Miss Rose last night."

"Thank you." Mya didn't even look at him.

Fine...be pissed off. Lad walked out past the masters and Jolee, ignoring their cold stares. He headed down to the basement. Exercise might relieve some of his anxiety, but he doubted it. The only thing that mattered was getting back to Lissa before war reduced his home to rubble.

"Hell of a time for a godsdamned war," Benj muttered as he and Jorren watched the First Army march past.

"Is there ever a *good* time for a war?" Jorren asked.

"I suppose not, but *damn...*" Benj spat into the gutter, swallowing several more inventive curses. There were too many people about, cheering on the departing army, throwing flowers and ribbons. He didn't want some hothead to misunderstand his ire. "We were stretched thin already. Every day we've got more fires and vandalism, and now they yank away our help? It'll make our jobs *twice* as hard! As if dealin' with Dreyfus ain't enough punishment."

Pulling double duty to keep an eye on the chief constable had put him in a sour mood. At least it was Jorren's turn to watch tonight.

The corporal's attention turned to a tight phalanx of cavalry coming up behind the foot soldiers. The massive warhorses pranced, slamming plate-sized hooves down on the cobbles. The leader, a gray-haired but robust knight, smiled and waved at the cheering crowds. His five squires, however, stared forward, grim faced. One, a flaxen-haired woman who looked far too young to be going to war, fairly glared as she fought to keep her recalcitrant mount under control.

"Look on the bright side!" Benj clapped his corporal on the shoulder. "You could be strapped to half a ton of nasty horsemeat for a three-week forced march, lookin' forward to nothin' but fightin' an army of pissed-off Morrgrey when you get there!"

Jorren smiled morosely and shrugged. "Sarge, do you think this might all be connected?"

"What connected?"

"The unrest in the city and the war in Twailin." Jorren scratched his jaw. "Like you said, the timing couldn't be worse."

"Could be." Benj frowned. "Morrgrey spies stirrin' up trouble in the city to tie up the army, then sendin' word back to their sultan. It'd sure make an invasion easier. Tough decision for the emperor, but if he kept the army here to help put down the violence, he might as well hand over Twailin."

Jorren's eyes left the column as the knight and his squires rode out of sight. "But *think*, Sarge," Jorren said in a lower voice. "What if it's the other way around? What if the Morrgrey invaded to lure the army out of Tsing? That would make it easier for whoever's inciting all this violence, wouldn't it?"

"A civil war?" Benj eyed the corporal and scowled. "Damn it, Jorren, as if I didn't have *enough* to worry about!"

Mya stomped up the steps into the carriage and flung herself into the cushioned seat. She'd tried all morning to banish her foul mood, but anger at Lad's selfish desire to abandon her had been stoked by Keyfur's prompt reply to her request for a meeting. The vehicle jostled as Lad boarded, but she refused to look at him. Couldn't he see that she needed his help if she was to have any hope of survival?

Need his help or just need him? Her conscience continued to battle with her heart, worsening her mood. *This isn't his war, Mya. You can't make him stay.*

The hackney lurched into motion. The drawn curtains cast the interior in a diffuse light, hopefully enough to hide the flush of her temper.

"You're still angry," he said.

Or maybe not... "And you're observant." She wasn't about to explain herself.

"You can't expect me to stay when my family's in danger, Mya."

"I don't."

"Of course you do."

Her temper flared. "No, I *don't*. I need your help, so I would *like* you to stay. That doesn't mean I *expect* you to! And don't assume you know what I'm thinking!"

He didn't respond, which was just as well. The carriage ride to the palace took longer than normal, delayed to avoid the departing army and the crowds of citizens bidding the soldiers farewell. She spent each extra minute in misery; this could be the last time they saw each other, but Mya clung to her anger, and Lad to his steadfast resolve to leave. By the time they reached the palace gate, the angry silence and claustrophobic atmosphere of the carriage had Mya's nerves as tight as harp strings.

"Miss Moirin." The guard at the palace gate nodded respectfully. "Master Keyfur is expecting you."

"Thank you." She drew the drapes back, grateful for a breath of fresh air.

To her surprise, the inner courtyard was virtually deserted. She'd assumed the palace would be a beehive of activity with a war brewing, but nothing looked different. *As if war's a normal thing.* The thought gave her chills.

Mya drew her daggers, placing them on the seat beside her. Lad never carried weapons. *He is a weapon. And he's leaving...* Stepping down from the carriage, she headed for the now-familiar postern door.

The lieutenant in charge gestured her through. "Welcome back, Miss Moirin. This way if you please."

My recognized the woman's piercing eyes beneath the rim of her helm. "Thank you, Lieutenant Tanse."

Inside, they stopped and submitted to the usual search. How odd that this was so routine now: catching a carriage to the palace; being greeted by imperial guards who knew her name, and greeting them in return; being escorted through the gilded passages to an appointment with the emperor or archmage.

Almost as if I truly belong here...

Through the corridors they passed until Lieutenant Tanse stopped at a nondescript door and knocked. The door opened immediately, and Master Keyfur's melodic voice sounded from within.

"Come in, Miss Moirin! Come in!"

Mya entered, then stopped so quickly that if Lad had not possessed preternatural reflexes, he would have bowled into her. "Oh, dear *gods*," she muttered as she gazed about.

Keyfur's chamber literally crawled with magic. The central rug writhed with runes so similar to her own tattoos that she had to look away. Across the room, a low table crawled on four lion's feet to an open spot amongst several deeply upholstered chairs, then froze in place. Pictures on the walls changed scenes, and knickknacks on shelves moved as if alive, one doll turning its tiny head to watch the two visitors, its blank eyes eerily aware.

Mya had been to the runemage Vonlith's home many times and had seen his collections of magical paraphernalia. That had seemed akin to a museum, while this was more like a menagerie. She was afraid to move for fear something would pounce upon her.

"Please, Miss Moirin, do come in." Keyfur raised a small glass ball in one hand as he approached. Inside the ball, a severed finger floated in liquid. "Come, come, nothing here will hurt you. Master Bloodhound, please join us."

Mya steeled her nerves and stepped forward, trying to ignore how the disembodied finger in the sphere followed her every move. Wizards were a curious lot, to be sure, but that was simply macabre.

Keyfur prattled on. "Your timing is impeccable; I was just about to send a message when I received yours. How did you know I'd solved the interference problem with my location spell?"

Mya's heart leapt. "I didn't, but that *is* good news!" Grinning, she glanced at Lad, but his blank expression reminded her of the reason for their visit. *Of course, he only wants to go home...* "We *actually* came to you for another reason entirely. My associate feels that, with the pending war, he needs to get back to Twailin. I realize that the needs of the empire surpass those of individuals. If you or Duke Mir's wizard are unable to spare the time, we can arrange—"

"Time?" Keyfur waved them to chairs. A platter of pastries and a blackbrew service now rested on the previously empty table. "Time is no problem. Please, sit and have a cup and a nibble. Preparations in Twailin are well in hand. Though I can make no promises, I believe Master Woefler could flick over here and back any time you wish. But why the rush?"

"The *war...*" Lad said, his tone incredulous. "Twailin is my home. I have...interests there that I have to see to."

"Oh, not to worry! Morrgrey's armies won't arrive in the city for weeks, at least. Duke Mir is still organizing evacuations of the southern counties." The wizard pulled the feather from behind his ear and waved it at the blackbrew service. The pot floated up to fill three cups. "Please, have something."

Mya lightened her blackbrew with fresh cream and helped herself to a lemon pastry, but Lad just sat there with his hands clenched, staring at first her, then the wizard. She sighed inwardly. Even now, he would brook no delay.

"Well, I'm sure you understand my associate's concern."

"Oh, of *course*. I'll send Master Woefler a message straightaway and ask him when he can arrange to come."

"*Thank* you." Lad said, his relief palpable.

Mya ignored him, her mind spinning ahead. If Keyfur had the location spell figured out, they could hunt down Lakshmi and end the guild war. She'd like Lad to be along on that raid, especially if they ran into Hoseph, but how could she convince him to stay? He was already suspicious of her motives, so she'd have to choose her words carefully.

"So preparations in Twailin are already underway? I imagine Duke Mir's been doing everything possible to fortify the city."

"Oh, yes!" Keyfur bit into a berry tart and sipped his blackbrew. "If the Morrgrey try to take Twailin, it'll be costly. Duke Mir's enlisted the aid of the Wizards Guild, and the city guard is forming a citizens' militia. They've already got over five hundred signed up."

Mya considered how Sereth and his assassins might apply their expertise to the defense of the city; their contribution could be significant. *If it's coordinated with the city defenses. But how...*

"When you send a message to Master Woefler, would you also send one to an associate of mine? I have old friends in the city who could help with the defense effort." Lad had told her of the unorthodox alliance between Sereth and captain of the Royal Guard. "Perhaps Captain Norwood would deliver it for me?"

"I'm sure he'd see to the delivery," Lad said, then looked to Keyfur. "I'd like to send a message of my own so that my...interests know I'm going to return as soon as possible."

"Of course!" Keyfur waved his feather, seemingly unconcerned. "But since you're here, let me test my modifications to the location spell. It'll only take a few minutes."

"Absolutely!" Mya bridled her excitement, or tried to. "The sooner we eliminate Hoseph and his associates, the sooner *everyone* will sleep easier." She cocked an eyebrow at Lad. "Right?"

He regarded her with poorly veiled suspicion. "That's true."

"Please go ahead, then, Master Keyfur."

"Excellent!" Keyfur finished his pastry and stood, suddenly bubbling with enthusiasm. "The problem, as you know, is interference. Location spells must be keyed to a specific person, but in this case, we're working with two people who share...um... attributes. The only other similar instance I've read of was in a case of identical twins." He retrieved a small wooden box, placed it on the table, and removed the lid. "I solved the problem with gold, of course."

"Gold?" Mya peered over the edge of the box. Tucked inside the gold-plated interior sat a cradle fashioned from gold wire atop her wrappings.

"Yes. Gold blocks certain magical energies, you see." The archmage placed the glass sphere with the finger inside in the wire stand and replaced the box lid, which had a hole in the center. He removed a small cover from another hole in one of the box's sides. "With this design, the box should shield the spelled sphere from you, and we can look for your culprit by directing the aperture in a search pattern." He demonstrated, turning the box this way and that. Mya leaned closer to peer through the hole atop the box.

"Um, it's pointing up."

"You can't watch," Keyfur chided. "It defeats the purpose of shielding."

"Can you position it so I'm blocked, then direct the aperture around?"

"Yes, that's what I planned..." Keyfur motioned her to get behind him, then looked down into the box. Holding it in front of him, he turned slowly while Mya shuffled sideways to maintain position behind him. "That seems to be doing the trick. It's pointing toward the city now."

"That little dance will be difficult to manage in a carriage," Lad pointed out, "and walking the street doing that is likely to get you killed."

Mya frowned at him. "That's a good point. We'll *have* to use a carriage, and you'll have to point the aperture in various directions."

"But if you're too close to the box..." Keyfur swung around and glared down at the device. "Yes, the thing just points up at the top aperture." Keyfur worried his lip in thought. "I know you want to go along on this search, Miss Moirin, but..."

"Going without me is *not* an option." *Lakshmi and Kittal are* mine! *I'm not going to be cheated out of this.*

"What if you added tubes to the two holes?" Lad suggested.

Keyfur blinked at him, his smile blazing. "That's *brilliant*! It'll restrict the angle of interference! I think that might just work."

"How long will it take you to modify the device?" Mya asked nervously. *If we could find Lakshmi before Lad leaves...*

Keyfur inspected the ceiling as he pondered his answer. "A day or two should be sufficient, I think."

Mya looked imploringly at Lad. "If Master Woefler isn't pressed for time, he can have you back in Twailin in a blink. Can you to stay a couple of days? Without your help, facing Hoseph and the others will be much more dangerous. If we fail..."

Lad's face might have been carved from marble for all the expression it showed.

He's thinking it through, Mya realized. *Think of your family, Lad... If we don't kill Hoseph...*

Lad frowned, then finally nodded. "I'll stay to help, but *only* if all's well in Twailin and Master Woefler agrees to take me back promptly when I need to go."

The weight of the world lifted off Mya's shoulders. "Thank you." She nodded to the archmage. "And thank *you*, Master Keyfur. We'll go so you can see to your tasks. Just send a message when you have news."

"Oh, I will. And here." Keyfur pulled a couple of pieces of parchment and quill pens from a desk drawer and handed them over. "Write your messages. I'll send them on, then get to work on this." He flicked the box with a finger.

They dashed off their notes and handed them over, thanking the wizard again before leaving. Mya concentrated on not bouncing with elation as they followed their escort through the palace. *With Lad's help, I've got a chance.* She couldn't keep a cold smile of vengeance from her lips as they boarded the carriage and she recovered her daggers.

I'm coming for you, Lakshmi…and I'm going to carve my runes from you with these very blades.

210

Chapter XVII

Less like you're for sale and more like you're just so pretty you can't stand yourself. Mya flounced into the pub with a bounce in her step, pursed lips, and a pang in her heart. *Dee taught me that.* His fate, if he was still alive in Lakshmi's hands, yawned like a pit inside her. *Focus, Mya! Dee's gone, and you're alive. Try to stay that way!*

Her entrance drew few passing glances. The Midtown pub wasn't nearly as rough as *Marley's*, and a slumming lordling wasn't uncommon, much less interesting.

Benj sat at a corner table, chair tilted back, tankard balanced on his knee, the same posture she'd seen before. He spotted her before she reached his table this time. He was probably expecting a disguise, and recognizing her dressed as a fop was easier than piercing the Downwinder getup.

"Constable," she said in a breathy voice, brushing off the chair with a lace handkerchief before sitting down.

"You're gonna damage my reputation dressed like that," he muttered, waving the barmaid over.

"Oh, stop." She flicked his shoulder with the handkerchief and tucked it away. "Wine, my good woman, something not *too* brutish." She produced a gold crown and set it on the table.

"Right away, milord." The barmaid curtsied and raised an eyebrow at Benj. "Another for you, Sergeant?"

"Hells, yes, Macie, but just one. I'm workin'. Oh, and the good lord's buyin'." Benj downed his ale and belched with impressive volume.

Macie took his tankard with a chuckle and left.

"No need to be disgusting," Mya murmured.

211

"Sure there is. I'm a disgusting person." He grinned at her with tobacco-stained teeth. "I'm serious about the outfit, though. I don't generally consort with blue bloods. Couldn't you have dressed like a trollop or somethin'?"

"No, I couldn't." Trollops generally displayed a good bit of cleavage, and her tattoos precluded that. "Sorry I missed our last meeting, but I've been busy."

"You missed our last *two* meetings, but I've been pretty busy myself, and not sleepin' half as much as I should." Benj always looked rough, unshaven, unwashed, and slovenly, but now he sported the red-rimmed eyes and sallow cheeks of fatigue.

"Have you learned anything about the social club?"

"Yep. Private club owned by a fella named Toffin, but he rarely goes there. Always at his townhouse on the other side of the Heights or his estate in the country. He's *stupid* rich, but has no title." He pulled a crumpled piece of parchment from a pocket and handed it to her under the table. "His address, and two others for our mystery lady. She visited Dreyfus twice more, but didn't go back to the social club. Once she went to a house in the Heights, and once to an inn in Midtown."

"Thanks." Mya glanced at the note before tucking it away.

Macie returned with Benj's ale and a bottle of wine. She presented the bottle, drew the cork, and poured a dram into the glass, which Mya sampled, leaving a smudge of lip rouge on the rim. At her nod, Macie filled the glass.

Mya handed over the gold crown. "That should keep the constable's tankard full for the afternoon, I think. The rest is for you."

"Thank you, milord." Macie curtsied with a smile, left the bottle, and hurried off.

"You're gonna stick out like an ogre at a court ball if you tip like that," Benj warned.

"That's fine." She flicked a hand dismissively and sipped her wine. It was quite good. "If anyone asks, tell them I'm from out of town. So, is this Toffin a shady sort?"

"Nope, he's squeaky clean. The club's aboveboard, members only, and *really* exclusive." Benj shook his head. "Hell, I can't even get a list of members."

Mya's Hunters had identified many of those who came and went from the building, from the high-society clients to the cooks, servers, and high-priced whores who serviced the rich with all manner of distractions. They'd also tracked numerous Alchemists and Inquisitors throughout the city, identifying potential headquarters for Lakshmi and Kittal. In fact, she'd recognized one of the addresses from Benj's list. There'd been no sign, though, of the masters themselves.

And no word from Keyfur yet. He was taking his sweet time modifying his tracking device. Lad was anxious, moody, and eager to go home.

"But this Miss Rose… I can't get a thing on her, and her visits are takin' their toll on Dreyfus. He's been as nervous as a long-tailed cat in a room full of rockin' chairs." Benj drank more ale, his face grim. "He busted a sergeant down to private this mornin' for tryin' to wrap up a case that had nothin' to do with the arsons."

"Interesting." Mya had been too busy lately to think much about Dreyfus. That lapse might be dangerous; there was certainly a connection between Miss Rose and the rogue assassins. Hoseph was the link, though how or why, she had no idea. "Has Dreyfus said anything to shed some light on what she's been telling him? Anything about Ithross or Hoseph?"

Benj shook his head. "Nah. Keeps to his office mostly. Only comes out to bitch that we're not workin' hard enough. Problem is, as soon as we start investigatin' one disturbance, another pops up. We lost our help when the army left, and we're runnin' ragged." He took a long pull of ale. "But enough about my woes. Have you discovered anything watchin' that club?"

Mya twiddled her fingers dismissively. "The obvious: sex, drugs, and gambling. Nothing to do with Dreyfus. We've tracked a few people who weren't blue bloods or working there, but we can't find the ringleaders, and we can't move until we do." At his raised eyebrows, she demurred. "This ties in to the mission the emperor has tasked me with. Sorry, but I can't say any more."

Benj didn't look at all happy, but he was used to keeping secrets. "Somethin's gonna break soon. I can feel it in my gut."

"So can I." She worried her lip. "I should get a line on the ringleaders soon. Then we can strike."

"Well don't expect any help from my caps! With those uppity up clients, we couldn't raid the place even if we *knew* it was full of traitors."

Good! Mya had hoped he wouldn't insist on some kind of joint effort. "Don't worry, my people can handle it. When we do, the arsons should stop."

"Can't happen soon enough for me."

"Me either." Mya smiled and pushed another gold coin across the table as she rose. "Thank you, Sergeant."

Benj scowled and pushed the coin back. "I don't take money but from the emperor's paymaster. I'm no snitch."

Mya pocketed the coin with a bow, her opinion of the man rising again. Who would expect intelligence, loyalty, and honesty in such a ragtag package? *That's his secret,* she supposed. *Always being underestimated. Not a bad strategy.*

Mya flounced out of the pub and up the street. Jolee had a carriage waiting only a couple of blocks away. The day was clear and stifling hot, but it had been a long time since she'd been out and about the city. She felt divorced from its rhythms. Her disguise was good, and walking helped her think. As always, she had too many questions and not enough answers: *Where could Lakshmi and Kittal be holed up? Why were they torching buildings and inciting violence? What was the link between Dreyfus, Hoseph, and Miss Rose?*

And how can I stop Lad from leaving?

A carriage clattered up the street behind her, which wouldn't have caught her attention except that the horses' hoofbeats shifted from a trot to a walk as the driver slowed his team to come up beside her. She fished a tiny mirror from her waistcoat, ostensibly to check her lip rouge. The carriage was a common hackney, and she didn't recognize the driver.

Heat flushed through her as the carriage door started to open, magic and panic in a jolt like lightning along her nerves. Had someone pierced her disguise or spotted the distinctive Jolee? Did Benj's deceptive appearance and helpful demeanor conceal a betrayal?

She tucked the mirror away and twitched her wrists. The daggers concealed in the lacy sleeves of her brocade jacket dropped into her hands. *Never again...* Every muscle tense, Mya prepared to fight to the death. *They'll never take me alive again...*

The coach came alongside.

"Mya!" The call was quiet, but clear...and familiar.

Mya whirled to face the carriage and the figure bracing the door open with a maimed hand.

"Get in," Lad said. "Keyfur's ready."

Kittal held up two vials. "Now remember: the blue is for you, the red for the boy. If you reverse them, well..."

"I'm not a fool!" Hoseph snatched the vials and tucked them into his belt. "You're sure the potions work?"

"I'm not a fool either!" The Master Alchemist sneered back at him. "Of course they work. We tested them last night. You should have an hour at the very least."

"That should be sufficient." Hoseph turned to Lakshmi. "And everything *else* is ready?"

"Yes, of course. If Dreyfus doesn't come through as we hope, we've got someone who will. *Timing* will be critical, however."

"I'm aware of that." They'd reviewed the plan a dozen times, working out every contingency. Still, Hoseph was the one walking into a dragon's den here. How many other plans had they thought flawless, only to have them fall through? How many times had he been confident of success, only to have unimaginable failure thrown in his face? An image of Tynean Tsing II, dead on the cold stone floor in a puddle of his own blood, fleeted through his mind before he forcibly dismissed it. Lad and Mya couldn't interfere this time. How ironic, then, that Mya would be the heart-blood of their effort.

"Chief!" A corporal burst into the constabulary headquarters, breathless and sweating.

Benj looked up wearily. *What the hell now?* The reports of violence had become so frequent, some caps didn't even pause their conversations. Personally, he was fighting to keep his eyes open. *Shouldn't have had that second tankard...*

The corporal dashed between the close-packed desks, jostling several and leaving a wake of spilled blackbrew, strewn paperwork, and cursing constables. "Chief Dreyfus! We got real trouble in Midtown, down near the wharves!"

"What now?" Dreyfus burst through his open office door like a grim thunderstorm. "Blendell, calm the hells down! Give me specifics! How bad—"

"Couple hundred Dreggars and Downwinders are riotin'. They got clubs, torches, axes, whatever they can get their hands on. They're throwin' cobbles, torchin' shops, and beatin' folks down! Sergeant Keeson's got four squads tryin' to hem them in and push them back across the river, but he's flanked and havin' to pull back."

"Benjamin, call in all Midtown and Heights squads! Pull in the Wharf patrols, too. Get everyone on this!" Dreyfus cinched his sword belt tight. "We'll drive those rabble-rousers back into the slums where they belong!"

Benj was already on his feet and moving, shouting orders, the haze of fatigue banished by a heady rush of urgency. As his messengers dashed out, he turned to his commander. "We're short of caps, sir! If this is as bad as Blendell says, we'll need more bodies. We could send a rider to the palace to request help from the Imperial Guard. Cavalry would sure be useful."

"You'll do no such *thing*!" The chief constable's face flushed, veins distending from his neck and spittle flecking his lips. "We don't need Ithross and his band of pampered milksops! Protecting the city is *my* responsibility. Let Ithross cower behind the palace walls and rot. I will *not* have him on my streets."

Benj stepped back, startled at the chief's reaction.

"Yes...sir." Benj turned away, shared an astonished look with Jorren. Had Dreyfus taken Miss Rose's ominous warning so deeply to heart that he'd risk his own caps rather than call in help from Ithross? The sergeant felt a twinge of guilt. *Maybe I should have told him she was full of shit.* But it was too late now.

Jorren jerked his head toward the door and whispered, "Do you want me to go to the palace anyway?"

"Hells, no!" Benj hissed. "He'll have us both in the lockup...or *worse.*"

The sergeant looked around at the bustling constables. There was order in the seeming chaos as some caps handed out shirts of mail and others distributed weapons. They knew their jobs and, by the gods, they'd do them to the utmost of their ability. "We can handle a riot. I just hope we can handle Dreyfus. He's headed for the edge. Keep an eye on him, will you?"

"Sure, Sarge." Jorren went to take a shirt of mail.

"Blendell! Where is he?" Benj scanned the crowd; the corporal was the only firsthand source of information they had.

"He scooted." Tobas pointed to the door. "Gone back to the fight, I guess."

"Mail, Sarge?" asked a corporal, holding out a heavy shirt of rings.

"Nah, I'm good." At Jorren's raised eyebrow, Benj patted his belly. "Tight around the middle. Too many tankards and pork pies. I'll be okay."

Dreyfus strode out of his office, resplendent in his own shirt of chain mail, bellowing loud enough to scatter constables like feathers in a tornado. "LET'S MOVE!"

Jorren cast his sergeant a wary glance, and Benj shrugged. There was nothing to do but follow their commander's orders. Their job was to keep the peace, and keep it they would.

Lad peered out through the narrow gap in the drapes, then at his companions. Keyfur hunched over his tracking device, his eye glued to the golden tube that protruded from the top, slowly moving the box back and forth, up and down. Mya sat scrunched in the corner, as far as she could get from the golden tube protruding from the front of the box. She'd insisted they go straight to the palace without stopping for her to change, and looked a little foolish in her brocade jacket and silk breeches. She'd removed the curly blonde wig and scrubbed off the makeup so the palace guards would recognize her, leaving her red hair disheveled and damp with sweat. Her expression shifted between anxiety, excitement, and nervousness, her garishly painted nails clicking together.

After taking a careful sighting from the palace, they quickly focused their search on the Heights and Midtown districts. For the past hour they'd been rolling through the streets in a narrowing search pattern. Lad watched the now-familiar scenery, tracing their route on the map in his head.

I wonder…

"I believe we're getting closer." Keyfur waved one hand without looking up from his device. "Turn left."

Mya thumped the roof of the carriage. "Left!"

They'd barely rounded the corner when Keyfur held up a hand again. "Wait! Stop!"

"What's the matter?" Lad asked as the carriage lurched to a stop.

"It's pointing…" Keyfur moved from one seat to the other, nearly sitting in Lad's lap, aiming the box this way and that, then finally tilting it. "It's pointing down!"

"Moirin." Lad peered out the window again. "Recognize the area?"

Mya peeked out between the curtains. "I don't believe it. We're only a block away."

"Away?" The wizard looked at her askance. "Away from what?"

"From a place we've been watching for *days*." Muscles bunched at Mya's jaw. "If we'd only known… Are you *sure*?"

"*Quite* sure, Miss Moirin." Keyfur sounded affronted.

Lad had a more pragmatic question. "Is it moving or stationary?"

The archmage stared into his little tube. "It doesn't appear to be moving. And it's pointing just…there!" He pointed down toward the back of the carriage. "As when we were searching for Miss Moirin, our target is definitely subterranean, though I can't say for sure if we—"

A pure musical note interrupted the wizard.

Lad tensed, ready to burst out of the carriage if need be. "What was that?"

"A summons." Keyfur put the box down and fished a crystal from a pocket. It pulsed a dull red color in the dim light. "Oh, my… Something dire has happened at the palace. I'm afraid I must hurry back."

"*Now?*" Mya's eyes widened and she shook her head rapidly. "No! We've just found the—"

"I'm *sorry*, Miss Moirin, but I must insist that you both get out of the carriage. I have to attend the emperor immediately!" The wizard's tone booked no argument, more serious than Lad had yet heard from the usually jovial fellow.

"You're going to *dump* us here?" Hysteria honed Mya's tone.

"Moirin." Lad put a hand on her knee. "We can do this without Master Keyfur, but we can't delay. We know where she is *at this moment*. If we wait, we could lose her."

"That's not the *plan!*" she insisted. "We've got a dozen other locations mapped. We've got to hit them all at once to prevent Hoseph from just blinking them away like he did before. I have to assign team leaders, position people, arrange backup contingencies." Her nails clicked incessantly. "We *know* the device works, so once Master Keyfur has resolved his problem with the emperor, we'll track her down again and—"

"No." Lad pulled his hand away. "I can't wait. The *war* won't wait. Either we do this now, or you do it without me."

Her teeth chirped as she ground them together. "I…suppose, but we can't just jump out of the carriage in broad daylight! They probably have people *watching*."

"Oh, I can fix *that!*" Keyfur pulled the feather from behind his ear. "Now, it's best if you clasp hands. Once you're invisible, you won't be able to see each other…obviously."

"Invisible?" Mya's eyes widened, but she did nothing to stop Keyfur as he swept the feather in a glittering arc, lightly touching them both.

Lad grasped Mya's hand as she started to fade from sight. "Thank you, Master Keyfur! We'll be in touch!" He opened the carriage door and pulled Mya out onto the street. The door slammed, and the carriage rumbled off.

"*Fantastic!*" Mya hissed in his ear, her breath faintly scented with wine. "Now what?"

"Now we go in and finish this. We'll use the secret entrance through the wine cellar." Lad tugged her in the direction of the social club, deftly dodging passersby.

"Alone? Are you mad? The place is full of assassins!" She tugged him to a stop.

"Alchemists and Inquisitors, not Blades and Enforcers." He pulled her to the side of the street to avoid a noisy group of well-bred young ladies strolling by, then continued on.

"But they're *still* assassins! We don't know how many there are."

"No, but you've already put a dent in their numbers and, as you said, they're scattered over a dozen hideouts." He squeezed her sweaty hand reassuringly, guiding her into the alley behind the social club. "We're *invisible*, Mya! We'll take out their guards before they even know we're there. This is the chance you've been waiting for!"

"But I'm not what I was, Lad. I'm not *invulnerable* anymore!"

Even without seeing Mya's face, Lad sensed her fear through the quaver in her voice and the tremble of her grasp. If they were to succeed here, he had to help her focus...and he knew how to do that.

He stopped and pulled her close. "You never *were* invulnerable, Mya. You can die. *I* can die. Lakshmi can die...and she's *here*. She's yours for the taking, but *you've* got to do it! You might never have a second chance!"

Mya's clenched his hand hard, and Lad knew he'd hit the mark. Nothing worked so well to banish Mya's fear as anger.

"Lakshmi and Kittal *will* die..." Her voice was so low that normal ears wouldn't have heard her.

"No fear, Mya."

"No fear," she agreed, her voice steadier, stronger now. "No pain. No mercy."

No mercy. Lad steeled himself. He didn't want to kill anyone, but if that was what he had to do to get home to Lissa and make her safe, so be it.

He pulled her onward, and they stopped at the back door. The clatter of pots and pans sounded from within. "Now all we need do is get through a barred door and past—"

Something banged on the other side of the door, and it opened. A man wearing an apron and holding several empty baskets stepped out.

"See you on the morrow, Mrs. Vexford," he called to the thin woman holding the door open.

"Bright and early this time, Mr. Smythe." She waved a ladle at his back. "And don't you forget my parsnips! I'll not answer if you…"

Lad tugged Mya's hand, and the two assassins slipped past the nagging cook. *Good thing she's skinny!* He pulled Mya into the scullery, their footfalls a whisper. They flattened themselves against the wall to evade a maid headed for the kitchen with a bag of flour, then the way was clear. Down the stone stairs he crept, Mya on his heels. The door to the wine cellar wasn't locked, and they eased inside.

"Well, *that* was easier than I dreamed possible," Mya whispered.

"Yes." Lad guided her through the wine racks to the one that concealed the hidden passage. "Now for the hard part."

Chapter XVIII

Hoseph held the vials Kittal had given him in the wedge of light slanting through the gap in the carriage drapes and shook them, watching the liquid slosh about inside. His future—the future of the empire—resided inside these small vessels. He placed them carefully on the seat beside him and sighed. *Patience...* The wait was wearing on him.

The rattle of wheels on cobbles drew his attention, and he peered out. His carriage was parked beside the main thoroughfare to the palace, a good place to hide in plain sight, amongst the dozens of other carriages carrying gentry to the pinnacle of the Heights District. A nondescript carriage rumbled by, straight for the closed palace gates.

Don't bother, he thought. Several carriages had already pulled up and been sent away. Usually open during the day, the gates had been shut soon after the arrival of a constable on horseback riding hells-for-leather.

This carriage stopped so quickly that the horses pawed and snorted. Curiously, instead of ordering the driver away, the guard gestured, and the gates opened. The carriage lurched forward, and the portal closed behind.

So they're not closed to everyone. Hoseph had no idea who the privileged passenger was, but it was reassuring that someone had been allowed to pass; his plan depended on it.

Trumpets blared, startling him, and he peered carefully out the window.

The palace gates were flung wide, and Captain Ithross rode forth atop a pale warhorse. Behind him followed two mounted standard bearers, their banners fluttering in the breeze, and rank upon rank of mounted imperial guards, all fully armed and armored, their horses stepping high.

Yes! Hoseph couldn't suppress a grin of satisfaction.

The contingent passed through the gate at a trot, drawing stares from nobles and passersby. Hoseph counted the ranks until the last one cleared the gate. Ithross raised a hand, and they broke into a thunderous canter, the crash of hooves reverberating from the surrounding buildings.

Finally! Lakshmi's plan had worked. The emperor's security forces now numbered dozens rather than hundreds, pitifully few for such a vast building.

Now it's my turn.

Hoseph leaned down. At his feet lay a thin boy, unconscious and snoring, a street urchin, abducted, drugged, cleaned, and dressed in finery. The priest popped the stopper from the red vial and poured the contents into the boy's mouth. Even before it ran empty, the young flesh began to flow like melting wax, resolidifying into a new shape. Duke Tessifus' youngest son now lay on the carriage floorboards...or so it seemed.

"Kittal seems to be as skilled as he is arrogant." Hoseph popped the cork on the blue vial and downed it without hesitation.

His gut wrenched, and he choked back a cry. *Damn Kittal! He didn't warn me that the transformation would* hurt*!* Beneath his liquid skin, muscles writhed like snakes. His bones shrank and twisted, his hips realigning with a pop into a new shape. He doubled over as his groin split open to swallow his testicles and penis, the organs altering inside him. Panting for breath through clenched teeth, he refused to scream. Finally, the pain eased, the transformation complete.

Thank Demia! Drawing a deep breath, Hoseph quickly shed the clothes that now hung loosely on his smaller frame. *One hour...* Though he had no time to waste, he marveled at this new flesh he wore: smooth pale skin, taut breasts, and a wisp of red hair between shapely legs. *Not my legs...Mya's.*

The potion, concocted from a bit of Mya's flesh excised from Lakshmi, had transformed him into the woman he loathed most in the world. Smiling grimly at the irony, Hoseph grabbed the clothes Lakshmi had given him, chosen for their similarity to those Mya wore when she'd been captured. The subtle caress of silk felt strange as he pulled on the scanties and camisole. He hurriedly donned the snug trousers, dark blousy shirt, belt, and soft boots. Lastly, he tucked his skull talisman into the shirt sleeve, and his vial of elixir into a handy pocket.

Ready, he thumped the roof of the carriage. "Drive on!" Hearing Mya's voice startled him and drove home the elegance of Kittal's potion; Hoseph didn't just look like Mya, he *was* Mya. *Now all I have to do is act like her.* That, he hoped, wouldn't be difficult.

The carriage surged into motion and approached the gate. Two guards crossed halberds, and a third strode up to the carriage door.

"I'm sorry, but no one is allowed into—"

"Not even the Heroine of the Coronation?" Hoseph fought to control his derision at the grandiose title—*If they only knew the truth about her*—and peered out at the guard.

"Miss Moirin?" The man swallowed hard. "I'm sorry, ma'am, but there's been trouble, and I was told—"

"You were told to admit no one. A reasonable precaution with riots in Midtown, but I daresay the emperor will want to see *me*." He leaned back so the guard could see the unconscious child. "I bring the son of Duke Tessifus at his bidding!"

"Tessifus?" The guard's eyes widened in surprise. "So *that's*—"

Hoseph tensed at the guard's surprise. Mya must have brought the other boys to the palace, but the gate guards evidently didn't know all the details. *Reasonable, but problematic.* Bluster would get him through here. "If the boy *expires* for lack of care on the palace doorstep, you'll be in a *lot* more trouble than if you disobey orders that *obviously* shouldn't refer to *me*!"

"Of...course, Miss Moirin!" The guard backed up and waved the halberd bearers aside. "Messenger! Inform Lieutenant Tanse that Miss Moirin's here bearing the son of Duke Tessifus!" A page dashed off. "To the postern door, driver. You'll be met."

"*Thank* you." Hoseph sat back and tried not to smirk.

The carriage rumbled through the outer court, the second gate, and finally the inner court. Hoseph gazed longingly at the vast flagstone-paved courtyard, the broad stairs that led up to the palace itself, the embodiment of the greatest empire in the world. It seemed an eternity since he'd seen it.

Soon enough, I'll be back for good.

The carriage proceeded to the postern door and jerked to a halt. A squad of imperial guards stood at attention, hands on weapons as their lieutenant approached and opened the door with a smile.

"Miss Moirin, you're making visits a regular habit! I'm told you've good news."

The officer's familiarity jarred Hoseph—*So like Mya to ingratiate herself with the menials*—but it worked to his advantage. "Indeed I do!" Smiling back, he stepped down and lifted the boy out of the carriage, wishing that the potion had also imparted Mya's enhanced strength. "But there's no time to waste. The boy's not well."

"Yes! At once!" The lieutenant snapped orders, directing two of her squad to escort him to an audience chamber, and sending messengers to summon Master Corvecosi, Duke Tessifus, and the emperor.

Hoseph hid a smile of relief. They'd counted on Arbuckle being summoned. At least he didn't have to argue to see the emperor.

He followed the guards through the familiar halls and up several flights of stairs, straining to appear as if the weight of the unconscious boy didn't tax him. They emerged into the Hall of Arms, a resplendent corridor hung with the coats of arms of every noble house of Tsing. Usually manned by no fewer than fifty guards, the long passage now sported only six.

Excellent!

He was ushered into an audience chamber and directed to place the boy on a divan.

"This way, please, Miss Moirin." The guard opened another door and waved Hoseph through. "You can await the emperor in the adjoining chamber while Master Corvecosi sees to the boy. It won't be long, but we've had some trouble and are short-handed."

"I don't mind." Hoseph stepped forward, but the guard blocked the door, looking expectantly at him. His smile faltered. "Something wrong?"

"The search?" The woman gave him a curious look. "For *weapons?*"

"Oh, of course." Hoseph raised his arms as the woman performed a cursory inspection. *So, their trust in Mya isn't absolute.* He'd never in his life undergone a search other than Mistress Jeffreys' magical frisk. Now, of course, they had no wizard to spare. "Please inform the emperor that I need to speak to him directly. There are other issues at stake here, matters he doesn't know of yet."

"I'll see he gets the message." The guard waved to a divan. "Please be comfortable. I'll have a servant bring refreshment."

"Thank you." Hoseph sat, girding his nerves, smiling amiably at the guards who took station at the doors. *Patience... Any minute now, our plans will come to fruition.* He was in the palace, and Arbuckle was on his way. *Nothing can save that useless weakling this time.*

The sounds of rioting greeted the constables well before they rounded the last corner.

"Hold up!" Dreyfus barked, breathing heavily from their jog from the constabulary.

Benj was winded, but not panting. It had been years since Dreyfus walked a beat.

"Heights squads with Tobas down Holly Street. Benj, reinforce the Wharf squads with yours on Wall Street. I'll take Midtown squads down the middle on Redway." Dreyfus sounded like a general on the battlefield. "Let's push this rabble back over the river!"

"Let's go!" Benj led his squad of grim constables one block west and around the corner. Ahead, a thin line of caps stood against a shouting mob. "Straight ahead, double time! Fill in the line. They're probably gettin' a little tired by now."

As they advanced, Benj thought about Dreyfus. Despite his reaction at headquarters, he seemed to have settled down to his old self. *A tussle will probably do him good.*

The street looked like a battlefield: broken windows, smoldering wagons, and a couple of bodies, either dead or beaten unconscious.

"Varne, back in formation," he called to a cap who stopped to check on a man lying still in the street, "We're here to stop a riot, not repair the damage."

Ahead, the mass of angry rioters saw them coming. They'd been held in check in the narrow streets, but the force of constables opposing them hadn't been able to push them back toward the river.

That was about to change, and the miscreants knew it. A new rain of cobbles, bricks, and debris flew at the harried constables. The rabble shifted uncertainly, ready to bolt, looking for a way around the line of caps.

"It's about damn time!" Sergeant Keeson bellowed as Benj tucked in beside him. "Five more minutes and they'd have swarmed into Midtown over our dead bodies!"

"Nothin' like gratitude..." Benj ducked a brick and surveyed their opponents.

At first glance, the motley clothing, dirty faces, and primitive weapons—pitchforks, clubs, and axes, with the occasional spiked board—pegged them as wretches from the city's poorest quarters, but Benj had been a cap far too long to be fooled. Their arms and legs were too well-muscled, their chests too thick, overall too well-fed for Downwinders. And their faces were grim rather than desperate, their grins derisive rather than defiant. Then he saw a few daggers tucked into boot sheaths, and knew something was very wrong.

"Downwinders, my arse," Benj muttered.

"They even look too beefy for Dreggars," Jorren agreed.

"Downwinders?" Keeson dodged a thrown cobble and glared at Benj. "Who the hells told you they were Downwinders?"

"Corporal Blendell." Benj kept his eyes on the surly mob as a burning torch flew with amazing accuracy. Fortunately, a quick cap knocked it down with a sword stroke.

"Blendell! Who sent him? Those are hired muscle, or I'm a two-crown trollop! I sent Clomferd! Didn't he get there?"

"Didn't see him." This was no place to figure out how they'd gotten the wrong information. "We'll sort it out later."

"Flamer!" Jorren shouted as a bottle with a burning rag at its neck arced toward them. It hit and burst into oily flames, sending nearby constables dancing aside and shouting epithets.

"Forward! Brace up!" Benj shouted as the mob surged toward the gap. "They're trying to break out!"

The constables responded with cool professionalism, leaping the flames and closing ranks, swords and daggers at the ready. With a howl, the mob came at them, weapons raised high. The two forces clashed hard. Though clubs and daggers were no match against yard-long steel wielded with coordinated skill, the rioters were surprisingly organized, stabbing with pitchforks and makeshift spears from the second rank. One cap was skewered before his comrades could knock aside the thrust.

"Cover him!" Jorren lunged over the fallen man to skewer the attacker in the throat.

"Forward!" Benj took a glancing blow from a club on the quillons of his dagger and drove his sword into his attacker's thigh. The man screamed and went down to one knee. A boot under the chin sent him sprawling. The constables fought forward, pressing the rioters back.

The cobbles trembled faintly beneath his feet, heralding the clatter of hoofbeats. Benj risked a glance over his shoulder. A couple of blocks away, mounted warriors wearing imperial colors rode straight toward them.

What the hell? Then he realized what he was seeing. *Imperial guards?*

"Split up! Let the chargers through!" The constables split left and right. The rioters stumbled back, eyes wide at the armored horsemen. Several turned and ran.

Without missing a beat, the Imperial Guard rode through the gap five abreast. The chargers, lathered from their dash through the city, advanced stirrup to stirrup. The riders, eyes grim beneath their helms, swords and shields at the ready, pushed the throng before them.

"Advance double time! Cover their flanks. Fan out at Riverway!" The constables trotted after the mounted soldiers at Benj's orders, exchanging astonished looks and colorful epithets.

As the mob beat a hasty retreat onto Riverway, the cavalry spread out on the wide avenue and merged with more imperials from other streets. The constables spread out behind them in support. The combined force pushed the rioters back, but to Benj's surprise, instead of scattering east and west, the rioters all fled across a single bridge, a hail of stones and bricks covering their retreat. Pressed hard at the bottleneck, a few of the rabble fell into the river, a fate worse than death as far as Benj was concerned.

"Hold!"

At the bellowed order, the imperial cavalry reined in. The riot was broken, and pursuing the culprits into the Dreggars Quarter would be more perilous than productive.

Benj looked around and caught a glimpse of Dreyfus. He snorted a laugh at the look of utter shock on the man's face. *So the imperials were as big a surprise to him as they were to me.* He wondered who would get busted for breaking the chief's orders to summon the aid.

Benj worked his way toward his commander. "Whaddaya think, Chief? Should we—"

The rattle of hooves cut him off as a squad of the mounted guards wheeled and approached. Ithross lifted the visor of his helm. "Well met, Chief Constable!" He swung down from the saddle, grinning broadly. "Seems like we got here just in time."

"What the *hell* are *you* doing here?" Dreyfus glared openly, still gripping his sword. "This is *my* city, and I'm *perfectly* capable of taking care of a simple riot without your interference!"

"Interference?" The captain's eyes widened, then narrowed dangerously.

Oh, shit. Benj regretted not informing Ithross of the whole Miss Rose situation. He'd hoped to solve that mystery without involving the captain, but now... "Please, sir, let me—"

Ithross cut him off. "Our aid was *requested*, Chief Constable! Your messenger said your constables were being overwhelmed."

"I *sent* no messenger!" Dreyfus rounded on Benj. "You sent someone, didn't you? After I ordered you not to! I'll—"

The sergeant backed a step. "I did no such thing, Chief!"

Dreyfus whirled back and stabbed a finger at Ithross. "You won't get away with this! False evidence! Accusations of treason! I'm sick of your *bullshit*! You think I don't know why you're here, you lying swine?"

"Chief Constable, you are out of line!" Ithross warned.

Benj stepped between the two men. "Wait! Chief, let me—"

Something buzzed past Benj's ear and clanged off Dreyfus' helm. A crossbow bolt clattered to the street.

What the...

Dreyfus shook his head, stunned, his eyes wide and wild.

More bolts buzzed, one striking an imperial guard in the chest, knocking him from his horse. Another pierced the neck of Ithross' mount. The animal squealed and reared, jerking its reins from its master's grasp.

"Archers!" someone bellowed. "On the rooftops! Behind us!"

Benj whirled, scanning the row of inns and warehouses, but another shout split his attention.

"The rioters! They're charging!"

A glance confirmed that the mob was indeed surging back across the bridge, those in the fore holding crude board shields. *Damn, this is a pretty trap!*

"Guard the bridge!" Ithross bellowed. "Don't let them pass!" As the ranks of chargers tightened along the edge of the river, two deep and stirrup to stirrup, Ithross' own squad set their mounts between the archers and their commander, shields raised high.

"Chief! What do you want us to do?" Benj eyed the milling constables waiting for orders, wondering which front to defend. Another hail of bolts buzzed down at them.

Dreyfus, however, just stood there, jerking his head this way and that as if looking for some hidden assassin. Ithross crouched to shield a fallen guard, knowing better than to give orders to the constables.

"Oh, *hell!*" Benj gritted his teeth and took command. "Wharf squads! Get into those buildings! Find a way up to the roof! Midtown squads, circle and cover the streets. Don't kill 'em and don't let 'em get away! I want those archers captured! The rest of you back up the cavalry!"

As constables scrambled to follow his orders, Benj ducked behind a mounted guardsman. Another hail of bolts buzzed down at them, striking steel, stone, and flesh. *Picked a hell of a day to leave my mail behind.* He tried to keep an eye on both the riverfront and the rooftops without getting shot.

"Chief! Don't!"

Benj whirled at Jorren's shout to see his corporal lunging at Dreyfus. The chief stood behind Ithross, thrusting a crossbow bolt down at the back of the captain's exposed neck. Jorren slammed into his commanding officer and they both crashed to the ground.

"What in the Nine Hells?" Ithross clapped a hand to his neck and jerked around. His hand came away bloody. He stared in shock to where Jorren lay atop Dreyfus, one hand clasped firmly on his commander's wrist and a forearm pinning his neck to the street.

"Get *off* me or I'll have your head!" Dreyfus screeched, the bloody bolt still in his hand.

"*No*, sir!" Jorren shouted in the man's ear. "I will *not* release you!"

Another bolt cracked against the cobbles perilously close to struggling pair, reminding Benj that they were still under fire. "Shields!"

"Imperial Guard, to me!" Ithross' bellow brought in several more mounted guards to form a cordon of steel between them and the archers.

Before Benj could sort out this mess—the chief trying to murder Ithross in the middle of a battle was almost too much to wrap his mind around—a scream from the roof presaged the meaty thud of a man falling to the street.

"I said I want them *alive*, gods damn it!" shouted Benj.

A constable waved a bloody sword down at him. "Got most of 'em, Sarge! Only that one dead."

"A little *help* would be nice!" gasped Jorren.

"Hold fast there, Corporal." Benj checked to make sure they weren't about to be overrun by rioters, but the mob had already fled back across the bridge. He snatched the bloody crossbow bolt from the chief constable's hand, then relieved him of sword and dagger as well. *What a gods-be-damned mess this is going to be.* "All right. You can let him up, but keep a hold on him. You two! Come over here and help Corporal Arryx."

"You tried to *kill* me!" Captain Ithross said incredulously.

As the burly caps hauled Dreyfus up, he cast a wild glare at Ithross. "You tried to frame me for treason! I know your plots! Frame me up and burn me at the stake!" He spat, but it fell short of the captain.

Ithross stared at him aghast, shook his head, and gestured to one of his guards. "Fetch a carriage. We'll be taking Chief Constable Dreyfus with us to the palace."

Benj stepped forward. "With all due respect, sir, as senior sergeant, I need to come along. I've got some...evidence relevant to this case."

"Evidence?" Ithross didn't look convinced.

"Yes, *evidence*." Benj raised his brow and gave the captain a piercing look; they couldn't very well discuss their joint investigation in public.

"All right, then." Ithross turned to Jorren. "Thank you for your quick action, constable. What's your name?"

Jorren snapped to attention. "Corporal Jorren Arryx, sir."

Benj clapped Jorren's back. "With what *you* just did, it'll be Sergeant Arryx soon enough."

"This is it?" Mya looked over the rack of bottles skeptically, still trying to control her frazzled nerves. *This isn't the damned plan!* She was supposed to be coordinating a multipronged assault on more than a dozen different locations, not infiltrating a secret headquarters herself with only one person to back her up. But Lad wouldn't relent. *Now or never…*

"Yes. Wait a minute. I'm going to listen." Lad released her hand, and Mya suddenly found it easier to think.

Focus, Mya! She took a deep breath and let it out slowly, trying to listen, but still couldn't hear a thing over her pounding heart.

"Two guards," Lad's disembodied voice whispered from inches away. "One on the right and one on the left."

"Which way to Lakshmi?" Without Lad's flawless sense of direction, they could blunder around forever.

"Through the door and off to our right, but I don't know how deep or what turns we'll have to take to get there."

"Fine." Mya took another deep breath. Her heart began to settle down. "This won't be easy. Kittal engineers some nasty alchemical traps, but if there are guards stationed right beyond the door, it's *probably* not rigged to explode."

"I never thought it *would* be easy." Lad sounded so calm, so sure.

No pain, no fear, no mercy…

Mya drew a fighting dagger, the hilt comforting in her hand. "Okay. Open it. I'll take the guard on the right, you the one on the left. *Quietly.*"

232

"Of *course* quietly, Mya."

Mya tightened her lips. *As if he needs me telling him to be quiet!* At least he was humoring her and not chastising. "Ready."

"Now!"

The third bottle from the right on the second shelf moved. Smoothly and quietly, the entire wine rack and the false wall behind it swung out on hidden hinges. The light from beyond was brighter than that in the wine cellar, backlighting the two guards. They turned to the opening door and squinted into the gloom, lifting their crossbows. Green glass shone pale at the tips of the bolts

"Arte, is that—"

Mya reached out, plucked the bolt from the nearer one's crossbow, and lashed out with her dagger, cracking the pommel against the woman's temple. The Alchemist fell like a poleaxed steer, but slow enough for Mya to catch both her and the crossbow before either crashed to the floor.

The other guard's head snapped back, and his crossbow leapt from his hands. Lad materialized, lowering both his unconscious foe and the weapon gently.

Mya checked herself; they were both visible. *Well*, that *was fun while it lasted.*

Beyond a small landing, another stair descended straight and deep. They paused, listening, but Mya heard nothing. Lad pointed at the unconscious guards, held up two fingers, and pointed down the stairs. His meaning was clear: two more guards below.

Mya held up a finger to wait. She cut the bowstring, tied the woman's wrists behind her back, lashed her bootlaces together, and finally stuffed a handkerchief in her mouth and bound it in place with her belt. Lad followed her example with the other guard, then pulled the wine rack door closed.

Lad pointed down the stairs, then leaned close, his whisper warm in her ear. "Fast or quiet?"

The choice depended on the positioning of the unseen guards below. If they were watching the stairs, a fast attack would give Lad and Mya a chance to take them down before an alarm could be raised. If the guards faced the other way, a quiet approach would be better. *But without knowing…*

Mya strained all her senses and caught the shuffle of feet, the distant clink and clank of glassware or pottery, the iron scent of blood from the gash on her recent opponent's temple, and an underlying tang of chemicals. That familiar smell stiffened the hairs on the back of her neck.

"Mya," Lad whispered, "we need to move."

She resisted the urge to bite her lip and nodded. "Fast."

Lad nodded, took a deep breath and let it out slowly, then plunged down the stairs. Mya followed as fast as she could, silently cursing her dandyish shoes. Lad bounded out from the stairs ahead of her, feet and fists lashing out. The two sharp impacts were loud to her ears, but provoked no cries of pain or alarm. When she reached the bottom, the guards lay sprawled unconscious on the floor. Lad stood over them, their crossbows in his hands and aimed down a hallway.

Mya froze in her tracks, ice water chilling her veins. The guard's face, the hallway, the scents and sounds all struck up a clangorous memory. Opium haze, pain, screams, and blood. "This is *it*!"

Lad glanced sharply at her.

She took a step back toward the stair, feeling as if the walls were closing in around her. "This is where they...held me."

"No *fear*, Mya," Lad whispered. "Remember! No fear. You can *do* this."

Mya looked into his eyes, pale hazel pools of calm. There was no doubt there, no judgment, no accusation of cowardice. He believed in her. She just had to believe in herself.

"No fear," she whispered, gritting her teeth against her silent screams.

"Good. Take care of the guards. I'll keep watch." He faced the far end of the hallway again.

No fear... No fear... No fear... Mya ran through the mantra again and again as she hauled first one unconscious guard, then the other, far enough up the stairs to be out of sight. She returned to find Lad several steps further down the corridor, his ear pressed to the nearest door.

She joined him and whispered, "Anyone?"

Lad shook his head and motioned them on to where the corridor turned to the right. Pausing there, he asked, "Layout?"

Mya nodded. "Long corridor here, common room at the end. Two near doors on the right, the second one is the laboratory I escaped through. There are more farther down, I can't remember how many. Another hallway branches to the left halfway down. It leads to…" She swallowed hard, her throat dry. "…where they held me."

Lad nodded again, then paused and closed his eyes for a moment, turned his head slowly left and right. Opening them again, he pointed one of the crossbows in the direction of the branching hallway. "Keyfur's spell pointed that way. Are there any other doors or branching hallways in that corridor?"

"No halls, but doors on both sides." Mya racked her memory, but couldn't remember how many doors there had been. *Some Hunter!* In her defense, she'd been drugged and had tried very hard to forget her time here. She did remember one detail, however. "The laboratory where they held me is at the end of that hall. It's a dead end."

He nodded and snatched a glance around the corner. "It's clear. Come on." Lad took off, moving swiftly and silently.

Mya followed more slowly, cursing her footwear once again. Down the corridor they raced, past the first door, then past the room that had been her escape route, Lad lengthening his lead with every stride. *Godsdamnit, slow down!* Laughter and clatter of dishes from the room at the end of the hall jangled along her nerves.

Lad dodged into the hallway to the left. The corner was only fifteen feet away now… Ten feet… Five feet…

Four assassins strode through the doorway at the far end of the hall. They stopped, faces going slack at the sight of her.

Mya froze, her feet welded to the flagstones. Her brain screamed, *Run! Run or die!*

One of the assassins finally found his voice. "Who the *hell*…"

Chapter XIX

Sweet shadow of death, grant me patience to endure this interminable waiting...

Though it felt like he'd been sitting here for hours, Hoseph suspected it had only been minutes. The blackbrew in his cup was still warm. He inspected the two stone-faced guards stationed at the doors, trying to look disinterested.

Do they usually post guards on Mya? He'd have thought saving the emperor's life would have bought her some trust. *Do they suspect something? Have I acted wrong?* He shifted, crossing his legs first one way, then the other, uncomfortable with his disconcertingly female body.

When the door latch finally clicked, he surged to his feet, the silver talisman firm in his grasp, ready to flee if necessary.

Two more guards entered, then a knight—*Sir Yanli*, he recalled—then the emperor himself. Several more menials followed, but Hoseph's whole being focused upon his quarry.

Arbuckle... Hoseph had to suppress the urge to lunge for the kill. One touch and not only would their plans be fulfilled, but he would frame Mya for the emperor's murder.

Not yet... Must get close... Patience...

"Your Majesty." Hoseph fumbled a curtsy.

"Miss Moirin, you truly astound Us!" Tynean Tsing III beamed with unabashed pleasure and strode forward, his hand outstretched.

Thank you, blessed Demia! Hoseph hadn't expected it to be this easy. He reached out his hand.

"Your Majesty!" With flash of colorful robes, Keyfur stepped around and in front of the emperor, waving his damnable feather. A shimmering barrier rainbow of light flashed between the emperor and Hoseph. "I *must* remind you of the security protocol when Captain Ithross is away from the palace. No one may touch your person."

That insufferable peacock! Hoseph's heart leapt in his chest. Keyfur had nearly killed him in the sewers. *But he helped rescue Mya, and I'm Mya.*

Arbuckle's brow furrowed. "Tennison, is that right? We don't recall such a protocol."

The imperial secretary stepped forward. "I'm not familiar with all the security protocols, Majesty. I must defer to Archmage Keyfur."

"And I must *insist*, else the good captain will have my head." Keyfur's flashed his brilliant smile, sweeping his robe in an arc as he bowed. "I'm sure Miss Moirin understands."

Fuming, Hoseph nodded in feigned deference. "Of course, Master Keyfur. It's good to see you again."

Keyfur's smile stiffened. "Yes. It's been...a whole thirty minutes since we parted. May I ask if you found what you were looking for?"

Mya's been working with Keyfur? Apprehension chilled up Hoseph's spine. *There's only one thing she could have been looking for.* Smiling, he played the only card he had. "Obviously! The youngest Tessifus boy's in the next room." *Please go take a look and let me get on with this!* "I was worried that he might be spelled. Haven't you seen him?"

"Congratulations on your success." Keyfur took a step closer. "And what about your charming companion? She didn't come with you? I would have liked to see her again."

He suspects... Hoseph ground his teeth. "I came alone for the sake of simplicity. My companion is fine."

"Master Keyfur, please! There's no need for this," Arbuckle waved a bejeweled hand at the shimmering shield between them, "and the inquisition. She is Our guest. We must insist—"

"What *I* don't understand..."

The wizard's interruption astonished everyone in the room. Even the guards exchanged troubled glances. Arbuckle stood with mouth agape. Keyfur seemed not to notice.

"...is why you changed *clothes* before bringing the boy here."

Clothes... Could his downfall be that simplistic, that inane?

"You bothered to change *clothes*?" Arbuckle knitted his brow and looked at Miss Moirin skeptically.

"Of *course* I changed clothes!" Hoseph argued desperately. "Mine were soiled with blood."

"You *had* no other clothes," Keyfur said softly, flourishing his feather.

Enough of this!

Hoseph clutched the silver skull, pulled the vial of elixir from his pocket, and whispered, "Shahallariva." Materializing behind Keyfur, he let go the talisman and invoked Demia's blessing, placing his glowing hand on the wizard's shoulder.

Keyfur collapsed into a heap of colorful robes and dead flesh.

A dash of elixir banished his pain and nausea, and he flicked the skull talisman back into his hand. "Shahalla—"

Breath left his lungs in a gasp as six inches of bloody steel plunged from his abdomen. All sensation of his lower body vanished, and his knees buckled. Reflexively, Hoseph thrust out his hands to break his fall. Glass shattered, shards piercing his palm. On the polished marble floor, elixir and blood mingled.

Demia preserve me! Hoseph clenched his teeth against a scream as the sword was wrenched from his body. The next blow would be fatal. Blood spraying from his lips, he spat out the invocation of soul searching.

When invoked with compassion, the magic allowed the dying to review their transgressions in life and ask forgiveness. Hoseph had made it a weapon, forcing his enemies to relive their worst moments. The dark wave of magic pulsed out from him. Screams and gasps filled the room, steel clattering to the floor as Sir Yanli and the guards collapsed. Arbuckle fell to his knees, clutching his chest.

Hoseph stretched out his hand, but Master Keyfur lay between him and his quarry. He fumbled for the skull talisman, then stopped. At the tip of the dead archmage's fingers lay a black sphere the size of a large pearl. Hoseph had seen it before, had felt its magic.

The fleshforge!

Hoseph snatched up the tiny sphere and popped it into his mouth, forcing it down his throat. All his pain vanished, a tingling sensation suffusing his lower body. Strength returned, and mobility with it. Hoseph stood, called the pearly light of death to his hand,

and strode toward Tsing's kneeling sovereign. The guards were already stirring, but Hoseph only needed a moment.

Finally... Standing over Arbuckle, Hoseph reached down with a glowing palm.

NO!

The voice exploded in Hoseph's mind like a clap of thunder, resounding throughout every bone in his body. The pearly light in his palm faded and winked out.

Hoseph stared at his hand in shock. *What in the name of...*

I care not for crowns or kings, my wayward son.

"Don't you *touch* him!"

Hoseph's head snapped forward as a heavy weight smashed into the back of his skull and set his senses reeling. The floor came up again, but this time he hadn't the reflexes to break his fall. His chin cracked against the polished floor, stunning him even further. Blood filled his mouth in a nauseating flood. Then, in a tingling instant, the pain vanished.

The fleshforge... It was still inside him, healing injuries even as they occurred. Hoseph rolled over to confront this new attacker.

The imperial scribe stood there wide-eyed, gripping the heavy tome in which he scribbled the emperor's every word. All around Hoseph, steel grated against stone as the imperial guards and Sir Yanli regained their senses and their weapons. Two guards grasped their sovereign's arms, pulling him to safety, while the rest closed in around Hoseph.

"Kill her!" ordered Sir Yanli.

Hoseph still gripped his talisman, but even if he materialized right behind Arbuckle, his touch of death had been denied him by Demia herself. *Failure...* He had only one option left. *But if Demia has revoked her blessings, will it work?* As the swords and halberds fell, he gripped the silver skull and spoke the invocation. He closed his eyes with a desperate prayer, *Please, Demia...*

Silence...

Nothingness...

The Sphere of Shadow...

Thank you, Demia! His beloved goddess hadn't revoked of all her gifts.

But why had she prevented him from killing Arbuckle?

...my wayward son.

Hoseph didn't understand. He had obviously done something to displease Demia. *But what?* Instead of belaboring the issue now, he focused on escape. Picturing his destination, Hoseph felt the palace wards. He couldn't cross that barrier, but he could travel within the palace.

He materialized atop the highest tower overlooking the seaward bluff. He staggered, but the pain and sickness of his transition passed quickly, healed by the fleshforge. *Even better than Kittal's elixir.* A moment later, a spasm gripped his gut, and the tiny black sphere surged back up his throat. He looked at it in his palm, considered what he had to do next, and popped it back into his mouth.

A thousand feet below sprawled the city, the blue of the sea beyond. Throughout the palace, the alarm would be spreading, every exit would be barred. Slowly but surely, they'd search and eventually make it up to this lonely spot. There was only one way out.

Carefully, Hoseph climbed up onto the battlement. Wind whipped through the bloody silk shirt, trying to tear him from the precipice.

Without a moment's hesitation, Demia's wayward son leapt from the parapet.

"Who the *hell...*"

Lad snapped around at the strange voice. Mya stood just in view, her eyes wide, staring down the corridor.

Damn!

He charged out of the side passage, acquiring targets and firing both crossbows as he cleared the corner. He cringed as the bolts struck. The first lodged in a woman's stomach, the alchemical tip shattering inside her. She screamed as the wound began to sizzle and smoke. The second hit the man beside her in the face. His entire head melted away as he fell.

More blood on my hands... But Lad had promised Mya he would kill if necessary, and he'd had no choice.

As the two other men shouted warnings and stumbled back into the room, Lad dropped the crossbows, bounded off the wall, and charged. Lakshmi was in the other direction, but leaving a room full of assassins between them and their exit was not an option. Mya's footsteps rang on the floor right behind him. She'd snapped out of her paralysis, at least.

Ahead, an arm swept around the edge of the door, and a foot-long cylinder of brass and glass flew down the hallway.

That can't be good.

Lad skidded to a stop and leapt to catch the cylinder. Before the bubbling alchemical explosive arrived, however, another assassin leaned out to fire a crossbow. The glittering green head streaked right at Lad.

When faced with multiple potentially lethal threats, prioritization is the key to survival. Remember!

Lad could catch the cylinder or dodge the bolt, but probably not both. If he dealt with one, he'd have to count on Mya to deal with the other. But Mya had frozen once already. Could he count on her?

No choice.

Twisting in the air, Lad batted the crossbow bolt out of its deadly trajectory. He reached out as the cylinder tumbled past, the liquid inside hissing and bubbling, but it brushed past his fingertips. If Mya missed, the explosion would fill the corridor. There was nowhere to hide.

Mya didn't miss.

The hissing cylinder slapped into her hand, and she whirled to throw it back.

Lad's feet hit the floor as the cylinder flew past him a second time. The assassin in the doorway dropped his crossbow and reached out for the deadly projectile, his eyes and mouth widening in panic. Lad didn't wait to see if the man managed to catch it, but turned to run, Mya at his side.

If we can just get around the corner…

Metal cracked on stone and glass shattered a split second before an ear-numbing explosion.

We're not going to make it.

Lad steeled himself for the blast. With an aching heart, he pictured his daughter's sweet face; he wouldn't make it home to protect her from the impending war. *I'm sorry, Lissa.*

Something sharp wrenched Lad's arm and yanked him aside. Mya wrapped her arms and legs around him, their faces so close their noses touched, her eyes squeezed tightly shut.

The world exploded.

Mya slammed into him, her mouth smashing his hard enough to chip a tooth. Heat washed past his face, a piece of shrapnel slashing his temple, but Mya took the brunt of the violence. The concussion knocked them flat and they landed hard, her weight knocking the breath from his lungs, their legs tangled.

As the smoke cleared, Lad gasped a deep breath, coughing at the stench of burned hair and singed flesh. He blinked, tasting blood, thankful that he hadn't been blinded, and saw Mya's face only inches above his. Her features were pinched, and her breath came short. She was alive, but hurt.

Moans and bellows from the direction of the common room told him some assassins had survived. The explosion would alert everyone in the complex.

"Mya, we have to move! How badly are you hurt?"

"Fuck me if I know!" she hissed through bloody lips. Her eyes blinked open. "No pain, right?" She tried to smile, but only managed to grimace. Gingerly, she pushed herself off him and stood, leaning against the wall, smoke wafting from her charred clothes. "I'm in one piece, I guess."

Lad rolled up, assessing the patches of pink, blistered flesh he could see through the gashes in Mya's ragged coat. The ridiculous brocade garment had saved her somewhat, but her hair had been burned away in the back, and bits of glass and debris had pierced her here and there. She winced as he plucked a shard of charred bone from the back of her neck and flicked it away. "You shouldn't have—"

"Shut up!" Mya glared at him. "I'll heal, you won't, and I need your help to finish this. Let's get moving!"

Now *that* was the Mya he knew.

Lad hurried into the side corridor. Mya followed, moving stiffly, obviously still in pain.

The corridor wasn't long, but had several doors. Through the ringing in his ears, he heard excited voices behind a door to the left. They couldn't fight everyone here, and too many had died already. He hurried past. If they could stay ahead of the response, they might get to Lakshmi and end this. She was still somewhere to his right.

He stopped at a door, gauging the angle and distance of Keyfur's location spell.

This is it.

Stealth was pointless now, so Lad simply opened the door.

The two guards at the other end of the short hallway were ready and, seeing two strangers, reacted immediately. One fired a crossbow, and the other threw an apple-sized glass sphere. Lad lunged forward, diving beneath the bolt, arm outstretched to catch the sphere before it struck the floor. He hit the floor hard, but rolled up with the sphere in hand. Steel flashed past his head, Mya's dagger missing him by inches. The blade buried in one guard's stomach, folding him over. The second guard reached for another crossbow bolt.

Lad put the glass sphere carefully down and charged the crossbowman. The man stabbed at him with the bolt, but Lad snatched it from his fingers and lashed out with a careful kick to the solar plexus. As the man folded, another careful blow to the back of the neck dropped him to the floor. Mya's victim lay clutching the dagger lodged in his stomach, his face pale. If they finished this quickly and got him some attention, he would live.

Lad smashed a crossbow to splinters and tossed a piece to Mya, whispering, "Wedge the hallway door shut."

While she did that, a voice from behind the inner door called out, "Jorry? What's going on?"

Mya dashed up, eyes wide. She pointed and whispered, "Kittal!"

Lad nodded and shouted back, "It's okay, Master Kittal! We got them. They're down."

Mya looked at him appraisingly, and he suppressed a smile. *Now who's thinking like an assassin?*

"Excellent!" said the voice from within. Shoes shuffled across a floor toward the door.

Beside him, Mya bent to pick up the unconscious crossbowman's quiver. Her hands trembled as she tied it to her thigh, but it wasn't fear this time. Her eyes burned with rage, her teeth gritted, her fists clenched on her daggers in a desperate need for revenge.

Lad knew that feeling, the empty allure of vengeance, and how it had very nearly destroyed his soul. *Mya doesn't deserve that.*

The latch clicked and the door swung open. In one swift move, Lad stepped in front of Mya and carefully punched Master Alchemist Kittal square in the nose.

As Kittal pitched backward, his nose spattered across his face, Mya shoved Lad aside. She didn't know if the blow had killed the Master Alchemist, but, if so, it had been too easy a death for what he'd done to her. No matter, she had other prey.

"Kittal!"

Mya turned to the cry. *And there she is...*

Lakshmi—the monster who had stolen her runes, the vile creature wearing her skin—seemed nothing more than an elderly matron in a colorful sari, her eyes wide and her mouth gaping as she stared at her compatriot on the floor.

Mya knew better. There were others in the room, but she left them to Lad. Lakshmi was hers. Ignoring the pain of her wounds, she stalked forward, her lips pulled back in a feral grin.

"*You...*"

Lakshmi looked at her then and her eyes narrowed. Unreadable emotions washed over that wizened face before it settled into an expression of contemptuous composure. "Mya."

"I want my *skin* back." Mya readied her daggers.

"And I want the rest of yours, dear." The Master Inquisitor smiled serenely as she pulled two colorful hand fans from her sleeves and spread them wide, the painted likenesses of serpents vivid on their faces. "To the victor go the spoils."

With graceful flicks of her wrists, Lakshmi sent a spray of tiny silver needles from the fans' stays. The miniscule missiles flew in twin lines that intersected where Mya stood, each one glinting in the lamplight like a tiny star, their tips black with poison.

Mya's legs flexed like released springs, launching her up in a twisting roll to evade the lines of death. Two of the needles tugged at her tattered jacket as they passed through the flapping hem, but none touched her flesh. She let steel fly from her hands, twin strokes of silver lightning among the spray of deadly stars. The daggers clanged against the painted fans as if they had struck iron.

Mya landed, drew her last fighting dagger, and stalked slowly forward. "Where's Dee?"

"Dee?" The old woman's eyebrows arched. "Well, not *here*. We took him someplace to...play."

Mya's heart lurched. *Play*... For the Inquisitor, that meant torture. But there was more in Lakshmi's eyes than amusement. There was calculation there. *She's lying! She's going to offer you a bargain next.*

"Drop your dagger, and I might—"

"Nice try," Mya seethed. Dee was gone, but Lakshmi was here...

Lakshmi flicked the fans again, and short blades extended from the stays. No longer than fingernails, they were edged like razors and black with poison.

They both moved at once, Mya lunging like a viper, steel flashing, and Lakshmi lashing out with the fans. Sparks flew when the blades clashed. Slashing and blocking with blinding speed, Mya darted beneath Lakshmi's guard to cut a furrow in the woman's wrist. Then the stays of the fan caught the blade and wrenched it from her grasp.

Mya stepped back, gauging her opponent anew. Every assassin could fight, but Lakshmi had spent untold decades as an Inquisitor, exerting her mind more than her muscles. And regardless of how many potions she'd imbibed or how many of Mya's runes aided her, she was still old. Mya, on the other hand, was a Hunter, her survival skills honed on the streets from childhood.

No fear...

She drew a bolt from the quiver at her thigh and lunged past the Inquisitor's guard. Lakshmi ducked in time to evade the glittering green crystal at the tip of the bolt, and clipped it off with another flick of a fan. The crystal ruptured when it hit the floor, spilling acid in a smoking puddle.

A new strategy clicked into Mya's mind. Drawing two more bolts from the quiver, she launched them at Lakshmi in quick succession. The Inquisitor blocked the deadly missiles with her fans, just as Mya had hoped she would. The green crystal tips shattered, and the acid splashed, eating away at the delicate fans and dripping down onto the Inquisitor's hands.

Lakshmi flung the fans away with a curse and plucked at the fine embroidery of her gown. A silken serpent peeled away from the fabric, coming to life in the woman's hand. She flung it writhing through the air at Mya, ivory fangs flashing.

Mya caught it by the tail and cracked it like a whip. As its fanged head spun away, she drew another bolt from the quiver and hurled it with all her strength at the Inquisitor. Lakshmi raised her draping sari as if mere fabric could stop the bolt...and it did. In fact, it absorbed the deadly missile. An emerald-tipped crossbow bolt now resided in silk thread on the magical garment.

I wonder who her tailor is? Mya thought distractedly.

Lakshmi pulled the bolt from her sari and threw it, but Mya knocked it aside. Several more silken projectiles flew: a poisoned dagger, a spider of horrific size, a monstrous wasp... Mya whirled and leapt, ducked and stabbed until there were none left.

As Lakshmi desperately searched her denuded sari, Mya drew two more bolts and advanced, backing the old woman against the wall. The wizened face now contracted in fear. Mya recalled the endless hours she'd spent lying strapped to a stone table, her skin sheared from her body like a sheep's fleece so this woman could strangle a few more years out of life, and felt not a morsel of pity.

No mercy...

"Wait!" Lakshmi screeched, her voice hoarse.

"No," Mya replied coldly. "I *won't* wait. I won't stop, and I won't *quit!*"

"I'll name you Grandmaster!" the Inquisitor bargained.

"I already *am* Grandmaster." Mya took another step forward, well within striking distance now.

Lakshmi's face hardened. "Kill me, and you'll *never* get your magic back!"

Mya considered that option for a moment, lying once again on a table while the skin that Lakshmi had stolen was stitched back onto her. Bile burned her throat. "Deal."

Mya feinted with the right-hand bolt, watched it absorbed into the Inquisitor's sari as Lakshmi blocked the thrust, then stabbed with the left. The crystal tip pierced the Master Inquisitor under the chin and ruptured against her spine.

Lakshmi jerked once, eyes wide, mouth agape, and acrid smoke trickled from between her painted lips. She fell in a colorful heap, dead before she felt even the slightest pain.

It hardly seemed fair.

CHAPTER XX

*M*other!"

The anguished cry reverberated through Mya's head. She looked down at the blood on her hands. *Mother?* Staggering back, she looked at the old woman dead at her feet. *Did I kill her again?* She shook her head. No, this wasn't her mother, and the voice wasn't hers.

Mya whirled.

Berta and another assassin cowered against the wall, hands open and empty. Lad stood over Kittal. The Master Alchemist wasn't dead after all, or even unconscious. Stretched out on the floor, tears streaking his blood-smeared face, one hand reaching out. His eyes weren't focused on Mya, however, but Lakshmi.

"Mother…" The final piece of the puzzle dropped into place, and it all made sense. Kittal's devotion to Lakshmi, his willingness to perform atrocities beyond redemption, hadn't been for power or gain.

I though him *a monster, but he was only trying to save his mother's life.* Mya felt suddenly sick. *I killed my mother.*

"Mya, we—"

Kittal's heartrending wail drowned out Lad's words. The Master Alchemist writhed on the floor, then curled into a quivering fetal ball, his shoulders heaving with pitiful sobs.

Click!

A low whine buzzed through the air, rising in pitch like a child's clockwork top spinning up.

"No!" Berta stared at her prostrate master, her eyes wide. "He just…killed us all!"

Lad flipped Kittal over, a fist to the nose knocking him unconscious. The Master Alchemist went limp, a small golden sphere rolling from his outstretched hand.

The whine grew louder, setting Mya's teeth on edge. Bolting for the door, she thrust out a hand. "Lad!"

Lad snatched the humming sphere from Kittal and pitched it to her. Mya caught it—it was hot to the touch and getting hotter—skidded to a stop at the door, and threw the device down the short hall. Grabbing the door to slam it shut, she stopped. The two fallen guards lay in the hallway. One was unconscious, but the other, still clutching her dagger in his gut, gazed desperately up at her.

"Shit!" Mya grabbed them by the scruffs of their shirts and heaved them into the room. The sphere hit the far door, the whining now so piercing she thought it would burst her ears. Shouldering the door closed, Mya heard a light *Pop!* just as the latch clicked home. With a tremendous roar, the shock wave ripped the door from its stout iron hinges and flung her across the room, smashing her against the wall.

All went black...

"Mya!" The voice seemed to come from a great distance, muffled by the ringing in her ears. Gentle hands rolled her over. "Mya...you...kay?"

Mya forced her way through the haze that swaddled her senses. Lad knelt over her, his expression dire.

"Ouch," she muttered, swallowing blood. She'd bitten her lip nearly through. "Am I alive?"

Lad looked relieved, but cupped a hand to his ear and shook his head. "What?"

His voice was still muffled. *The explosion...*

Motion over Lad's shoulder caught Mya's attention, and she blinked as a figure approached from behind him. *I must have hit harder than I'd thought.* What she saw didn't make sense. She couldn't be gazing into a mirror...could she?

"It's...me..."

As the wind of free fall whipped through his clothing and howled in his ears, Hoseph gauged his position. Past the outer curtain wall, past the immense blocks of the palace's foundation, past the sheer wall of the bluff... The ground rushed up at him.

Now!

He invoked the talisman's power, desperately hoping that he'd passed beyond the lowest reaches of the palace wards. Transiting through the Sphere of Shadow, he pictured his destination, relieved to discover no barrier. He had to warn Lakshmi and Kittal of his failure, and that Mya was seeking the Tessifus boy.

He coalesced from the mists into chaos. Dust filled the air, and he almost coughed out the fleshforge before swallowing it forcefully to relieve the anguish of the transition. As the pain ebbed, he squinted through the dust. *One of Kittal's damned explosions!* Debris and bodies littered the floor, one in particular, a splash of color that drew his eyes. *Lakshmi! I'm too late.*

Across the room, someone crouched over a prostrate form that sported a mop of short red hair... *Mya!*

She moved, her head lolling. "Am I alive?"

Not for long!

Tentatively, Hoseph invoked Demia's blessing. His palm glowed pearly white, and he breathed a sigh of relief. Though the emperor seemed to be off limits, the power had not been utterly revoked.

The young man crouching over Mya cupped a hand to his ear, shook his head sharply.

Lad!

Fear and frustration shook Hoseph to his boots. *I don't dare—*

"What?" Lad said, leaning closer to Mya.

His senses must be dulled by the explosion! Steeling his nerves, Hoseph stepped forward, glowing hand outstretched. Even if Lad *did* look around, he would only see Mya approaching. Confusion ought to buy Hoseph time enough to touch him. With a surge in his gut, the fleshforge started to come back up. *No!* He swallowed hard. Trying to kill both Lad and Mya, he might need it. One last step and he reached down.

Just one touch...

Mya squinted at the glowing hand—*her* glowing hand—wondering for an instant, *Why would I be carrying a light?* before her subconscious screamed what her concussion-addled mind had yet to realize.

Hoseph!

Panic pierced the ringing in her ears and the fog shrouding her mind. As the glowing hand descended, she flung Lad out of its reach. Cheated of her target, the other Mya snarled and lunged for her, glowing hand extended. Mya snatched her assailant's forearm, holding the lethal hand easily at bay. *Not as strong as me, then…* She squeezed hard and felt bones crack.

The other Mya—*Not me…it has to be Hoseph!*—screamed through clenched teeth. Instantly, the broken bones beneath Mya's hand moved, squirming back together to become solid once again.

My healing, too? She fought through the pain and confusion. *Even I didn't heal that quickly!*

It's magic, her lucid mind insisted. *A potion maybe…*

Right. Heal this! Holding the glowing hand at bay, she pulled another bolt from her quiver and jammed it into the other Mya's chest. The crystal tip ruptured, splashing acid, but even as the silk shirt and underlying flesh sizzled and burned away, as the other Mya screamed in pain, the pink skin reformed, healing instantly and completely. *Well, shit!*

The other Mya—*It's Hoseph!*—fought frantically to reach her, eyes wide with desperation.

Mya caught a flicker of silver from the corner of her eye. A tiny silver skull on a thin chain arced up toward Hoseph's free hand. She'd seen that before.

Remember! screamed her subconscious, and Mya saw Dee and Hoseph struggling…a tiny silver skull flipping into Hoseph's hand…and just before he dissolved into mist, he said a word…

Mya reached for the glittering skull. If she didn't get it before Hoseph, she'd suffer the same fate as Dee.

Would I see him again? she wondered. The silver skull felt oddly cold as her hand closed around it.

Hoseph pried at her fingers. "Give it to me!"

"Where's Dee?" Mya demanded. "Where did you take him?"

"You'll *never* find him!" Hoseph scratched at her fist with his nails. "Give. It. To. *Me!*"

This thing took him somewhere...

"We'll look for him together." Mya spoke the word. "Shahallariva."

Hoseph's eyes—*My eyes*—flung wide, his mouth gaping. Futilely, he fought to pull free from her grasp. "Noooo!"

Mya watched her mirror-self dissolve into a smoky mist, chilled to realize that the same was happening to her. As if from a distance, she heard someone call her name, but couldn't prevent herself from slipping away, all sensation fading, then...nothing.

Lad shook his head and blinked, momentarily stunned by being slammed into the wall. For a moment, he thought he was seeing double, Mya grappling with herself. But no...they wore different clothes. Then he noticed the glowing palm.

Hoseph!

He surged up, pain lancing through his head with the sudden motion. Black mists began to swirl around and through the two Myas, devouring them both.

"Mya! No!" Lad lunged, reaching for the Mya he knew to be real, the one wearing the ridiculous brocade jacket scorched by two explosions, but he passed through the mists like a bird through a cloud. When he rolled to his feet and looked back, there was nothing.

Gone... Lad stared at the spot where the two Myas had struggled. Injury and death were always possible on a mission like this, but to watch Mya simply vanish, after all they'd been through... Why did that make him feel so alone?

Remaining focused is key for survival. Remember!

Lad shook off the numbness and assessed the situation. They'd beaten the masters, but the Tessifus boy was still missing, and Lad had no intention of leaving the child to be a pawn in Hoseph's plan.

Where to start? He didn't know if Hoseph might return, had no idea how many assassins were left in the lair, and didn't relish his chances of finding the boy and escaping without Mya's help.

No choice. He looked to the two assassins, a severe-looking woman with the stained fingers of an Alchemist, and a man in fancy clothes, both of them still recovering from the blast. "How many assassins are here?"

The two exchanged a glance, and the woman nodded to Kittal. "May I check on Master Kittal?"

"He'll live, and he's not your master anymore," Lad stepped over Kittal and faced them. "I need answers. How many assassins are here?"

"Um…" The woman pursed her lips. "Maybe twenty."

"Berta!" The man in the fine linen jacket and doeskin leggings shot her an admonishing glare.

"Accept it, Reynolds! We've lost." Berta looked back at Lad. "Most of the Inquisitors are out at this time of day, and the Alchemists are usually in their labs, though I don't know how many are left.

Lad considered. With the assassins they'd already neutralized, his odds weren't entirely dismal. "Do you know where the Tessifus boy is?"

Berta looked to Reynolds, who just shrugged and looked away. "Yes. I'll take you there."

Lad cocked an eyebrow at her. "You're being very helpful."

Berta shrugged. "The war's over as far as I'm concerned. I'll tell you whatever you—"

Lad felt it before he followed her wide-eyed stare, a light puff of air.

Black mists were coalescing in the spot where Mya and Hoseph had vanished.

Hoseph was returning.

CHAPTER XXI

*W*hat *in the names of all the gods…*

Mya hadn't known what to expect using Hoseph's magical trinket, but she *had* expected to go *somewhere*. But this…

This is…nowhere.

All of her senses were blank. There was literally nothing here: no up or down, no inside or outside. She would have been disoriented, but there was nothing to orient *to*. She had nothing but her own thoughts.

Am I dead? she wondered, but no, that didn't make sense either. There *was* an afterlife, of that she was sure, something more than this, anyway.

What had gone wrong? Maybe it took more than just holding the little silver skull and reciting the word to use it properly. Maybe only Hoseph could use it, Demia's high priest. Maybe he had banished her to this place.

Whatever this place is.

Refusing to consider that depressing alternative, Mya set about finding some way out. She was a Hunter, skilled in observation and problem solving. Though she had no senses, she had her intellect, she could think. Even magic had rules. She should be able to reason her way out of this. Banishing all preconceptions, she reached out with the only thing she had left: her mind.

A cool veil enveloped her. Of course, it was neither cool nor a veil, here in this nothing place, but that was the impression it left in her mind. But if there was really nothing here, what was this? Only one answer came to mind. *The silver skull—its magic.* She stretched out further, straining, seeking. Yes, there was something else there, too…

I'm not alone.

The realization both horrified and encouraged her. The presence—that was the only way she could think of it—was cold, angry, an icy malevolence that clung to her like a leech.

Hoseph!

Repulsed by both the sensation of his mind and the notion of Hoseph's touch, she mentally shuddered and pushed it away. *Let go!*

And he was gone.

No, not gone, not entirely. She could feel him still—icy hate, now swirling in a cloud of fear outside the cool veil—nearby but not connected to her any longer.

And if I can feel him, maybe there's something else out there.

No longer haunted by his specter, Mya cast out even further with her mind. There was more to this place than she'd first perceived: shifting shadows and eddies, matter and emptiness, thought and thrumming energy.

Then…something else…something *more.* It came out of nowhere, like a suddenly building thundercloud, heavy and oppressive, rushing in, down, through, and past her as if she didn't exist. Mya heard—no, not heard, but *felt*—a cacophony of thoughts, minds, voices, and feelings, like a tornado of leaves all spinning together. In one vast rush, it continued on, then vanished.

And Hoseph vanished with it.

Startled by the speed and ferocity of its passing, Mya huddled within herself, then reached out tentatively. It had taken Hoseph—*Consumed? Absorbed? Assimilated?*—and left her totally alone. *Why?*

That question provoked another. *Could this be where Hoseph brought Dee? Hoseph said I'd never find him…he's got to be somewhere. Perhaps he's wandering here in the nothingness like me.*

Mya wasn't sure if that was comforting or not. She knew one thing, however. *I may not be dead, but unless I can figure out a way to get back to where I started, I may as well be.*

Logic compelled her first option. *If Hoseph's trinket got me here, maybe it can get me out. Shahallariva.*

Something stirred, a gentle pressure like waves in a pond beating against her, within her…but nothing changed.

Damn it!

The pressure still pulsed in and around her, but it didn't do her any good if she couldn't induce it to take her where she wanted to go.

Mya quelled an upwelling of panic and thought hard. The word Shahallariva brought her here, but maybe it took a different word to take her back. Maybe every place in the world had its own word. She could guess forever and still not get it right.

So here I stay until I figure this out! Come on, Mya. You need to get back! Lad's standing there alone in Kittal's office... The room appeared in her mind's eye, clear in every detail. She felt the pressure building, pulling.

Kittal's office emerged from a swirling black mist, clearing, solidifying under her feet. Mya's senses returned, reviving the scent of smoke, the acrid tang of blood on her tongue, the pain of her injuries.

Lad whirled around—*so fast, so graceful, so beautiful*—and lunged. Clamping one hand onto her wrist, he swept her legs out from under her. Mya yelped in surprise and hit the floor hard. Before she could even catch a breath, he had her legs entangled in his, his chest pressed against hers, and her wrists pinned to the floor. She'd been taken completely flat-footed, still disoriented from the transition.

As her head cleared, she realized what must be going through Lad's mind. *Two of me...he doesn't know which I am, but I can give him a hint.* Smiling up at Lad, Mya flexed her hips against his. "If you want to get *frisky*, we should probably wait until we're alone."

Lad blushed, but his hard expression didn't change. "Finish this phrase: No fear, no pain..."

"No mercy," she said. "*Now* can I get up?"

Lad released his hold, got up, and extended a hand to her. "Sorry. I had to make sure you weren't Hoseph."

"Hoseph's gone." Mya swayed on her feet, dizziness and pain swirling through her head like the void she'd escaped. She closed her eyes to suppress the room's spinning.

Lad's sure hands gripped her by the arms. "Are you all right?"

"Just the knock to the head, I think." She smiled at the concern on his face, then looked down to her hand. She still clutched the little silver skull. The thin silver chain, once secured around

Hoseph's wrist, now dangled in an empty loop. *I got you, you bastard...* She tucked it in her pocket. "How long was I gone?"

"Only a few seconds. We've still got problems."

Mya could hear assassins beyond the short hallway. Both doors were destroyed, so there was nothing to slow them down if they decided to attack. *Enough of this...*

Striding over to Lakshmi's corpse, she knelt and considered the woman. She might have been a great asset to the guild if not for her greed.

Not greed...fear. Fear of death.

Mya's realization triggered an unexpected empathy. Lakshmi's fear of dying had driven her to horrific extremes. *That's what fear does.* It chilled Mya to think that her own fears could pervert her into such a creature. It seemed that the only way to avoid that was to abolish the fear, face it head on and overcome it.

Easy to say.

She looked at Lakshmi's bare leg sticking out from beneath her sari. The runes—*my runes*—had ceased their whirling and dancing. They were just tattoos now, the magic forever gone. *If only...* Abruptly, Mya pulled the onyx ring from Lakshmi's finger. Enough regret; it was time to look forward.

No fear...

Picking up one of her daggers lost in the fight, she approached Kittal, still prone on the floor. "Is he dead?"

"No. Unconscious." Lad watched her warily, reached out and grasped her shoulder as she leaned over the Master Alchemist. Heat blazed from his palm, a sure sign that his magic was primed. "Mya, don't."

Mya shrugged off his hand in annoyance. "Don't tell me what to do! No mercy, remember?" She immediately felt guilty for the outburst, but relieved when Lad stepped back. This was *her* decision.

Other than a bloody nose, Kittal looked asleep. What had made him such a monster? What kind of life must he have had under Lakshmi, the manipulative Inquisitor. What pressure had he been under, to join the guild, to become an Alchemist, to serve her every whim...his mentor, his colleague...

His mother.

Mya held up her dagger. After what Kittal had done to her, he deserved to die... But knowing *why* he'd done it, she'd reconsidered. *What would I do to bring my mother back, to make her alive again, to wash the blood from my hands?*

Mya lifted Kittal's hand and severed his ring finger with surgical precision. Cleaning the dagger on the former Master Alchemist's coat, she sheathed it, then wiped the blood off the ring. Straightening, she turned to face Lad.

"Once I wondered how you could forego vengeance and give Kiesha a peaceful death after what she did." She dragged in a deep breath and let it out. "People sometimes do horrible things for love. I can't forgive what Kittal did to me, but I wonder if I might not have done the same in his place."

Lad relaxed visibly. "Mya, you aren't—"

A raised hand cut him off. "Never mind. This war is *over*. More killing isn't what I want."

"What *do* you want?"

Mya coughed a laugh. *Such a loaded question...but I can't tell him the truth.* Pulling herself together, she said, "I want my *guild* back...whole." She stepped over Kittal to the two assassins cringing by the wall. "Berta."

The Alchemist curtsied stiffly, her face as pale as a sheet. "Grandmaster."

Grandmaster... I like the sound of that.

Mya proffered one of the onyx rings. "You're my new Master Alchemist if you want the job. By putting on this ring, you're declaring loyalty to the guild, not me. If you have any problems with what I'm doing, I expect you to bring them directly to the guildmaster or me, not work behind my back." She nodded to the fallen masters. "You see where *that* gets you."

The woman's face flushed and she gaped at Mya. "After...what I did to you?"

"Not you, Berta." Mya hooked a thumb over her shoulder at Kittal. "Him. You gave me what little mercy you could. Now, do you want this or not?"

"I..." Berta paused, deep in thought, but without a hint of avarice, greed, or elation on her face. "Yes, I want it."

"Good." Berta held out a hand and Mya dropped the ring into it. When the woman had slipped it onto a finger, Mya nodded in satisfaction. "You'll get the rest of your people back soon."

"They not dead?" Berta asked in surprise. "We were told—"

"You were told lies. Why would I destroy my own guild?" Mya wanted to smile at the woman's dazed expression, but she kept her mien serious. "Now call off your Alchemists and see to your injured, *Master* Berta."

"Yes, Grandmaster." Berta hurried over to the guard groaning beside the shattered door with Mya's dagger still stuck in his liver.

Mya turned to the other assassin. "And you are…"

"Senior Journeyman Inquisitor Reynolds, Grandmaster." He bowed stiffly, his expression carefully neutral.

Inquisitors… She wondered if any of them ever showed their true feelings. "Do you know where Lakshmi was keeping the youngest Tessifus boy?" Mya edged her question with steel and held up the second ring to make her point clear.

Reynolds licked his lips—*One of his tells, no doubt*—and she knew he lusted after it. "I do, Grandmaster."

"And are you willing to serve under the same conditions I gave to Berta?"

"Yes, Grandmaster."

"Then this is yours." Mya handed him the ring. "Keep in mind what happened to your former master before you get too proud of your new position. Now go check on the boy, but don't bring him yet. I have a few things to do."

"At once, Grandmaster!" He slipped the ring on and dashed across the room. There he touched a piece of molding on the wall, and a section of seemingly solid stone swung out to reveal a short passage. He left it open and vanished within.

Mya turned to find Lad staring at her with amusement. "What?"

He smiled. "I was right. You're good at this."

"At what?" She glared at his mirth.

"At being Grandmaster."

She snorted a disgusted laugh. "You're just trying to justify tricking me into taking the job."

He laughed. "Probably, but you're still good at it."

"Thanks. Coming from the *worst* guildmaster in the history of the Assassins Guild, that means…almost nothing."

He shook his head. "I was a pretty poor guildmaster, wasn't I?"

"You were." Mya twisted her sore neck. Her aches and pains were very slowly subsiding, which was good. The war might be over, but her work to rebuild the guild had just begun.

Lad had to admit it; Mya surprised him. After what she'd been through, his greatest worry was that her thirst for vengeance would destroy her, or worse, make her into something that *he* had to destroy. But she'd shown Kittal mercy, even appointed as master one of the people who had assisted in the Master Alchemist's atrocities. She cared more for the guild than her thirst for revenge.

She seemed whole again, her riven soul somehow healed. She was still a stone-cold killer, but her good heart had not been broken. Now Lad simply stood back and watched Mya do what she did best.

"You were just following orders, I get that," the Grandmaster said as she paced slowly in front of the assembled Inquisitors and Alchemists. "But now you'll be following *my* orders. If you don't like it, there's the door; use it. If you leave, you'll never come back. If you decide to stay, there'll be no retribution, but know that there'll be *changes* around here. We're going to do things differently, be more innovative, and everyone will benefit."

There were a few hard looks and some outright belligerence, but Berta and Reynolds took the wayward souls firmly in hand. The rest of the assassins just seemed relieved, happy even, that the conflict was over.

Lad watched…and watched…and watched as Mya took care of this task, spoke to that person. He finally wondered if she was deliberately stalling. The Morrgrey still marched toward Twailin; he had to get home.

"Mya…"

Mya held up a finger. "Almost ready. Just one more thing…"

Berta and two more Alchemists escorted Kittal into the room. The man glanced briefly to the corner where his mother's body had been, but all that remained was a dark stain. He turned back toward Mya, his face blank.

Mya stared at the former Master Alchemist for a full minute, tapping one toe. Not one of her tells, which probably meant she was doing it on purpose. Lad began to worry, wondering if he'd been wrong before. Would she execute Kittal now? Had she just waited so the man would have to face his death instead of being dispatched while unconscious? When she spoke, her voice was crisp and firm, but Lad could detect the slight quaver.

"Not too long ago, I signed your death warrant for what you did to me." The muscles at her jaw bunched and relaxed. "One of the best things about being Grandmaster is that I can change the rules. I'm not going to execute you, and I can't very well turn you over to the authorities, but I can't just let you go either. So, if you wish, you can remain with the guild. You'll have no official position, and you won't command anyone. Under Berta's supervision, you can conduct whatever alchemical research you want, with the stipulation that all your results belong to the guild. It's either that or you remain the guild's prisoner. Your choice."

Kittal just stared at her without comment.

"Well, think about it." Mya waved him away, and he trudged out of the room after Berta. "What's next?"

Lad stepped forward. "*Mya…*"

She looked at him and pursed her lips. "All *right*. Reynolds, fetch the Tessifus boy."

"Finally!" Lad whispered.

They didn't have long to wait.

"Don't touch me. Do you know who I am?" The high, shrill voice echoed down the corridor and grated on Lad's ears. A young boy strutted through the door. Reynolds followed, rolling his eyes.

The new Master Inquisitor bowed fluidly and said, "He's all yours."

Mya smiled at the boy. "Well, young Lord Tessifus. We're going to take you home! What do you think about that?"

The boy met Mya's pronouncement with a pout. "Who are you? Your hair looks funny! Where's Mistress Lakshmi? She promised me another puppy. The last one died—stupid thing."

Mya's smile wavered. "My name's Moirin. Mistress Lakshmi has gone away, but that's okay. You're going home! Aren't you anxious to see your family?"

"Whatever." The kid shrugged and looked around as if bored.

"Was he like this when he arrived?" Mya asked Reynolds quietly.

The Master Inquisitor had the decency to look ashamed. "No, he *was* a pretty good kid. But the conditioning…"

Lad looked pitifully at the errant child. He hated to imagine this boy raised—under the guidance of Lakshmi and Hoseph—to be a new Imperial Grandmaster along the same lines as the last: arrogant, cruel, disregarding of anyone or anything beyond his own desires. *That's not going to happen now. Maybe his family's love will undo what's been done.*

By the time they'd gotten into a carriage and set out for the palace, Lad's sympathy had shifted to the boy's family. Lad was used to a fussy child—Lissa could be a handful—but this kid was nothing short of a petulant little brat. He complained, demanded, and insulted throughout the trip. Lad considered a gag, but didn't want to anger anyone at the palace. He still needed the emperor's good will to get home.

Home… He looked at Mya staring out the open carriage window and wondered if he would ever see her again. She looked pensive and somewhat sad. He wondered if she was thinking the same thing.

"Are you all right?" he asked.

She looked at him. "Yes, just thinking."

"About…"

"About Dee. I think I might know what happened to him."

Lad arched an eyebrow. "What?"

"I'll tell you later." She shot a meaningful glance at the boy, then turned back to the window.

Lad nodded and they rode on, enduring a continuous barrage of petulance until the palace finally loomed ahead.

"We're here!" chimed Mya with more relief than elation.

"It's about time!" snapped little Lord Tessifus.

"More guards at the gate than usual," noted Mya as the carriage rolled to a stop.

Lad peered out the window. "And the portcullis is closed. Keyfur said something was amiss. Evidently it was something significant."

"Sorry, the palace is off limits to—" The guard went abruptly silent, his eyes wide, and he took a half step back from the coach. "Ah, Miss Moirin! How…uh…are you?"

The guard seemed unduly nervous to Lad. They'd been here once already this morning, and Mya seemed to be well regarded.

"Fine, thank you. I don't have an appointment, but I've got a delivery for the emperor and we need to speak with Master Keyfur."

"Lieutenant, it's *Miss Moirin*," the guard called to his superior.

Yes, there was definitely tension in the guard's voice. Lad touched Mya's knee and gave her a significant look. She returned a minute nod; she'd heard it, too.

The lieutenant hustled over, glanced in the carriage, and waved them forward. "Take it slow, driver. You may have to stop. They're doing some work on the inside gate." He, at least, seemed calmer.

The driver waited until the portcullis was raised, then lashed his team forward into the tunnel that led to the inner courtyard. The sound of the portcullis dropping behind them startled the horses. The carriage rumbled to a stop, but the inner portcullis remained closed.

Lad tensed, peering out the window at the arrow slits and murder holes lining the tunnel. They were trapped. He looked to Mya, but she made a forestalling motion.

"What's going on?" the young noble demanded.

"I don't know." Mya clicked her nails together.

At least I'm not the only one who's nervous. Lad listened carefully. Armor clanked and feet tromped along the corridors above and alongside the tunnel. Soldiers stepped into sight beyond the inner portcullis, crossbows creaking as they were cranked and loaded. "I don't think they're happy to see you this time, Miss Moirin."

Mya peered out the carriage window and frowned. "I think you're right."

CHAPTER XXII

My arse is gettin' numb.

Benj shifted in the ridiculously ornate chair, wondering how all the highfalutin couriers tolerated sitting in such things. He, Jorren, and Dreyfus had been cooling their heels for nearly half an hour, and he'd had just about enough.

He wondered what was taking so long...and what was up. First an imperial messenger had arrived at the scene of the riot, and Ithross had raced off with most of the Imperial Guard, leaving a squad to escort a carriage with Dreyfus and the two constables. Then they'd been ordered to wait in this room until they were called.

I hope whoever's gonna call does it soon, or I'm not gonna be able to stand up.

Finally, Ithross entered with a clatter of steel, his face stormy. He was still in his armor, but his neck was swathed in a bandage. "I'm sorry for the delay, but there was an...incident while I was out of the palace."

Benj's eyebrows shot up. "Incident?"

"Another attempt on the emperor's life. He survived, thanks to his *scribe*, of all people, but Archmage Keyfur was killed, and the assassin escaped."

Another *assassination attempt?* Benj recalled the suspiciously beefy rioters. "Just when you *happened* to be outside the palace? Didn't mention this before, but those rioters—"

"Were probably mercenaries. This *supposed* riot seems to have been orchestrated to deprive the emperor of protection." He glowered at Dreyfus. "Now, follow me." Ithross turned on his heel and marched off.

Dreyfus didn't protest as Benj and Jorren each took an arm and hauled him from his chair, and didn't say a word during their long trek through the palace. He just plodded along, head hanging, like a man being lead to the gallows.

Or that neck chopper the emperor's so fond of. Benj shared a look with Jorren, who just shook his head.

Eventually they stopped at a door and Ithross knocked, conferred in hushed tones with the guard who answered, then waved them in.

The room surprised Benj not in its grandeur, but in its stark functionality. Shelves of scrolls, books, and ledgers lined three of the four walls, and above the door hung the banners of the four Imperial Armies and the Imperial Navy. The emperor sat at a broad table strewn with papers, his secretary hovering at his shoulder. His Majesty was writing, his quill pen scratching along at a feverish pace. He didn't look up.

A man sat in the corner with a huge ledger in his lap, a pen poised. *The Imperial Scribe.* Glancing at the newcomers, he scribbled in his ledger. A golden star pendant hung on a light blue ribbon around his neck, gleaming in the lamplight.

Huh! Benj stared. *Scribe gets the Star of Tsing for saving the emperor's life, and all I got was more work.*

The emperor finished writing with a flourish and handed the parchment to his secretary. "Tennison, have that copied that fair, then bring it back for Us to sign. We'll send it by the fastest possible messenger."

"At once, Majesty." The secretary handed the parchment to an assistant, who ducked out the door.

Tynean Tsing's attention turned to his guests, but he didn't rise. "Gentlemen, forgive the wait. We've been busy."

They all bowed, though Dreyfus had to be encouraged by one of the guards.

"We have been informed that Chief Constable Dreyfus tried to murder Our captain of the Imperial Guard." The emperor sat straighter, his eyes flinty. "Who's the one who witnessed this firsthand?"

"I did, Majesty." Jorren bowed low. "Corporal Jorren Arryx, Tsing Constabulary."

"Give your account of the event, Corporal Arryx," the sovereign ordered.

"There's not much to say, Majesty. When everyone's attention was on the rioters, we were ambushed by some archers. One shot hit the chief's helmet, and several more hit some of the guards and their mounts. While everyone's attention was diverted, Chief Constable Dreyfus picked a crossbow bolt from the ground and stabbed it at the back of the captain's neck. I then...intervened."

The emperor shifted his attention. "Do you contest the corporal's account of your actions, Chief Constable Dreyfus?"

Dreyfus glared at Ithross with fire in his eyes. "He wants me *dead!* First he kills Otar, then he tries to frame me. He wanted me ruined, and that didn't work, so he set up those marksmen to murder me."

"Tried to have you murdered?" The emperor's brow furrowed as he looked at Ithross. "Captain?"

Ithross shook his head. "I have no idea what he's talking about, Your Majesty."

"Of *course* he'd say that! What do you expect? And of course you believe *him* over me!" Dreyfus' face flushed scarlet. "It's a conspiracy!"

Aw, crap. Benj cleared his throat. "If you'll pardon me, Majesty, I might be able to clear some of this up."

The emperor's eyes snapped to his. "Go ahead, Sergeant Benjamin."

Uncomfortably aware the eyes of the emperor and Ithross on him, he related the information he and Jorren had gathered during their surveillance of Dreyfus, including Miss Rose's visits to the chief constable and the gist of the first conversation, though he omitted Miss Moirin's name.

Dreyfus was the first to respond. "You've been *watching* me? You son of a bitch! I *knew* I should have—"

"Chief Constable!" Tynean Tsing's voice rang off the walls with all the authority of his office. "Sergeant Benjamin is the only reason you're not *already* in the dungeon. You were observed consorting with the late Captain Otar, who was meeting with High Priest *Hoseph.*"

Dreyfus' eyes widened. "I didn't—"

"*Then*, evidence found in Otar's quarters implicated you in a plot of regicide. Your sergeant, however, argued that the evidence was suspicious, and that you were being framed. *We* ordered him to watch you and report his findings to Captain Ithross." The emperor's eyes shifted again to Benj. "It *seems*, however, that the sergeant has been negligent with his reporting."

Benj endured the emperor's baleful stare. "Sorry, Majesty. What with all the arson and double patrols and such lately, I didn't have a chance to make it up here."

The emperor pursed his lips, then turned back to Dreyfus. "The truth of all this will come to light in time, but what We know for a *fact* is that you attempted to murder Captain Ithross." The emperor sighed and folded his hands. "We hereby strip you of all rank and position. You're to be held in the palace dungeons until your trial, Mr. Dreyfus. Take him away."

Dreyfus slumped as if every ounce of energy had suddenly been drained from his body. He quietly acquiesced as a squad of imperial guards led him away. An uneasy silence fell over the room.

"If I may, Majesty," Benj said, waiting for the emperor's nod. "The chief's been actin' right strange lately, not like his self at all. Now, to have him actually attack the captain? It's way beyond just bein' twitchy. We don't know nothin' about this Miss Rose. She could have spelled him or doped him up as well as feedin' him lies."

The emperor nodded. "Tennison, have Master Corvecosi see to him."

"Yes, Majesty."

Benj felt strangely sorry for Dreyfus—the man had been driven over the top—but at least all this sneaking around was over. He saw a large ale, a greasy pork pie, and a soft bed in his future. *And it can't come too soon.*

Tynean Tsing, however, wasn't done with him yet. "Sergeant Benjamin, we charge you with the investigation into who was behind the manipulation of your former commander and bringing the perpetrators to justice."

"Yes, Your Majesty." Benj bowed.

"As chief constable, you'll have free rein with the constabulary, but if you need additional resources, you may call on the palace."

Sergeant Benjamin choked. "Wha— What? *Me*, chief constable?"

The emperor and Ithross both smiled at him, and Jorren gave him a little nudge and whispered, "Good luck with *that*, Sarge!"

"You *are* senior sergeant, are you not? And you've shown great initiative and doggedness, not to mention loyalty and dedication, in this investigation. We think you'll make a fine chief constable."

See if I ever save your *life again...* Benj cleared his throat, at an uncharacteristic loss for words. "Thank you, Majesty, but...well, just between you, me, and the lamppost, I'd make a *crappy* chief constable. I'm a street cap. Always have been, always will be."

"We see." The emperor sighed. "Can you recommend someone for the position?"

"Ahhh..." Benj wracked his brain. *Tobas? No, he's a bit slow on the uptake. Keeson? Too much of a hothead.* None of his colleagues struck him as chief constable material, but it would have to be one of them. *Unless...* Grinning, he clapped Jorren Arryx on the shoulder. "*Sergeant* Arryx here is ripe as a plum for the job!"

"What?" Jorren stared at Benj in shock.

"Ripe as a plum and sharp as a tack, he is!" Benj clapped him hard again. "Your Majesty couldn't make a better choice!"

Tynean Tsing sat back in his chair, his brow furrowed. "Sergeant? We thought he was a corporal."

"Only 'cause I ain't had a chance to file the paperwork yet. I'm promoting him for savin' Captain Ithross' life. He'd make a *great* chief constable. He knows the city like the back of his hand! And he was a squire candidate, you know. Only reason he's not a knight is 'cause of some political bullshit."

The secretary gasped.

"Oh! Sorry, Majesty."

"But I—"

"Sergeant Arryx, you haven't been given leave to speak!" The emperor still looked grim, but one corner of his mouth twitched. He raised a hand. "Tennison." He whispered something to the secretary.

"At once, Majesty," The secretary went to the door and whispered to someone outside, then feet could be heard running down the corridor.

The emperor went back to his papers, scratched something on one, and looked at another.

Benj stood quietly, staring straight ahead. He could feel Jorren's glare on him like a hot poker nearing his skin, but refused to look. Jorren *would* make a great chief constable, whether he'd admit it or not. *And I get to go on drinkin', whorin', and not shavin'.* He just wished they'd get on with it.

A knock sounded on the door, and a message was whispered to Captain Ithross. Benj wondered if messages ever got screwed up with all the retelling.

Glowering, the captain stepped to the emperor and said in a low voice, "Your Majesty, Miss *Moirin* has arrived with a…package. She's being detained between the courtyards."

"Miss Moirin?" The emperor sat up straight with a startled look.

Why would the emperor be scared of Miss Moirin? Benj wondered. *With any luck, the package is Hoseph's head on a silver platter.*

The emperor resumed a neutral expression. "It doesn't seem likely they would try the same gambit twice, Captain, but We'll leave the security to your discretion."

"Yes, Majesty!" Ithross hurried out.

Moments later, a servant arrived with a large tome. Tennison flipped through the pages, then presented the book to the emperor, pointing at several entries.

Tynean Tsing read, then tapped on the book as he looked up. "Well, We see that you were *indeed* a squire candidate, Sergeant Arryx, with extremely high marks in your examinations. Frankly, they're higher marks than most *successful* candidates." He pushed the book aside and finally stood. "We suspect it was *indeed* some political bullshit at work."

A guard stifled a snort of laughter, and the scribe smiled. Benj forced a somber face, though it was a struggle.

"So, Sergeant Arryx, if you've no objection,"—he squinted wryly at Benj—"We will appoint you to the position of chief constable."

Jorren bowed deeply to the emperor. "I have no objection, Your Majesty."

"Excellent." The emperor held out his hand, and Tennison put something in his palm. Holding up a small gold star, Tynean Tsing pronounced, "Chief Constable Arryx, We charge you with keeping the emperor's peace within the walls of the city of Tsing. We also thank you for your service this day, as I'm sure Captain Ithross does as well." He held the insignia out to Jorren. "Put this on, if you please, Chief Constable Arryx.

"Thank you, Your Majesty." Jorren pinned the star to his collar and bowed again.

"You are welcome. Now, We must see to other matters." The sovereign snapped his fingers, and the ranking guardsman escorted them out.

That worked out well! Benj flashed a grin at his new commander.

Jorren leaned close and grumbled, "I'm never going to forgive you for this, you know."

"Oh, I know." Benj chuckled and clapped the new chief constable on the shoulder. "But I'll put up with your grousing if you'll put up with the paperwork."

"Miss Moirin!"

Mya leaned out the carriage window. "Yes?" She couldn't make out who had spoken with the sunlight of the courtyard backlighting the portcullis, but several more imperial guards stood among the crossbowmen.

"Please exit the carriage—Miss Moirin only!—and walk slowly toward the inner portcullis." Mya recognized Captain Ithross' voice now. "Keep your hands visible, and no weapons."

"This is bizarre!" Mya handed her daggers to Lad and climbed down from the carriage. The arrow slits and murder holes lining the walls and ceiling bristled with arrows and spears. If she made a wrong move, she'd be riddled. *What did I do to deserve this?*

Beyond the portcullis stood Captain Ithross and Lieutenant Tanse. The crossbowmen stepped back just out of reach, their weapons trained on her.

"Captain, Lieutenant. What's wrong?"

"That's what she was wearing earlier," Tanse said to Ithross. "The *first* time she arrived."

Mya cocked her head. "The *first* time?"

"Miss Moirin, why did you come to the palace earlier?" Ithross asked sternly.

"I had a message from Master Keyfur to meet him here."

"May I see the message?"

Mya patted her pockets before remembering. "I haven't got it. My colleague—Bloodhound, you remember him—got the message, picked me up, and we both came here. He's in the carriage if you want to speak with him."

The captain brushed off her offer. "And what business did you have with Master Keyfur?"

What the hells is going on? "He helped me track down someone, but he was called back to the palace, an emergency, he said. But why don't you ask him? What's going on? I've got the...ah..." she lowered her voice, as her mission was still supposedly a secret, "third boy here."

Lieutenant Tanse snorted. "So did the *other* Miss Moirin."

The other Miss Moirin? Suddenly everything clicked into place. "Hoseph! He was here looking like me, wasn't he?"

"*Someone* looking very *much* like you was indeed here not an hour ago," said Ithross dryly. "So you understand our need to—"

Mya raised her hands. "Absolutely, I understand. I saw him, too, looking like me, but wearing a maroon shirt and black trousers. You'll be pleased to know that he's dead."

Ithross' brow arched. "That *is* good news, but please, tell me the lieutenant's name, if you would. Just to confirm."

"Tanse. She escorted me and Master Bloodhound to Keyfur's quarters this morning. But why not just call the archmage down here to verify the truth of what I'm saying?"

Ithross clenched his jaw so hard Mya thought his teeth would shatter. "Archmage Keyfur is dead."

Mya stumbled back. *Keyfur...* His bright smile, his brilliant robes, and that ridiculous feather behind his ear. *He saved my life...and now he's dead.* "Was it Hoseph?"

"Apparently." Ithross waved a hand. "Open the portcullis. Thank you for your patience, Miss Moirin. We'll take you to the palace."

Mya boarded the carriage as it passed. "I suppose you heard that."

"Of *course* I didn't hear it," complained the Tessifus boy. "You were way over there, and *he* wouldn't let me out of the carriage."

"I heard." Lad looked grave. "If Keyfur's dead, how can I get home?"

"We'll figure something out. There must be *some* way to get word to Master Woefler."

"Very well." He didn't sound much consoled.

The imperial guards seemed subdued as the three guests were checked at the postern door and escorted to the familiar adjoining audience chambers. Master Corvecosi took possession of the argumentative Tessifus boy for an examination while Mya and Lad settled down in the other chamber to await the emperor. The boy's screeching protests could be heard through the closed door. For once Mya accepted the offer of refreshments. The light, fruity vintage washed the rancid taste of dust and chemicals from her throat.

She leaned back against the hard chair and winced. "Ouch!" She reached around and tried to feel what had stabbed her.

"Hold still." Lad probed through the holes in her jacket and shirt, his fingers warm as they ran lightly over her skin. He jerked, and pain lanced through her.

"Ow! What are you doing?"

He showed her a bloody shard of metal. "You've still got bits of shrapnel in your back, some of it already healed over. You need to have it taken care of."

"Or spend the rest of my life sleeping on my stomach." She sighed. "I'll get Berta to take care of it, though without my magic to block the pain, it's not going to be as pleasant as the last time."

"The last time?" Lad cocked an eyebrow.

"Dee." Mya smiled forlornly at the memory. "He spent hours pulling shrapnel out of my back once. He was very patient...and gentle." She drowned the lump in her throat with another sip of wine.

"Dee would be." Lad put a hand on the tattered shoulder of her ridiculous brocade jacket. "You've *got* to stop throwing yourself in harm's way."

Mya blinked at his concern, and felt a pang in her heart. Even soot stained and with a bloody gash across his temple, he was the most beautiful human being she'd ever known. *And he'll soon be off to Twailin.* "Lad, I need to tell you something..."

"Right! You were going to tell me about Dee."

Shit! Mya gulped her wine and put the glass down. "Yes, about *Dee.* I think I might know what happened to him."

"Oh?"

Mya told him of the chaotic emptiness where she had marooned Hoseph, and of the presence that whisked him away. "Maybe that's what happened to Dee. When it passed me, I thought I felt…something. Not thoughts exactly, but…maybe emotions."

"Dee's emotions?"

"I don't know." She shrugged miserably. "I wanted to ask Keyfur about it, but…"

"Hoseph was a priest of Demia. Maybe someone at the temple would have an answer."

"Maybe." She gritted her teeth. "But what I *really* wanted to tell you—"

The door to the adjoining audience chamber opened, allowing them to hear what was going on next door.

"Jondi! Oh, my little Jondi!" The man's tear-choked voice rang true, only to be interrupted by the Tessifus boy.

"Father, I'm starved! I want some lunch. Oh, and I want a puppy."

No more was heard of the reunion of father and son as several imperial guards marched in, followed by a knight and two squires. The emperor came next, his face set in a strange expression somewhere between elation and anguish.

Mya rose and curtsied. "Your Majesty."

"Miss Moirin! Once again you have delivered us from—" He stopped and stared at her. "Gods of Light, you've been injured *again!* And your companion as well. I'll get Master Corvecosi in here as soon as he's completed his examination of young Lord Tessifus."

"Majesty, I'm fine," Mya assured him.

"No, she's really not," Lad said.

"I *am* fine!" Mya glared at him, then turned back to the emperor. "I'll have my wounds taken care of presently, Majesty, but Master Corvecosi *does* need to know what I've learned about the boy. It seems that his abductors weren't just planning to pressure the duke by threatening his son. They were conditioning the youngest to eventually take the throne as their puppet."

The emperor's brow knitted. "But he's only a child, and his elder siblings would inherit before he did."

"Yes, which is why they would also have to be eliminated. I don't know how much of the conditioning has taken hold, though I imagine his parents could tell. They were apparently giving him drugs to make him more receptive. They were playing a very long-term game, Majesty, but it's over."

"Welcome news in the midst of an otherwise dreadful day, Miss Moirin."

"We heard that Master Keyfur was killed. I'm so very sorry, Majesty."

"You're not to blame in this, Miss Moirin. In fact, you have paid Us back in full by returning the Tessifus boys and eliminating that loathsome priest once and for all." The emperor stepped forward, much to the consternation of his guards, and held out a hand. "Thank you. Your task to the Crown of Tsing is fulfilled."

Mya shook his hand. "Disposing of Hoseph was my pleasure, Majesty. I just wish I could have done it sooner. I liked Master Keyfur very much, and I couldn't have completed my task without his aid. In fact, I'd probably be dead if he hadn't helped find me."

"And I would *certainly* be dead, twice over now, if not for your and Master Keyfur's aid." He squeezed her hand warmly, then released it and took a step back. "And for that, you have Our sincere thanks. If there's anything at all We can do for you, merely ask."

Lad nudged Mya's arm.

"As a matter of fact, Majesty, there is. My associate here was good enough to come up from Twailin to help find me and aid in my mission. I owe him my life several times over. I promised to get him back home before the armies of Morrgrey arrived. Master Keyfur was going to help us, but... Is there another way to get a message to Duke Mir's wizard, Master Woefler?"

The emperor frowned. "Until We can recruit a new archmage, We're bereft of magical aid. We are sending Duke Mir a missive, which he should receive in about six days, barring any mishaps on the road."

"Six days?" Lad's hand closed hard on Mya's arm. "I need to *go*!"

The emperor looked askance at him, and the guards stiffened. To ease the tension, Mya patted Lad's hand, then pried his fingers from her arm. "I know, but—"

"If you choose not to wait, We can provide you with a mount and an imperial writ of passage," the emperor offered. "It's the least We can do."

"Thank you, Majesty. I accept. I think that's my best chance to get to Twailin before the war does." Lad bowed, but didn't sound happy.

Six days on horseback, riding alone through ogre-infested mountains? There had to be a better way, some magic or... "The Wizards Guild!"

"What?" Lad looked at her askance.

"Tsing's got a Wizards Guild. They might not be up to Imperial Archmage standards, but one of them might have some way to get you there quickly, or get word to Woefler."

"We'll send someone immediately." The emperor signaled to a guard. "Tell Master Tennison to send someone to the Wizards Guild to see if any of their members can either magically travel or get a message to Twailin. Cost is not a factor."

Mya glanced at Lad. "Is that all right with you? If they can, it'd save you days."

"I'd still like the horse and writ," Lad said, looking to the emperor, "just in case."

The emperor smiled. "Of course. And in the meantime, I insist that Master Corvecosi attend to your wounds, Miss Moirin."

Mya opened her mouth to protest, but found Lad's hand on her arm again. "You really *should*, Moirin. I'll wait long enough to say goodbye, I promise."

"I..." Mya swallowed hard. *So much to say...* "Then yes, thank you, Majesty, I'll take you up on the offer of Master Corvecosi's services."

"Good!" The emperor waved a hand, and guards hurried up to escort them away.

CHAPTER XXIII

Lad stood at the sitting room's open windows, gazing out at the lavish palace gardens while he waited. Life proceeded apace out there, gardeners trimming hedges, others tending the flowerbeds, troweling dung into the rich, dark earth. He could smell it from here. One maid cut armfuls of blooms, while another piled them in a long, shallow basket, discarding those with the slightest imperfection. *They'll probably adorn the emperor's dinner table tonight.*

It all seemed incongruously peaceful, knowing the Morrgrey army was marching toward the city of Twailin and his family.

Gauging by the progression of the sun along the high palace wall, he estimated he'd been waiting at least an hour. Lad looked at the parchment in his hand. The writ granted a swift horse from the imperial stables, and permission to exchange mounts as necessary at the courier posts that dotted the road to Twailin.

I should just take a horse and go, but... He'd promised to say goodbye to Mya. Who knew when—or if—they'd see one another again. Besides, if the Wizards Guild came through, he could be home this afternoon rather than next week. The logical thing to do was to wait for their answer, but doing nothing galled him.

A little while later, the door to the adjoining chamber opened and Corvecosi came out, an assistant behind him carrying a satchel, a bundle of bloody towels, and a basin that clinked and clanked as it shifted.

The imperial healer met Lad's questioning look with his usual smile. "She's fine, though she may be clumsy for a bit from the salve I used to deaden the pain."

276

"Thank you, Master Corvecosi," Lad said as the healer headed for the outer door.

The smile flashed again. "It's my job, young man."

Corvecosi had left the inner door open, and Lad spied Mya sitting on a bed in the next room, pulling on boots. The emperor had once again provided clothes, but these, at least, were practical.

Lad went to the door. "Feeling better?"

"Not really." She looked pale and wobbled a little as she stood. "Lightheaded, and my back's numb. But numb is better than screaming while he cut into me, I guess." She shivered slightly and shook her head.

"Well, it's over, and you're better off for having all that stuff out of you. Aside from wound fever, a piece might—"

"I already got the lecture on the dangers of untended shrapnel wounds, thank you." She walked past him to the outer room, smelling of antiseptic and burned hair, which was now even shorter.

"He trimmed your hair, as well?"

She reached up and fingered her shorter locks self-consciously. "Corvecosi's assistant trimmed the burnt parts off."

A knock at the outer door made him tense.

"Yes?"

A guard leaned in from the hall, admitting a young woman in imperial livery. She was breathing hard, sweating, and smelled faintly of horse and leather.

"Message for you, Miss Moirin. From the Wizards Guild." She held out a scroll.

"Stay a moment, please." Mya took the scroll, cracked the wax seal, and read the note. Her lips curled down, and she glanced up at Lad. "No good. None of the guild wizards can travel that distance. They're sorry they can't assist, blah, blah, blah." She crumpled the parchment in her fist.

Lad heaved a sigh. It was the road, then. He faced the messenger. "Would you please go to the stables and tell them to saddle a horse immediately. A *fast* one. If there's any argument, tell them I've a writ from the emperor."

"Yes, sir." The young woman hurried out.

He turned to Mya. "I'm sorry, but—"

"Hang on." Mya stepped past him, closed the door, and turned to face him. "I've got something—"

No more delays! "Mya, if you're trying to keep—"

"Just shut up and listen!" Mya looked straight into his eyes. "I *know* you're anxious to get home, but this is no little jaunt you're considering. What if I could get you back to Twailin this afternoon?"

"But the wizards—"

"No wizards," she said as she reached into her pocket, "just me." Pulling out her hand, she dangled a little silver skull on a chain between them. "And this."

Lad caught his breath. "Hoseph's *talisman*? Are you *crazy*?"

"I've *already* used it once. Twice, really, if you consider the round trip." Mya's tone was blasé, but her unconscious tucking of a wisp of hair behind her ear betrayed her anxiety.

Lad was torn. To get home today would be ideal, but… "It's a huge risk. Maybe it only worked before because Hoseph was with you. That…nothing place you told me about, we could get stuck there."

"I don't think so." She bit her lip. "And it wouldn't be *we* initially. I'd test it alone first. If I don't come back, you can take your horse and go."

He stared at her, shocked speechless. *Mya risking her life just to get me home quickly?* His puzzlement must have shown on his face.

"I've seen Hoseph transport people safely with it, Lad. One way or another, I'm *going* to use it." Her face brightened. "*Think* about it! Being able to instantly travel anywhere will do me a world of good as Grandmaster."

Not so much altruism after all. "Well…if you're going to use it anyway… Go ahead and try it."

"I can't do it in the palace. There are wards against it."

Lad rolled his eyes. *Another delay.*

"Don't!" Mya snapped. "I'm *not* putting you off! Just come with me in the carriage. As soon as we're beyond the palace wall, I'll try it."

A flicker of suspicion—*A trick?*—but he quashed it. Mya had changed. "All right. Let's go."

Their escort saw them down to the courtyard where their carriage waited. Next to it stood a groom holding the bridle of a long-legged gelding. At Lad's request, he tied the reins to the back of the carriage. If Mya's experiment didn't work out, Lad could leave directly.

If it doesn't work out...

Mya's thoughts apparently ran along similar lines. She fidgeted as they boarded, and jumped as they jerked into motion. Looking out the window of the carriage as they entered the tunnel to the outer court, she clicked her nails, then abruptly clenched her hands. She knew Lad could read her tells.

Lad felt like he should say something, but he wasn't sure what, so he considered her in silence. She was still pale, but he didn't know if it was from blood loss or nerves. Otherwise, she seemed like the old Mya. *Except for her hair.* The style, shorn almost to fuzz in back, but longer in front, gave her head a strange, forward-tilting look, but made her neck look very long and slender.

"I think I like your new haircut."

"What?" Mya's eyes snapped to his, sharp as her daggers.

"Your hair." He pointed to the back. "If you're not careful, you'll set a new fashion trend."

She shook her head and looked away, but her fingers crept up to touch at the bare stubble at her nape.

The dark of the second tunnel cast her face in shadow until they emerged back into the sunlight and the outer court. Then they were beyond the palace walls, the horses picking up the pace as they headed down through the Heights.

"Well..." Mya fished Hoseph's silver talisman from a pocket and gazed at it. "I guess I better find out if this thing works."

Lad's heart suddenly skipped a beat. "Mya, wait! It's not worth the risk."

"It's not *your* risk to take." She looked at him and quirked a sardonic smile. "I *promised* I'd get you home, Lad. Wish me luck."

With a whisper, the dark mists swirled, engulfing and consuming her. Within seconds, she was gone.

"Good luck." Lad stared as the last of the mists dissipated in the breeze from the open window and wondered if he'd ever see Mya again.

Oblivion…

Well, so far, so good. Mya paused, her Hunter's curiosity aroused. *What* is *this place?*

She stretched out her mind as before, felt the cool tingle that she recognized as the talisman. *Hoseph's talisman.*

Mya considered that and tried to follow a logical path to an answer. Hoseph was a priest of Demia, and Demia was the Usher of Souls, so perhaps this was where souls were sent after death, some kind of purgatory where souls waited before Demia sent them on to their just rewards.

But I'm not dead, and I'm not just my soul. My body's here too, right?

That was the question, wasn't it? If a person travelled body and soul to this place, then was abandoned—like she had done to Hoseph and what Hoseph had likely done to Dee—were they still here? Were they still alive?

Since she survived, it seemed logical that others would. *They have to be! Dee…*

But even if he was here, how could she find him? Without a voice, she could hardly shout out his name. Perhaps emotion—she'd sensed Hoseph's fear and rage, and the roiling emotions of whatever had taken him. But what emotion could she use to find Dee? Mya wasn't particularly adept with emotions.

Thoughts, then.

Thoughts seemed to precipitate consequences in this place: she'd abandoned Hoseph with a thought, invoked the talisman by simply thinking the word of activation, and returned to the place she'd pictured in her mind.

It's worth a try.

Mya thought about Dee, recalling the sound of his voice; the look of his face and his long, lean body; the feel of his fingers skimming her skin… Little vignettes ran through her mind: Dee doing her paperwork, cooking dinner, dressing her in one of his disguises, practicing with his tiny crossbows, making love to her, attacking Hoseph to save her life. Mya felt hollow, a yawning emptiness within her. Dee had helped her so much, and she had appreciated him so little...until the end.

Mya wished she could cry to relieve her heartache. She may not have loved Dee the way he wanted, but she had treasured him as a colleague and friend, and now he was gone.

I miss him so much... DEE!

Something heard her.

From everywhere and nowhere, a maelstrom of emotions rushed in and engulfed Mya like a raging sea. Love, hate, hunger, greed, desperate loneliness, terror... The feelings swept through her, threatened to drown her in a cacophony she couldn't silence.

Mya panicked, straining to focus through the din. *Safe... I need to get somewhere safe...* She pictured the one place—the only place—she'd ever felt truly safe. *Shahallariva!*

It was dark. Pitch dark.

For a moment, she didn't know if it had worked, but she felt her hands and feet, heard her heartbeat, and drew a breath. Then, gradually, a diffuse light rose, illuminating her surroundings, and she sighed with relief.

Home... The only place she'd ever truly felt at home: her apartment beneath the *Golden Cockerel* in Twailin. *It worked!* Triumph surged through her. The world was hers.

She wandered through the rooms, the glow crystals in silver sconces brightening with her passage. Everything was as she had left it: the pin-studded map on the wall, the books beside the couch, the bare walls of her exercise room that had once sported mirrors...until she smashed them all. *Paxal must have closed it up before going with Dee to Tsing.* Mya wondered if he would return to Twailin now that the guild war was over. She hoped not. It was comforting to know he was nearby even if he wasn't always doting on her the way he had here.

Maybe I'll buy him a new inn to run in Tsing, use it as my headquarters. The urchins could live there, too, free from the dangers of the streets. Who knew where things would go from there. But, even if he did come back to Twailin, with the talisman, she could visit any time she wished.

Twailin... Lad! I can bring him home...and visit any time I like!

But the flash of hope died in the light of cold logic. Lad didn't love her. He only loved his family. He wasn't part of the guild any longer, abhorred it, in fact, and everything to do with it. *And I am* the *guild…*

Love is a weakness, Mya, get over it. It's never going to happen. Move on… Her conscience was right and she knew it. Still, it hurt. But pain— both physical and emotional— was so familiar now that it was simply part of her. Part of being alive.

Mya had the guild and the whole world at her fingertips. It was more than enough.

Clasping the little silver skull, Mya invoked the talisman and transitioned into the dark void. Thankfully, she sensed nothing; the storm of emotions was gone. That was good. She didn't need any distractions. Hoseph had been able to pop into a moving carriage, but then, Hoseph had been using the talisman for years. She remembered the mercenaries he'd brought into the orphanage, materialized with the trip-strings they'd strung up in the hallways transecting their bodies.

Get it right, Mya…

She pictured Lad in the carriage, felt a pressure like a gentle but steady hand urging her along. Mya pictured herself moving along with it, said a little prayer to the Gods of Light, and thought, *Shahallariva.*

Lad's tense face appeared through a swirling fog, relaxing as she solidified. "Where have you been? I thought that…maybe…you weren't coming back."

Mya reached over and slapped Lad's knee. "It worked! I was just in Twailin, in the *Golden Cockerel.*"

Lad's face lit up like a beacon. "Then I guess we should return the emperor's horse, since I won't be needing it. *Thank* you, Mya."

Mya sighed and flopped back against the cushioned seat, her face aching with a grin. The ability to travel instantly was a game changer. She'd be able to keep tabs on the most far-flung branches of the guild, actually meet her guildmasters instead of governing from afar. *No intermediaries or messengers required.*

She raised her hand and dangled the silver skull, gazing at it. "What I don't understand is why this even works for me. I'm not a disciple of Demia."

"Maybe you should be," Lad said. "She *is* Keeper of the Slain, and if there's anyone who might be in her good graces, it's the Grandmaster of Assassins. Perhaps *she's* interested in *you*."

Mya found that thought disquieting. She remembered an old Jesti curse, "May the gods take interest in you."

"So, now that you know it works…"

Mya raised a forestalling finger. "Hold that thought. I've got to do something. Meet me at Embree's headquarters. Shahallariva." Mya took the vision of Lad's gaping mouth into the void with her.

You're being petulant, you know, chided the voice in the back of her mind.

I know, Mya thought, only half-shamed. She'd promised to take Lad home, and she fully intended to, but she couldn't resist prolonging it a bit longer. Picturing her destination, she invoked the talisman.

As Embree's office resolved around her, there came the scuff of boots and screeching chairs on the floor, shouts of alarm, steel hissing from sheaths, the flash of silver streaking at her.

Mya twisted away and flung out a hand, felt something bite into her palm.

"Stop!" she shouted, realizing how foolish she'd been. What did she expect, materializing into the middle of a nest of assassins?

"Grandmaster!" Clemson was the first to recognize her.

"Good gods! Grandmaster, I'm sorry!" Noncey rushed forward, a horrified expression on his ashen face. A thin chain trailed from the buckle in his hand to a blade embedded in Mya's hand. "I could have *killed* you!"

"Not your fault, Noncey." Mya jerked the blade from her hand, hissing at the pain. The chain recoiled into the buckle, and Noncey replaced it on his belt. He passed her a kerchief for her hand. "I've always wondered what that belt buckle was for."

"How in the Nine Hells…" Clemson cleared her throat. "Pardon, Grandmaster, but we thought you were Hoseph, misting in like that."

"Hoseph's talisman." Mya dangled the silver skull for them to see, then tucked it away. "You got my message, didn't you?"

"Yes, but quite frankly, we thought it was a ruse. Only two of you to clean out two factions of assassins?" Embree gestured around his disorganized office. "We were getting ready to vacate the premises."

"It wasn't a ruse. The war's over. Hoseph's gone, Lakshmi's dead, and Kittal is under guard." Mya wrapped her bleeding hand, accepted a chair, and filled them in on all the details. Her tale transformed their worry to elation.

"This calls for a celebration!" Embree rummaged through a crate and pulled out a bottle. Filling four glasses, he handed out the celebratory drinks.

Mya raised her glass. "To our victory. We're *finally* one guild again!"

"One guild!" They all toasted and drank.

The whisky burned a smoky track down Mya's throat, and she sighed in contentment. The war was over, the guild was hers. *And Lad will go home.* Her mood dropped a notch.

As if summoned by her thoughts, an urgent knock at the door heralded Lad's arrival. He stopped at the sight of them relaxing with crystal tumblers in hand, and he cocked his head in that gesture she found so endearing. "Mya..."

Damn! Smiling brightly, Mya raised her glass. "Bloodhound! Sit and join us for just one drink, then I'll take you—"

Lad raised a hand with an easy smile. "There's no rush." He accepted a glass from Embree and pulled up a chair. "On the ride here, I thought about it. Tonight would be a better time to take me back, so we don't surprise anyone."

"Good idea." Mya peeked under the kerchief wrapping her hand, but the wound had already closed to a thin, pink scar. "I've had way too many surprises already for one day."

Chapter XIV

Lad staggered slightly as the familiar rough wooden stalls and straw-strewn floor of the *Tap and Kettle*'s barn coalesced around him. One of the mules huffed in surprise, and the horses shifted uneasily, but relaxed when they recognized his scent. He breathed deep the air of home, heard the distant sounds of the inn, could almost taste Forbish's fresh bread.

Twailin... Family... Lissa...

He released Mya's warm hand and turned to her. "Thank you for bringing me back. I know it was risky. That place...I felt like I was dreaming or something."

Mya leaned against a worn post and crossed her arms. "You get used to it, and it was a risk I was going to take anyway. You just had to trust me."

"I *do* trust you." The words came without thought, and Lad realized with surprise that he meant them. For the first time in...well...ever, he had no suspicions of Mya. They'd been through too much, shared too many risks, saved each other too many times not to trust each other now. And what was more, he'd truly seen a change in her. Mya had been through hell, but it hadn't broken her. She was still an assassin, but her heart had grown.

"Well, I better be—"

"Don't rush off. I want to say something to you."

Mya cocked a wry eyebrow, opened her mouth as if to say something, then closed it again and shrugged.

Where to start... The beginning seemed like a good spot, their beginning. He gestured to their surroundings. "Remember what happened here?"

"Of course," Mya glanced around, nodded toward the rafters. "I hid up there. You wiped out half my team, then I captured you using a poisoned ring."

"Not a promising start to our relationship."

"No," Mya admitted. "But as you once said, we were both slaves then. Things have changed. *We've* changed. You've got a family to look after, I've got my guild." She chuckled and ran her fingers through her hair.

"Being Grandmaster should be easier now, anyway, but you've got a lot to do."

Mya rolled her eyes. "Tell me about it! I've got to set up my own headquarters, find a place to live, appoint a new guildmaster, touch base with the other guildmasters, get a new assistant—" She stopped abruptly and dropped her gaze. "I *really* miss Dee. That's probably going to be the hardest thing to get used to. Not having anyone to talk with anymore. *Really* talk with." She laughed, but it rang false to Lad's ears.

"You can talk to *me*, Mya. I'm not Dee, but—"

She snorted a laugh and shook her head. "No, you're not."

"Why is that funny?"

She looked up at him. "It's not funny, it's ironic."

"Why?"

Her eyes twinkled in the soft light. "Dee was loving, witty, attentive, and really, *really* good in bed."

Lad thought for a moment, then said, "So, you're saying I'm not witty?"

Mya laughed again, this time with true good humor. "Well, *sometimes* you are, I suppose. As for the rest, we'll never know, will we? You'll be here in Twailin, and I'll be off in Tsing."

Lad stepped closer. Dressed as he'd first met her, in soft leather trousers, boots, and a blousy shirt, but with her hair cut so differently, she looked…quite nice. He reached out to flick the little silver skull dangling from the chain at her wrist. "Just a blink away. If you ever need…someone to talk to, laugh with, spar with, have a glass of wine with…you've got a friend."

Mya stared at him, her eyes bright. "*Are* we friends?"

"Yes." Lad wasn't sure how to say what he wanted to say. Mya was the one who had a way with words. "We're more alike than not,

Mya. We've shared things that other people could never understand. If we can't turn to each other, who *can* we turn to?"

"You're saying you would *want* me to visit?" She sounded truly surprised.

"Yes, I'm saying…" He cleared his throat. "…that maybe what we have…could grow."

She blinked at him. "But Wiggen…"

Lad shook his head. "This isn't about Wiggen. I'll *always* love her. My heart still breaks when I think about her, and no one will *ever* replace her. But our relationship is…different."

Now Mya looked wary. "We have a *relationship*?"

"Well, friendship, anyway. I'm not promising anything, Mya, but perhaps, if we were to get to know each other better, sit down and talk about things that have nothing to do with the guild or killing or emperors or wars. Get to know each other for who we *really* are. Then, maybe…"

"You know what I think, Lad?" Her voice sounded strange, quivering, tense like he'd never heard it.

"No, I don't."

"Fuck maybe!" Mya grabbed Lad's shirt and pulled him into a fervent kiss.

Lad could have stopped her, but he found that he didn't want to. Her lips weren't Wiggen's, but they were earnest and very soft. He kissed her back for the first time, honestly, openly, and passionately.

Lad had no idea where this might lead, but it didn't matter. They had time to figure that out. Mya was more than just Grandmaster, and he was more than just a father and innkeeper.

Together, they could be themselves, whoever they were deepest in their souls.

Mya closed her eyes against the warm breeze that flowed in through the carriage window. *No hiding behind dark curtains anymore.* For the first time in the better part of a year, her life was resuming some semblance of order. Not even a week had passed since she'd returned Lad to Twailin—her heart skipped a beat remembering their farewell—but it had been a productive time.

She'd moved into a comfortable townhouse high in Midtown with a view out over the city. *My city*, she thought with satisfaction.

Her household staff consisted mostly of assassins, but she'd managed to procure an excellent cook who had willingly adopted Paxal's recipe for mulled wine, and knew how to brew a proper pot of blackbrew. Mya's new personal assistant, a dour but able Inquisitor named Veera, with a head for figures and a penchant for finery, had chosen the gown Mya currently wore. Deep blue, it made the most of her figure, accented her hair, and covered her tattoos. Nice, but devoid of Dee's sense of style and personal little touches.

Work was going equally well. She'd settled the Tsing Guild firmly on her new course. She'd visited Sereth and reveled in his straightforward professionalism without any fawning or obsequiousness; they'd known each other too long for that. He was solid and loyal, and she expected great things from him. She planned to visit him again soon to check on the progress of the war. She'd also sent messengers to the other provincial guildmasters informing them of events past, new policies, and that she'd visit each of them soon.

Her carriage pulled to a stop, and she suppressed a sigh. *But into every smoothly flowing stream, stones will be tossed…*

"Miss Moirin to see the emperor at His Majesty's invitation," her driver announced to the imperial guards manning the palace gates.

Invitation…more like a summons.

The letter, delivered yesterday by imperial messenger, had read, "His Imperial Majesty Tynean Tsing III requests your presence at the Imperial Palace tomorrow at midday for a formal audience."

An imperial guard peered into the coach window. "Hello, Miss Moirin. Good to see you again."

"Thank you."

The coach rumbled into the inner courtyard and pulled around in a wide circle, stopping before the main entrance, not the postern gate as she was accustomed. *I guess I rate the front door now instead of the servant's entrance.* A liveried footman opened the door and held out a white-gloved hand to assist her down the single step.

Captain Ithross awaited her in full dress uniform at the bottom of the steps, a genuine smile on his usually stern face. "Miss Moirin. Welcome."

I either finally made it off his "suspicious persons" list, or the emperor ordered him to be nicer.

"Thank you, Captain." She took his proffered arm and they ascended the steps, a squad of imperial guards falling in around them. "I don't suppose you'll tell me what this is about."

"I'm afraid I can't, Miss Moirin. His Majesty forbade it."

Forbade? That raised the hairs on the back of her neck, or would have if they weren't shorn so short. They stepped inside the palace and strode through the towering foyer. *And no search for weapons this time, either.* Mya considered Ithross critically as they began their trek through the opulent palace corridors. Such trust from him seemed uncharacteristic, but he didn't appear anxious at all. Whatever the reason for this summons, it had earned her some credibility, at least.

Hopefully it won't take all afternoon. Mya had a guild to run.

They turned into a wing of the palace she'd never seen before. From a nearby room came the sound of laughter and clinking glasses, the clatter of dice and the flip of cards.

Gods, I thought this was to be an audience with the emperor, not some social occasion. She had better things to do than paste on a false smile, make small talk, and flatter noble egos.

"Is there a celebration going on?" she asked Ithross in a stage whisper.

"Oh, that's just the courtiers in the Hall of Revelry." He flicked a hand dismissively. "They rarely stop reveling, even when the empire is at war."

Mya glanced into the chamber as they passed. The privileged of Tsing sat upon opulent chairs and divans, playing games, chatting, drinking, and laughing. *Good work if you can get it.* Then something caught her eye, and she stopped short, yanking Ithross to a halt. The squad of guards clattered to a stop, nearly bowling into them.

I'll be damned to all Nine Hells if Lad wasn't right. Several of the women and one man sported hairstyles cut very short in back and longer in front, shockingly similar to Mya's explosion-induced coif.

"Is something wrong, Miss Moirin?" Ithross asked.

"Um...no." Mya curbed her fascination and resumed walking, but not before numerous eyes in the room spotted her, and whispered conversations began in earnest.

"That's *her*!"

"...beautiful gown..."

"...thought she was taller..."

"...never would *dream* she was a commoner."

Heat prickled Mya's neck, but she marched on. The last thing she needed was more notoriety. Assassins did their best work in the shadows.

The laughter and sounds of revelry faded as she and her entourage walked on. They finally reached a pair of double doors and stopped. The four guards posted there snapped to attention, and two of them swept open the doors.

The audience chamber was small and comfortable, with tall glass doors providing a splendid view of the city. Mya focused instead on the dozen or so people occupying the room. She started as a herald cracked his staff twice on the polished floor and announced her. Everyone turned and beamed at her.

Gods of Light and Darkness, what the hell is this about? Mya released Captain Ithross' arm and curtsied.

"Miss Moirin, We're *delighted* to see you!" The emperor strode forth, flanked by a knight and several imperial guards, none of whom intervened as he walked right up and stuck out a hand. "You look splendid!"

"Thank you, Your Majesty." She blushed when he kissed her hand instead of shaking it.

"We believe you've met Our cousin, Duke Tessifus, and his three sons, although the young lords may not remember you." The emperor dragged her by the hand into the midst of the duke's family.

"Pleased to see you looking so well, Miss Moirin." The duke shook her hand warmly and introduced his sons. "You recognize Bollins, Wexford, and Jondi, I daresay, having saved them from ignominious ends at the hands of those kidnapping fiends. I'd also like to introduce my wife, the Duchess, and my daughters, Cloitia and Breethe."

"Delighted." Mya shook hands, curtsied, and smiled. The three boys looked well enough, though the youngest seemed put out for some reason. The duchess gushed praise for her actions in rescuing her family, and thrust her daughters forward as if presenting them to potential suitors. Breethe, a delightful little girl of twelve or so, also sported Mya's hairstyle, and fairly bounced on her toes when she shook her hand.

"You've created quite the rage with your daring do, Miss Moirin!" little Breethe exclaimed. "They call it 'The Tilt,' you know! I *insisted* that mummy let me have one!" She flipped her short hair ecstatically.

"It looks lovely on you," Mya said, wondering whether she should tell the girl how she'd gotten hers. She decided against it. The family had been through enough trauma.

The duke stepped in again, patting his exuberant daughter on the shoulder. "You gave me my family back, Miss Moirin. The entire Tessifus clan is eternally grateful." Duke Tessifus pulled an oblong mahogany box from the inside pocket of his jacket and presented it to Mya. "Please accept this gift."

"Why, thank you, Milord Duke!" Mya curtsied as she took the box.

"Open it! Open it!" Breethe bounced on her toes some more, brimming with excitement. "I helped pick it out!"

Mya opened it and caught her breath. A row of perfectly matched rubies, each as large as an almond, glittered on a golden bracelet. She struggled for the right words, and failed. "Oh...my."

The duchess clutched Mya's arm and gushed, "It's a *trifling* token, really. You gave me my *sons* back!"

Mya looked at the bracelet—it was hardly trifling, even by a duke's standards—then at the Tessifus family. They all—except for Jondi—looked so pleased with her that Mya banished the notion of telling them that she'd only rescued the boys to foil the plots of her enemies, not out of any sense of compassion or duty. "Thank you, milady. I'll treasure it." *Or sell it and pay off my townhouse!*

Duke Tessifus took his wife by the arm. "And if ever you need *anything* that House Tessifus can provide, you've but to ask."

"You're very gracious, milord." Mya curtsied.

"Well done, Milord Duke." The emperor beamed and stepped forward.

The duke took his cue, said his farewells, and ushered his family out of the audience chamber.

"Now it's time for Us to reward you for your services to the empire, Miss Moirin." The emperor maintained his smile.

Mya tried not to fidget as his entourage repositioned themselves, not in the usual semicircular arrangement to protect their lord, but two precise lines. Mya chilled at the formality, wondering what her reward might be. *If a duke's warrants a king's ransom in jewels…*

"Without your intervention," the emperor intoned, "We would have died before We took the crown. Without your willingness and courage, Duke Tessifus, perhaps *Emperor* Tessifus, would have been subject to extortion by Our enemies. Indeed, the duke and his two elder sons would have *died* to fulfill the plot you foiled. Without your devotion and miraculous skills, the empire would now be in the hands of murderers, torturers, and fiends."

"I didn't do it *alone*, Majesty," she demurred.

"Tennison." The emperor held out a hand, and his secretary placed a ribbon-bound scroll of fine vellum into it. This he handed to Mya. "This document confers upon you the title of *Lady* Moirin, and bequeaths to you the lands of a small estate to the north and east of the city formerly owned by Baroness Monjhi."

Holy shit! Mya felt like the scroll in her hand might burn her. *A gods-be-damned title?*

Swallowing her apprehension, her thoughts strayed to the myriad ways this would benefit the guild: *influence, intelligence, access…* Of course, she'd have to make the occasional social appearance, but she was accustomed to wearing disguises and assuming roles. *Just be humble and take it, Mya…*

"Majesty, I don't know what to say. You're too kind."

"We are no such thing." He waved a hand dismissively, "You've *earned* the title and its attendant privileges as a reward for your services. By accepting it, you may, at your pleasure, visit the palace without invitation, enjoy the numerous amenities here, and…consort with other nobles, though that's a dubious pleasure, in Our opinion."

Mya couldn't help but grin. "Excepting your Majesty's company, of course."

"We're happy you think so." Tynean Tsing face brightened. "So, the empire has repaid its debt to you, and now We would like to repay Our own *personal* debt…privately."

Privately? Mya felt a rush of apprehension as he took her hand and placed it on his arm. *What the hell?* She went along as the emperor strolled toward the balcony. The guards started to follow him, but the sovereign stopped them with a raised hand.

Captain Ithross stepped forward. "Please Majesty, not the balcony. The antechamber perhaps. We can secure both doors, and there are no windows."

"The antechamber is not *suitable* for this, Captain," the emperor said without breaking his stride. "The balcony is much more conducive to…*private* conversation. And We won't be requiring your services either, Verul. Some things need not be recorded for posterity."

The scribe bowed and closed his ledger.

Uh-oh. Mya glanced helplessly behind her as the captain and imperial scribe stepped back. The guards remained staid, but Tennison's expression vacillated somewhere between apprehension and joy. *What the hell is going on?*

They emerged onto the balcony, and the emperor closed the glass doors behind them. "Beautiful, isn't it?" He swept his hand to encompass the view.

"That it is, Majesty."

The balcony jutted out over the sheer bluff. Far below, the buildings of the Heights District appeared small, and diminished even further down the hill. From this distance, the river actually looked picturesque, a blue-green ribbon winding through the city to the huge bay, where dozens of ships lay at anchor. Beyond, the azure ocean stretched to the horizon.

Now that they were alone, the emperor's formality seemed to ease, his posture relaxed, and his face became more amiable. "So, as We said, We owe you a great personal debt, one that We can never repay. We have…*I* have decided not to *try* to reward you. Instead, We are honored to offer you this…" Dipping into a pocket of his jacket, he drew forth a small velvet box of the most beautiful blue hue, as pure as the sea and sky, and proffered it to her.

Oh. My. Dear. Gods. Of. Light. Heat that had nothing to do with the temperature of the air flushed her face. Her mouth gaped, but Mya, usually so glib, could think of nothing to say. *Couldn't* speak, actually, around the lump in her throat. "I...I...I..."

Tynean Tsing's smile became suddenly strained. "Please consider Our situation, Lady Moirin, if you would. We're beset with powerful enemies, and the situation with the Tessifus boys made Us realize that loved ones could be used against Us."

Love is a weakness... Mya swallowed the lump.

"We once offered you a position at Our side as Our bodyguard. Now We're offering you a position at Our side...as Our empress. You're the most capable woman We've ever met, a true hero of the Empire. You charm us with your wit and your poise, your dedication and your frankness. We *know* that you would protect Our children better than any number of guards or soldiers. *Please*, Moirin, be my empress... Be my wife."

Mya clutched the balcony balustrade to keep her knees from buckling. Sweat prickled her neck, and she gasped to breathe with the thrice-damned corset squeezing her ribs. The view swam before her, the city...the empire...a plum ripe for her hand. All her life she'd sought power, schemed for it, killed for it. She hadn't planned on donning the Grandmaster's ring, but she'd fought, bled, and been tortured to make the guild her own. Now she was being offered the keys to the empire.

Imperial Grandmaster of Assassins...

The tiny box beckoned, and Mya knew what she'd find inside...if she accepted.

Slavery.

The word popped unbidden into her mind, and her thoughts snapped to clarity. As empress, she'd be ensconced behind palace walls, guards constantly on her heels, her time strictly scheduled, expected to pump out imperial heirs. That was no kind of life for an assassin. She *liked* her work, enjoyed the freedom, the planning and scheming, and even the danger.

But the power... she mused. The emperor might have his advisors, but she would wield the power of intimacy. *A new Imperial Grandmaster, the first of a dynasty...*

Are you insane? You think you'd be any better than the last one? screamed her conscience.

What am I thinking? Mya fought to hide her sudden revulsion as she considered what she might become if she accepted this offer. Power was like a drug to her—*If a little is good, more must be better, right? Wrong!*

Though the lure was strong, she'd seen what that kind of power did to people, and that was *not* who she wanted to become. Frankly, she'd rather cut off her hand than open that little blue box.

But how do I tell him? How could she speak the truth without revealing too much or insulting his pride?

Mya took a deep breath and faced the emperor. "Majesty, you don't really *know* me." He started to speak, but she held up a forestalling hand and plunged onward. "Please. You know what I've done, what I'm capable of in the physical sense, and you think this would make you and your heirs safe. What you *don't* know is the *real* me. It takes a certain kind of person to succeed in my line of work. Ruthless, you might say. Dangling this kind of power in front of such a person is like dangling meat in front of a well-trained dog. They may ignore it for a while, but sooner or later, the temptation becomes too great, and they *snatch* it."

The emperor paled, and the hand holding the box wavered. "I…We see."

Oh, gods, what am I doing? she wondered, but preserved.

"I hope you do, Majesty." She hated the pain in his eyes. He clearly hadn't expected to be turned down. *Who turns down this kind of offer?* "Please don't think that I'm not tempted or that I don't honor your offer, but I know myself. I'm not a *bad* person, but I am a *dangerous* person. I would make a *very* poor empress. You deserve better. The *empire* deserves better."

"Well." A sad smile flickered across his lips as he tucked the box back in his pocket. "We see that you have saved Us once again, this time from Ourself."

"No, Your Majesty." Mya also handed the ribbon-bound title back to him, albeit reluctantly. *Way too tempting,* she reminded herself. *Just be Grandmaster; that's more than enough.* "I'm saving you from *me*."

Epilogue

Dee!

The voice called out from the swirling chaos of the Sphere of Shadow…and Mystral heard.

Like a pinprick, it triggered memories acquired from one of the newest minds caught up in the unceasing maelstrom that was Mystral. She had existed here in the Sphere for eons untold. Driven near madness by the seclusion and sensory deprivation, she'd gathered together the banished and the lost…for company. The many became one, and that one was Mystral.

She knew each intimately: their dreams and desires, their fears, their loves and hates, their entire lives. Together yet still separate, they could not harm her, nor could they break free. Despite their differences, they all shared one desire—to *live* again…to feel, taste, touch, breathe again.

And this voice in the mists offered that.

Mystral surged forward with love, burning with hatred. *Two* recognized the voice. As they warred impotently with one another, Mystral sifted through their knowledge and, in it, found her key to escape this prison.

All her minds—mortals, demons, necromancers, even dragons— reveled at the opportunity revealed.

Mystral the Banished would be free. A new god would be birthed into the world, and none could stand against her.

The voice was gone now. *She'll be back.* Mystral would wait, and she would be ready. The voice was her key, and the key had a name.

Mya…

About the Authors

Chris was born and raised in Oregon, Anne in Massachusetts. They met at graduate school in Texas, and have been together ever since. They have been gaming together since 1985, sailing together since 1988, married since 1989, and writing together off and on throughout their relationship. Most astonishingly, they have not killed each other, or even tried to, at any time during the creation or editing of any of their stories...although it was close a few times. The couple has been sailing and writing full time aboard their beloved sailboat, *Mr. Mac*, since 2009. They return to the US every summer for conventions, so check out jaxbooks.com for updates and events. They are always happy to sign copies of their books and talk to fans.

Preview Chris and Anne's novels, download audiobooks, and read the writing blog at jaxbooks.com. Follow their cruising adventures at www.sailmrmac.blogspot.com.

Novels by Chris A. Jackson

From Jaxbooks
A Soul for Tsing
Deathmask

Weapon of Flesh Series
Weapon of Flesh
Weapon of Blood
Weapon of Vengeance
*Weapon of Fear
*Weapon of Pain
*Weapon of Mercy
(* with Anne L. McMillen-Jackson)

The Cornerstones Trilogy
(with Anne L. McMillen-Jackson)
Zellohar
Nekdukarr
Jundag

The Cheese Runners Trilogy
(novellas – also on Audible)
Cheese Runners
Cheese Rustlers
Cheese Lords

From Dragon Moon Press
Scimitar Moon
Scimitar Sun
Scimitar's Heir
Scimitar War